long way
home

Long Way Home

Copyright © 2022 by Melissa Grace

First paperback edition: October 2022

Cover art by Elle Maxwell

Cover copyright © 2022 by Elle Maxwell

ISBN: 978-1-7355646-5-4

www.melissagracewrites.com

long way home

MELISSA GRACE

Also by Melissa Grace

Home Is Where You Are

Home Again

Author's Note

Dear Reader,

Long Way Home contains sensitive topics such as child abuse, domestic abuse, and substance abuse, and is intended for audiences 18 years and older. While these subjects may be difficult to read about, it has always been my desire to tell stories that are true to real life. Trauma and healing are deeply ingrained in the Midnight in Dallas series because I think those are two of the most devastating and beautiful parts of the human experience.

There's something healing about feeling seen and understood, about feeling loved. It is my hope that if you are reading this and find pieces of yourself among the pages, that you will know that you are so very loved.

Love Always,

Melissa Grace

For Jen.
Now it's your turn.

"If you don't like the road you're walking, start paving another one."

—*Dolly Parton*

ONE

Jo

"Convention attendees I spoke with remain hopeful they'll get a refund, but they don't expect it anytime soon. The CEO of Geeks and Ghouls Fan Fest, Josh Freeman, could not be reached for comment, but we'll keep you updated as more details become available on this breaking story." The camera remained focused on me as I prepared to deliver my outro. "For Channel Eleven News, I'm Jo Kingsley, reporting to you live from the Donald E. Stephens Convention Center. Back to you in the studio, Neil."

"And we're out," Riggs said, bringing the camera off his shoulder.

"Geeks and Ghouls?" I rolled my eyes as I handed him the mic. "There's a congressman being indicted on fraud charges right now, and I'm out here covering a Geeks and Ghouls con artist?"

"He really puts the *con* in *con*vention." Riggs flashed me a toothy grin.

My lips quirked. Riggs and his dad jokes got me every time. He'd been my cameraman for the entire six years I'd been a field reporter at WSTQ Channel Eleven, Chicago's leading news station.

"The only people being conned right now are us." I knew I was pouting, but I didn't care. "I can't believe Kimber is the one reporting on Congressman Tilly." Riggs loaded the van, and I smoothed my hands over my sleek black skirt. "I'm never going to make it to CNN like this—let alone get the morning anchor position. I'll be back doing those fluff pieces, like the one I did a couple of months ago about the Irish Setter."

Riggs hopped out of the van and slammed the door shut. "Ruffles? But you loved that piece."

"That's not the point." Ruffles was a well-loved therapy dog, and I had covered her retirement party. I also may or may not have cried. Okay, fine, I cried like a baby. "You can't be Daniel Kingsley's daughter and report about puppies and rainbows."

Riggs placed his hands on the sides of my shoulders. "You're a damn good reporter, Jolene. You're one of the best I've seen in my fifteen years at the station."

My face softened. It felt paternal when Riggs called me by my given name instead of my nickname, and it reminded me of my mom, who loved Dolly Parton so much she named me after her favorite song. I was never sure what to make of my own mother naming me after one of music's most-hated man stealers, but she always said she loved the story behind how the song got its name. Dolly had famously looked out into the crowd and saw a pretty little girl with red hair and green eyes —much like mine—and asked her for her name. The rest was history.

"You really think so?" I finally asked.

"Absolutely," he insisted in his thick Chicago accent.

"You're a shoo-in. You've got the chops, kid. You've been here twice as long as Kimber, and you practically live at the station. You're gonna get that anchor job tomorrow. Harper's probably taking it easy on ya right now to make the transition a little easier, you know? Give you a break before you take the big job."

I twisted my lips to the side. "I hope you're right."

Harper Leslie was the CEO at WSTQ, and I'd never known him to take it easy on anyone, least of all me. You didn't get to be my father's daughter without a certain level of expectation. When you heard names like David Muir, Lester Holt, Brian Williams, and Daniel Kingsley, you thought of groundbreaking news stories, *not* therapy dogs named Ruffles.

It was bad enough that everyone assumed I was the weather girl instead of the woman delivering the evening news. It wasn't my fault I had a case of RFF—Resting Friendly Face—and a spray of freckles across my cheeks that made me look far less than my thirty-one years. Whether I was standing in line at the grocery store or had my feet in stirrups at the gyno's office, everyone saw my face and assumed I was game for a chat. It was one of the reasons I only wore black. My wardrobe could look serious even if my face couldn't.

"We need to get you back to the station," Riggs said, opening the door for me. "Isn't tonight the big night with Aiden?"

My stomach twirled like Michelle Kwan doing a triple lutz at the Olympics as I climbed into the van. "Yep, tonight's the night."

Aiden and I had been together for a little over a year, and I knew this was the night he was going to propose. He'd said he wanted to take me to dinner to talk, and we were going to

Prosecco, the very same restaurant where we'd had our first date. While that alone wasn't exactly a flashing sign that he was going to put a ring on it, the three-carat rock I'd found in his coat pocket a few days ago most certainly was.

Riggs got in the driver's seat and started up the van, and a sweet voice sprang to life on the radio over a melancholy melody. *"Caught somewhere between who you want to be and who you are. Your dress in shades of gray, trying to blend in with the walls of this crowded bar."*

"I love this song," Riggs said, turning up the volume.

"Who is it?" I asked as I pulled my phone from my pocket and began going over my notes for the next day's stories.

He shook his head. "How do you not know who this is? It's Midnight in Dallas. They're huge."

I shrugged. "I guess I don't listen to the radio much." The name did *sound* familiar, but I'd probably heard it on TV or something.

My fingers tapped across the screen, the song quickly forgotten, and I shuddered when I got a good look at my nails. *Oh Mylanta.* I couldn't get engaged with my nails looking like they'd been gnawed on by a beaver. I tuned out the sounds of Riggs singing along to the radio as I used the front-facing camera to inspect the rest of my appearance.

My eyes looked tired. I *was* tired. I'd been getting up at three a.m. for the last nine years—first as an intern, then as a news desk writer, then as a field reporter.

At least I'd washed my hair that morning instead of caking on another layer of dry shampoo. I was in desperate need of a blowout, but there wouldn't be enough time for that. My phone rang as I studied my reflection, a photo of my dad and I smiling inside his office at CNN flashed across the screen.

"Hi, Dad," I answered, bringing the phone to my ear.

"Are you ready for the big day?" he asked. I could tell from the soft sounds of road noise that he was in the car too, though I couldn't remember the last time he actually drove. My dad liked to spend his travel time working from the back of his Escalade. He planned every single day down to the second. In fact, he'd probably penciled in just enough time for this phone call.

"I am," I sang. "But I've got to get through the big night first!"

"Big night? Does this mean you're covering the Tilly case after all?"

"Unfortunately, no. Tonight is my dinner with Aiden. He's proposing tonight, remember?" I bit back my disappointment. He'd already forgotten about my dinner with Aiden, which wasn't surprising, really. My dad could remember details of stories he covered decades before, but things like my love life weren't exactly headline news in Daniel Kingsley's world.

"Ah, right." My dad liked Aiden well enough. Or maybe he liked the way Aiden didn't complicate my career goals. Aiden didn't care about the long hours I put in or if he didn't see me for a few days at a time. He knew my career was important to me and never tried to make me feel guilty about it.

He didn't ask a lot of questions about my job, but I didn't mind. When I was with Aiden, I got to unplug from the craziness of my day-to-day life and just exist. Once the new car smell of our relationship had worn off, he'd been content to stay in and watch TV most nights that we spent together, which was perfect for me because I hadn't stayed up past nine p.m. for as long as I could remember.

"I'm headed back to the station to finish up and get ready for dinner."

"That's nice," he said. "Well, good luck." There was a brief pause, and I heard his muffled voice giving directives to the driver. "And how's your mother doing?"

He asked me this question nearly every time we spoke, and every time it hurt for me to answer. He never said as much, but I knew he missed her.

"She's good. She and John left for Hawaii this afternoon." John was my mom's boyfriend, and he worshiped the ground she walked on, which was something my father never did even on his best day. For all the ways John was a lovable teddy bear, my dad was a cactus. Or a porcupine. Or something equally as prickly.

"That's good to hear." He cleared his throat. "Listen, Jo, I've got to run, but I can't wait to hear about how everything goes tomorrow."

"Thanks, Daddy," I said as Riggs pulled the van into the Channel Eleven parking lot. "I'll keep you posted. I love—"

I didn't bother finishing my sentence because he had already hung up.

Riggs had barely parked the van when I launched myself from the vehicle and scrambled inside to send out a few last emails and tidy my desk. *A cluttered desk is a cluttered mind.* And I needed to start tomorrow, the day I would be named Channel Eleven's newest morning anchor, with a clear head.

"Hey, Jo." I turned and saw Carina, my friend and one of the best news writers at Channel Eleven, walking toward me. "You ready for tomorrow?"

I took in a shaky breath. "Yep. I'm ready."

"You've got this in the bag," she assured me. "And what

about tonight? Are you ready for that?" She wiggled the fingers on her left hand at me.

"Definitely," I said. "Everything is going according to plan."

Carina playfully rolled her eyes. "You and your plans."

"Well, Confucius said that those who don't plan long ahead will find trouble at their door."

It was true. If there was one thing my father had instilled in me, it was that I always needed a plan. I couldn't leave my life, or my career, to chance.

She snickered. "You are the only person I know who can quote Confucius and not sound like a total asshat "

The alarm on my phone trilled a sharp reminder that I needed to get out of there if I was to stand a chance at making myself look presentable.

"Peas and rice! I've got to go." I shut down my computer and grabbed my purse.

Carina shook her head. "You know, it wouldn't kill you to say *fuck* or *shit* or *damn*. It might even feel good—let some steam out of that kettle."

I pretended I didn't hear her. "Wish me luck."

"I won't." She smiled and crossed her arms. "Because you don't need it."

"Thanks, Carina." I gave her a quick hug. "I'll see you later."

As I hurried out the door, I knew she was right. I'd never relied on luck. Everything I'd planned for, everything I'd worked hard for, had always been mine. And everything taking place over the next twenty-four hours would be no exception.

Everything is going according to plan.

"AFTER YOU." AIDEN HELD THE DOOR FOR ME AT PROSECCO as the smell of garlic butter and simmering marinara beckoned me inside. His normally broad grin was tighter than the little plastic retainer I wore every night to keep my teeth straight, but I knew he had to be nervous. It *was* a big night, after all.

He looked dapper in his gray suit, and when he smiled at me, my heart fluttered. As a pharmaceutical sales rep for a company selling cosmetic fillers, he had to be charismatic. It was no wonder he was one of the leading reps in the state, which had afforded him the ability to buy the giant diamond he was about to place on my finger.

"Thank you," I said as we strolled inside.

"Good evening," a hostess greeted us. "Do you have a reservation?"

"Yes," Aiden replied. "It should be under Aiden Christopher."

The hostess squinted down at her iPad, flicking her finger across the screen. "Ah, yes. Christopher, party of two. Right this way." She grabbed a couple of menus from the podium and led us through the dimly lit restaurant to our table.

As Aiden took his seat across the table from me, I noticed beads of sweat had already formed along his hairline. He loosened his tie as a server brought two glasses of water to our table with a promise to return for our drink order.

"This is nice," I said, reaching across the table and taking his hand in mine. "It's been a while since we've had a date night that consisted of something besides me falling asleep during a movie on the couch."

He cleared his throat as his eyes did a quick sweep of the restaurant. "Yeah, it has."

"I feel like I haven't gotten to talk to you all week." I took a sip of my water. "How was the training?"

"Hmm?" His eyes flitted about as though they were watching an erratic fly buzz about the room.

He's nervous. This is so cute.

"The training you were out of town for?" His job had been extra busy, and he'd been out of town more than he'd been home. But that was okay. I spent so much time at the station that I didn't really mind. In fact, aside from my Wednesday phone chats with my best friend back home in Nashville and the occasional happy hour with Carina, my social life was pretty much nonexistent, and I liked it that way. Less distractions, like my dad always said.

"Oh, right," he began, but the server returned before he could finish.

"Can I start you off with anything to drink? I can give you a few more minutes if you'd like," he said.

"I think we're ready to order. I'd love a glass of Pinot Grigio and the Calabrese." I smiled and passed him the menu. I hadn't even glanced at it because I always got the same thing when I came to Prosecco.

To be fair, I did that everywhere I went. If I didn't venture off script, I wouldn't be met with any surprises. I had the same protein shake for breakfast and a grilled chicken salad with extra veggies for lunch every single day. I went to the same spin class three days a week, and I'd had the same haircut since I was twenty-three. I even got the same nail color anytime I went to the salon—Blush Crush.

"And for you sir?" the server asked as Aiden studied the menu, something he rarely did when we came here.

"Um, I'll uh... I'll have the Petto di Pollo," Aiden answered.

"And to drink?"

"Water, please."

"Perfect. I'll get these in for you, and I'll be back with your wine in a moment."

I waited until the server had disappeared before I spoke again. "No Carbonara this time?"

He shrugged. "I just needed something different. Something a little lighter."

So, he was going a little off-script. That was okay because everything else was going according to plan. I was about to check two huge things off my life's to-do list: land an anchor job and get married before I turned thirty-five. Maybe we weren't getting married *yet,* but I knew once we got engaged and moved in together that marriage was just around the corner. It wasn't something we talked about, but it only made sense for that to be where we were headed. We already had the routine of an old married couple as it was. Things had become predictable...comfortable. So what if I got more sleep than orgasms these last few months?

We made small talk over dinner, mostly Aiden rambling on about work, but I struggled to keep up. My mind was too busy thinking about the proposal. I wondered how he would do it. Would the ring appear inside a glass of champagne or atop a decadent dessert? Would his voice drop low so that only I could hear him, or would he gently clink his butter knife against the crystal glassware, politely requesting the entire restaurant's attention?

The server returned for our dishes and asked if we were interested in dessert.

"No dessert," Aiden said quickly. "Just the check."

I felt a pang of disappointment. *Okay, so it won't be*

covered in something sticky or gunked up with a bunch of chocolate. That's not necessarily a bad thing.

Aiden's forehead glistened with sweat. "Listen, Jo, I think you're great."

Here it comes. I took a deep breath and released it, a smile spreading across my face.

"You're driven, focused, and you've got such a kind heart," he continued. "Which makes what I'm about to say..."

"Yes, I'll marry you!" I blurted out before he could even ask the question.

Aiden's face crumpled. "Wait, what?"

"I'm sorry. I got a little ahead of myself there." My cheeks pinked. "Go ahead. Ask me."

He looked around to make sure no one could hear him and lowered his voice. "Jo, I'm not asking you to marry me."

"Oh." I frowned. "But...I found the ring."

Aiden pressed his lips together and pushed his hand through his hair. "You found that," he said flatly.

"I did," I admitted. "You were clearly trying to surprise me, and now I've gone and ruined it."

"There is no surprise."

I shook my head. "I don't understand."

He paused, and in those few seconds I imagined all of the different possibilities he might suggest. Maybe he wanted to get a house outside the city first or adopt a dog. "I...we can't see each other anymore."

My voice came out razor-sharp. *"What?"*

He startled, glancing around nervously. "Will you please keep your voice down?"

"You're breaking up with me?" Dear God, I was going to throw up. "But I saw the flippin' ring!"

"It's not for you, Jo."

All of the air whooshed out of my lungs, and my entire body went rigid as though the blood in my veins had frozen. "What do you mean it's not for me? Who's it for?"

He closed his eyes for a few seconds before looking at me again. "Abigail. My girlfriend."

Tears stung my eyes and my cheeks burned. *Stupid. I'm a stupid, stupid girl.* "You've been cheating on me?"

He huffed out a breath. "Actually, I've been cheating on her."

"I don't…"

"I've been cheating on her with you."

The room turned upside down in a sea of red. I pressed my palms to the sides of my face as the cogs in my brain spun wildly before finally clicking into place. "I'm the other woman. I'm a *homewrecker*."

"Did you really never wonder why you'd never met anyone in my life?" he asked. "Why I never took photos of us and posted them on social media?"

I shook my head. *No. This can't be happening.* "But…you don't have social media."

"*Everyone* has social media," he countered. "Did you really never wonder why I never brought you to my place the entire time we were together?"

"You said you had roommates. That you preferred to come to my place so we could be alone."

"Abigail *is* my roommate," he admitted.

I seethed. "Are your parents even dead?"

He looked away and cleared his throat.

"Oh my God," I cried. "What is wrong with you? Who *does* that?"

"Will you please keep your voice down?"

"I will *not* keep my voice down," I shouted.

"Jo, I'm sorry," he said. "I didn't mean for this to happen."

"Which part, Aiden?" I shot back. "Cheating on your girlfriend for over a year? Breaking my heart? Turning me into the villain of a freaking Dolly Parton song?"

"At least it's a good song?" he answered, and my nostrils flared. "I'm scum. I know I am. But I'm trying to do the right thing here."

"Well, somebody should give you a cookie," I spat. "Congratulations on finding some freaking morals. How...why...I thought you loved me."

Silence again. My heart sank with the reality that I wasn't losing Aiden at all. He was never mine to begin with.

"You'll find someone. Someone far better than me." Aiden tried to reach for my hand, but I snatched it away.

"Darn right I will," I fumed, rising to my feet. "I gave a year of my life to you, Aiden. How could you do this to me?"

"I'm so sorry, Jo," he said, his face turning as red as the tomatoes they put in the marinara. "Please forgive me."

Out of the corner of my eye, I saw a full glass of red wine on the table where two women were sitting beside us. I lunged for it and threw it in Aiden's face.

"What the hell is wrong with you?" one of the women shouted.

"Sorry. It was an emergency." I was sure I looked positively deranged. "This stand-up guy here will buy you another one."

Aiden opened his mouth to say something else, but I cut him off, anger rumbling deep in my chest.

"You can go screw yourself, Aiden. I hope Abigail doesn't like orgasms since she won't be getting any for the rest of her life."

"Oh shit." The lady whose wine I'd stolen raised her brow at me. "Is his dick small?"

"Microscopic," I said, looking at him one last time before turning my attention to the woman. "Sorry about your wine."

She shrugged. "Sorry about his tiny penis."

My rage grew legs and carried me out the door into the chilly October night. It wasn't until I was outside that I started to cry.

TWO

Derek

"DUDE, WHAT IS WITH YOU?" My cousin Dallas threw his drumsticks on the floor, sending them clattering at my feet. "You're playing like you just picked up the bass yesterday."

Jax, the lead singer of our band, Midnight in Dallas, turned and gave Dallas a pointed look. "That's a little dramatic, don't you think?"

I shook my head, and Jax gave me an apologetic look. "I'm sorry. My head isn't in the game today."

"Yeah, no shit," Dallas fired back. "Your head hasn't been in the game for a long time."

There wasn't anything I could say to that. He was right.

"You need to calm the fuck down, man," Luca said, lifting his guitar strap over his head and propping the inky black Fender against the amp behind him.

"That's rich coming from you." Dallas rolled his eyes. "You can't be bothered to show up on time, so you can stop with the self-righteous bullshit."

"The only one being self-righteous right now is you." Jax pressed his lips together in a firm line.

"Jax, you can barely remember the words to songs you fucking wrote, man." Dallas threw his hands up. "What is with you people? Am I the only person who still cares about this fucking band?"

"That's enough." The voice of Cash Montgomery, CEO of our record label, boomed through the small practice hall. Dallas opened his mouth to speak, but Cash held his hands out as though he could physically stop whatever words he was about to say. "I mean it, Dal. You need to knock it off or I'm going to sick Antoni on you when he gets back in town." Antoni was our manager and friend who had no problem letting us know when we were being assholes.

"I'm sorry, guys," I said again. I couldn't even make an excuse, and I definitely couldn't tell them the truth.

"Don't apologize," Cash said gently. "Everyone has an off day."

Dallas huffed. "Been a lot fucking longer than a day."

Cash glared at him. "That's it. Rehearsal is over. Pack it up."

"What?" Dallas exclaimed. "We still have an hour left."

Cash crossed his arms over his chest. "Not anymore you don't. You fellas need to go relax." He pointed at Dallas. "Especially you."

"Fuck this shit." Dallas nearly knocked over his cymbals when he rose to his feet.

"That's real mature," Jax muttered.

Dallas shot him daggers before bursting through the double doors.

Jax turned to me and squeezed my shoulder. "I'm sorry, man. He'll cool down."

I gave him a weak nod as I removed my bass and placed it back in its case.

"Or he won't," Luca added, unhelpfully. "But Dallas is an asshole, so who cares?"

"Pot, meet kettle," Jax joked.

Luca shrugged. "At least I *know* I'm an asshole. Dallas acts like he's God's fucking gift to music."

"Look, you guys have some time before the CMAs," Cash said. "You're just a little rusty. Artists go through this all the time."

I'd been going through it for nearly a year. I hated letting Dallas and the guys down, but after letting myself down for so long, I'd become kind of an expert at it.

"Cool," Luca said, packing up his guitar. He started toward the door. "I'm headed to the bar."

I wrinkled my brow. "It's only noon."

If he heard me, he didn't let on. The doors closed with a click behind him.

"Okay then." Cash raked his hand through his hair and sighed. "Get some rest, you two." He pulled his phone out of his back pocket and glanced at the screen. "It appears Ella is in need of some hush puppies and a Crunchwrap Supreme."

Jax snorted. "At the same time?"

"I swear, my fiancée has a gut made of steel." Cash chuckled.

"Liv and I are taking the kids to the park to burn off some of their energy," Jax said as we headed for the door. Liv was Ella's best friend and Jax's wife.

"What about you?" Cash clapped me on the back. "What are you getting into this afternoon?"

"Nothing much." There was no family waiting for me to come home. Just an empty apartment. Sometimes I wished I had someone—until I remembered that was one less person I would let down.

"You're welcome to come to the park with us," Jax offered.

My phone vibrated against the fabric of my jeans. I pulled it out and saw I had five missed calls. That was two more than I'd had when I got to rehearsal. I shoved my phone back in my pocket. I didn't want to deal with those calls earlier, and I definitely didn't want to deal with them now.

"I have some photos to edit, so I'll probably work on those," I said. " Maybe practice a bit so I'm ready for rehearsal tomorrow morning."

"You were fine today," Jax insisted. "Really. Don't stress it."

I'd been in music long enough to know the truth. And the truth was that lately, I'd sucked. Part of what made our music so good was that we played with feeling, channeling our emotions into every note. But it had become clear that I didn't want to be there. Going through the motions was no longer good enough to hide the dread that weighed me down every time I picked up my instrument.

"Thanks, man," I said, starting toward my motorcycle with my bass slung across my back. "I'll see you guys tomorrow."

I climbed on my bike and started the ignition, the motor vibrating to life. As I pulled out of the parking lot and headed toward my condo, I tried to pretend I was driving someplace else. Somewhere that didn't make me feel like I was suffocating.

Anywhere else.

Anywhere but here.

"THANKS AGAIN FOR MEETING ME," I SAID TO ELLA LATER that afternoon as we walked inside the Nashville Humane Association. Well, *I* walked, and Ella sort of waddled, her hands cradling the melon-sized bump of her stomach.

"Are you kidding me?" she asked. "I wouldn't miss it. Sorry I was a little late. I had to stop by the bakery. I had a dream about these mocha cupcakes with candied bacon on top, so Katie made them for me."

I scrunched up my nose. "Sounds disgusting, but if anyone can make those flavors taste good together, it's Katie."

"Anyway, you were my good luck charm when we came here and found Bradley Cooper. Hopefully, I can be the same for you."

To be clear, we found a *dog* she decided to name Bradley Cooper. She did not, in fact, find Bradley Cooper, the actor, at the animal shelter.

"How've you been feeling?" I asked as we waited for the receptionist to finish with another guest. I'd grown close to Ella the year before when she'd first realized her feelings for Cash. Her twenty-year-old daughter, Grace, had even become like a little sister to me.

"Pregnant," she answered quickly. "I feel very pregnant. Not going to lie, I thought this part of my life was done a long time ago, and I'm definitely not one of those women who enjoy being pregnant. I'll be so happy when we have that baby in our arms, but until then, I reserve the right to be miserable."

"Well, you look great. You're glowing."

"That, my dear, is sweat. Because that's what I do when I'm pregnant. I sweat all the damn time. God, it's like a hundred degrees in here." She fanned herself with her hand.

"Anyway, Cash is happier than a pig in shit, and Grace is so excited to be a big sister, despite the fact that she's technically old enough to be this kid's mom. They're both spoiling me rotten, so I really shouldn't gripe, but I'm still going to." Despite her complaints, she smiled. Even though this baby was a complete surprise, I knew she was happy.

"Sorry about your wait," the receptionist said. "What can I do for you today?"

"We'd like to see the dogs you have available for adoption," I answered.

"Of course," the perky brunette said, a big grin stretching across her face. "Aw, y'all are so cute. Getting that baby a furry brother or sister?"

"Oh, no," I said. "She's not my wife. She's my manager's fiancée." The receptionist raised her brow. *I should have just said 'yes' and moved on.* "He's not *just* my manager. He's my friend too."

The woman blinked rapidly, and Ella stifled a laugh.

"You know what… the more I talk, the worse it sounds." I chuckled, but the receptionist was unmoved.

"Uh, so right this way," she said, leading us through a set of doors to the side of the desk, deciding, thankfully, to ignore what I'd said.

I poked Ella in the arm and whispered, "Gee, thanks for the help."

She giggled. "What? I thought you had it under control."

"All of the info about each dog can be found on the cards to the right of their kennels," the woman said. "If you want to spend time with any of the dogs, let one of us know. I'll be out front if you need anything." She avoided eye contact with both of us as she returned to her desk.

"So, what made you decide you were ready to become a

fur dad?" Ella asked as a German Shepherd-looking dog licked her fingers between the wires of the cage.

"I think I'm tired of coming home to an empty house. At least this way I won't just be talking to myself. I can say I'm talking to the dog."

"Nice try, but you'll still be talking to yourself," she teased.

I chuckled. "I know. I just think it would be nice to be needed by someone. Someone—or some*thing* as the case may be—who won't think I'm a total failure when I mess up or don't exactly meet expectations."

"I take it Dallas is still being a dick?" Ella wasn't exactly known for her subtlety.

"Yeah," I said with a sigh. "But he also isn't entirely wrong. My heart isn't in the music right now."

"It hasn't been for a while," she said gently.

I was immediately self-conscious. "Did Cash say something?"

"No, no." She glanced up at me. "Not at all. I just…Well, I've noticed when I've seen you play or talk about the band. Like when Liv or Jax or Cash talk about music, their eyes light up, and they get all smiley and happy. But when you talk about it…" She chewed her lip thoughtfully for a moment. "It's like someone has turned all the lights off inside your eyes. You look like your dog got run over." A chihuahua yelped from the kennel across from us, and Ella winced. "Poor choice of words. I'm sorry."

"You're not wrong," I admitted.

She knelt to greet a dog whose hair was so long it obscured his vision, then glanced at the info card. "What about this one? He's only a couple of months old."

I shook my head. "He won't have a hard time getting

adopted. I want to find the dog nobody else wants." I blew out a long breath. "I don't know, Ella. Maybe I'm just burnt out."

She gave me a soft smile as we continued to look through the kennels on either side of us. "You're not burnt out, Derek. You want a different life than the one you have, and that's okay. You're allowed to want something else."

"Even if it hurts everyone I care about?" I asked. "Even if it completely ruins their lives?"

"Listen, I love you, kid," she said, "but you don't have that much power. If you decide this life isn't for you, it's up to everyone else involved to take care of themselves. You aren't responsible for their happiness."

I looked down at my feet, my fingers grazing the cold metal of the kennels, until a sound that was half-bark, half-cry, caught my attention. I crouched in front of the small dog whose belly was so round it almost grazed the floor. Its little toothpick legs pranced, and its tail stood at attention.

"Hey there," I said to the pup. "What's your story?" I glanced at the card on my right which told me that Izzy was a fourteen-year-old female Jack Russell and Rat Terrier mix. "I like your name, Izzy girl." Her ears perked as she cocked her head to one side.

"If you're going for the one nobody else wants, I think you may have found your match," a voice said from behind me. I turned to see a young guy with a broom who had been cleaning so quietly that we didn't even hear him over dogs' barks and whines. "Sorry. I didn't mean to eavesdrop. But Izzy here has been with us a long time. She was found on the streets with another dog, a much younger one who got adopted the first week he was here. Izzy may be a little old lady, but she has a lot of love left to give the right person. I'd have taken her myself if I didn't already have a house full. She's made a lot of strides since she's been here. Used to be real skittish, but now, she's a total lover."

I knew before he'd even finished speaking that she was going home with me.

"I'll take her," I blurted.

"Derek, are you sure?" Ella asked. "I love you and your big, gooey heart. But an older dog could be a huge undertaking."

I nodded and looked back at where the dog stood on her hind legs, reaching her paws up at me. "I know. But Izzy deserves a second chance, don't you think?" I glanced over my shoulder at the worker. "I'll take her," I said again.

The guy beamed and set his broom aside, starting for the door. "Awesome! I'll go up front and get someone to come help you get all the paperwork sorted."

I knelt in front of Izzy, slipping my fingers through the cage. She whined and licked me, her tail waving around like a magic wand. "You hear that, girl? You've got a home now. You get to finally live the life you've always deserved."

Izzy barked and danced in a circle as though she was putting on a show for Ella and me.

Ella squeezed my shoulder. "You know, Izzy isn't the only one that deserves to live her best life. You deserve that too."

I sighed and acknowledged the familiar longing that lived tucked away in my chest like an old, worn library book. It was getting harder and harder to push those feelings down.

"Maybe you're right," I said.

Ella snorted. "I'm always right. It's one of my most endearing qualities."

I chuckled, but my mind was a million miles away as my

phone buzzed in my pocket. I didn't even look to see who it was because I already knew.

It was hard to think about best lives or new beginnings when my old life was bound and determined to never let me go.

THREE

Jo

A FEW HOURS AFTER DINNER, I laid sprawled across my bed like a starfish. Even in my drunken state, I knew downing an entire bottle of Chardonnay had been a bad idea considering the most I ever drank in one sitting was a glass of wine or champagne. The ceiling fan spun along with the room, causing my tears to dry in a salty film on my face.

How had I become the woman Dolly Parton warned us all about? My mom's favorite song had become a self-fulfilling prophecy, and now I was *that* Jolene.

One minute I thought I was getting engaged, crossing another milestone off my to-do list, and the next I was a home-wrecking adulteress who melted down in fancy restaurants. I'd never had a problem keeping my cool under pressure. It was part of my job. To report the news and report it well, you had to be able to keep your emotions in check. You had to be Even Steven in the most high-pressure situations and focus on the facts.

I sucked in a ragged breath. *Okay. What are the facts? First off, I am now single…*

An acidic burp gurgled deep in my stomach, and I thought about what my father would say when he found out. He'd tell me I was better off because relationships only hold people back. He'd say I needed to put all my focus on my career. That this was a blessing in disguise. And maybe he was right.

I was about to get the promotion of a lifetime. When I was the new morning anchor for WSTQ Channel Eleven, I wouldn't have time to plan a wedding. I wouldn't even have time to miss Aiden.

My phone buzzed from beside me on the bed. I picked it up when I saw my best friend's name and squinted at the screen in an effort to stop the words from swirling.

Katie: So??? Where's the ring pic?!

I dropped my phone and it bounced with a soft thud on the mattress. I couldn't tell her yet. Not now. I needed to have some good news to sandwich it in with. *I got the promotion, and oh, by the way, my boyfriend who was supposed to be proposing dumped me for his soon-to-be fiancé, and I made a scene in public about his tiny penis.*

It wasn't even *that* tiny. I smirked to myself. *Okay, yes, it is. I'm supposed to be focusing on facts after all.*

And it could have been worse. At least Aiden wasn't living with me. Short of a few articles of clothing and a tooth-brush, there was nothing left to show that he'd ever been here. He didn't write cute notes on Post-Its and leave them on the mirror. There was no shared furniture or a dog over which a custody battle would ensue. With one trip to Goodwill, it would be as though Aiden hadn't existed. Like I'd never even been loved. *Had I been loved at all?*

My stomach churned, wine and Italian food bubbling like a pot of spaghetti sauce turned up way above a simmer.

I might have been alone, but at least I still had my apartment in the city. Sure, it was barely over five hundred square feet and above a dry cleaner that I was pretty sure was a front for a money laundering operation. But it was ten minutes from the station, and I didn't need a lot of space anyway. Working as much as I did hadn't allowed me to furnish the place the way I would have liked. It was functional, which was really all I needed. It wasn't like I had a lot of free time to spend at home.

Home. Even after all the years I'd been here, it didn't really feel like what I thought a home was supposed to feel like. Where it should have been warm, it was cold. Where it should have been full, it was empty. I'd thought that getting engaged to Aiden would change all of that.

A light tinkling sound came from above me. I blinked slowly, willing the ceiling to stop turning pirouettes above my head. My eyes narrowed on the crystal globes of the fan as I saw a small, dark spot slide from the base of the fan to the glass.

"What the…"

The small spot grew larger, and as I raised up on my elbows to get a closer look, a flash of black fell in my field of vision.

"COCKROACH!" I shrieked and flung myself from the bed where a roach so big I could have shot it with a rifle was crawling on my duvet. I wriggled my entire body, shaking off the heebie-jeebies as I stepped slowly toward the door with my back against the wall. "No sudden movements, Jo. No sudden movements."

The cockroach stopped in its tracks as though it knew I was talking to it. Its little antenna waved menacingly in my direction, and I yelped.

"You stay right there, Mr. Roach," I said, taking slow

steps toward the door. "Don't come any closer." I reached the doorframe and bolted to the kitchen where I kept a bottle of Raid under the sink. Clutching the container like a shield, I crept back to the bedroom, a soldier heading into battle. It struck me that a fiancé would have really come in handy at that moment. Because what were fiancés good for if not killing Godzilla-sized cockroaches in the middle of the night?

I held the Raid out in front of me with a trembling hand as I crossed the threshold to the bedroom, cocked and loaded, ready to kill.

But the roach was gone.

"No, no, no, no," I cried, crouching to look beneath the bed. I tossed the pillows, scanned the walls, looked behind and inside the nightstand, but it was nowhere to be found. "Well, this is just craptastic."

I pressed my palm against my forehead as I considered my options, but I decided that no matter how lonely I was, I did *not* want the warm body in my bed to be that of a cockroach. So, with my bug spray in tow, I grabbed my phone and darted to the bathroom, slamming the door closed behind me. I tore my bath towel off the rack and shoved it in the crack where the door met the floor.

My mouth was dry, and I really wished I'd grabbed a glass of water on my way into hiding, but I wasn't willing to risk my cover now. Instead, I ran the cold water from the bathroom faucet and bent to guzzle it straight from the spout before splashing my face with it. I turned the knob, cutting off the stream, and raised my gaze to the mirror. Mascara streaked down my face, my eyes were red and puffy, and my hair looked like it might have been the cockroach's living quarters.

I sat on the edge of the tub, placing the bug spray and my

phone beside me. I wasn't supposed to be coming home alone tonight. *I should have had a fiancé, but now I was cohabitating with a cockroach the size of a small dog.*

My phone buzzed against the tile, and I glanced down at the illuminated screen.

Katie: You must be out celebrating still! I'm off to bed but I expect a ring photo waiting for me when I wake up. XOXO

A fresh batch of tears stung my eyes. Tomorrow, I would tell Katie everything. I would endure the pitying glances from my coworkers when they found out I got dumped. Tomorrow, I would get the promotion and start working on a new plan that didn't include Aiden.

My stomach lurched and bile burned the back of my throat.

But tonight...Tonight I was going to throw up.

"I HOPE THAT I CAN COUNT ON YOUR DISCRETION," AIDEN said over my voicemail the next morning. "I know what I did was wrong, but we're both adults here."

I rolled my eyes. Apparently, I'd put the fear of God in him after making a scene at the restaurant, though, I wasn't sure why he was worried. It wasn't like I knew any of his friends or family, and I wasn't interested in hunting him down on social media to exact some sort of revenge The whole thing was embarrassing enough. All I wanted to do was forget about it.

"Anyway, I feel bad about the way we left things," he continued. *Really? You feel bad about me throwing wine in your face? I can't imagine why.* "And even though I know you probably don't believe me, I really am sorry for—"

I pulled the phone away from my ear and hit the garbage can icon, sending his apologies into the trash where they belonged. The last thing I cared about was how sorry he was. I placed my phone screen down on the desk and leaned back in my chair.

Carina approached with a wary expression on her face. "You look like shit."

I winced. "Can you keep it down? I've got a headache from h-e-double-hockey-sticks."

"Hell," she corrected. "And you look it, too, girl. Did you do a little too much celebrating last night? Let's see that rock."

The corners of my eyes burned as I cast my gaze downward. "There is no rock."

"What?" She grabbed my left hand, confirming it with her own eyes. "What happened? I thought—"

"Yeah, well, so did I," I said, withdrawing my fingers from hers. "Turns out the ring was for someone else."

"*Excuse me?*" Carina's jaw dropped. "Someone *else*? He was cheating on you? Do I need to hide a body? Cause I'm pretty sure I've watched enough true crime documentaries to figure out how to dismember a corpse."

I recoiled. "I don't know whether I'm impressed or disturbed." I sucked in a deep breath. "Actually, *I* was the other woman." I could see her wheels spinning as she worked out the details in her mind.

"Damn. He's got some nerve pulling that shit when your name is Jolene." She was clearly trying to make me laugh, but the joke was already old hat in my mind. I'd only thought about it all night on the cold tile of the bathroom floor with the bottle of Raid clutched in my arms like a teddy bear. Carina squeezed my shoulder. "I'm sorry, Jo."

I forced a smile. "I'm fine. Really. It's a blessing in disguise."

"Damn right it is," Carina said. "You're not gonna have time to worry about what's-his-name once you're crowned the new morning anchor." She glanced at her smartwatch. "Speaking of, we should get to the conference room before the guys get all the good donuts."

"I can't even think about food right now." I scrubbed my hands over my face and blew out a nervous breath. "Do I really look that bad?"

She wrinkled her nose. "One sec." She disappeared around the corner and returned a few seconds later with a tube of lipstick. She popped the lid off and turned the tube until a rosy shade of rouge appeared. "Put this on."

I did as I was told while Carina fluffed my hair, fussing with the pieces that framed my face. Once she was satisfied, she took the lipstick from my hand and dotted the color along the tops of my cheekbones, blending it with her fingertips.

"Better," she said with a satisfied nod. "I can't do anything about the fact that you're dressed like you're going to a funeral, but Rome wasn't built in a day."

I looked down at my black shift dress. "What's wrong with my dress? I always wear black."

"Let's go." She ignored me and grabbed my hand, pulling me toward the conference room where everyone had already started filing in.

I sat at my usual spot near the head of the table across from Kimber Sutton, the darling of WSTQ. She'd only been at the station for five years, but she'd come to us from one of the top news outlets in Los Angeles. Kimber was the kind of woman who smelled like expensive perfume—the kind of girl you can bet never got picked last for anything in life. Her Instagram feed was full of idyllic snapshots of her perfect life that she shared with her nearly twenty thousand followers and guidance on how the rest of us peasants could manifest magic into our own lives. As though simply wanting something bad enough could make our dreams come true.

Speaking of dreams, she also happened to be engaged to Chip Kasey, Channel Eleven's Emmy Award-winning weatherman extraordinaire. He was exactly the kind of guy you'd picture with the woman who had everything she could have ever possibly wanted. He was handsome, devoted, and probably had no problem killing Kimber's cockroaches. Who was I kidding? Kimber had probably never even seen a cockroach in real life before.

"Good morning, Jo." Kimber's toothpaste commercial smile greeted me, and I groaned inwardly. Did she really have to be that perfect this early in the morning? "That lip color looks great on you."

"Thanks," I replied, plastering a phony smile across my face as Riggs entered the room.

"Hey, Jo," he said, taking his seat near the other side of the table. "How'd it go last night?"

Carina shot him a glance from the refreshment table and shook her head as she took a bite of a powdered sugar-covered donut.

"That's right," Kimber purred as Chip dropped into the seat next to her. "I heard last night was a big night for you. I want to see your ring."

Before I could come up with a reason why I wasn't wearing a ring that didn't include my boyfriend breaking up with me for his actual girlfriend, Harper Leslie entered the room, closing the door behind him. "Good morning, everyone."

I folded my hands in my lap, thankful that in just a few minutes, the focus would be on me being the new morning anchor instead of my non-existent engagement.

"Before we get started, I wanted to say congratulations to Kimber for that outstanding coverage on Congressman Tilly," Harper began. "That was first-class reporting. Well done."

Kimber turned on a bashful smile and pretended to be embarrassed as we applauded her.

Harper turned his attention to our program director. "Jeremy, give me the rundown on what's happening this week."

Jeremy cleared his throat. "Well, we have a piece coming up about the new wing at the veteran's hospital, and we're working on…" I barely listened as he recapped the upcoming stories, making sure to insert an occasional nod to make it look like I was paying attention. Kimber caught my eye and smiled, her blonde hair glistening like a halo around her head.

Her looking gorgeous while I sat there looking like I'd spent the night sleeping with cockroaches did nothing to help my sour mood, but I smiled anyway.

"As you all know, there are some changes happening at WSTQ. We're saying goodbye to Hannah as she moves on to Philly." Harper's voice pulled my attention back to the head of the table. "That means we need another anchor to do mornings. Hannah's leaving behind some big shoes to fill. We need someone the public can rely on. Someone they can count on to deliver the tough stuff with grace and aplomb."

Grace and aplomb. Yep. That's me. I'm the aplombest person in this room. Is apolmbest even a word?

My nerves popped to life like popcorn in a microwave. I'd

kind of thought Harper would tell me I got the promotion privately before sharing the news with everyone.

He must have wanted it to be a big surprise. Crap. I probably should have prepared a small speech.

Harper continued addressing the room, glancing at us over his sleek tortoiseshell frames. "This individual needs to be able to carry this morning show on her very capable shoulders, and I have no doubt she will do exactly that. The person we've chosen for the job has devoted a lot of time to this station. Her name has become synonymous with good journalism, and I know this program will thrive with her as the face of our morning show."

My heart thudded out of my ears, pulsing behind my eyes. *This is it. This is what I've been working for. Everything is going according to plan once again.*

A proud smile spread across Harper's face. "So, without further ado, let's congratulate our very own Kimber Sutton."

What...

The edges of my vision turned red, and the room swayed.

The...

The cheers and applause sounded like they were happening under water, and I was floating somewhere above them.

"What the fuck," a voice shrieked, causing the entire room to go silent. A couple of people, including Carina, gasped as their attention snapped toward me.

Oh God. Oh no. It was me. What am I doing?

"Excuse me," Harper said, his nostrils flaring.

"I said, *what the fuck.*" I slammed my fists on the table and rose to my feet. "*Kimber?*"

"Oh shit." Carina covered her face with her hands.

"*Sit* down," Harper ordered.

"I will not sit down." I pointed my finger in his face as the word vomit poured from my mouth. "Do you know how many personal days I've taken in ten years? *Three.* Three days. I've worked every holiday. I stay late every night. I've filled in everywhere you've asked, and I have devoted my entire life to this station. Even when you assigned me the most asinine stories, I gave them everything I had. This show is supposed to be on my very capable shoulders. *Mine.* Do you know why? Because it's all I have left. My boyfriend who was *supposed* to be my fiancé dumped me for the woman he actually *wants* to be his fianceé. I have no one to kill my cockroaches, and now you're telling me I've given my life to this station for *nothing?*"

"*Enough,*" Harper boomed. "Sit down, Ms Kingsley. Now."

More word vomit bubbled up from the depths of my stomach.

Wait. Oh no.

Actual vomit. *Exorcist* style puke erupted out of me with a volcanic force that could have shaken the earth. The room gagged as regurgitated white wine sloshed out of my body and onto the table. It splashed Harper's glasses and even managed to land in Kimber's hair.

"Oh my God. I'm going to be sick." Kimber lurched from her seat, and Chip trailed after her, tossing a disgusted look at me from over his shoulder.

Harper cringed and rose from his seat, removing his glasses. "Someone please escort Ms. Kingsley to the bathroom so that she may clean herself up and collect her things—"

"Mr. Leslie, I'm so sorry," I whispered as Carina jumped to her feet and rushed toward me.

Harper cut me off with a look that gripped me around the throat. "Because *she* no longer works here."

With that, he stormed from the room.

Panic rose in my throat as Carina placed her hands on my arms. Her lips moved, but I couldn't hear anything over the high-pitched ringing in my ears. Everything moved in slow motion as she guided me toward the door.

My coworkers craned their necks as the train-wreck that was my life passed through their view.

Nothing to see here, people. This crash had no survivors. My life was officially over.

FOUR

Derek

IZZY CAME to the side of the bed and scratched the mattress the next morning when she heard me stir. I couldn't help but laugh at how cute she was, how big her ears looked compared to the rest of her little body. I'd offered for her to sleep in my bed, but she was cozy in the oversized gray bed I'd placed on the floor nearby.

I stretched, sliding out from under the covers and rose to my feet. Izzy's tail whipped around in circles, but when I crouched to pet her, she cowered.

"It's okay, girl," I said softly, stroking the top of her head.

She snorted and peered up at me. I moved my hand away, and she came closer, but when I reached to pet her again, she shrank to the floor.

I sat beside her and extended my hand. She army-crawled toward me and nuzzled her nose into my fingers.

"Someone hurt you before, didn't they?" I asked, and she tilted her head in response. "I know you don't know me well yet, but I promise I'm never going to hurt you, okay? I don't expect you to believe me yet. I know it takes time to trust again after what you've been through, and I've got all the time in the world. You take as long as you need."

Izzy licked my hand and crawled across my legs, inching closer so she could sniff my pajamas.

"You and me, we're not all that different," I explained, holding out my other hand for her to sniff. "I've been let down by people before too—people who were supposed to care for me. The people who were supposed to love and protect me. But I'm not going to do that to you. I'm going to make the rest of your days the way they should have been all along. I promise."

The pup let out a gentle whine before standing on her hind legs, placing her front two paws on my chest, and giving me a slobbery lick on the chin.

"You're a good girl, Izzy," I said with a smile, and her tail spun in tiny cyclones as she covered my face in kisses. My phone rang from the nightstand, startling her. "Sorry, girl." I reached for it and groaned as I glanced at the name that flashed across the screen. *Might as well get this over with.*

"What?" I snapped in lieu of a hello.

"Derek...I...I've been trying to reach you." She tripped over her words, clearly shocked that I'd even picked up.

I blew out a long breath. "I know, Mom."

"I left messages."

I knew that too. I hadn't listened to a single one of them. She didn't call unless she wanted something, and I was sure today would be no exception.

"How are you, son?" she asked. Even after all these years, her voice still sounded like broken promises.

"What do you need, Mom? Do you need some money? How much?"

The line went quiet for a moment. "I don't need money, Derek. I'm calling to talk."

"Well, that's a first," I spat, my own words stinging me like a slap to the face. Even if it was true, she was still my mother. And no matter how complicated our relationship was, I still loved her...somehow.

"I'm sorry for that, Derek." Her voice wavered. "I know you may not believe me, but I am. I've been doing a lot of thinking. I have more regrets than I can count, and not being a good mother to you is at the top of my list."

I'd had enough counseling over the years to know words like this were often a trap coming from her. She wanted me to argue with her; to tell her she'd been a good mom. But that wasn't the truth. Years ago I would have taken the bait, but I was older now...wiser.

"Is that what you called to talk about?"

Another beat of silence. "No. I suppose it isn't."

"What is it then?"

"I'm calling to talk to you about your father," she said finally. "I think you need to come see him. At least call him."

Here we go. "Mom, I'm not calling him. I have nothing to say to that man."

She sighed into the phone. "I know he wasn't perfect, but he's still your dad."

"And I have the therapy bills to prove it," I fired back.

"I'm calling because your father is sick."

I scoffed. "Nothing a fifth of whiskey can't fix, I'm sure."

"He's dying, Derek." Her words hung in the air like a dense fog. The kind so thick that you can't see anything else around you. My entire body went numb as it washed over me. "Your father is dying."

I WAS EVEN MORE DISTRACTED AT REHEARSAL THAN USUAL, and everyone could tell. It began with me forgetting to even plug in my bass and had ended with Dallas storming out once again. I couldn't blame him for being upset with me. He didn't understand. He didn't know that the band had always been a means to an end for me.

Dallas was more like a brother to me than a cousin, but there were some things I didn't want anyone to know. Even him. But deception came at a cost. Pretending to be someone I wasn't made my bones ache. It had all gotten so heavy.

Too heavy.

My dad's behavior had finally caught up with him. I should have been sad. I should have wanted to extend an olive branch. But when I thought about my dying father, all I felt was anger. He had squandered away his life. This was *his* fault. And part of me blamed my mom for enabling him all these years. For not walking away. For not choosing me.

Deep down, I also blamed myself for not being good enough to be chosen by either of them.

Jax sighed as the door to the rehearsal hall clicked closed behind Dallas. "Try not to let it get to you, man."

That was impossible, but I forced a smile and pretended it wasn't. "Yeah."

"Listen, I think I'm going to cancel rehearsals for the rest of the week," Cash said, shoving his hands in his pockets.

Jax flashed him a worried glance.

"I don't know, Cash." I scrubbed my hand down my face. "I think I need all the rehearsal time I can get right now."

"I think you need the break more," Cash replied. "Sometimes we have to take a step back in order to move forward."

Luca wrinkled his nose. "Here's some real advice. Go home and get drunk."

I shook my head. Typical Luca. "Because drinking will clearly make my playing much better."

He smirked. 'Well, it can't make you any worse."

"Thanks," I said. "Thanks a lot."

Luca laughed. "I'm kidding. Mostly."

"We'll take the rest of the week off. I've got to head out to LA for a couple days anyway," Cash went on, ignoring Luca.

"Didn't you just get back from there?" Jax asked.

Cash blew out a breath. "Yep. I feel like I've been there more than I've been here lately, but I've been signing more talent, and they all happen to be in LA." He turned his attention to me. "No practicing whatsoever. We'll pick back up on Monday."

"What about Dallas?" I asked. "He's going to be pissed."

"I'll worry about Dallas," Cash said. "Get some rest. Do something that has nothing to do with music. Recharge your batteries."

I hesitated. The last thing I deserved was a break. "Okay."

Cash clapped me on the shoulder. "A break will be good for you. For *all* of you."

"Don't have to tell me twice," Luca said. "I'm out of here."

Jax packed up his acoustic guitar. "Are we still on for Sunday dinner?"

Cash nodded. "Yep. I'll be back Saturday night, so we're still hosting."

"Crunchwrap supremes for everyone," Luca said. "Pregnant Ella is my favorite."

Cash chuckled as we started for the door together. "For your information, I will be cooking up a southern feast."

Jax turned to Luca. "Why don't you ever have to host Sunday dinner?"

He shrugged. "Because I don't technically live here. And the only thing in my hotel mini fridge is vodka."

Jax shook his head and laughed. "I don't understand why you won't move here already."

Luca was the only one of us who hadn't made the move to Nashville. He still had his apartment in Kentucky, where we were all from, opting to stay in hotels while we were recording or rehearsing.

"Because I don't want to host Sunday dinner," Luca said, pushing through the door. "Not having you guys up in my shit is just an added bonus."

"Don't worry. I'll always find a way to be in your shit," Cash joked as he broke away and headed toward his car.

"See you guys Sunday," Jax called over his shoulder.

Luca and I walked together in silence over to where his car was parked next to my motorcycle.

"You really were shit today, man," Luca said finally. "Is everything okay?"

"Not really," I responded before I had time to make up a lie. I was so tired of lying.

Luca leaned against his Tesla. "You want to talk about it?"

I couldn't help the shock that registered on my face.

Luca laughed. "I know. I'm not exactly Dr. Phil. Feelings aren't really my thing. That's more of Cash or Jax's territory. But even my cold, dead heart can see something is up."

I let out a slow breath.

"Listen, this opportunity doesn't come around often." He crossed his arms over his chest. "You know I can only be a good person like twice a year."

I choked on a laugh. "True." I rested my hand on the seat

of my bike. "I've just… I've been distracted lately. I haven't felt like myself, and this morning I got some bad news about a family member."

"Shit," he said. "Is that why Dallas is being so touchy?"

"Dallas doesn't know."

"I thought you said it was a family member?"

"I did."

He looked at me quizzically. "But…"

"It's my dad."

His eyes widened. "Fuck, man. I'm sorry."

"My dad and I…" I trailed off. "I have a complicated relationship with my parents." I sucked in a deep breath. "My dad is a drunk and a pretty mean one at that."

"Shit. And Dallas—"

"Doesn't know," I cut him off. "And I'd like to keep it that way."

Luca narrowed his eyes, studying me before saying anything else. "Okay. It stays here."

"My dad's dying," I blurted. "Cirrhosis. My mom called and told me. I just don't know if I can forgive him for everything he put me through, but I know I should. He's fucking dying."

"And?" Luca raised his brows. "Him dying doesn't negate anything he did to you."

"What if he wants to make amends?"

"So what if he does?" he asked. "Look, I know a thing or two about assholes, okay? If I find out I'm dying tomorrow that doesn't change the fact that I was a fucking dick while I was alive. Nobody owes me shit. And you don't owe him anything either."

"But—" I began, but he cut me off.

"But nothing. This isn't about him and what he wants. It's about what *you* want, man."

"Yeah," I said, unsure if I really believed that. What if what I wanted could potentially hurt the people I cared about? "I appreciate it, brother. I guess I've got a lot to think about."

"There's nothing to think about. It's really that simple. The only person you owe shit to is you. Don't ever forget that." He poked me in the chest before maneuvering around to the driver's side of his car.

"Thanks." I gave him a faint smile. "You have any other sage words of wisdom for me, Brené Brown?"

"Yeah," he shouted over the vehicle. "Life is hard. Like my dick."

"There's the Luca I know," I muttered with a laugh. He started the engine and threw the car in reverse, peeling out of the parking lot, leaving me wondering if I would ever be brave enough to show the world my true self.

FIVE

Jo

My entire life had imploded in the span of twenty-four hours.

Carina helped clean me up in the bathroom, whispering soothing words while I sobbed uncontrollably. She'd tasked Riggs with gathering my things from my desk into a cardboard box and gently let me know we'd been in there for forty-five minutes in an effort to coax me out of the stall. It was funny how humiliation could mess with your sense of time. When I saw Riggs waiting for us with my belongings in hand, it struck me how pathetic it was that what was left of my career fit so easily inside such a small box. And the box wasn't even full.

As we were leaving, I saw one of the news trucks pulling out of the lot, no doubt on the hunt for the day's big story, a glaring reminder that I wasn't the one chasing down headlines anymore. Instead, my life had *become* the story. *Breaking News: Local woman burns her entire life to the ground. This and more after your morning traffic report.*

I stared out the window of Carina's Honda Accord, while

Riggs followed behind us in my white Ford Focus. I was practically catatonic and in no state to drive, as Carina folded me into the passenger seat. A sad sounding song played over the radio, and I recognized it as the one Riggs had been listening to the day before. *"Your dress in shades of gray, trying to blend in with the walls of this crowded bar. But all I see when I look at you are sunsets and a night sky full of stars. I don't care about your scars, 'cause honey, I see who you are."*

"You picked a hell of a time to start cussing," Carina finally said, trying to lighten the mood as she turned the radio down. I couldn't force myself to laugh. What had I been thinking? Why had I blown up like that? That wasn't me. I was the nice girl. The do-as-everyone-expects girl. The don't make-too-many-waves girl. Not the girl from every episode of *Snapped.*

"It's gonna be okay," Carina assured me as we made the turn onto my street. "Everything is going to be…*shit*."

The car crawled to a stop, and I snapped to attention to see pure chaos. Fire trucks, ambulances, and police cars lined the street blocking off my—

"Where is my apartment?"

There was nothing but smoke and flames lapping at the sky in the space where my apartment building had been when I'd left that morning.

My body went numb, and I had the distinct feeling that I was watching my life on a movie screen. There was no way this could be real. I noticed the Channel Eleven news van parked up ahead, and to add insult to injury, Kimber was standing in front of the rubble, reporting live from the worst day of my life.

A police officer flagged us down, and Carina rolled down

her window. "You can't be here," the officer warned. "This is an active crime scene. You need to move out."

"But my friend lives here." Carina gestured toward me. "She lives, er, lived above the dry cleaner."

The officer's face was the visual representation of *yikes*.

"What happened?" I choked out.

"What's your name?" The officer knelt so he was looking at me through Carina's window.

"Jo," I answered. "Jo Kingsley."

"You look familiar," he said. "Aren't you a reporter or something?" He gestured over to the Channel Eleven van. "With those guys?"

I gave a weak nod. I didn't have the energy for that explanation.

"Did you know anything about Mr. Lucas, your landlord?" he asked, glancing back at a squad car where my landlord was in the backseat.

I shook my head. "Only that he didn't charge much for rent." And that he was every bit as intimidating as Don Corleone. "I rarely saw him."

"Well, let's just say that Mr. Lucas was running more than a dry cleaner out of that building," he explained. "He apparently owed somebody a lot of money, and that somebody didn't get it so they burned the place down."

"Maybe...Maybe they'll be able to put it out," Carina said tentatively. "At least we could get some of your stuff out."

"I'm afraid it's going to be a total loss," the officer said. "You're lucky you weren't home, Miss Kingsley. This could have been a lot worse."

I understood what he meant, but the last word I would have used to describe myself at that moment was *lucky*.

"There are resources available to help you," the officer

said. He reached into his pocket and pulled out a card, handing it to Carina. "Take this. I'm happy to assist any way I can. Do you have somewhere you can go for now?"

"She can stay with me," Carina assured him.

"Good. I'm going to need to get your information for the detective." He motioned in the direction of a woman who oozed authority out of her pores, and handed Carina a small notepad and a pen from his other pocket.

I nodded as I quickly wrote my name and phone number on the pad.

"She may call to ask you a few questions," he added. "Now, I'm sorry, but I'm going to have to ask you ladies to move out of here. This is still a very active crime scene."

"Of course, Officer," Carina said. "Thank you."

I glanced in the side mirror and saw Riggs gawking in disbelief as we pulled away from the curb with him close behind.

"I'm sorry, Jo," Carina whispered. "I'm so sorry."

We made the short drive to Carina's house in silence. I'd really lost everything. What was I going to do? I'd always had a plan. Every second of my life had been meticulously accounted for, but now I found myself without a job, an apartment, or a boyfriend.

As we pulled into the driveway of Carina's townhouse, an overwhelming feeling washed over me. I longed for something familiar, to be cocooned in a place that felt safe. She squeezed my hand before we got out of the car. Riggs parked behind us and jumped out of my tiny Focus, ran toward me, then wrapped me in a bear hug.

"I'm so sorry, Jo."

"I want to go home," I said, tears forming in the corners of my eyes.

"I know, honey," Carina replied sympathetically, placing a hand on my arm. "But your home is basically a bonfire at the moment."

I shook my head. "Not that home. Nashville. I want to go home to Nashville." I wiped at my eyes with the backs of my hands, the start of a plan forming in my mind. "I've got some money saved up." *A benefit of not having much of a social life.* "I need to go there and clear my head. Is that crazy?" I wasn't used to coming up with a plan on the fly, but to be fair, I also wasn't used to losing everything. Perhaps I was losing my mind too.

"I don't think that's crazy," Riggs said gently. "But are you sure? Maybe we can talk to Harper, get you your job back."

Carina's face summed up what a terrible idea that was. "I don't know. Harper's not really the forgiving type." She tilted her head as she looked at me. "Listen, I'm going to tell you what my grandmother always told me. Sometimes the universe, God, however you want to put it, slams the door in our face when something isn't meant for us. Because it knows we're too stubborn to walk away on our own. I don't know if that means you should go to Nashville or somewhere else, but I think it's telling you it's time for a change."

Her words settled in my soul like the wind after a storm, and just like that, my mind was made up. "I'm gonna do it. I'm going home."

"When?" Riggs asked.

"Now," I answered, taking in a shaky breath. "Right now. Before I lose my nerve."

"Are you sure?" Carina asked.

"The only thing I'm sure of right now is that I need to get

out of Chicago," I answered. "If I don't, the universe is likely to hit me with an asteroid the way things are going."

Riggs looked doubtful, but Carina's face filled me with confidence that I was making the right decision.

"Let's go inside and get you a change of clothes. I'll pack you some snacks." She turned on her heel, headed for the door. "And you should probably take a shower. You kinda smell like the inside of a toilet."

I scrunched up my nose.

"We're going to miss you, kid," Riggs said, placing my car keys in my hand. "You're going to come out on the other side of this. Remember it's always darkest before the dawn."

I believed it. Because even though the sun was shining, it was dark as night inside my heart.

An hour later, I was traveling down I-65 South with the one box of belongings left to my name, a dress that smelled like vomit, and a care package from Carina. She'd given me a pair of leggings and a sweater to change into, and a bag packed with more snacks than I could ever need on the nearly eight hour drive to Nashville. Not that I felt like eating much anyway.

I'd turned my phone off before I left Carina's house when I saw that a junior staffer at Channel Eleven had the sheer audacity to text me for a statement about my apartment burning. I knew Katie had probably tried me too after not getting that engagement ring shot, but I was afraid that the second I heard her voice I'd fall apart. I could fall apart after I got to Nashville but not a second before.

The radio bounced between stations as I traveled, until I got tired of adjusting the dial to stop the static interference. Instead, I concentrated on nothing but the road before me and the sounds of cars thundering by.

I was running on pure adrenaline when I made a pit stop at a Target after I stopped for fuel. I quickly picked up a few toiletries, makeup, a phone charger, and a couple of outfits to get me through the first few days back home. The cashier eyed me as she scanned each article of clothing, all of which were black. Perhaps it would have been a good time to really do something crazy, like buy something red, but I could only handle so much change at once.

The anesthetic only trauma could provide had started to wear off and reality had set in by the time I drove through Kentucky. I was jobless, homeless, and alone. Hours bled into vivid shades of orange and pink as the sun set—a bright light that quickly faded to nothing, just like me.

Even though I hadn't been home to Nashville in years, I still remembered my way around. My mom had long since moved to Boca Raton, but Nashville was where my happiest years had been. My heart still called it home. By the time I got on I-440, my shoulders started to relax.

I eased off the interstate in the darkness and made a couple of turns I still knew like the back of my hand, pulling in the gravel driveway behind Katie's house. I knew better than to use the front door. That door hadn't been opened in years because it had a tendency to get jammed. The backdoor was the one we always used.

The neon clock on the dash told me it was just after nine p.m. I cut the engine and took a deep breath as I got out of the car, stepping carefully across the old stone path. I raised my hand to knock on the door only to have it ripped away from my hand, and there stood my best friend wearing green flannel pajamas and a look of complete shock.

"Jo!" Katie exclaimed. "Oh my God!"

"Surprise," I said weakly, the sound of her voice causing my eyes to well up with tears.

Her face fell, instantly knowing that something was very, very wrong. "I've been worried sick about you. I tried texting and calling, and then you missed our FaceTime date tonight. And now you're *here?* What happened?"

I collapsed in her arms, every emotion I hadn't allowed to surface yet barreling out of me with the force of a freight train.

"YOU ARE *NOT* A FAILURE," KATIE INSISTED, HER ARM LOOPED through mine where we sat huddled under a cable-knit throw on her tufted gray sofa.

I wiped at my face with the sleeve of my sweater. "I have no fiancé, no home, no job, and no prospects."

"First of all, this will always be your home. Secondly, Aiden is a garbage human being, and I hope that every time he wants to sneeze, he can't." She rested her head on top of mine. "And lastly, you *will* have prospects. You're Jolene-freaking-Kingsley. You're the same Jo who wrote a letter to the editor of The Tennessean when we were thirteen after you saw that kid from our Social Studies class waiting for the bus in a drainage ditch off Hillsboro Road. Because of you, the mayor installed covered bus stops at every stop in the district."

I sighed, and she squeezed my hand.

"The very same Jo who convinced our entire senior class to volunteer to cook Thanksgiving dinner for that nursing home over in Sylvan Park."

A faint smile formed on my lips. "That was pretty cool."

"Hell yeah, it was. And remember when you interned for WKRN the summer before you moved to Chicago? When you met that sweet woman who ran Project NENA? You found out they weren't getting a lot of donations for the kids for Christmas, and you convinced the station to host a toy drive for them. You got actual Titans football players to come out and take photos with people in exchange for gifts. Because of your determination all of those kids had presents to open Christmas morning." Katie nudged my knee with hers. "My point is, this *just* happened. Literally today. And regardless, you're still a badass. Your job didn't make you a badass. You're a badass all on your own."

"What if I never actually become a lead anchor? What if I've climbed as high as I can?"

Katie shook her head adamantly. "That's not possible. Even if you've climbed as high as you can in the news business, there's no limit to how far *you* can go. You're so gifted, Jo."

I snorted.

"I'm serious. You see people and what they need. I think that's when you've always shined as a reporter—when you're making a difference."

"I haven't done anything like that in ages," I admitted. "I kinda started to believe those stories were a waste of time. With every one I did, I heard my father's voice echoing in my mind that they weren't *real* news."

She shrugged. "Maybe that's what Daniel Kingsley thinks, but what do *you* think?"

I chewed my lip.

"Have you considered that maybe that's why you're always so exhausted and stressed? Doing those stories, helping people—that's what's always filled your cup." She moved so she was sitting cross legged on the couch, facing me. "Every week when we talk, you are stressed out of your mind. And I know there are good types of stress and bad types of stress. When I get a big order at the bakery or someone wants me to craft some elaborate wedding cake, I get stressed. But it's the good kind. The kind that sets your world on fire. The kind that makes time pass by fast because you love every second of what you're doing. You haven't been that kind of stressed in a long time."

She wasn't wrong.

"What happened to you sucks, and in no way am I taking away from that," she continued. "But maybe what feels like the end is really only the beginning."

I couldn't help but to crack a smile. One of my favorite things about Katie was her unwavering optimism. "That belongs on the inside of a fortune cookie."

She laughed, and I was amazed at how much better I felt simply being in her presence. "It really does." Katie reached for my hand. "Come on. Let's get some rest. Everything looks better after a good night's sleep."

I snorted. "It'd be hard pressed to look worse."

"Yeeeeah." She put her arm around my shoulders as she guided me toward the guest room—the room that used to be mine when I lived with her during college. "You've definitely had an epic stroke of bad luck, but it's only going to get better from here. I just know it."

For the first time in my life, I, Jo Kingsley, didn't have a plan, but I was starting to wonder if that was all the plan I needed.

KATIE AND I HAD COFFEE TOGETHER BEFORE SHE LEFT FOR work the next morning. Dark circles framed her hazel eyes, and I felt a little guilty for showing up like I did, throwing off her whole night. She insisted she was glad I was there, and I believed her. But she was clearly exhausted, and in my despair the night before, I hadn't picked up on just how tired she'd looked. It wasn't the kind of fatigue from one rough night—it was the kind caused by a lot of them.

"There's some cinnamon rolls in the fridge if you want one," Katie called as she ran out the door. We planned to have dinner when she got off work, and I made a mental note to ask if she was feeling okay. I knew her job as head-baker at Livvie Cakes Bakery and Cupcakery kept her busy, but I also knew she loved it.

She'd left me my old key in case I wanted to go out, but I decided to hang at the house. I soaked up the scent of sugar and fresh apples, still familiar even after all these years. I spent the morning curled up in my old room before getting up and tracing my fingers along the many picture frames that lined the hall.

Katie's house had been in her family since the early 1920s. It first belonged to her great grandparents, but when they died, they left it to her grandmother, who had raised Katie. We spent many a summer day eating Purity ice cream out of tiny cups and playing board games on the back porch. As we got older, we helped Granny in the kitchen, peeling apples for pies or chopping onions for a stew. We hardly turned on the TV, too entertained by each other's company and Granny's singing.

The summer after we graduated high school, Granny's health began to fail rapidly. But she made sure Katie would have a home for as long as she wanted, leaving the little brick house on Sharondale Drive to her. I spent a lot of time there, helping Katie care for Granny, and helping Katie care for herself. Soon after Granny passed, she asked me to move in. Even though it belonged to her and Granny, it had always felt like home to me too.

When I finally turned my phone on, I saw I had a voice-mail. I tapped the screen, placing it on speaker before pressing play.

"Jolene, this is your father." His stern voice caused me to jump. "Why am I finding out from someone at our Chicago bureau that you were *fired*? Do you understand what this could do to my reputation if it gets out? Call me immediately."

The message was timestamped from earlier that morning. It was no surprise my dad had heard the news before I'd told him. He knew everyone, but more importantly, everyone knew him.

I swallowed the lump that formed in my throat. I couldn't deal with my dad yet, so I called my mom instead and filled her in. She was ready to jump on a plane, but I assured her there was nothing she could do and that she and John should enjoy their trip. She finally calmed down when I told her I was in Nashville with Katie.

I also texted Carina and Riggs to let them know I was safe, though maybe not entirely sound.

At a quarter to six that evening, I got out of the shower to find that Katie had sent me a text.

Katie: Soooo we got this last minute catering gig for tomorrow night. Some bigwig that was willing to pay double for us to do it at the last minute. But that means I've got to stay late and prep everything.

Jo: Oh no! That's okay. We can do a late dinner! I'll wait for you. You know I've got nothing but time.

Katie: It's gonna be LATE late. By the time I finally get home I'm going to be wiped. We just ordered some sandwiches. I'm so sorry. I promise I'll make it up to you.

Jo: It's really okay. We have lots of time. I'm not going anywhere. Literally. I have nowhere to go. LOL

Kaite: YET!!! Speaking of, maybe you should still get out tonight. At least for a drink or something!

A drink did sound good, and it might be nice to be around people. And since it was a week night, I could be around people without being around *too* many people.

Jo: Maybe I'll do that!

Katie: You should! Got to get back to it. Have fun!!!

I snorted. I wasn't sure I knew what fun was anymore. But a drink couldn't hurt.

SIX

Derek

MY THOUGHTS KEPT me company all night. I tried reading and listening to one of my favorite piano playlists, but the voices from my past were too loud. I finally gave up around seven a.m. and took Izzy for a long walk, grabbing a cup of coffee at the place on the corner with the good cappuccinos. Normally I would have asked Dallas if he wanted to come with me since we lived in the same building, but things had been tense between us for a while.

The more my heart pulled me away from music, the more we butted heads. I couldn't really blame him. For a long time, the band *had* been my life. *I* was the one flipping the script. It was *my* spirit being tugged in another direction.

When I got home and released Izzy from her harness, one of the many framed photos in the foyer caught my eye. I'd taken it outside of Tootsie's, where a couple of street performers were playing for the crowd gathered on Broadway. The joy I got from looking at that picture made me feel treasonous.

It was one of my favorites. I loved the contrast of the electric signs against a twilight sky. But what I loved most were the faces the people in the picture wore. There were two men, probably in their sixties, one with a harmonica and the other with a guitar. They were lost in whatever song they were playing, their faces creased with happiness. Off to the side, a young couple stood by. The woman leaned into the man beside her, smiling broadly, her fingers clasped around his arm. The man's eyes were closed, his lips pressed to the top of her head.

That was my favorite part of taking pictures. The people. The humanity nestled inside the images.

Our manager Antoni's uncle, Wayne Hartford, was the one who helped me understand what I loved most about photography. I'd spent a few weeks with him in New York over the summer where he'd become my mentor. Wayne had been a photographer for Vogue for nearly fifty years, retiring only a couple of years ago. Even though I had no interest in fashion, I was thankful for the opportunity to soak up what information I could.

The first day I was there, he showed me the gallery wall in his office that showcased a collection of his most acclaimed work. "You see, Derek," he'd said. "The clothes in these pictures, the jewelry, the extravagance—none of that matters. People don't look through the pages of Vogue like it's a damn Sears & Roebuck catalog. Ah, but you're probably too young to remember those. Anyway, look here." He pointed to a photo of a young Kate Moss in a simple pantsuit that hung loose on her slender frame. "Tell me what you see."

"Well, she's blonde. She's pretty," I'd said. "The clothes look good on her."

"Dig deeper, Derek," he urged me. "What do you *see*? Look at her face, at her expression. Look at her eyes."

I studied the photograph for a couple of moments. "She looks confident. Like she doesn't need anyone. Like maybe she doesn't even want anyone."

"Yes!" he exclaimed. "Yes, young man. You are exactly right. *This* is why I was so successful. It was never about the clothes. It was about capturing how the clothes made people feel—the kind of life they could live in those clothes, the kind of person they wanted to be. Photography is its best when it's untampered with. No fancy lights. Just raw beauty and emotion. Those are the pictures that tell the best stories."

What I got from Wayne was worth its weight in gold. I still couldn't tell you the difference between Versace and Gucci, but after my time with him I started finding beauty everywhere. Photography had been a hobby of mine for a long time, but the more I studied it, the more I longed to capture the raw emotion that defined the human experience in all of its messy, beautiful glory.

A knock at the door brought me back to the present. I opened it to see the doorman walking away, a package left on the welcome mat. "Thank you," I called after him, and he waved.

I scooped up the package and shut the door. "Izzy, I believe you have a present here."

Her paws pitter-pattered across the floor as she ran to me, ears at full attention. She followed me to the kitchen island where I opened the box and pulled out the perfect Izzy-sized backpack and wind goggles. My motorcycle was my primary ride, so I needed a way to bring Izzy along with me.

She eyed me suspiciously when I knelt with the backpack in my hands for her to smell. Once she was satisfied, she tentatively wagged her tail and licked my hands. I scratched behind her ears, causing her back leg to thump against the wood floor.

"What do you say we give this a try?"

———

IT TURNED OUT THAT IZZY LOVED GOING FOR A RIDE. HER paws rested on my shoulders piggyback style, and she barked greetings to everyone we passed, smiling big with her pink tongue flapping in the wind. We spent the day cruising around Nashville, stopping to enjoy lunch on the patio at 12 South Taproom. Later in the afternoon we got coffee and a pup cup before heading back home. Izzy promptly returned to her cozy bed, completely zonked from her day of fun.

My mom tried to call again, but I didn't answer. I'd told her when we'd last spoken that I needed some time to think, but I still didn't know what to say.

I found myself restless, so much plaguing my mind that I finally decided to go out a little after eight thirty that evening. I hopped on my bike and ventured over to East Nashville. It was rare that I was ever recognized for being in the band without the rest of the guys around me, and it definitely never happened on the east side. Midnight in Dallas was far too mainstream for anyone hanging out over there. I loved that I was often able to fly under the radar.

That was one of the perks of playing bass. I remembered laughing the first time I saw the Tom Hanks movie *That Thing You Do* because they didn't even give the bass player a name. They just called him "The Bass Player". It was such an accurate depiction. Few people really cared much about the bass player outside of the context of the band, and that was perfectly fine by me.

I parked along the curb and walked up Woodland Street, finally pushing through the doors of 3 Crow Bar. The place was packed with people dressed like flappers, monsters, various animals, and puns. My favorite was the guy with the Gene Simmons face paint who wore a beret. *French kiss. Clever.* The fact that it was Halloween had completely slipped my mind. I'd known it was coming up soon, but I'd been so lost in my own head that I'd somehow managed to forget just *how* soon.

Finally, I was able to squeeze my way to the bar.

"What can I get you?" A bartender dressed like Marilyn Monroe briefly lifted her eyes from the fireball shots she was pouring.

"An Old Fashioned please," I said, prying my credit card and driver's license out of my wallet, sliding them across the bar.

"So what are you supposed to be?" she yelled over the noise. "A biker dude?" She checked my ID and mixed the drink, handing it to me with a tiny black straw.

I looked down at my usual uniform of dark jeans, a T-shirt, and my leather jacket. "Uh, no. I guess I'm an actual biker dude." I chuckled. "I honestly didn't even realize it was Halloween."

"Nice." She swiped my card and nodded at me approvingly. A rowdy guy dressed as Batman leaned over the bar a few feet down, trying to get her attention, and she rolled her eyes. "I can see tonight's going to be a blast."

I gave her a sympathetic smile as she handed me my card along with the receipt and a pen. I scribbled in a five hundred dollar tip, placing the receipt face down on the bar. I may not have been able to do anything about drunk assholes, but hopefully that would make her night a little better.

The bar was full of goblins and ghouls that were already three sheets to the wind at nine p.m. I settled toward the back of the bar when a girl with a forest fire of red hair drew me in. She was standing near the back wall, wearing black leggings, an oversized black sweater, and black booties. There wasn't a pair of animal ears in sight. It appeared she hadn't gotten the Halloween memo either.

She had the face of a Disney princess, with a wide-eyed gaze and the perfect cupid's bow. Her eyes were focused on a spot I couldn't see, and she held her drink with both hands.

A guy dressed as a box of tissues with the words 'Blow Me' on the front sauntered over to her. The girl tried to pretend she hadn't heard him, but finally, he touched her arm so she was forced to acknowledge him. *What a douche.*

Even as uncomfortable as she clearly was, her face looked sweet and approachable. I had a feeling she didn't have much control over that.

The guy put one arm around her, talking animatedly with his other as though he was explaining how it was possible for a jackass of his magnitude to exist.

She raised her shoulders to her ears and physically tried to take a step away, but he didn't get the hint. The dude was not going to let up. Her lips pinched together in a tight smile, indicating she was clearly in misery. I had to do something.

"There you are! I've been looking all over for you." Confusion swept over her face as she tried to decide if she actually knew me or not. I leaned in and gave her a light, one-armed hug, not wanting to cause her any further discomfort. "You look like you needed some help getting rid of this guy," I whispered in her ear before pulling away.

"Hey," she said in mock surprise. "I didn't even see you come in. How are you?"

'Blow Me' dude looked pissed, narrowing his eyes as he sized me up. "Are you her boyfriend or something?"

"Just a friend," I answered, wanting to make it clear to her that I came in peace, only wanting to help—even if she was the most beautiful woman I'd ever seen. "My friend Matt is her boyfriend. Good guy. Bodybuilder. Drives a motorcycle."

She smirked. "Yep. We've been together for a year now."

"I introduced them actually," I continued, reaching my hand out to shake his. "Nice to meet you, by the way. I'm Derek. What's your name?"

He rolled his eyes, ignoring my outstretched hand as he walked away. I shifted my gaze back to the breathtaking woman in front of me. "Good thing he won't be sticking around long enough to find out that Matt doesn't exist."

SEVEN

Jo

"Oh my God! Thank you so much," I said, grabbing my rescuer's arm. "That guy was such a creep. You totally saved me."

His laugh was throaty and velvety. "Don't mention it. You want me to hang with you until your friends get here in case he decides to try again?"

I noticed the faintest stubble along his perfectly angled jaw. He looked like a knight in a shining leather jacket with the face of Prince Charming.

"Actually, I'm not meeting anyone. I came by myself," I answered. "I'm realizing now that may not have been the best idea. I was supposed to have dinner with my friend, but she ended up having to work late." I paused for a moment, glancing at him over my drink. His short blond hair was pushed back off of his face in that messy on purpose sort of way. Wow, this guy was cute. "What about you? Are you meeting anyone?" With the luck I'd been having lately, he was probably waiting on his girlfriend.

"I'm not meeting anyone either," he said, leaning in so I

could hear him over the noise in the bar. He smelled like cinnamon and really good coffee. "I just needed to get out of the house for a while."

"Well, Derek—it is Derek, right?"

"It is."

I held my hand out to him. "Derek, I'm Jo. Can I buy you a drink for saving me from a box of Kleenex?"

He took my hand in his, the callused tips of his fingers sending shivers down my spine. "I'd love to have a drink with you, but I'm buying." He nodded in the direction of the bar, and I followed as he snaked through the crowd. "What would you like?"

"A Cosmopolitan would be great. Thank you."

"Another Old Fashioned?" the bartender asked.

He nodded. "And a Cosmopolitan, please."

She quickly went to work making the drinks, and Derek turned back to me. "So, did you also not know it was Halloween, or are you a Halloween scrooge?"

"Um, both?" I chuckled. "I definitely didn't know it was Halloween, but I also haven't dressed up for Halloween in ages. I'm usually working." The humiliation from the day before came rushing over me and made my entire body flush.

"But you're off tonight?" he asked. "That's good, right?"

He had no idea what a loaded question that was. I considered saying yes. I *should* have said yes. That was a lot easier to swallow than the truth. "Well, I sort of got fired yesterday." *Oh wow, okay, so you're just going all in, huh, Jo?*

Derek's eyes widened. "I'm so sorry. Are you okay?"

There was something about his gentle presence that made me feel like I could be completely honest with him—like I *wanted* to be. "Oh most definitely not," I answered, stone faced. Then I burst out laughing. Wild, crazed, unfettered laughter.

A smile spread across his face, and suddenly, he was laughing with me. "I take it that it's a funny story?"

"If I told you about my last couple of days, you probably wouldn't believe me," I said as the bartender returned with our drinks.

Derek paid the tab and turned toward me, handing me my Cosmopolitan. "Try me."

We sliced through the crowd and found a quieter spot to stand near the back of the bar. "Well, on Tuesday, the boyfriend I thought was going to propose let me know that he was, in fact, going to propose." I took a swig of my drink. "To someone else. He'd been cheating on me. For a year."

"Damn, Jo," he said. "That's brutal."

"And somehow that's not even the worst part. I went home and drank all of my feelings, and a cockroach fell on my bed so I slept in the bathroom," I barreled on. "Then, I went to work the next day—I'm a reporter in Chicago. At least I was. I thought I was getting promoted to anchor, but it went to Kimber instead. And in what was possibly my worst moment, I yelled at the CEO. Not only did I yell, but I *cursed* which is something I never do. Then, I proceeded to projectile vomit all over him and the entire conference room."

"No!" Derek cringed on my behalf. "You're kidding!"

I swished the pink liquid in my glass. "But wait, there's more," I said in my best news reporter voice. "So, my boss fires me, because of course he does. And then I go home to find that my landlord is like a drug dealer or something, and my apartment is on fire. So I left. I left Chicago and came home to Nashville."

He pressed his palm to his forehead, his mouth agape.

I gasped, realizing I had just word-vomited all over this kind, beautiful man. "And oh my God, I sound like a crazy person right now. I'm so sorry. I don't even know what I'm thinking." What was with me? It was like what happened with Aiden had tipped some invisible scale, causing a volcano of emotions to erupt inside me. And they just kept bubbling up, making it impossible to act like a civilized member of society.

"No, it's okay. Really," he assured me. "Sometimes we just need to get it all out. Honestly, I've had a pretty crappy couple of days too."

"Do you want to tell me about it?" I asked. "I may not be the best person to give advice since my life is basically in shambles, but I'm a good listener."

He raked his teeth over his bottom lip, pausing for a moment as though he wasn't sure how to respond. "I found out my dad is dying."

What I'd lost suddenly felt inconsequential. "Oh, Derek. I'm so sorry."

"Thanks," he said, giving me a faint smile. "I have a complicated relationship with my parents. My father...He put my mom and I through hell." He took a sip of his drink. "Now that he's dying, I don't know what to do. My mom wants me to talk to him and wipe the slate clean, but he wasn't a great guy, and him dying doesn't change that. So, do I go there and forgive him so he can feel better for what he did to me and my mom?" His blue eyes, full of the hurt he'd endured, shined down at me, and I wished there was something, anything, I could do to fix it.

I tilted my head, considering his question. "Did he ask for your forgiveness?"

"No." He squinted and pursed his lips. "No, he didn't."

"I think forgiveness is a very personal thing," I began. "He might never ask for forgiveness, but that doesn't mean you can't do it for *you*. Forgiving him doesn't have to grant him access to you, unless you want it to. It doesn't mean you have to allow him in your life. I think forgiveness is when you take back the power over your pain and begin to heal."

"Wow, Jo." He chuckled softly. "I thought you said you wouldn't give good advice. That was…That was beautiful."

My cheeks burned. "It would seem I'm full of surprises lately. Now, if I could just make some sense out of my disaster of a life."

Derek gazed down at me, tilting his head. "There's this new bar I've been hearing about that just opened up down the street. It's called The Stockroom—part of some old abandoned warehouses," he said. "They're supposed to have really great live music. What do you say we check it out and spend the rest of the night trying to forget about all of this for a while? Just two walking disasters having some fun."

My stomach twirled. "I'd say that sounds like a really great idea."

EIGHT

Derek

"It's somewhere up here on the left," I said as we walked along the sidewalk. Why was I suddenly so nervous? She was gorgeous, but it was more than that. Her entire presence sparkled. Even dressed in all black, she was vibrant and full of color.

Talking to Jo came easily, more easily than talking to anyone else. Perhaps it was because she didn't have any preconceived notions about who I was or who I should be. Or maybe it was because she'd been so vulnerable with me that it had allowed me to feel comfortable doing the same.

The sign for The Stockroom came into view at the corner, people in costumes scattered out front. Loud music spilled out into the street, as I opened the nondescript black door. "After you."

We approached a small podium where someone who looked like they belonged inside a nightmare awaited us. They pointed to a sign that showed the price of admission. I handed the ghoulish creature my credit card, and they returned it to me with the charge slip. After I signed, they pointed toward another black door that was vibrating from the sheer volume of the music on the other side A muscley bouncer dressed as a skeleton stood in front of the door with his arms crossed.

Jo glanced up at me. "That's some intense music."

It certainly wasn't what I normally listened to, and I was second guessing my suggestion as the raging guitars assaulted our ears. "Yeah, it is. Are you sure you want to go in?"

"Totally sure." Her wide eyes suggested otherwise.

"Let's do it," I said, approaching the skeleton.

"Do you have any sharp objects on you?" he asked.

I shook my head.

"Nope," Jo answered. She waved the small wallet-sized purse she was carrying in her hands. "This barely fits my phone, let alone my katana."

"Good luck." The skeleton smirked as he opened the door. "And remember, don't touch the actors, and they won't touch you." With that, he gave us a little shove and closed the door.

"Actors?" Jo asked. "What kind of show is this?"

"Also, where is the show?" I took in the eerie purple glow of the small, dark corridor.

"Must be through here." Jo started through the shadows, and I followed behind her.

As we reached the end of the hall, a looming figure appeared out of the darkness, causing us both to scream. It got close enough for me to see that it was, in fact, Michael Myers who was tilting his creepy face at us. He must have been seven feet tall. No wonder he always survived in the movies.

"Peas and rice!" Jo shouted, nearly taking me down as she jumped backward. "Alright, you got me. Now, can you tell us where the music is?"

Michael Meyers breathed heavily through the nose holes of his creepy mask, cocking his head to the other side.

Jo laughed nervously. "Why isn't he saying anything?"

He remained silent and leaned in toward Jo.

"Ohhhhkay," she said, grabbing my arm and pulling me down another dark corridor to the right. "They're really serious about this Halloween business around—" She screeched mid-sentence when a loud bang pierced our ears, and a cloud of smoke surrounded us. A dark figure wielding a large machete appeared out of nowhere. I jumped in front of Jo as she screamed. "What is going on here?"

Machete guy held the shining blade menacingly over our heads.

"What kind of concert is this?" Jo cried as we pushed our way through, the boogeyman following on our heels.

Once he turned back down the hall, we stopped for a moment to catch our breath. We were propped against the wall when a whispered '*boo*' came from beside my head causing me to almost leap into Jo's arms.

"What is wrong with you people?" Jo lunged at our assailant who was dressed in a full black bodysuit so they blended in with the wall. "We're just trying to find the live music, and nobody will tell us anything! We get it, it's Halloween, but for the love of Pete can you just tell us where to go?"

The person in black burst out laughing.

Jo crossed her arms over her chest. "What's so funny?"

"You're in a haunted house," a high-pitched voice answered from behind the body suit. "Scaring you is literally the whole point."

"I thought this was The Stockroom," I said. "The sign said—"

The shadow person cut me off. "Their door is around the corner. This is The Nashville Scream."

Jo and I burst into laughter, and the person in black ripped off their mesh black mask, revealing a very non-scary looking young woman.

"Did you guys really just come to a haunted house by accident?" she choked out between guffaws.

We were laughing so hard we couldn't answer with more than a nod of our heads.

"I've gotta be honest," she said with a chuckle. "That's impressive for all the wrong reasons. You can go back the way you came and get your money back, but if you want to stay, tonight's proceeds are going to the Northeast Nashville Alliance."

Jo gasped. "Project NENA? No way!" She turned to me. "I covered their Christmas toy drive a while back when I interned for one of the local news stations."

I looked at Jo, the question dangling in the air. "So, should we stay?"

"We have to," Jo insisted with a smile. "It's for the kids!" She grinned as she reached for my hand, guiding me through the darkness.

"I guess we're staying then," I said, not at all disappointed that Jo might have a reason to get even closer to me.

WE WERE CHASED OUT OF THE NASHVILLE SCREAM BY TWO guys wielding chainsaws, and we stumbled out onto the sidewalk, laughing our heads off.

"I can't believe we did that," I said, adrenaline coursing

through my veins. "I thought you were going to pee yourself when that clown came out of the floor."

Jo was doubled over giggling. "I think I probably did a little."

"That was actually really, really fun," I said.

"I haven't done anything like that in forever."

"Me either." I couldn't think of a time in recent history where I'd laughed that much.

"But you've proven you can't be trusted to pick where we go. We're likely to end up at a slaughterhouse or something."

"I guess that means you'll have to decide where we go next."

She raised her brows at me. "You mean that didn't satisfy your quest for fun?"

A smile swept across my face. "Maybe I just want to spend more time with you."

I could see her cheeks blush in the glow of the streetlights.

"Okay then," she said, turning on her heel and heading back down Woodland Street. "Let's see what we can find." She looked up at the signs of the various bars and businesses, peering in windows to see what each place offered. Finally, she stopped in front of The Soda Parlor. "Yes. This is it."

I opened the door for her, and the sugary scent of waffle cones welcomed us.

She closed her eyes and took in a deep breath. "Doesn't that smell divine? I don't know when I had ice cream last. It's been years."

"What?" I asked, with feigned disbelief. "No ice cream, no haunted houses. Do you just hate fun?"

She laughed as we approached the menu that hung on the wall. "I don't hate fun, but up until the last seventy-two hours, I always had a plan for everything. My days were always scheduled, and I rarely ventured off script. I even ate the same giant salad for lunch every day for the last five years."

"Okay, now I'm sad," I teased. "There's so many great lunch options you're missing out on. There are actually these really cool things called sandwiches. You should try them sometime."

"Ha. Ha." She scrunched her nose at me. "I mean, that's just what was instilled in me from such an early age. When your dad is Daniel Kingsley, the world expects greatness at all times. That means acting perfectly, eating perfectly...basically doing everything perfectly."

"Holy shit. Your dad is Daniel Kingsley? The news guy?"

Jo chuckled. "I see his reputation precedes me." She scanned a finger down the menu. "Ooh I want that!" She landed on a Halloween themed sundae called The Cereal Killer that consisted of a double chocolate waffle, topped with cereal milk flavored ice cream, Fruity Pebbles, and chocolate sauce.

"That sounds like a very festive sugar coma," I said. "I like it. Let's make it two."

We got our desserts and sat in a corner booth by the old school pinball machines that lined the walls.

Jo took a large bite, sliding the spoon slowly between her lips. "This is heavenly." Her lips *did* look heavenly, and I wanted to know what they felt like...what they tasted like. How could the guy who'd broken up with her want to kiss anyone else?

I cleared my throat. "You said you've always tried to honor your dad's legacy. Is that because that's what you wanted to do?"

She shrugged. "I guess I never really had a choice in the matter." She took another bite of her ice cream. "I loved it in the beginning—at least parts of it. I loved helping people tell their stories and the fast pace of a newsroom. I guess I got to a point where it stopped being about the stories and became about being the best." Her lips turned down slightly. "About being like my dad so maybe he would, I don't know, *notice me*." She pressed her palm to her forehead. "There I go again with the word vomit. What about you? What do you do?"

"Photography," I answered without thinking. Talking to Jo made me want to be who I longed to be, rather than who I was.

"That's awesome!" Her eyes lit up. "Tell me what you love about it."

And I did. I told her all about Wayne and every single thing I loved about photography, and it felt good. Like feeling the sun on your skin after a week of rain.

"That must be really cool," she said finally, once our desserts had disappeared and only melted remnants remained. "Getting to do something you love, something you're passionate about."

I immediately felt like a fraud. An amazing girl was sitting in front of me, and I was lying to her. I started to come clean, but she spoke again before I could.

"Have you ever felt like you've completely lost your way?" she asked. "Like nobody knows who you really are because maybe you forgot who you were too?"

My chest constricted, and I nodded. "You have no idea."

Her phone dinged, and she sighed, pulling it out of her bag. "Oh! My friend is home from work. I should probably get going."

"Yeah, of course," I said, unable to hide the disappointment that crept into my voice. "Let me walk you to your car."

We tossed our garbage on the way out the door and started slowly down the street.

"Thank you for tonight." She nudged my arm with her elbow. "I can't tell you how much I needed this. I mean, without you I'd probably be listening to Kleenex guy's dissertation on why I should go home with him."

I chuckled. "I'm glad I could save you from such a tragic fate."

"So, this is me." She pointed to the Ford Focus parked on the street in front of us. "Seriously, Derek, this was so fun."

God, she was pretty. The freckles scattered across her face reminded me of some intricate constellation, and I was thanking my lucky stars that I got a close-up view.

"I'd really like to—" I began to tell her that I wanted to see her again, but was stopped mid-sentence when Jo stood on her toes, pressing her mouth to mine. Her pink lips were soft as marshmallows and far sweeter than the ice cream sundaes we'd had. I slid my hand around the back of her neck, gently pulling her closer, catching a whiff of warm sugar and crisp apples that made me hungry all over again. It was chilly out, but she was like curling up in front of a fireplace. I never wanted to leave her warmth.

She broke our kiss and ran around to the driver's side of her car, leaving the air feeling colder than it actually was. Where was she going? It couldn't end like this.

"Wait," I called out. "Can I have your number? I'd really like to take you out on a proper date."

She thought for a second and started back toward me, but quickly shook her head and returned to her car. "I'm trying out this new thing where I don't make plans because they've been a disaster lately." She ran a hand through her auburn hair. "And you...You're too good to mess up, Derek."

No, no, no. I didn't like this. "But how will I see you again?"

"I have to believe that if we're supposed to cross paths, the universe will make it happen."

I waved my phone at her. "Why trust the universe when you could give me your number?"

"Because what would be the fun in that?" She shot me a smile that was an arrow right to my heart before getting in her car and driving away.

NINE

Jo

"WHAT WOULD BE the fun in that?" I mocked myself as I gave Katie the play-by-play of my evening on the couch over a cup of Earl Grey tea. I explained everything from Kleenex guy to the haunted house to me fleeing the scene after kissing a handsome stranger. "Who even am I? Who says things like that? I'm so stupid."

"You are not stupid," she insisted. "It was cute, flirty, and dare I say, *fun*?"

"Katie, in what world do any of those words actually describe me?" I pressed my fingers to my temples. "I'm an uptight goody-two-shoes. I'm Daniel Kingsley's daughter. I'm about as cute, flirty, and fun as...I don't know...a tampon."

Katie cackled, nearly spilling her tea. "I'm sorry, but *what?* A tampon?"

I shook my head and laughed. "Yeah, a tampon. Tampons aren't fun. They don't make you feel excited and full of life. Just the opposite, actually. They're boring and functional, and they fill you with dread."

"I think that depends on who you ask," Katie protested.

"If you were afraid you might be pregnant, you might be very happy to need a tampon."

I rolled my eyes and sighed. "I don't know why I'm even worrying about it. It wouldn't have been smart to give him my number anyway. I'm a walking disaster. I'm still trying to regain my footing. It wouldn't be right to bring someone else into that."

"But what if you run into him again?" she asked. "You said yourself that if the universe wants you to cross paths again, it'll happen. So what would you do if you saw him?"

"I'd say the chances of that happening are slim to none."

"But it *could* happen," Katie reminded me. "So? What would you do?"

I leaned my head back against the cushion.

"You know, it's okay to hope for it. It's okay to want somebody in your life."

"But my life is—"

"A mess," Katie filled in for me. "So? I don't know anyone whose life isn't at least a little messy. Honestly, I hope you do run into him again. He sounds like he could be good for you."

"How so?"

"We've been best friends since the sixth grade, Jo. The last time I saw you this excited about a guy was when Bryce Anderson asked you to Homecoming sophomore year," she said. "You seem lighter tonight. Like someone lifted this giant boulder off your chest."

I sucked in a deep breath through my teeth. There was no point in arguing because she was right, and we both knew it. "I should have given him my number, shouldn't I?"

She shrugged. "I mean, maybe. But I also think it's really romantic and exciting that you left it up to chance."

"It's only romantic and exciting if I run into him again," I pointed out, frustrated with myself all over again. This wasn't a fairytale. This was real life, and in real life you couldn't leave things up to the universe. Amazing things like that didn't happen by chance, right?

Katie shook her head. "Even if you don't, the fact that you let go and did something totally spontaneous is romantic and exciting all on its own." She paused for dramatic effect. "But I definitely hope you run into him again."

I giggled. "Well, I won't. Because I'm never leaving your house again."

"Oh yes, you are," she informed me. "You're coming to Sunday dinner with me at Ella's house this weekend."

"I think that's so sweet that you've found a family of friends here," I said. "But I wouldn't want to intrude on that. You should go and have fun."

"Don't be silly. Any family of mine is going to become family of yours," she insisted. "They're going to love you, and I know you'll love them too. Besides, it would be good for you to know a few people here besides me."

"Are you sure you don't mind me going with you?" I asked. "I feel like I've kind of crashed your whole life."

"Oh, stop. You haven't crashed anything. I'm really glad you're here," she promised. "It feels good to have you home. I've missed you."

I smiled over at her. "I've missed you too. And it feels good to *be* home." I took a sip of my tea. "How have things been here? I know work keeps you pretty busy, but are you getting enough rest?"

She shrugged. "I probably don't get as much rest as I should, but who does? Things are good. Work is crazy in a good way, but I guess I'm realizing I'm not in my twenties anymore. I tire out easily, and my body doesn't respond to stress quite the same way it did when I was younger."

I narrowed my eyes at her. "Have you been to the doctor? Just to be safe?"

"Not recently," she admitted. "But really, I'm fine. Promise. So…Have you talked to your dad yet?"

I snorted. "My dad talked to my voicemail. He knows I got fired."

"But does he know what Aiden did to you? That your apartment burned down?" she asked. "That's kind of a big deal."

"Honestly, I don't know that either of those things would even register on my father's radar. I guarantee you he's more concerned with whether I've started applying for jobs yet." I picked at my nail polish. "Which I guess I should do."

"Give yourself some time, girl," Katie said. "Figure out what you want to do, not what your dad wants you to do. You need some relaxation in your life, Jolene Kingsley." She rose to her feet and disappeared from the room for a moment. When she returned to her seat, she had two plastic shopping bags with her, and she emptied the contents of the bags, item by item. "I went by Walgreens on the way to work this morning. We've got clay face masks, hot oil treatments for our hair, heated neck wraps, these eye gel thingies that looked really cool, toe separators, and some fun, sparkly holiday nail colors. Oh, and some kind of treatment that's supposed to make our feet feel like a baby's butt. I don't know. There was a cute little old lady cashier that suggested it, so I had to get it."

I burst into laughter and threw my arms around her. "I love you so much."

"I love you too," she said, before pulling away to present

me with three glittery bottles of polish. "Now, do you want sparkly purple, red, or navy?"

"It's a tough choice, but I'm going to go with purple."

She turned the bottle upside down to read the name and choked on a laugh.

I grinned. "What's it called?"

She handed it to me so I could see for myself. I nearly dropped the bottle when I read the name on the bottom:

The Universe Is Calling.

"DON'T BE NERVOUS," KATIE SAID, CARRYING A BLACKBERRY pie as we approached the front door of her friend Ella's house on Sunday. "They're going to love you."

I smoothed my hands over my black sweater dress. Before we reached the top step, the door flung open and a gorgeous young woman who looked to be in her early twenties beamed at us. "Hey, Katie!"

"Grace!" Katie greeted her with a hug. "This is my best friend, Jo."

I reached out my hand to shake hers, but she flung her arms around me instead like we were old friends. "Oh, uh, wow, hi," I said, taken aback.

"It's so nice to meet you," she greeted me. "Come on in." We followed behind her as she led us inside. "Now, I must warn you that my mom is pregnant right now, and well, she's a little—"

"GOOD GOD IT'S HOTTER THAN SATAN'S LEFT TIT IN HERE," a woman's voice shouted.

Grace and Katie snickered, and my eyes grew wide.

"Let's just say she's not handling it well today," Grace

whispered as we rounded the corner into the kitchen where an older version of Grace stood, one hand on her baby bump, the other fanning her face with a potholder.

"That's Ella." Katie pointed her out. "And that's her fiancé, Cash." She nodded toward a nice-looking man who was frying chicken in an electric skillet. "The one making the mashed potatoes is Dallas." This time, she pointed toward a really hot guy whose hair was pulled into a bun. I'd heard a lot about Dallas, and now I could see why.

"Top Chef Katie!" Dallas exclaimed, and I noticed Katie tuck her hair behind her ear, a soft giggle rising out of her. I nudged her subtly with my elbow, but she pretended I didn't.

"Can we eat yet?" a guy with fair skin and dark hair asked, taking a swig from a glass filled with amber liquid. "I'm wasting away here."

"That's Luca," Grace informed me as a cute red-headed guy wrapped his arms around her from behind. "And this is my boyfriend Sam."

It was impossible not to notice that Sam, Dallas, and Luca were good-looking. Like abnormally good-looking. Ella, Cash, and Grace were gorgeous too, but those guys could have been movie stars. Wait…How had Katie met them again? My mind tried to recall when these names had been introduced in conversation a few years before. I thought she'd mentioned they'd all connected because of her boss, but there was more to the story. What *was* it?

"Ooooh! Fresh meat!" A voice called from the kitchen table. It belonged to a guy with the most perfect eyebrows I'd ever seen. He wore a shimmery black top and sat next to a guy that could have been in a J Crew catalog. "Hey, sugar. I'm Antoni, and this is my husband Nate." Nate nodded a hello.

Why were all of these people so beautiful? And why

hadn't Katie said, '*oh, by the way, my friends are all super-models*'? Or had she, and I'd just been too preoccupied to notice?

"You cannot ride Bradley Cooper like a horse." I heard a woman's voice as a couple entered the room with their two small kids, who were chasing after a scruffy looking dog. *Wait. Bradley Cooper is here? Maybe they really are movie stars.*

"Bradley Cooper is our dog," Grace explained, sensing my confusion. "And that's Liv and Jax and their kids, Jonathan and Chloe." *More unreasonably beautiful people.*

"Hi!" Chloe squealed as Jonathan ran through the kitchen.

Katie presented me to the group as though she was Vanna White, and they had all just bought a vowel. "Everyone this is—"

"Jo?" A voice came from behind me causing a chill to run down my spine. It was a voice I would have recognized anywhere.

I turned to see him standing there, all smiles and soulful eyes wrapped in a leather jacket. The universe was, indeed, calling. And had he somehow gotten even more gorgeous since I last saw him?

"Wait," Katie cocked her head to the side. "What?"

"Derek." I gulped "Hi."

"Hold on," Dallas said, his interest piqued. "How do you guys know each other?"

"Yeah, how *do* you know each other?" Katie asked, her brows drawn together.

"Um," I managed, my cheeks burning.

Derek took a step toward me, causing my heart to flutter in my chest. "We actually met the other night. On Halloween. We accidentally went to a haunted house together."

Katie's eyes grew wide, her mouth falling open. Ella looked on curiously as she fanned herself.

"Oh my God," Grace chirped. "That's so cute."

"Who *accidentally* goes to a haunted house?" Luca asked.

Grace laughed and rolled her eyes. "Ignore him."

It wasn't hard to do exactly that when Derek was standing so close to me, like we were the only two people in the room. My lips tingled as I remembered what it felt like to kiss him.

I looked over at Katie, trying to communicate with her through telepathy, begging her to please wipe the look of shock off her face. Derek and Ella exchanged a glance, and I noticed her give him a nod. *What does that nod mean? Is that code for something?*

"Okay, everyone," Cash announced, oblivious to what was going on. "Let's eat."

With everyone's attention off me and Derek, I turned to face him. "Wow…Fancy seeing you here, huh?"

He laughed that velvety laugh that made me melt as he leaned into me. "So, does this mean you're going to give me your number now?"

TEN

Derek
___

Jo GAVE ME A SHY SMILE. "It would seem the universe wanted us to meet again, and who am I to deny the universe what it wants?"

I couldn't believe my luck. When Jo drove away Halloween night, she'd left me with nothing but the taste of her on my lips. She hadn't given me her number, not even a glass slipper to help me find her again. Now, here she was in Ella and Cash's kitchen, the very same place I'd told them about her the day before over coffee. In a matter of seconds, I'd gone from thinking I may never see her again to finding her standing amongst everyone I considered family.

Ella gave me a satisfied grin. She'd told me she thought I'd see Jo again, that it was too great a story to be finished, and she'd been right. It was as though our conversation had conjured her out of thin air.

"Jo, come sit over here," Ella encouraged her, pointing to one of the middle spots at the main dining table. Ella's dining set only sat six, so she added a long folding table at one end to extend it. We were sandwiched in like sardines, but it only emphasized the tight knit, chaotic feel of our Sunday dinners.

"Yes, get over here," Antoni insisted. "I promise we don't bite."

"Speak for yourself," Luca said, chomping into his dinner roll.

I sat on one side of Jo while Katie sat on the other. Multiple conversations happened at once as we all served ourselves. Jax told a story about how Jonathan had gotten his head stuck in the banister, and Ella was animatedly recapping an episode of some TV show with Grace and Liv. Antoni and Luca were sparring over whether or not drinking before eleven a.m. was acceptable if the drink wasn't a mimosa or a bloody mary.

Jo and I reached for the green beans at the same time, and her fingers grazed mine, sending a jolt of electricity coursing through me. Her cheeks flushed, and I gestured for her to take them.

"So, Jo, Katie said you're visiting from Chicago," Dallas said after everyone had started to dig in. "What do you do there?"

Jo dabbed at the corners of her mouth with her napkin. "Well, I'm...I *was* a reporter for a news station there. I'm in between jobs at the moment, though." She shifted uncomfortably in her chair, and Katie gave her shoulder an encouraging squeeze.

"How long are you in town for?" Cash asked.

I wanted to reach for Jo's hand. Though she'd told me everything that happened, I knew that was far different than sharing all the intimate details of what she'd been through with an entire table of people.

"That's to be determined," she answered politely. "My

apartment kind of, um…burned down. I'm staying with Katie until I can get things figured out."

"Oh shit," Dallas said. "I'm so sorry. Are you okay?"

Liv took a sip of her sweet tea. "Is there anything you need? Clothes and things like that?"

"Aunt Liv gets tons of stuff from designers and brands wanting her to wear their stuff," Grace explained.

Liv nodded. "I'm sure I can load you up with lots of fun things."

Grace chuckled. "The clothes are definitely a perk to knowing Aunt Liv."

"And the skincare," Katie added.

Ella sighed dreamily. "Can't forget the skincare."

Jo blinked. "Wow, thank you. That's so nice of you." She paused for a moment. "Are you a model or something?"

"Oh, God no," she answered with a soft laugh. "Jax and I play music together."

"And when I'm not making music with her, I'm playing with these guys," Jax added, gesturing around to me, Dallas, and Luca.

Jo tilted her head toward me, brows pinched together. "You're in a band?"

And that's when I remembered I'd omitted this little detail about my life.

Grace looked at her with wide eyes. "Yeah, he's in a band. Only one of the biggest bands in the world."

"What's it called?" she asked me, but Dallas answered.

"Midnight in Dallas," he said politely before shooting me a questioning glance, probably wondering why I'd withheld that information. I couldn't really explain why I hadn't told her, and I knew she was probably wondering the same thing. But there was something about her that made me want her to know the me that existed outside of the band. Because that was the only version of myself that actually *felt* like me anymore.

A wave of recognition swept over her face. "Wait, *you're* Midnight in Dallas? I just heard one of your songs on the radio for the first time a couple of days ago. It was really lovely." She turned to Dallas. "So, are you the lead singer?"

The table erupted in laughter.

"Honey, the only place that boy sings is the shower," Antoni quipped.

"Very loudly, I might add," Jax said. "One time, our hotel reservations got messed up, and I got stuck sharing a room with him. It was like getting a private concert from a dying cat. I swear the whole floor could hear it."

"Actually, Jax is the singer of the group," I explained. "Dallas plays drums, Luca is our lead guitarist, and I play the bass."

"Katie, why didn't you tell me you were friends with real, bonafide rockstars?" Jo whipped her head around to face her.

Katie opened her mouth to speak, but Luca answered instead. "Probably because she knows we're really just a bunch of losers."

"Are you embarrassed of us, Top Chef Katie?" Dallas quipped, pinning her with a devilish grin.

"Of course I'm not embarrassed of y'all," Katie replied, not missing a beat. "Okay, well, maybe Luca."

"Touché," Luca said, and we all cracked up.

"I'm a little behind the times." Jo took a sip of her wine. "I probably haven't updated my playlist since the first iPod came out. Work was always so hectic that when I was in the car I rarely ever had music playing," Jo said.

"So, what I hear you saying is that you're a psychopath," Luca teased. "Seriously, no music in the car? Who hurt you?"

"Don't feel bad, Jo," Grace interjected. "Cash doesn't know who anyone is either."

Cash chuckled. "Hey!"

"Fun fact," Grace continued. "He didn't even know who Bradley Cooper was."

"Okay, even I'm not *that* far removed from society," Jo joked before turning back to me. "So, when we were out the other night, nobody stopped you. Isn't that what people do when they see celebrities, you know, out in the wild?"

"People in Nashville are pretty good about leaving famous people alone," I said.

"Unless they're tourists," Ella corrected. "The tourists always lose their shit."

"It helps that I'm the bass player too," I said. "People don't really notice me as much as they do the other guys. You could probably replace me on stage with just about anybody and no one would bat an eye."

Dallas flashed me another probing stare. "That's not true. The band only works with all of us. That's why we always have to be at our *best*." He emphasized that last word and aimed it straight at me.

"No shop talk at Sunday dinner," Cash said with a smile and a pointed look at Dallas.

"So, I guess now's not the time to talk ideas for the next album?" Dallas prodded.

I groaned inwardly. I'd known this was coming. I'd known it was only a matter of time before we had to get back in the studio, but the idea of being cooped up in a sound booth made my heart race.

"Definitely not," Cash replied.

"So, what do the rest of you do?" Jo asked casually. "Are you all musicians?"

"I work with Cash at his record label," Grace answered. "Sam is in music too. He's on our label along with these guys." She gestured around the table.

"I manage all of these fools," Antoni explained. "And Nate here is a model. We got married earlier this year, so he got grandfathered into our little dysfunctional family."

"I manage Livvie Cakes," Ella said, "and I have no musical abilities whatsoever."

"Or baking abilities," Katie mock-whispered.

"Hey!" Ella balled up her napkin, throwing it at her.

"It's a little known fact that Ella doesn't cook," I said, "At least nothing that doesn't come from the freezer section."

"Pizza rolls are my specialty," Ella quipped.

"So, Jo," Luca spoke, taking a pull from his drink. "Are you into my buddy Derek or not? Cause I've always had a thing for redheads."

I kicked Luca hard beneath the table, and he winced.

"Luca," Cash warned.

I knew it was too much to hope for Luca to be on his best behavior.

"What?" Luca shoveled in a bite of macaroni and cheese. "I'm just joking. Unless you're not into him. Because in that case, I'm definitely not joking."

I scrubbed my hands down my face. "Why are you like this?"

Luca leaned back in his chair, placing his hands behind his head, clearly amused by himself. "I'm just saying, what if this is a sign? I like redheads, Jo *is* a redhead."

Jo propped her elbow on the table, leaning her head onto

her hand. "The only signs I'm seeing here are red flags, Luca." She gave him a playful smile.

Everyone, including Luca, burst into peals of laughter.

Damn. A lot of people would have been put off by Luca, but she'd held her own, beating him at his own game.

Ella nearly choked on her water. "Oh my God. That was brilliant."

Dallas was laughing so hard that tears had started to form in his eyes. "I kind of love you for that."

"I like you, Jo," Luca said, nodding approvingly. "This one's a keeper."

I couldn't have agreed more.

———

"HEY, WAIT UP," I CALLED OUT TO JO AS SHE STARTED toward the door. Sunday dinner was over, and everyone was saying their goodbyes, filtering out into the night. "Are you trying to leave without giving me your number?"

"I thought maybe we'd leave it up to the universe again," she teased.

I chuckled, handing her my phone. "Not a chance, Cinderella."

She tapped out her number and hit send, causing her phone to ring once from inside her purse. "It's not a glass slipper, but I guess it'll do." She handed my phone back to me with a smile.

"I'd love to take you out," I said, opening the door for her. "Do you have any free time this week?"

Jo looked up at me, her eyes glittering in the glow of the porch light. "All I have is free time."

"How about Friday?" I asked. "The CMAs are on Thursday. We're part of a Johnny Cash tribute performance, so we're rehearsing a lot until then, but after that I have some time off."

"Friday sounds great," she answered as Katie joined us on Ella's front stoop.

She squeezed Jo's shoulder. "Ready to head out?"

"Sure." Jo smiled at her then turned back to me. "So, I guess I'll talk to you soon?"

I nodded. "You can count on it."

Katie flashed me an excited smile as she and Jo bounded down the walk.

"So, Katie's friend seems cool," Dallas said, sidling up next to me as I started toward my bike.

I watched as Jo and Katie pulled away in Katie's old VW Bug. "Yeah, she is."

"You two really hit it off," Dallas continued.

I inhaled the crisp November air. "She's…She's really something."

He clapped me on the shoulder. "Any girl that can go toe to toe with Luca and hold her own is okay in my book."

We laughed as we reached the end of the drive where my bike and his car were parked.

"You could have told me you met somebody, man." Dallas shoved his hands in his pockets. "That's really great."

I couldn't bring myself to meet his eyes. Normally, I *would* have told him about something like this, but with how tense things had been between us, I wasn't sure how he'd receive it.

"Look, I know I've been hard on you lately," he said, as though he were reading my mind. "I've been a dick, and I'm sorry about that. Things have just been…I don't know." He blew out a sharp breath. "It feels like everything's changing, you know? It all started when Liv and Jax got together. I love that girl to death. You know I do. She's brought a lot of good into our lives. But it's like ever since they started their own thing, the band's kind of taken a backseat. Cash is going to have less time to give once the baby's born, and again, I'm fucking happy for them, but..." He trailed off for a moment, then shook his head. "Then there's Luca. I'm concerned about his drinking, but every time I ask him about it, he tells me to fuck off. So, what I'm trying to say is, you're the one I've always felt I could count on. And lately, it just feels like your heart just isn't in this anymore."

I didn't know how to tell him. How to tell him my heart had never been in the band, at least not completely. "I'm sorry, man. I—"

"No, I'm the one who should be sorry," he said. "Listen, I know it's just a rough patch. I should have given you the benefit of the doubt. You've never let me down, and I know you're not gonna start now. No matter what, it's you and me, brother."

Guilt surged through my veins, cold as ice, as he held out a hand to me. I grasped it, and he pulled me into a one-armed hug.

"See you tomorrow," Dallas said as he walked to his car.

I raked my hands down my face as his tail lights disappeared down the street. My phone vibrated in my pocket, and I pulled it out to see a message from Ella.

Ella: I told you I didn't think the story with Jo was over. In fact, I think it's only the beginning. ;)

Just thinking about Jo filled me with hope. There was something about her that made me want to show her exactly who I was...to be completely honest with her. Maybe one day I'd find the courage to do that with everyone else too.

ELEVEN

Jo

"You could have at least told me they were famous. Like legit, real-life rockstars," I said to Katie on Monday morning from where I sat cross-legged against the wall in the back of Livvie Cakes, where Katie was the head-baker.

"I did." She hesitated for a second. "Back when I first met them, remember? I was freaking out because they're one of my favorite bands."

"Oh…" My lips curved downward, and shame tinged my cheeks pink. I'd been so self-focused that I'd either forgotten that important detail, or worse, never heard it to begin with.

"To be fair, I think you were reporting on that hospital shooting at the time," she continued as she filled a pastry bag with buttercream, clearly willing to give me far more credit than I deserved. I remembered that shooting at Northwestern Memorial and the many terrified people I'd spoken to over the course of that week, but I couldn't remember something so important to my best friend, and *that* was a problem.

"It doesn't matter," I said softly. "That's no excuse. I'm so sorry. I've not been a very good friend, have I?"

"You've been a little distracted," she admitted. "But I think we all go through seasons like that. Don't be so hard on yourself."

I nodded and forced a smile, making a silent vow to be the friend she deserved. A forced break from work would be good for me in more ways than one.

"I mean it. We're good," Katie assured me, placing a cupcake in my hand. "Now, try this. It's one of our new ones."

I did as she asked and closed my eyes, the perfect blend of gingerbread, brown sugar, and coffee dancing on my tongue. If Christmas had a flavor, this was it. "Oh my God. What's this one called?"

"Santa's Brew," Katie answered, moving to the island in the middle of the kitchen. "We used to wait until after Thanksgiving to add our holiday flavors to the menu, but people love them so much we had to start serving them the first full week of November."

I took another bite. "You are a baking wizard."

"Actually, I didn't come up with that one," she said as the door between the front of the store and the kitchen opened, and a pretty girl with light brown hair piled in a messy bun walked in. "That was McKenzie's creation." Katie nodded in the direction of the girl who had just entered. "My friend Jo was just complimenting your Santa's Brew cupcake."

The girl stopped in her tracks.

"This is amazing," I gushed, holding up my half-eaten cupcake. "A masterpiece."

McKenzie blinked at me before turning toward Katie. "Sydney just called in. Her dad is in the hospital again."

"Poor Sydney. Did she sound like she was holding up okay?" Katie asked.

McKenzie gave her a blank stare. "Not really?"

"I need to send some flowers over there. Vanderbilt, right?" Katie looked up from the cupcakes she was working on. "I know that leaves you on your own up there. I can call Jacob and see if he can fill in."

"I don't need help," McKenzie said quickly. "I mean, I don't mind working alone. Besides, I think Jacob has friends in town."

Katie nodded. "Right. Well, as long as you're sure you're good."

"I'm good." She started back toward the door. "I better get back up front."

"Nice to meet you," I called to her.

"Yep," she said as the door closed behind her.

I snorted. "Guess McKenzie won't be one of my Nashville friends."

Katie laughed. "Don't take it personally. That's just McKenzie. She's a little…"

"Stand-offish?" I finished for her.

"She's different." Katie chuckled. "But she's so good at what she does. Our whole Christmas menu? All her ideas."

"Really?"

"She also came up with a lot of our lunch and catering menus after we expanded the business, and she's a hell of a barista too," she answered. "I honestly don't know how I ever worked without her. Sometimes, she'll literally hand me something I need before I even ask for it."

"What do you think her story is?"

Katie shrugged. "I think maybe she's just one of those people who doesn't make friends at work. Maybe she likes to keep her personal and professional lives separate. And honestly, if she keeps doing what she's doing and she's good with the customers, I'm happy. We haven't had help as good as her in…well, ever."

I polished off the rest of my cupcake. "As long as you're happy. And speaking of happy…" I dusted the crumbs off my hands. "Why haven't you told me about Dallas?"

"I have."

"You have. *That* I remember, but you didn't tell me you were in love with him," I fired back. "I'm pretty sure it's mutual too, *Top Chef Katie*."

Katie rolled her eyes. "We're just friends."

"There is a land called Denial, and you are the queen."

"You and Derek, on the other hand," she said, completely ignoring me. "You two have some serious chemistry. He couldn't take his eyes off you the whole night."

I laughed. "How did this get turned back around on me? We're talking about you and Dallas." My phone rang from my purse beside me on the floor.

Katie's eyes lit up. "Maybe it's Derek."

Hope swelled in my chest as I retrieved my phone and immediately retreated when I saw the name on the screen. *No such luck.* "It's my dad." I sighed and rose to my feet. "May as well face the music. I better take this outside."

"Good luck," Katie called as I started toward the back door.

"Dad," I answered my phone as I pushed my way outside.

"Jolene, what on earth is going on? *Fired?*"

I sucked in a deep breath. "It wasn't my proudest moment, but yes, I was fired. But there's something else I need to tell—"

"The news business is like a small town high school. Everybody knows everyone and news travels fast. You're lucky I was able to keep this quiet."

"Yes, but—"

His voice escalated to a yell. "Do you understand how busy I am? And now I have to go kiss some blow-hard's ass to try to get you your job back."

"I don't want my job back," I blurted. "I'm in Nashville."

"You're *where*?"

"Dad, my apartment burned down," I said. "So much happened in the span of twenty-four hours. I needed to get away from there."

"Are you alright? Were you there when it happened?" The sharp edge of his voice turned smooth.

"I wasn't there. It happened while I was still at work... while, well, you know."

"We can get you another apartment, Jolene, but jobs like this are hard to come by," he said gently. "Why don't you go stay with that boyfriend of yours?"

"We broke up." I didn't bother telling him the details because I knew they didn't matter to him.

He let out an exasperated sigh. "Where are you looking for jobs? I'll make some calls."

"I haven't started looking. This all just happened last week, Dad. I don't even know what I want to do yet," I said. "I've just been thinking and...What if news really isn't for me? What if I'm not actually good at it?" *What if I don't love doing it anymore?* I knew better than to ask that out loud.

"That's ridiculous." He scoffed. "You're a Kingsley. Journalism is in your blood. It's practically your birthright."

"I think I need to take a few days and clear my head. I—"

"Don't worry. I'll make some calls and help you get out of this mess."

"But, Dad, I think—"

"I've got to go. I just got to my next interview," he said, cutting me off. "I'll be in touch soon."

"Okay," I said. "I love—"

The line went dead, and I stared at my phone for a moment. I wished it came as a shock that my dad was more concerned about my job than the fact that my apartment had become a fire pit or that my relationship had ended. But it didn't. Work was the only thing we'd ever really connected on. That was all Daniel Kingsley knew.

Maybe I *was* being ridiculous. Maybe I needed to get back to Chicago or at the very least give Harper Leslie a call. My dad was right. Journalism was all I'd ever done.

I hung my head and was about to shove my phone in my pocket when it vibrated in my hand. Derek's name appeared, and I smiled when I opened the message.

Derek: No getting away now, Cinderella. See you Friday.

I couldn't help but be curious about Derek. There was something about him that made me feel...alive. Free. Like maybe there could be life outside of the newsroom. A life *period.* Of course, there was zero chance we could work. I'd be leaving once I found a job, and he had a demanding career of his own. He was a rockstar for crying out loud. How far could this really go? Any time we spent together had an expiration date. But a couple of dates couldn't hurt, right?

———

I EXAMINED MY REFLECTION IN THE FULL LENGTH MIRROR IN Katie's bedroom late Friday morning. She'd taken the morning off just to help me get ready for my date with Derek, who would be picking me up at eleven a.m. He'd told me to dress comfortably, which for me usually involved a black pantsuit or a smart, black dress. I was pretty sure that wasn't what he had in mind, so Katie had helped me piece together an outfit with some of the clothes Liv had generously given me—clothes that were meant for a gorgeous celebrity, not a woman who almost exclusively shopped at Ann Taylor and Target.

"Are you sure it isn't too much?" I asked, looking back at Katie, who was sprawled across her bed.

The outfit I was wearing wasn't unusual for anyone that wasn't me. Black leggings that looked like leather, hugging my body with an almost supernatural level of strength. A pair of leopard print booties and a chunky emerald-colored sweater that hung a little off my shoulder. My hair fell in loose waves around my shoulders, and I'd kept my makeup simple, opting for just a little mascara, blush, and a rosy lip gloss.

Katie made a face as though that was the most absurd thing she'd ever heard. "It's perfect. It's casual and comfortable, and bonus points that it's not all black. You look amazing."

Even I had to admit I looked good. Like a woman who knew what she wanted and, more importantly, *got* what she wanted. Someone like Kimber. Not the girl whose boyfriend belonged to someone else or the woman who puked in front of a conference room full of people.

"But is it *me*?" I questioned, tugging at the hem of the sweater. "Maybe I should just wear the dress I wore to dinner on Sunday."

"Why?" Katie asked, rolling off the bed and bounding to my side. "You look hot!"

I pushed my hands through my hair and let out an exasperated sigh. "I just feel like people take me more seriously when I wear black."

Katie chuckled. "Well, good thing you're going on a date and not a job interview. It's supposed to be fun. Besides, a dress isn't a great idea because he drives a motorcycle."

My mouth fell open. "He drives a *what?*" I thought back to the night we met, when he rescued me from that creepy guy by telling him about my nonexistent boyfriend who drove a motorcycle. I'd thought it was all made up. I'd noticed a bike outside Ella's house, but I'd just assumed it belonged to Luca.

She gripped me by the shoulders. "Breathe."

I inhaled deeply through my nose.

"What's the worst that could happen if you aren't taken seriously?" she asked. "Or if you stop taking *yourself* so seriously?"

I blinked as I considered what she said. "I started wearing all black to look more professional, to hide my Resting Friendly Face. So I didn't always look so nice and approachable."

"But you *are* nice and approachable."

"Being nice doesn't get you anywhere in this business," I explained. "Like my dad always said, if you're nice, they think you're the weather girl or there to fetch the *real* reporters coffee. When I landed a big interview or broke a story, I wanted people to believe I deserved to be there."

"Jo, you always deserved to be there," Katie said gently. "Having a big heart isn't a character flaw. It's what makes you *you*. I happen to think you're pretty damn fabulous as you are. And these leggings make your butt look ah-mazing."

I laughed as a loud knock came from the back door.

"He's here," Katie squealed, squeezing my arm. "Are you ready?"

I appraised my reflection one last time and wiggled my shoulders, attempting to shake out the nervousness that had built up inside me. "Ready."

"I'll get the door." A few seconds later, she emitted a high-pitched shriek. "Oh my God! Is this your new dog? She's precious!"

I rounded the corner of the hallway, and my heart swirled around like snowflakes in a Chicago snow storm. But I certainly didn't feel cold. Heat rose from my core as I drank Derek in. He looked every bit the part of a rockstar in his ripped jeans and leather jacket. I remembered the way his lips felt on mine, and the fire in my belly roared. I wondered what it would feel like to curl up into his chest. He was the perfect height. The top of my head would make the perfect resting spot for his chin. His arms were the kind you could make yourself at home in—warm as a cozy blanket and a cup of hot cocoa.

"Isn't she adorable, Jo?" Katie's voice pried me from the clutches of my daydream, and my eyes landed on the goofiest, cutest dog I'd ever seen. Derek had her in a backpack, her paws draped over his shoulders like he was giving her a piggyback ride. Her tongue hung out of her mouth in what looked like a happy grin as she peered at me through big goggles.

I burst out laughing as I moved closer to the door. "Who is this?"

"This is Izzy," he answered, flashing me a smile that made my knees turn to liquid. "I hope it's okay that I brought her along for our date."

My heart fluttered, and my words caught in my throat. "I think dogs should be present for all dates if you ask me," Katie said, saving me from my speechlessness as she scratched Izzy behind the ears. "Isn't that right, Izzy?"

"I'd be offended if you didn't bring her," I said finally. "Look at that smile!" I reached a finger out to boop her nose just as Derek turned his head, causing me to poke him right in the mouth. My cheeks burned, and he laughed. "Sorry, I was going for Izzy. But your smile isn't too bad either "

"It's okay. I'm already used to her stealing the show. She gets a lot of attention when we're out and about." His grin told me that as cute as Izzy was, she wasn't the only reason they got so much attention.

"So, where are you and Izzy taking Jo today?" Katie asked.

"If you don't mind, Izzy has asked that it be a surprise," Derek teased. "But what I *can* tell you is that we are going to take full advantage of this beautiful day. Unless, of course, Jo hates the outdoors, in which case, I have no idea what we're doing."

I rubbed the top of Izzy's head. "I'm as basic as they come. I live for fall and pumpkin spice everything, so it sounds like Izzy and I will get along just fine."

"Well, you guys have fun," Katie said, turning toward me. "I've got to get ready to go to work, but I'll see you later?"

"Yep," I answered.

"I promise I won't keep her out too late," Derek added.

Katie tossed a smile over her shoulder as she headed down the hall. "I wouldn't be upset if you did."

"Trying to get rid of me already," I joked. "I see how it is."

"So, shall we?" Derek asked.

"Yes, we shall." I beamed up at him, and he opened the door for me. Even the cool November air wasn't enough to tame the heat rising in my body as he placed his hand on the small of my back.

"There's just one problem," Derek said as we approached his shiny black motorcycle.

"And what's that?"

"I'm going to need you to wear Izzy. Is that okay?"

"Are you kidding? I demand that I wear Izzy. Literally nothing in this world would bring me more joy."

He laughed. "Perfect." He grabbed a leather jacket from a side compartment on the bike and held it open for me. "It gets pretty chilly, so you'll need to wear this." He helped me into the jacket, and it swallowed me up in his delicious scent. "It's a little big, but it'll keep you warm." He removed Izzy's backpack from his shoulders and placed it onto me, securing the straps. The pup greeted me with a lick on the cheek. "Now, have you ever ridden on a motorcycle before?"

I shook my head.

"Okay, well, first things first." He stepped closer to me and gently reached in the pocket of the jacket I had on, pulling out a wide pair of glasses and tucking them on my face. "Wind glasses."

"Look, Izzy!" I said. "We match!"

She let out a happy yelp.

Derek slipped on his own glasses before reaching for the red helmet that was strapped to the seat. "And, of course, you'll need to wear this."

I took the helmet from his outstretched hand and attempted to put it on, struggling to maneuver it over the glasses.

He tucked my hair behind my ears, his fingers grazing my cheek. "Let me help you."

"Okay," I said, and our eyes locked. For a second, I

thought he might kiss me. In fact, I hoped he would. Instead, he cleared his throat and eased the helmet on me, checking to make sure it was secure. He flipped up my visor so I could still hear him even after he plunked his helmet on his head.

"Biker chick is a good look for you." He licked his lips and got on, straddling the seat, causing the heat at my center to spread to a wildfire level of intensity. "Hop on."

Holy Moly, no man has the right to look this good.

I nodded, and he held his arm out to steady me as I slid on behind him. "Now what?"

"You're going to want to get closer to me, and hold on tight."

He guided my hands to his chest as the inside of my thighs hugged the outside of his, and his fingers lingered over mine as I gripped his chest.

"Like this?" I asked.

"Exactly like that," he answered.

"Was this just your ploy to get me close to you?" I teased.

"No," he replied with a chuckle. "But it's certainly an added bonus."

I gripped his jacket to prevent myself from running my hands all over his body. "Alright. Helmet on, stay close. Anything else?"

"Yep," he said, reaching back to push my visor down. "Enjoy the ride."

The bike roared to life, rumbling beneath us, and Izzy gave an excited bark as we cruised out of the driveway and onto the street.

TWELVE

Derek

"THIS SOUP IS PHENOMENAL," Jo said, taking a sip from her thermos. "Where did you get it?"

We were sitting on a large flannel blanket amongst the trees just off the Natchez Trace Parkway, inside the Franklin city limits. The parkway stretched all the way from Nashville to Natchez, Mississippi and was known as one of the most beautiful drives during autumn. I'd taken the scenic route to the Parkway, partly because it was such a beautiful day, but mostly because I wanted to feel Jo close to me for as long as possible.

I grinned, placing a small handful of treats beside me on the blanket for Izzy, who eagerly gobbled them up. "Actually, I made it."

Jo pressed her palm to her chest. "You made me soup? From scratch?"

The smile on her face made the immersion blender I'd purchased solely for the purpose of making the soup completely worth it. I'd never even heard of an immersion blender until Dallas had told me about it.

"I had a little help," I admitted. "Dallas had the recipe, and he walked me through it. The turkey and gouda sandwiches with apple slices were his idea too."

"Delicious," she said. "It's the perfect pairing."

"Dal has become pretty great in the kitchen since he met Katie. And what he's learned, he's tried to teach me."

"That's really sweet. I take it you and Dallas are pretty tight?"

I nodded. "He's my cousin, but really he's more like a brother."

She took a bite of her sandwich. "He and Katie seem close."

"I'm pretty sure he's in love with her," I said. "And everyone knows it but him."

"And Katie," she added, taking another bite, causing a few crumbs to fall into her long hair. "Wow, I'm a disaster."

I chuckled and reached my hand over, gently tugging the tiny pieces of bread from her loose curls. "The most beautiful disaster I've ever seen."

Jo's cheeks flamed pink, and she raked her teeth over her bottom lip. "You really didn't have to go through all this trouble for me. This is incredibly sweet."

"You deserve for people to be sweet to you," I said simply. Seeing her happy made me want to be the one to put that smile on her face all the time.

"Honestly, other than Katie and my mom, nobody else has ever cooked for me."

I took a sip of my soup. "Not even that ex of yours?"

"Especially not him." She chewed thoughtfully for a moment. "I should have seen the writing on the wall."

I tilted my head. "How so?"

"We didn't even have an actual relationship. Not really,

anyway. After those first couple of months, we stopped going anywhere together. He never did anything special, like cook for me. The most he did was order UberEats, and he always got my Chinese order wrong."

"Why did you stay with him?"

Even with the sad smile that played on her lips, she was still beautiful. Surrounded by a patchwork quilt of autumn colors, she was the most breathtaking woman I'd ever seen. "It was better than being alone. I was just so lonely." She took a sip of her apple cider, a wistful expression settling on her face. "So lonely that I settled for scraps of a relationship and convinced myself it was the main course. I was so stupid."

"Don't beat yourself up." I said, touching her shoulder. "Love is never wasted."

"That's just it, though. I didn't love him, and he definitely didn't love me," she confessed. "I had built my entire life around my career. My dad instilled that in me ever since I was a kid—that I had to be dedicated or someone else would snatch the opportunity from me. So, instead of finding someone I really cared about, I settled for what was available all in the name of not being alone. But I ended up alone anyway. I left my home, my mom, Katie, everything that I loved to chase a dream I'm not even sure I want anymore."

"Wow," I said. "You don't miss your job?"

She shook her head. "I mean, I miss Riggs and Carina. They were the only real friends I had there. I even miss Kimber."

"She's the one that got the promotion, right?"

Jo nodded. "And she deserved it too. I can't believe how awful I was to her. I was just so…jealous. I thought it was about the job, but really, I was just jealous that she not only seemed to get everything she wanted, but that she *knew* what she wanted at all. I want to apologize to her, but I don't know if she'll even talk to me again. I don't know if *I* would talk to me again."

"If it's in your heart to apologize, I think you should do it," I said, scratching Izzy's ear to keep myself from reaching for Jo's hand. "Sure, there's a chance she won't want to hear you out, but I think you need to do it so maybe you can start to forgive yourself."

She chewed her lip. "Speaking of forgiveness…How are you feeling about things with your dad?"

"I don't know, honestly." I sighed. "There's so much wrapped up in this thing. I'm angry with him, and I'm angry at myself."

Her forehead creased. "Why are you mad at yourself?"

I rubbed my hand along my jaw. If I told her the truth, that I had been lying to everyone I cared about, would that change her opinion of me? I knew the second the thought popped into my mind that it wouldn't. If anyone would understand living a life you didn't really want, it was her. My gut told me I could be my true self with Jo.

"I have the life I have because of my dad. I got into music to get *away* from him." I looked down at my hands. "And by the way, I'm sorry I didn't tell you about the band the night we met. I didn't mean to lie to you."

"It's okay. I was wondering why you hadn't mentioned it, but I didn't want to pry."

"My dad was an alcoholic," I began. "A raging one at that. He was awful to me and my mom. Dallas lived close by when I was a kid, so I hung out there a lot of the time or just played in the neighborhood with him and Jax. Anything to avoid being home."

"Oh my God, Derek." Jo reached across the blanket, covering my hand with hers.

I cleared my throat. "When we started playing music, it became a way to escape my life. I would spend hours with Jax and Dallas listening to records, and then Dal's dad got us guitar lessons. I loved it simply because it got me out of the hell my home had become."

Her eyes creased at the corners, and she nodded solemnly, listening to every word I said.

"By the time I got to college, I was too far in. Dallas wanted to start a band, and I couldn't let him down by giving up music. He wanted that band more than anything, and it wasn't like I hated playing. But it didn't do for me what it did for Dallas or Jax or even Luca. So, I made an agreement with myself that I'd stick it out for a while. I figured we would play for a few years and then real life would catch up with all of us. Because how many people actually make it in this industry, you know?"

She raked her teeth over her bottom lip. "And then you did."

I blew out a breath. "We did. I didn't have the heart to back out. Dal's my family, and he'd been my saving grace all those years. I couldn't quit on him."

"I don't know Dallas, but he seems like he's a pretty reasonable guy," she said gently. "Knowing what you'd been through, I'm sure he would have understood."

"That's the thing. He doesn't know."

Her eyes widened. "Oh…"

"I couldn't tell him. I couldn't tell anyone," I admitted. "I was too scared of what my dad might do."

"But…No one ever suspected something was off? Your aunt or uncle maybe? A teacher?"

"My dad was a mean drunk, but he was also smart." I swallowed hard. "He knew better than to leave bruises in places anyone might see. And he was the kind of guy people liked and respected. He was a pretty successful mechanic, the guy everyone trusted to fix their cars. You'd never suspect he came home from work at night and beat his wife and kid. My uncle, Dal's dad, could tell we weren't close, and I think he always tried to compensate for that by including me in whatever he and Dallas did."

She peered at me thoughtfully. "What was your uncle's relationship with your dad like?"

"They never got along," I explained. "My father was convinced that his mother would have preferred to have Dallas' dad as a son. After my grandparents passed away, our parents had this huge falling out because my dad thought he'd somehow been cheated out of a bunch of money from their estate, which wasn't true. It was split equally between my dad and Dallas' mom, but the difference is that my dad blew his entire inheritance on booze and cigarettes in about six months."

"I'm so sorry. That you had to go through that. That you've dealt with it alone." She tilted her head toward me. "What about your mom? How has she handled all of this?"

I scoffed. "She's always made excuse after excuse for him. And I know she's a victim here too, but it's complicated. Because as my mom, I think she owed it to me to, I don't know, demand better. Or at least get me out of harm's way. I was just a kid."

"Did she ever try to leave?"

"She did," I said. "We were on the way to the car, and he must have suspected something was up, so he came home early. My mom made up some story about me needing supplies for a school project I'd forgotten about, which of course, I got punished for."

She winced.

"Please don't feel sorry for me. I've had a lot of therapy over the years, but aside from my therapists, I've never been able to bring myself to tell anyone else the truth. Because part of that truth means I don't want to do music anymore, but I don't want to let Dallas and the guys down. They've been the best family I ever could have asked for, and the last thing I want to do is disappoint them. But I'm so tired of pretending. It feels like I'm lying to everyone I care about, and I don't know... I guess it just feels good for someone to know me." My eyes met her dazzling ivy-green ones. "It feels good for *you* to know me."

She blushed. "I like knowing you. But I think if anyone deserves to know the real you, it's the people you love." She reached over and scratched Izzy behind the ear. "Like Izzy. Isn't that right, girl?"

Izzy barked and gleefully pounced on Jo, licking her face. Jo squealed as she let the tiny dog push her to the ground, continuing her assault of kisses.

"Get her, Izzy," I encouraged with a laugh.

"Is she like this with everyone?" she asked, shielding her face with her hands.

"Honestly, no," I said. "I haven't had her for long, but she definitely hasn't taken to anyone this fast. You must be pretty special."

Izzy spun in circles and let out a sound that was some-where between a dog howl and a pigeon coo. She jumped up so that her front paws were on my chest as she turned her onslaught of kisses on me.

"That's right, Izzy," Jo cheered. "Take him down!"

I laughed, collapsing on the blanket next to Jo, as Izzy darted between the two of us. "Okay, okay! Is this what you wanted?"

Izzy yipped, and her tail whipped in circles as she returned to kissing Jo.

I rolled over so that I was facing her, my head propped on my hand. "You know, I think Izzy has the right idea."

She giggled. "You want to lick my face too?"

"Not exactly." I chuckled and got Izzy's attention with a few more treats. She followed the trail of biscuits to the bottom of the blanket, allowing me to move closer to Jo. Our laughter subsided and settled into a gaze so intense it made my breath catch in my throat. I touched her peaches and cream cheek with my thumb. "But I would really like to kiss you."

Her eyelashes fluttered along with my heart as she whispered, "I'd like that."

I brushed her hair from her face before I leaned down, touching my lips to hers. A soft sigh escaped her, a drop of gasoline on the fire that had started burning for her the first night we met. She gripped the back of my neck, pulling me closer as we melted together. Our mouths collided, two lost souls seeking each other. She tasted sweet, like mulled wine, and her lips were cool as the autumn breeze on my skin. It was the kind of kiss that both took your breath away and gave you life, filling your lungs with hope.

When we finally broke our kiss, I leaned my forehead against hers. "I don't know what you're thinking, but I really don't want this date to end." I kissed her once more. "And I'd really like to do a lot more of that today."

She answered by pressing her lips to mine. "Then I'd say we're on the same page. However, I really, really have to pee, and I would prefer to not have to do that behind a tree."

I chuckled. "How about we pack up and continue this date somewhere else? Somewhere with indoor plumbing."

"Perfect," she said, and Izzy barked her agreement.

I stood and helped her to her feet. Once we'd packed everything up, I grabbed Izzy's leash and pulled Jo into me.

She placed her hands on my chest as she gazed up at me, her eyes sparkling. "How are you real? How is this real?"

"What do you mean?" I asked as the breeze caused the trees to shed their leaves all around us.

"Just a few days ago, my whole life went up in smoke," she said. "But now, I'm standing here with the sweetest man I've ever met in the middle of a snow globe of leaves."

I grinned. "A snow globe, huh?"

She nodded. "This entire day feels like I'm living in a snow globe."

"How so?"

"Because the world inside a snow globe is perfect. It captures all the magic of a single moment. But to truly see the beauty of it, you have to shake it up first," she said. "You've come along and kind of shaken up my world, but this moment...It's perfect."

"Yeah, it is," I agreed, and Izzy ran in excited circles around our feet.

"Uh-oh." Jo laughed as Izzy bound us together with her leash.

And with one final tug, Jo and I were falling.

THIRTEEN

Jo

———

WHAT WAS it about Derek that had me acting like someone else? I kissed him the night we met, and I had never once kissed a stranger, even in my college years. And I certainly wasn't one to kiss on a first date, at least not *that* kind of kiss. A peck on the lips maybe, but kissing Derek was…different. It felt intimate, raw, vulnerable. It was the kind of kiss that led somewhere, somewhere I *definitely* had never gone on a first date. But as strange as this all was for me, I felt more like myself than I had in ages. And it felt *good*.

We spent the afternoon strolling through downtown Franklin with Izzy, talking about anything and everything. He told me about growing up in Kentucky, and I told him more about my life in Nashville before I'd moved to Chicago. I'd never had a first date, or any date for that matter, that had felt this good or lasted this long. I often found my mind drifting to other things I could or should be doing while I was out with a guy, but not with Derek. I couldn't get enough of him. Seven hours somehow felt like seven minutes.

The more I learned about Derek, the more I wanted to

know. I loved seeing the world through his eyes. He found beauty in the things most people overlooked. The way moss grew in the cracks of the sidewalk and the symphony of scents that wafted out into the streets—notes of bitter, sweet, and sour punctuating the air. The way an elderly couple held onto one another as they walked in front of us, lines etched in their hands, a treasure map of happy memories. He pointed it all out to me, my arm threaded through his. And I couldn't help but to want more of that. More of him.

Finally, as the sun set, he asked if I'd come over and let him cook dinner for me. I didn't want our date to end, and there were far worse ways to spend a Friday night than having a gorgeous man make me dinner. So we made the short drive to his apartment in Midtown, waved at the doorman on our way in, and stepped onto the elevator. Derek pressed the button for the seventeenth floor, and our fingers intertwined as the doors closed, as though we were a couple who held hands in elevators all the time.

I let out a contented sigh as we entered his apartment. It smelled like him, warm and comforting.

"So, this is it," Derek said, releasing Izzy from her leash and harness. The foyer was lined with a gallery of framed photos that I studied carefully. Each one was a candid shot. Some were even faces I recognized.

There was a gritty looking photo of Luca, a glass tumbler in his hand and a far off look in his eyes. Next to it there was a photo of Liv and her husband on stage, eyes locked on each other, and one of Ella looking adoringly at Cash as he kissed the top of Grace's head. There was even one of Katie, Dallas, and Antoni laughing around someone's dinner table.

Sprinkled in throughout were pictures of people I didn't recognize. A photo with two older men caught my eye, one had a harmonica and the other a guitar, while a couple stood nearby looking young and in love. One of a lively crowd in a bar, some faces caught mid-conversation, while a young woman off to the side sat alone.

"Wow," I said, my eyes lingering along the photographs. "Did you take these?"

"Yeah," he answered, quietly. "I did."

"I recognize some of the faces, but who are the others? Friends or family members?"

He shook his head. "People I don't know. This is a collection of some of my favorite photos I've ever taken. Moments I thought were beautiful."

My eyes found his. "Derek, these are incredible. You have such an amazing gift. You see people. Not as they present themselves to the world but as they really are."

"Thank you." He smiled softly. "That's what I love about photography. You're freezing these moments in time, and along with that, the people. In all their happiness, their pain, their beauty."

I listened to him, enchanted by the way his eyes lit up as he described his photos to me and what he loved about each one.

"Amazing," I said. "You are…amazing."

He chuckled. "You may want to withhold your judgment until after I cook you dinner since I don't have Dallas to walk me through it this time."

"I can help. I'm no Katie in the kitchen, but she's taught me a few things over the years."

"You can help by having a glass of wine and hanging out with me while I cook," he said. "I may not be the best chef, but HelloFresh helps me fake it."

I laughed as my phone pinged from my purse.

"You get that, and I'll get the wine. Red or white?"

"Red," I answered.

"Red it is," he said over his shoulder as he headed for the kitchen.

I pulled my phone from my bag as I followed behind him. A message from Katie flashed across the screen.

Katie: Sooooo?!?! How's it going?

I smiled as I tapped out my reply.

Jo: He's incredible. He's actually making me dinner!!!

The text bubbles immediately burst to life.

Katie: OMG! That's precious! Sounds like he really likes you!!

She added a pink heart emoji.

Jo: The feeling is entirely mutual.

Katie: This makes me so happy!! Derek is one of the good ones.

Jo: He's really something special.

I glanced up as Derek walked toward me, two glasses of wine in his hands. He'd shrugged off his jacket when I wasn't looking, and I drank in his lean, muscular arms in his snug, black long-sleeved tee. All the moisture evaporated from my mouth, and my brain short-circuited, sending visions of Derek in various states of undress dancing like sugar plums in my head. I wanted each of those visions to come true. As soon as humanly possible.

I had never slept with someone on the first date, but I'd never had a date with someone like Derek. He made me want to be in the moment, and in this moment, I wanted him.

"Everything okay?" Derek asked.

I fired off one last text to Katie.

Jo: Don't wait up. :)

I took the glass from his waiting hand. "Everything is

perfect."

DEREK MADE A DELICIOUS TOMATO BASIL PASTA FOR DINNER
and toasted a baguette with olive oil and garlic. Our conversation flowed as easily as the wine, warming me from the inside. When I finally glanced at the clock on the wall, it was well after nine p.m. I was amazed that even after being together for so long, we managed to continue talking long after the wine was finished and the dishes were washed.

He showed me the rest of his apartment. It was understated and cozy, just like him, with lots of muted colors, soft fabrics, and warm lighting. After he gave me the tour, I found myself in front of Derek's wall of beautiful moments again, drawn there like a moth to a flame. I studied each image as though there might be a quiz afterward.

"I wish I could see the world through your eyes," I said when I felt his arm brush mine as he moved to stand beside me.

"I wish you could see yourself through my eyes." His voice was low, a light rasp tickling at the edges.

My cheeks burned. "What would I see?"

His tongue flicked across his lips. "The most exquisite woman I've ever met. A woman who doesn't realize the grace and strength she possesses."

I closed the small gap left between us. "What else do you see?"

He let out a shallow breath and tucked my hair behind my ear. "I see a woman who doesn't know what she's doing to me."

"Show me what I'm doing to you," I whispered.

His eyes searched mine for any doubts, but there were none. No hesitation, no doubts, no questions. Just me and Derek.

I gripped the back of his neck, crushing my lips into his. Stars exploded behind my eyes, sparkling all the way down to my core.

Derek slid his hands down my back, cupping them under my butt as I jumped into his arms and wrapped my legs around him. Normally, I'd have been too in my head to do something like that, worried I'd get dropped or that he'd trip. But with Derek, I knew he'd be there to catch me.

He didn't break our kiss as he carried me to the bedroom, where he gently placed my feet on the floor. The room was dimly lit by a bedside lamp that cast the softest glow over the navy walls.

I tugged his shirt over his head, revealing his tanned chest and a gray scale tattoo of a phoenix covering the left side of his rib cage. I traced my fingers across the drawing and the outline of his abs, then trailed my fingers along the v shape that disappeared beneath his jeans.

"Good God," I whispered, and he chuckled.

I knew he was hot, but he looked like a freaking underwear model for Calvin Klein. I could feel my old ways creeping in like shadows in the night, but before I could over-analyze or think ten steps ahead, I ripped my sweater over my head, tossing it to the ground. I wanted this. I wanted *him*.

His nostrils flared as he took in my black lace bra, and I thanked God and Liv for the body-hugging leather leggings.

"Damn, Jo." His fingers grazed along my collarbone and the straps of my bra. "You're beautiful."

Any doubts that could have threatened to surface were instantly put to rest when his eyes met mine. He looked at me like I was something rare, something special. Like he never wanted to stop looking at me.

His lips found mine in a long, slow kiss before he turned me so my back was to him. He guided me a few steps to the left so we were standing in front of a modern floor mirror. I leaned into him, my head falling back as he kissed down my neck.

"I want you to see what I see," he whispered between the kisses he gently placed on my skin. "And I want to see all of you."

Our eyes caught in the mirror as he swept his fingers down my shoulders and along the length of my arms, leaving goosebumps in their wake.

His hands settled at my hips, lingering at the waistband of my leggings. "May I?" he asked.

Unable to form words, I nodded my reply as I kicked off my booties. I watched our reflection as he slowly slid the material over my hips, leaving my black thong in place. My heart raced as I looked at him looking at me, taking in the way he treated my body with such care, like a delicate gift he was unwrapping.

"I want to see every beautiful inch of you," he said as he knelt on his knees, pulling my leggings down bit by bit, reveling in each new inch of exposed skin. With his hands on my legs, he placed open-mouthed kisses along my skin.

My knees turned to jelly when his fingers grazed my inner thigh. We weren't even completely naked yet, and already this was the most intimate sex I'd ever had. He rose to his feet, eyes locked on mine in the mirror.

"I love the way you look at me," I said as his fingers hooked beneath my bra straps, pulling them off my shoulders.

"Good." His breath was warm as he whispered against my

cheek. "Because I love looking at you."

His hands found the clasp of my bra and twisted it loose, sending shivers and lace down my arms. I let the fabric fall to the floor as Derek turned me to the side, kissing the tops of my breasts.

Our reflection played before me like a scene in a romantic movie, only somehow, I was the star. My nipples perked as Derek's tongue slipped across them, and I closed my eyes, letting my head fall back.

His hand gently grasped around the back of my neck as his lips grazed my skin. A soft whimper escaped my mouth, which ignited something in him, his kisses becoming more urgent.

"I've never wanted anyone as much as I want you." Derek pressed his forehead to mine while his hands smoothed down my bare back.

I let my fingertips travel the length of his torso stopping at the button of his jeans as he quickly kicked off his shoes. Even in the dim lighting, I could see how much he strained against the denim.

"I want you too," I murmured, not taking my eyes off him as I tugged the button open, pushing his jeans to the floor. He stepped out of them, and every nerve in my body sprang to life as he pulled me into his arms, his erection pressing against my hip.

My hands took on a life of their own and shoved his gray boxer briefs down his legs, leaving Derek naked before me. I took him in my hand and stroked him lightly, and he released a moan so low it was almost a growl.

"How does that feel?" I asked, enjoying the reaction I elicited from him.

"So good. God, you have no idea." He pressed his hips

into mine and gripped my panties. "I don't know how much longer I can hold back before I rip these off of you."

I pressed my lips to his, and his tongue slipped out to meet mine, but I pulled back, teasing him. "What are you waiting for?"

His eyes darkened, and in one sweeping movement, my thong was on the floor. He quickly moved to the nightstand and retrieved a condom before backing me up against the wall. He kissed his way down to my core and dropped to his knees in front of me. He grazed his thumb tenderly over my clit, and I gasped.

"Yes," I said, gripping Derek's hair as he placed a kiss at my center, and I bucked against his mouth. His tongue slipped into my folds, teasing and tantalizing me.

"Tell me what feels good to you," he whispered and pressed his tongue into me with a little more pressure. "Does that feel good?"

"Uh-huh," I managed to squeak out. "Just like that." My muscles tightened as his tongue flicked and licked in the perfect cadence. "Faster," I begged as I moved my hips to meet the stroke of his tongue.

Continuing his pace, he slid his finger inside of me, and I cried out, twisting his hair in my fingers. "Derek, I want you. I want to feel all of you."

With one last slip of his tongue, he stood and ripped the condom open, rolling it over his length. I wrapped one leg around his waist and took him into my hands, guiding him inside me.

He eased his way into me slowly, and I bit down onto his shoulder, burying my face in his neck. I wasn't used to sex like this, and I certainly wasn't used to guys the size of Derek. Or guys that knew what they were doing with their tongues.

"Damn it, Jo," Derek murmured into my ear. "You feel so fucking good."

I wasn't one to curse, but he felt fucking good too.

So. Fucking. Good.

"Take me from behind," I panted. The words popped out of my mouth before I could stop them. I'd never once asked for what I wanted in bed—or against a wall—before. But with Derek, I felt safe enough to ask for what I wanted. To be who I wanted.

I turned and braced myself against the wall as he entered me again. His pace was slow and rhythmic as he slipped in and out of me.

"Do you like that?" he asked, pressing his body into mine and slipping his fingers softly over my clit.

I was rendered speechless, so I nodded my answer emphatically, guiding his other hand over my breast. He took the lead, pinching my nipple between his fingers, moving inside me faster and faster.

A scream was building inside me as he stroked my clit in rhythm with each and every thrust.

"I can't wait to feel you come." His voice was low and husky in my ear as he grabbed my hips, quickening his pace. "I want to make you come undone."

And undone I came, his words sending me over the edge. I cried out, his name spilling off my lips in a breathy sigh as he drove into me harder, deeper.

"Fuck," he grunted, burying his face in my neck with one last pulse.

I moved my hand behind me and into his hair as our bodies hummed, clinging to the lingering waves of desire.

When he slipped out of me and removed the condom, I immediately missed feeling him inside me. Derek had awakened a longing within me that I didn't know existed. Probably because I didn't know sex like that existed.

My body melted into his like butter on bread as he pulled me into his arms, and I buried my face into his shoulder. We held each other like that until a shiver shuddered through me.

He pressed his lips to the side of my head "Let me get you a shirt. As much as I love looking at you with your clothes off, I don't want you to be cold."

I wanted to *live* in his shirts and anything that smelled like him. "Thank you. I'm just going to go to the bathroom."

"Want something to drink?" he asked as he handed me my panties from the floor and crossed over to the dresser, pulling out a long-sleeved gray T-shirt for me.

"Some water would be great," I answered, slipping the shirt over my head.

He kissed my nose before pulling on his underwear. "One water coming up. Restroom is over there if you need it." He pointed toward the ensuite bathroom before leaving the room, and I made my way over.

Once inside, I closed the door and leaned against it, catching a glimpse of my reflection in the mirror above the vanity. My hair was mussed and wild. My face was flushed, mascara was smudged beneath my eyes, and my lips were slightly swollen from all of the kissing. Derek's shirt hung loosely on my body, the sleeves falling just past my fingertips. I couldn't help the smile that crept across my face. Even though I looked like a mess, I'd never felt more beautiful or content. Gone was the uptight version of Jo who needed a plan for everything, and in her place was a woman who was happy to live in the moment.

I just hoped more of those moments would include Derek.

FOURTEEN

Derek

I woke to the sound of a long, rattling snore. My eyes flew open to find Jo shaking with silent laughter, covering her mouth so as not to disturb Izzy who had somehow managed to jump on the bed in the middle of the night. She was laying belly up between us, her little toothpick legs in the air, sawing logs.

"I don't know whether to be concerned or impressed that your tiny dog snores like a bear," Jo whispered.

"Both," I said, choking on a laugh.

Izzy's paws twitched as though she was running on air, and she let out a soft yip, still dead asleep.

"Oh my goodness." Jo pressed her palm to her chest. "She's having a puppy dream."

"I've never seen her do that before." I grinned as one side of Izzy's mouth twitched as though she were an Elvis imper-sonator. "This is the first time she's gotten in the bed too. I guess she just needed you to stay over. Look how comfortable she is."

"I love her." Jo beamed. "I've always wanted a dog."

"I guess that means you're just going to have to spend more time here," I said. "You know, to hang out with Izzy."

"Just Izzy?" she asked, raising her brow at me and biting her lower lip.

With her red hair flaming wildly around her, she looked like some sort of mythical goddess.

I reached my hand over my snoring dog to touch Jo's cheek. "Definitely not just Izzy."

I was leaning in to kiss Jo when a loud *ttttttttthhhhhhhhh-ppppppppptttttt* stopped me in my tracks.

Jo's eyes widened as the putrid smell of rotten eggs surrounded us.

"That was not me," I said as Jo gagged and covered her mouth, falling back on her side of the bed.

"Sure, blame the dog," she teased, stifling a giggle. "There's no way a smell that lethal came out of something so small."

Izzy shook herself awake, sniffed the air, and immediately jumped off the bed.

"I believe we have just been the victims of a fart and dart," I said, holding my nose.

Jo dissolved, rolling out of the bed and onto the floor. "I can't..." She dry heaved, covering her mouth with her hand. "Woman down."

Izzy saw this for the opportunity it was and ran to her side, dancing excitedly, causing two more loud and happy farts to come flying out of the dog's ass.

I howled as Jo gagged, and Izzy let out a satisfied bark.

"Help," Jo cried as the pup covered her face with kisses. She laughed so hard that no sound came out. "Oh God, I think she's singed my nose hairs off."

My phone trilled from its spot on the nightstand, interrupting our laughter. I saw my mom's name flash across the screen, and I groaned, my mood crashing down in an instant.

"What's wrong?" Jo asked.

"It's my mom," I said, letting the phone ring through to voicemail. It was only a couple of seconds before a text came through. I glanced down at the screen to see two simple words staring up at me.

Please, Derek.

I pushed my hands through my hair and blew out a breath.

Jo crawled back into bed, her hand gently stroking my shoulder.

"She still wants me to go see my dad," I said. "And I don't know what I want. Honestly, I'm scared."

"Of what?"

I thought about her question. I knew I'd been avoiding even thinking about my dad because every time I did, my heart raced, and I got a nervous pit in my stomach that felt like it might swallow me up. "What if I go there and he's exactly the same asshole he's always been?" I asked. "What if he doesn't feel any remorse for what he did?"

She considered this for a moment, tilting her head. "Is that really what you're afraid of?"

"What do you mean?"

"It's just…If that's the case, then nothing has really changed, right? If he's still a jerk, you leave with the knowledge that you did everything you could," she said. "In my experience, things staying the same isn't what's scary. Even if what isn't changing is awful, it's the devil you know and all of that." She ran her fingers through my hair. "I think what's scaring you is the possibility that he has changed because you're not sure if you can forgive him even if he has."

I felt like the wind had been knocked out of me.

"And I think you're scared of the old wounds seeing him could break open," she said softly. "You going requires you to be vulnerable, to open yourself up to hearing what he has to say, and that's scary. It's okay to be afraid, but just because it's scary doesn't mean it isn't worth trying. If anything, it might help you find some closure. Because once he's gone..."

"I'll never get that chance again," I finished for her. "And like you said the night we met, forgiving him doesn't mean I have to let him in my life. Even if he doesn't ask to be forgiven, I can still do it for me."

She nodded.

I scrubbed my face with my hands. "Why does this have to be so fucking hard?"

"Would it help if you had someone go with you?" she asked. "Maybe you could tell Dallas?"

I shook my head. "I like the idea of not going alone, but I'm just not ready to tell him or any of the guys yet. I think that's more than I can handle at this point. They'll be upset that I didn't tell them sooner, and it'll become this big thing. That's not where I need my focus."

"Well," she began. "It's not like I'm doing anything right now. I could go with you. Izzy and I could hang out at a hotel while you talk to your dad. I know we haven't known each other that long, but—"

"You'd do that for me?" I asked.

She threaded her fingers through mine. "I would."

"That would mean a lot to me," I said. "Just knowing you're there."

"Then I'll be there."

I placed my hand behind her head, my fingers tangling in her hair as I pulled her closer, pressing my lips to hers. "Thank you," I whispered.

I leaned in to kiss her again, but was startled by the sound of a loud growl. Izzy was nowhere in sight.

Jo's cheeks flushed. "Yeah, that was my stomach. I guess I worked up quite an appetite last night."

I chuckled and kissed the tip of her nose. "Then let's get you some breakfast before we do it all over again."

"ARE YOU SURE WEDNESDAY IS OKAY?" I ASKED, POLISHING off the last of my french toast. We were finishing breakfast at Fenwick's and making plans for Jo to go with me to visit my dad. "I feel bad taking you away in the middle of the week."

She snorted. "Yeah, you're really going to be interrupting my plans to rewatch every episode of the *Golden Girls* while pretending to job hunt." She speared the last piece of her waffle with her fork. "Oh, and actively avoiding my dad's phone calls. He's already called me twice today, by the way."

I took a sip of my coffee. "If it's any consolation, I think what you're doing is pretty fucking cool. You're taking some time to figure out what you want to do." I noticed Jo's cup was empty, so I refilled it from the carafe on the table.

"You might be the most considerate, thoughtful guy I've ever met," she said, placing her elbow on the table and leaning her head against her hand.

I chuckled. "How so?"

"Let's see." She folded her hands on the table. "You saved me from that weirdo on Halloween, you took me on the most wonderful picnic where you made me soup, and you cooked me dinner." Her voice dropped to a whisper. "Not to mention all the...*other* things you've done for me in the last twenty-four hours. And now you're refilling my coffee cup before I can even reach for the pot."

"That's how it should be," I said. "Anything less is unacceptable."

"But it's not like that. Not with other guys," she replied. "Not even a little. So, honestly, I have no idea how someone like you is even...*available.* Are you sure there's not a line of groupies just waiting to kick my behind that I need to be worried about?" She pretended to glance around for potential attackers. "I'm not a violent woman, but I'm pretty sure I would fight them. For Izzy, of course. And the butternut squash soup."

"Of course." I grinned. "And no, there's no groupies. I haven't even dated anyone in a long time. Nothing beyond a date or two anyway."

She looked at me in bewilderment. "How?"

I shook my head. "I don't know. I guess for a long time I worried I'd end up disappointing them once they knew I wasn't really into this whole music thing or the fame that comes along with it."

"Well, I happen to like that about you," she said. She paused for a beat, raking her teeth over her bottom lip. "Have you ever gotten a box of chocolates, one of those really fancy ones? Where the candies are almost too pretty to eat? Then you bite into one only to find out it's coconut. I imagine that's what a lot of famous people are like. Beautiful, but the inside is...underwhelming. But not you. You're like...a truffle."

"A truffle, huh?"

"Oh! Or the strawberry cream. I mean, everybody loves cream filling." She grimaced. "Wow. That might be the dorkiest thing I've ever said."

I laughed, my insides melting like I was that box of

chocolate sitting in the sun. "It might be the dorkiest thing anyone's ever said, but I like it."

She giggled, and I was overcome by how adorable she was, wearing her leggings from the day before and one of my hoodies. The zipper had slid down a little, and the sweatshirt was so oversized on her that it fell slightly off one shoulder. Her eyes glittered, framed by the remnants of her smudged eyeliner, and her hair shook as she laughed, grazing her clavicle. God, she was stunning. I opened my mouth to tell her that but was interrupted by a woman's voice.

"Jo?" the voice said, approaching our table. "Jo Kingsley? Is that you?"

"Lindsey!" Jo beamed, rising from the table to hug the blonde woman in front of her.

"How've you been?" Lindsey asked. "Girl, I thought you moved to Chicago."

"I did," Jo answered. "I'm kind of...between jobs at the moment."

"Listen, honey, that's okay," Lindsey replied easily. "The in-between is where the magic happens."

"Derek," Jo said, turning her attention to me. "This is Lindsey Langley. She's the founder of Project NENA."

I recognized the name from the haunted house we'd found ourselves in on Halloween. "Oh, awesome! Jo was telling me about your organization recently."

Lindsey looked at me with a flicker of recognition. If she did know who I was, she didn't say so, which I appreciated.

"Yeah, we went to the haunted house that was benefiting Project NENA," Jo explained, leaving out the part about how we accidentally got there.

"I'm so glad," Lindsey said.

"So, how are things going?" Jo asked her. "The Christmas drive is in full swing now, right?"

Lindsey's face fell. "It is, but donations have been on a decline these last couple of years. It's nothing like when you helped us, Jo. We haven't had that kind of magic in a long time. Last Christmas, I had to dip into my savings just so we didn't have to turn away any families. Our services have had to be cut pretty significantly."

"What?" Jo's eyes widened. "Lindsey, I'm so sorry. What can I do to help?"

"Can you perform a Christmas miracle?" Lindsey joked. "Make people care about the people that live in their community?" She sighed. "We're having a little party for the kids the first Saturday in December. It'll be much smaller than it was back when you covered it, but we're still having it. It might be the last year, though. If things don't improve…well, I guess I'll cross that bridge when I come to it."

Jo's face grew determined. "I will definitely be at the party. In fact, I'm going to see to it that it's restored to its former glory, and I'm going to think of a way to help you increase donations." She dug her phone out of her purse that was sitting in the booth and handed it to Lindsey. "Here, give me your number. I'll call you this week for all the details and get to work."

Lindsey tapped her number into Jo's phone before wrapping her up in a hug. She turned her eyes to me. "She's a good egg, this one."

"Yeah," I agreed with a smile. "She is."

"Thank you, Jo," Lindsey said. "I'm meeting a friend over there, so I'm going to run, but I'm so glad I bumped into you."

"It was nice to meet you." I waved.

"You too," Lindsey said before disappearing to the other side of the restaurant.

Jo plopped back in her seat, her eyes laser focused on the table in front of her. "I've got to do something to help Project NENA gain some major exposure. Something good. Something really good."

I nodded thoughtfully, an idea forming in my mind. "Well, it's too bad you don't know any Grammy award-winning bands who would do a benefit concert."

"Yeah." She sighed. "That would be..." Her words trailed off as her head snapped to attention. "Wait, you would do that? But I know how you feel about the music thing, Derek. I don't want you to do that if it makes you at all uncomfortable."

"How can I not do it? It's for the kids!"

Jo's smile stretched across her face. "You think the guys would be up for it? And Liv?"

"I know they would," I answered. "What if we did one in the spring? That way we can raise money and increase awareness early on next year. But until then, we'll make sure they have everything they need for their party and then some."

"Oh my God, Derek. Thank you, thank you, thank you." She beamed at me with gratitude. "I can't tell you how much this means to me. I...wow. You're just...wow. Okay, what if we..." Her hands fluttered as she launched into a flurry of ideas, whipping out her phone to jot down some notes. The smile on her face could have lit up the darkest room. There was a spark in her eyes, and a fiery passion in her voice.

I settled in and poured myself another cup of coffee, listening as she rattled off dozens of ideas at rapid-fire speed. I couldn't help the grin that tugged at the corners of my mouth.

She must have caught me looking at her because she stopped mid-sentence. "What?" she asked, her smile matching mine. "Why are you looking at me like that?"

"You're really fucking cute," I said. "Did you know that?"

She blushed and picked up right where she left off, making plans, not missing a beat. And I knew I'd play a million benefit shows if it meant seeing her smile.

FIFTEEN

Jo

My phone rang through my speakers, courtesy of my bluetooth. I knew without even looking that it was my dad. He had sent multiple text messages over the last few days asking about the status of my job search, and I had given him some version of the same answer every time.

Still looking, Dad.

I'm keeping an ear out for opportunities.

I'll keep you posted.

The truth was, I hadn't even started. I knew I'd have to sooner than later, but this was the first break I'd had in years. Between staying with Katie and my savings, I had a rare opportunity to coast for a bit.

I'd been spending my days helping Katie accomplish some tasks around the house. Katie wasn't one to complain, but I could see how tired she was. She'd mentioned wanting to paint the bedrooms, so I had her pick out the colors she wanted, and I did it for her while she was at work.

But I couldn't tell my dad that I was doing anything but looking for a job. He wouldn't understand. His entire life revolved around strategizing about how to reach the next benchmark in his career, to earn more money, to be better. The goal post was always moving.

"I take it you're still screening your dad's calls." Katie glanced over at me.

"You bet I am," I said to Katie as I pulled into the parking lot at Livvie Cakes late Tuesday morning.

"And hey, before I forget, remind me later that I need to find a doctor and set up an appointment."

Her forehead creased. "Is everything okay? You're not feeling sick, are you?"

"Not at all," I answered, cutting the ignition. "It's been years since I even had a check up. Self care kind of fell to the back burner, and after what happened with Aiden, I think I should get...you know...*tested*. Just in case." I paused, flipping the visor mirror down, checking my teeth for any errant seeds from the everything bagel I'd had for breakfast. "Especially since I wasn't expecting to be having s-e-x again quite so soon." My cheeks flamed.

Katie squealed. "And you're going to Kentucky with him tomorrow!"

It was hard not to get excited about going away with Derek, but I knew this wasn't exactly a pleasure cruise. "I don't really know what to expect," I admitted. "I'm just going for moral support. He needs a friend." I hadn't told Katie the entire reason for the trip because it wasn't my story to tell. All I'd said was that Derek needed to have a difficult conversation with his parents, and he wasn't ready for Dallas or anyone else to know about it.

She raised her brow at me. "I think you two are more than friends at this point."

"We haven't put any labels on it," I said quickly. "And we don't need to. I'm going with the flow."

Of course, that hadn't stopped me from wondering what exactly Derek and I were doing. When we were together, I was immersed in the moment, enjoying it for what it was. But when he dropped me back off at Katie's, I couldn't help but feel a little sad, knowing we had to have an expiration date.

"*Mmmhmm*," Katie said, opening her door and getting out of the car.

"What do you mean *mmmhmm*?" I exclaimed, opening my own door. "No *mmmhmm*. I mean it. Besides, how long can this thing really last? He's in a band. I'm eventually going to find another news job to appease my father or run away and join the circus. Either way, I don't see how we can make it work long term."

Katie shut the door and looked at me over the car. "What happened to going with the flow?"

I made a face at her as I shoved my door closed with a thud.

"Anyway," Katie continued as I fell into step beside her. "I think you two could make it work if it's something you want. Derek really likes you, Jo. I mean, you're going to Kentucky with him for a reason even Dallas doesn't know about."

"Which, by the way, you are sworn to secrecy." I held out my pinky to her in a promise, like we'd done a million times before when we were kids. Without missing a beat, she linked her pinky with mine. "And I really like him too." I grinned just thinking about him. We'd spent the majority of the day together Saturday after breakfast, and even though we didn't see each other Sunday or Monday, we'd texted so much that my fingers hurt.

"Of course you do," Katie said, bumping my shoulder

with hers. "And that makes it hard not to want to look a few steps ahead, but I think that's all the more reason you've got to stop yourself. You don't want to psych yourself out before you've even had a chance to figure out what this is yet."

I sighed as we reached the door to the bakery, deciding to redirect my nervous energy to Project NENA. "Are you sure Ella will be on board with catering the Christmas party for the kids? I know it's a big ask."

"She's going to love the idea," Katie said, opening the door. "Ten bucks says she cries when you tell her about it." She chuckled softly to herself. "Pregnant Ella is a crier. The other day, I walked into the office and found her bawling her eyes out. I thought something really terrible had happened. Nope. She was just watching a video of a cat who had taken in some baby squirrels."

I pursed my lips as Katie hung up her purse and tied on her apron. "I cry at those videos, and I'm not pregnant."

"Do you also cry when Sonic runs out of nuts for your hot fudge sundae?" Katie asked. "Because she cried about that too."

I laughed. "Okay, no, I definitely don't cry about that."

"Listen, that was devastating, okay?" Ella said, bursting through the door that led to the front of the store, clearly having overheard our conversation. "I'd been thinking about that sundae all afternoon, and what kind of sundae doesn't have fucking nuts on it?"

Katie and I grinned with amusement as Ella's eyes filled with tears.

"Shit," she cursed, fanning her face. "Sorry. Pregnancy hormones are a bitch, and I'm so damn hungry right now." She looked over at me as she slipped the hairband from around her wrist, tying her blonde hair in a ponytail. "If you stand still long enough, I'll eat you."

"Do you want me to go get you something?" I asked. "I'll go to every Sonic until I find one with nuts."

She waved me off. "It's okay. Thank you, though. Cash is bringing me Taco Bell. And Dallas is bringing Chinese food from that place on 8th on his way to the band's writing session." She leaned against the counter and crossed her arms, resting them on her belly. "Luca's having a pizza delivered. Oh, and Derek PostMated some hot chicken from Prince's." Ella beamed proudly.

"I hope Jax and Liv sent you some Tums," Katie teased. "Because that sounds like heartburn waiting to happen."

"Close," Ella said. "They had UberEats bring over some donuts from Five Daughters earlier."

"How?" Katie asked. "How did you pull this off?"

"And wait, isn't Five Daughters just down the street?" I added.

Ella snorted. "What was I going to do? Walk there? I'd be sweating like Jake Gyllenhal listening to the ten minute version of 'All Too Well.' No thank you."

"How did you get everyone to send you food?" Katie pressed, clearly amused.

"I watched the squirrel video, and I called them." Ella flashed us a mischievous grin. "Never underestimate the power of a crying pregnant lady."

Katie's shoulders bounced with silent laughter. "You're awful, Ella. Absolutely awful."

"Or brilliant," I said with a shrug.

"Thank you," Ella chirped. "I'm glad someone appreciates my resourcefulness. And it's not like I'm going to eat it all.

It's for all of us." She turned her gaze to me. "You can stick around after our chat, right, Jo?"

"Heck yeah," I said with a smile.

"So, what was it you wanted to talk to me about?" Ella asked.

I launched into my speech about Project NENA, complete with a clip from the toy drive I'd hosted years ago. I'd also made sure to have Lindsey send me some videos of the kids at last year's party to show her.

As Katie had predicted, Ella cried.

"Of course we'll help," Ella said through tears. "This is… such a beautiful thing you're doing, Jo. And this Lindsey woman sounds like an angel on earth. I just…This makes my heart so happy." Tears streamed down her cheeks, and she threw her arms around me.

It was at that moment that McKenzie came through the door and immediately froze.

"Did Sonic run out of nuts again?" she asked, causing us all to holler with laughter.

Ella released me from her grasp and pulled her phone out of her pocket. "I can't let these tears go to waste. Who wants ice cream sundaes?" She began tapping away furiously on the screen before bringing the phone to her ear.

McKenzie shrugged. "I mean, if you're buying, I won't say no. Anyway, your pizza's here."

"We'll be right there," Ella said before turning her attention to her phone, her voice wavering. "Antoni? Could you do a favor for me?"

Katie and I stifled a laugh as McKenzie shook her head and disappeared back through the door to the front. We listened as Ella delivered an Oscar-worthy performance, convincing Antoni to go to Sonic. So convincing that he didn't even ask why she wanted *four* hot fudge sundaes. Pregnant Ella got what pregnant Ella wanted.

She ended the call with a satisfied nod. "Ice cream will be here in half an hour." She threaded her arm through mine and held out her hand to Katie. "Come on. Work can wait. We're having a feast to celebrate."

"What are we celebrating exactly?" Katie asked with a laugh. "Your keen ability to manipulate people into bringing you food?"

"Well, yes, that," Ella answered. "And our new friend Jo."

"*Our* new friend? You do know she's been my best friend for ages," Katie reminded her jokingly.

"*My* new friend Jo. I have pregnancy brain." Ella waved her off as we reached the front of the bakery. She checked to be sure there were no customers in the shop, then opened the pizza box that waited on the counter. "Everyone take a piece."

Katie and I did as we were told but McKenzie scrunched up her nose.

"Ew," she said, reluctantly picking up a slice. "Are those anchovies?"

"Here's to friends that bring us food," Ella said, holding out her piece of pizza. "And new friends who just fit right in, like a missing piece to a puzzle." Her eyes welled with tears once again. "Dammit, I can't stop crying."

Even though I knew Ella's pregnancy had her feeling extra emotional, it still warmed my heart that she had given me her stamp of approval.

"To hormones," Katie chimed in, holding her slice up with Ella's. "And to Jo."

"You guys," I cooed, joining my piece of pizza with theirs.

"Do we really have to eat this?" McKenzie asked, and we all dissolved once more.

I took a bite of the pizza and instantly regretted it as the salty fishiness of the anchovies assaulted my tongue. My face screwed up involuntarily.

"You okay there, Jo?" Ella asked.

I smiled through the horrible taste, because other than the disgusting anchovies, I was okay. I was more than okay. I was happy. Even though I hadn't been back in Nashville for long, I could already see the beginnings of a life here for me. A life with Katie, with new friends.

Maybe even with Derek.

SIXTEEN

Derek

"FUCK, I'M SO NERVOUS," I said to Izzy and Jo as I paced the living room floor of our AirBnB early Wednesday evening. We had driven to Louisville in Jo's car earlier that afternoon, and I had been trying to work up the courage to go see my parents ever since we'd arrived. I'd sent my mom a text earlier in the day letting her know I would be there around seven p.m. With thirty minutes to go, I was down to the wire.

Jo rose from her spot on the couch and came to stand in front of me, gripping my arms with her hands. "If you're not ready, you don't have to do this. You can cancel. We can head back to Nashville in the morning."

"No, I need to do this." I swallowed hard. "For me."

"Do you want Izzy and me to go with you?" she asked. "We can sit in the car and wait for you. Whatever you need, I'm here."

I shook my head. "It's okay." I pulled her into my arms, resting my chin on her head. "Just knowing you'll be here when I get back helps."

"Izzy and I will be right here waiting for you," she said

softly. "And when you get back, we can talk about it, or we don't have to say anything at all. I'll support you however I can."

"Okay." I blew out a nervous breath. "I need to get going."

"I set the keys on the table by the door." She placed her hands on either side of my face and pulled me down to her, pressing her forehead against mine. "You can do this," she whispered. "You're going to be okay. No matter how this turns out, you're going to be alright."

"Thank you." I kissed her softly. "For everything."

"Let me know you made it, alright?" she said. "And take as long as you need. Don't worry about me and Izzy girl. She's going to be helping with finalizing some details for the Project NENA party." Jo looked back at Izzy who was sprawled out on the couch. "Look at that. She's already lying down on the job."

I kissed Jo once more, wishing I could pack up her belief in me and take it with me. I needed every bit of confidence I could get. "See you in a bit," I called as I walked out into the cool November night.

The streets of Louisville were different, but still familiar. New strip malls and condos may have altered the way it looked, but the well-worn asphalt beneath the tires felt the same. Anxiety washed over me as I drove, revealing potholes I thought I'd long since filled.

By the time I turned onto my old street, my palms were sweating, my fingers erratically drumming the steering wheel. I sucked in a sharp breath as I pulled into the driveway of my childhood home, the uneven gravel causing the car to sway slightly as though it was warning of the rocky road ahead. And even though it had been nearly ten years since I'd been back to this house, I felt the same sense of dread as I got out of my car.

I shook out my shoulders as I walked up the old concrete pathway to the front door with the faded welcome mat, and a motion light blinked on. Before I could raise my hand to knock, my mom opened the door.

"I thought I heard you pull in," she said, holding the door open. Once I was inside, she placed a hand on my arm. "Let me get a good look at you." I studied her as she did the same to me, and what I saw broke my heart. The deep lines etched into her face made her look far older than her fifty-five years. Her blonde hair was almost white now, pulled back in a low ponytail.

It had been a couple years since I'd seen her. We'd met for dinner while the band was in town. She'd needed money again—that time it was for a new water heater. She'd always worn the effects of her marriage one way or another. Whether it was the bruises she hid, the lines stamped into her skin, or the sadness in her eyes. Seeing her always filled me with conflicting feelings. She was my mother, so I loved her. And in a weird way I missed her. But it was almost like missing something you never really had. My dad may have been a monster, but I believed my mom had the ability to be a better parent. But she was wrapped up in him so tight, it was as if he'd suffocated the goodness right out of her.

Guilt surged through me when I saw the bags under her eyes. I knew this was hard on her. She'd given up everything for my dad. Even having a relationship with me. And all she had left to show for it was this house, that from the looks of it, was falling apart. It was clear that none of the money I'd sent her over the years had gone toward its upkeep. The paint had become dingy from years of neglect and cigarette smoke, and

I noticed a couple of poorly patched holes in the drywall. I didn't have to ask what happened. I already knew my father had a penchant for putting his fist through walls in fits of rage. Blood would be dripping down his hand, but he was so drunk, he wouldn't even feel it until the next day.

My mother pulled me into her arms, reeking of tobacco and some overly sweet perfume she'd no doubt doused herself in to mask the smell of the smoke. "It's good to see you, son."

"Yeah," I said quickly. "You too."

Her mouth turned down slightly, telling me she knew I didn't really mean it. Standing in the house I'd grown up in was nothing but a painful reminder of the home I longed for and never got. The parents I wanted and never had. My dad wanted his booze, and my mom wanted my dad, but neither of them wanted me.

"Who else knows?" I wondered if I'd be faced with Dallas finding out before I had time to even process my own feelings.

She looked down at her feet. "Just you. Darryl doesn't want anyone else to know. At least not until...closer to time."

When she looked back up at me, her eyes were shining with tears.

"Come on," my mom said, guiding me with her hand on my arm. "I'll take you to your father. He's been waiting for you."

She led me down the hall as though I didn't have the place memorized. I could have found my way to their bedroom blindfolded. It was a side effect of having to sneak around the house in the middle of the night just to get a drink of water because if my dad noticed me in his drunken stupor, he'd take the opportunity to rough me up.

The walls in the hallway were still the same, mostly bare,

save for one of my parent's wedding photos and a couple of pictures of me from elementary school. We never took any family photos. We weren't really a family. Not in the ways that mattered. And the walls, which were nothing but a nicotine stained time capsule, reflected that.

I followed my mom to the last door on the right, and she gently pushed it open. "Darryl? Derek is here to see you."

My nose was hit with the nauseating scent of antiseptic mixed with air freshener before I'd even fully stepped into the room. The television was playing an old episode of *Criminal Minds,* but my dad wasn't looking at the screen as he laid in his bed. Instead, he appeared to be staring off into space, not budging at the sound of my mom's voice.

"Darryl," my mom said his name again, louder this time. "Did you hear me? Derek's here."

I saw him sigh before he turned to face us. His skin was yellowed, and his eyes were glassy. He nodded at me in acknowledgement but said nothing.

"Hey," I said.

"Have a seat." My dad gestured to the worn armchair at his side.

"Can I get you something to drink?" my mom asked.

I shook my head. "I'm okay."

"Wanda, will you bring me some juice?" my dad asked.

"Of course," my mom answered, quietly leaving the room.

I didn't know what to say or where to begin. What the hell were you supposed to say to your dying father who'd treated you like shit your entire life?

Clearly my dad didn't have any ideas either because he simply returned to staring off into space until my mother entered with a blue tumbler. She handed it to him before popping a straw into the top.

"Thanks," he grunted. "Do you mind giving us a minute? We have some father and son things to discuss."

She nodded, her mouth curling into a small, hopeful smile. "If you need anything, just holler."

I wrinkled my brow. *What the fuck does that mean?* We'd never had anything to talk about. My father's version of talking usually consisted of insults and backhanded compliments. And then there was the yelling. So much fucking yelling.

My mom closed the door, and my dad took a long drink of his juice before finally looking at me.

I cleared my throat, unsure of what to say. "I'm sorry you're sick," I finally managed.

My dad barked out a laugh. "No, you're not. You think I deserve this. Go on. Say it."

"That's not true," I said, and I meant it. No matter how awful he was to me, I didn't feel anyone *deserved* something like this.

He took another sip from his drink. "I may be a lot of things, but I ain't stupid, kid. I know you'll be glad when I'm gone."

I stared at him a moment, my brows knitted together. "Why do you think that?"

"I know what you think of me," he said. "I know you think your mother and me are beneath you now that you're all rich and famous." He waved his hand dismissively. "You left us here living in this shithole."

My stomach clenched, and I had to force myself to take a deep breath. "I don't know what you're getting at, Dad. I've sent you money countless times, and somehow none of it seems to have gone to repairing this house."

"You could have bought us a better house. You could have

bought us a fucking mansion, I bet."

And there it is. He'd told me I was worthless my entire life, but once I had a modicum of success, he felt he was owed something. The only words we'd exchanged over the last few years had always been about money.

"So you could drink yourself to death in a fancier place? Is that what would have made the difference? If you'd had a bigger home, would that have made you a better father?" The words tumbled out of me before I could catch them. "I fucking tried. I tried to get you to go to rehab. I would have paid for you to go anywhere, to any facility you wanted, but you turned me down every time."

"I don't need your bullshit rehab," he spat, taking another slurp from his tumbler.

For the first time since being there, I saw him. *Really* saw him. The man I used to fear had become an emaciated shell of himself. His words were still combative, but he was weak.

"You're right. You don't anymore, because it's too fucking late. The damage is done," I said. "But it didn't have to be like this."

"There you go with your holier than thou shit. You think you're so much better than me."

"No, I don't think I'm better than you," I said quietly. "I *know* I am. I don't put my fists through walls or hit my kid or my fucking wife when I'm drunk. I take care of the people I love. I give a shit about more than just my fucking self."

He seethed, his knuckles turning white as they gripped the cup. "Still the same self-righteous wimp you always were." He shook his head and took another drink. "Always swore your mom must have messed around with the mailman or something cause there's no way a chicken-shit like you could be my kid."

My pulse pounded in my ears. "And you know what? I wish I wasn't your kid. If I could have picked, I would have picked someone else."

"That makes two of us."

"Why don't you tell me why I'm really here, Dad?" I asked, cutting to the chase. "Because you certainly have no interest in making amends, and I have no interest in being here any longer. So what is it? What do you really want?"

He blew out a breath but didn't answer.

"How much?"

"At least enough to cover the funeral costs and get her out of debt."

"And how much debt are we talking?"

He paused, taking a long pull from his juice. "About a hundred grand."

"For fucks sake." I pressed my head into my hands. After a moment, I raised my eyes to him. "Of course, I'll take care of her. You may be okay with leaving mom in a fucking mess, but I wouldn't do that." I paused, gathering my thoughts. "But I want something from you in return."

He raised his brows in question.

"I want to know why," I said quietly. "Why weren't we ever enough for you?"

"Your mother was enough for me."

"No, she wasn't. It's never been just the two of you in a relationship together." I leaned forward in my chair. "It was you, mom, and Jack Daniels or Jim Beam."

"A little drink never killed anyone." He let out a chuckle, seemingly amused.

"I'm glad you think this is so funny," I said. "When I leave here tonight, and when you're gone, do you know what changes for me? Absolutely nothing. Because you can't lose something you never had, right? But you know what changes for *her*?" I pointed toward the door, referencing my mother who was undoubtedly sitting in the next room just waiting to cater to my dad's every whim. "Everything. Because she gave up her entire fucking life for you."

He wrapped his lips around the straw, but this time I took the cup from his hands.

"What the fuck are you doing?" he yelled as I unscrewed the top, the scent of whiskey burning my nostrils.

"You've got to be fucking kidding me." I threw the tumbler against the wall causing what was left inside to splash onto the floor. "You selfish bastard."

My mom burst through the door. "What on earth is going on in here?"

"You're still giving him alcohol?" I asked incredulously. "He's literally dying from cirrhosis, and you're *still* giving him fucking whiskey?"

She cowered, her mouth turning downward.

"Why would you do that? Why would you keep giving it to him?" I demanded.

"Because he wants it," she said softly, her eyes welling up with tears. "It makes him happy. I just want him to be happy, Derek."

I scrubbed my hands down my face. "It's just…It's so fucking sad. Because he doesn't give a damn about your happiness."

"I love him." Her voice was almost a whisper.

"Well, I hope you love him enough for the both of you," I said. "Because he doesn't give a shit about you or anyone else."

"You know what? Fuck you, kid," my dad growled. "Fuck you and the high horse you road in on. We don't need you. I never wanted you anyway! Your mother was too nice to say it, but I'm not. You were a fucking mistake."

His words hit me like bullets, knocking me back in my seat. We stared at each other for a moment, not saying a word. I realized how much I'd hoped he'd seen the error of his ways. That he'd regret the time he lost with me. That he'd feel a speck of remorse for the torment he put us through.

But he had none. There was nothing in his eyes, no feeling. The only person that had changed was me. Jo's words about forgiveness from the first night we met echoed in my mind.

I rose to my feet. "I'll give you the money," I said quietly. "I'll have it wired to your account tomorrow."

"Darryl," my mother cried. "You said you wouldn't ask him. You promised me!"

I held my hand out to stop her. "It's fine, Mom. I want you to have it. I want you to be taken care of. You've always deserved that." I turned my attention to my father. "And I want you to know that I forgive you. Even though you're not sorry, I forgive you."

His face wavered slightly, and I thought for a second that something had gotten through to him. "I don't need your fucking forgiveness."

"Well, tough shit." I shrugged. "I'm giving it to you anyway. Maybe you don't need it right now, but there may come a moment when you wish you had it. When you're staring down the door between this world and the next, when you have to answer to a power higher than you or me, you may want it then. And you have my forgiveness, but I won't be here to tell you again." My voice threatened to break, but I continued. "Because when I walk out that door, I'm not coming back. My conscience is clear. You can't make someone love you, but I'll be damned if I'm going to be your whipping post one minute longer."

"Derek," my mother sobbed. "Please don't go. I'm so sorry."

"And I forgive you too. I love you, Mom. I do," I said as I made my way over to her and kissed her cheek. "And I know you love him, but it's okay to love yourself more."

"Derek," my mom pleaded.

"I guess deep down I've been waiting, hoping that you would eventually choose yourself," I said. "I guess I hoped maybe you'd choose me too, but I can't do this anymore. *I've* got to choose me now. Someone has to."

With that, I walked out of the room, down the dingy hall and straight out the front door. I didn't look back, and I didn't stop until I was standing beside Jo's car.

That's the moment I fell apart.

SEVENTEEN

Jo

After Derek left, I flopped on the couch with Izzy. She curled up next to me, resting her head on my belly. I still had a lot of work to do for the Project NENA party, but I was restless, worrying about how Derek's visit was going. I wanted to believe his dad's illness had helped him understand all the ways he'd failed his son. That Derek would be able to spend his father's last days with him and that maybe they'd both be able to find some peace.

But I hadn't wanted to fill Derek with false hope before he'd left because I truly had no idea what his dad would do. All I knew was I would be there to support him no matter the outcome.

I blew out a shaky breath. I needed a distraction.

I could always call my dad back.

That thought caused a shrill burst of laughter to bubble out of me, making Izzy startle.

"Sorry, girl," I said, petting her on the back. I reached for my phone on the coffee table and scrolled through my contacts until I landed on the name I was looking for, then pressed the FaceTime button.

After three rings, Carina's face filled the screen, surrounded by a throng of people. "Jo! Hey! Can you hear me?" In the background I could swear I saw Kimber's profile.

"Kind of," I said.

"Look who it is," Carina said, panning the phone over to Riggs.

"Jo!" Riggs beamed, shouting over the noise of the crowd. "How's Nashville?"

"It's great," I answered. "It's been good to be back home."

"Hang on, Jo," Carina's face filled the screen again. "We're at a bar for a work thing. We're going to step outside so we can talk to you."

"That's okay. I can call you back later," I said, but she didn't hear me.

The faces on the screen jostled around, camouflaged by the dim lighting.

A few seconds later, I heard the sounds of a door creaking open and footsteps shuffling.

Finally, Carina's face reappeared, Riggs standing behind her. "Sorry about that! How are you, girl? Wait, did you get a dog?"

Izzy had popped her head up to see what was going on.

I chuckled. "No, this is Izzy. She's...my friend's dog."

"Your friend Katie?" Carina asked.

I shook my head. "She belongs to a new friend. His name is Derek."

Riggs raised his brows, and Carina's mouth gaped open.

"And what kind of friend is this Derek exactly?" Carina asked.

I blushed, covering my face with my hand. "A really cute one."

Carina squealed.

"That's great, Jo," Riggs said.

"How's the job hunt going?" Carina asked.

"It's not, really," I answered. "I've kinda put that on hold for a minute because I've been doing some volunteer work with this group called Project NENA." I launched into a brief description of their mission and what I was doing to help them.

"That's the kind of stuff we need to see more of on the news," Riggs said, his voice filled with pride. "People helping people."

"So, what's new with you guys?" I asked. "How are things at the station?"

"Same shit, different day, my friend," Carina quipped. "We miss you, though."

"I miss you guys too," I said, pausing a moment. "How's Kimber doing?"

"She's good," Carina replied cautiously.

"How've the ratings been since she took over the anchor spot?" I asked.

Trepidation flickered in her eyes.

"It's okay," I assured her. "It's not going to hurt my feelings. I messed up with Kimber. How I acted that day...That wasn't like me."

"We know, and I think everyone else does too," Riggs said. "You still would have been good for the job, though." I appreciated his belief in me, but that didn't change the facts.

"But she was the better choice," I replied. "She was always the better choice, and I want her to do well. I want you all to do well. We were a team."

Carina gave a resigned sigh. "The ratings have actually gone up these last couple of weeks. The audience has really gravitated to her."

I smiled. "That's great. Kimber was the right person for the job."

"She's actually why we're here tonight," Carina explained. "It's her birthday."

"You should get back to the party," I insisted. "We can talk later."

"I'll call you soon," Carina promised.

"And send us the information on Project NENA so we can donate," Riggs added. "We'll share it with the crew too."

"Thanks, guys," I said. "Good night."

"Bye." Carina and Riggs waved into the camera before disconnecting the call.

Izzy raised her head off my stomach, her ears perked.

"What?" I asked her.

She let out a soft yip and laid her head back down.

"Alright, alright," I said, reaching for my computer on the coffee table and pulling it onto my lap. "Geez. I'll get back to work."

I spent the next hour responding to emails from businesses who were donating and confirming some vendors for the Christmas party. My heart exploded at the kindness that was continuing to pour in. Since Saturday, I'd managed to link up with some of the old contacts from my internship to garner some media attention. Then they connected me with even more people who helped me land coverage on every local television station, a couple of radio stations, and the newspaper. Plus, I'd been able to generate some buzz about the involvement of Midnight in Dallas and the benefit concert in the spring.

It felt good to be productive, useful. It felt even better knowing I was helping others. For so long, I'd been focused on getting ahead in my career that I didn't know how much I craved this, how much life it gave me....Working with Project NENA, doing something good—my soul felt lighter than it had in years.

I was so focused on what I was doing that I didn't hear Derek come in until he was in the living room.

"Hey," he said wearily, and I snapped to attention. His eyes were red-rimmed, his brows drawn together.

"Hey…" I placed my laptop on the coffee table and jumped to my feet, rushing to his side. "Are you okay?"

He shook his head and raked his teeth over his bottom lip.

"I'm so sorry, Derek," I whispered, wrapping my arms around him. "I'm right here, okay? I'm not going anywhere."

When he finally returned my embrace, the force of it nearly knocked me over, and a million emotions spilled out of him all at once, waving their white flags in surrender.

"I GUESS I DIDN'T KNOW HOW MUCH HOPE I WAS HOLDING onto that he'd changed," Derek said, his warm breath tickling my skin. "Or that she would have."

Once Derek settled, we ordered a pizza, and then I'd led him to the bedroom where we'd changed into our pajamas. Even with the heat on, it was chilly, so I wrapped us in a cocoon of blankets where he'd told me about the heart-breaking visit to see his dad. We were lying in bed, face to face, with Izzy nestled between us.

"Of course you held onto hope." My eyes searched his. "They're your parents. Our families are the ones that are supposed to love us unconditionally." My thoughts flickered to my own parents. My mom was always that loving, supportive force in my life. Her only dream for me was that I was happy. My dad, on the other hand, had very distinct views on what I needed to do and who I needed to be. His love felt contingent on whether or not I made him proud. "Realizing you won't get that love from them…It's a big loss."

"But you know what?" he continued. "It's *their* loss."

"It is," I agreed gently. "But I think people often use that saying as a way to lessen their own sense of loss. You're in pain, and you don't need to make that smaller or put a positive spin on it. Not for me."

"Maybe it's time I get back into therapy and work through this shit." He sighed and then traced his finger along my cheek. "Something hit me in the car on the way back here tonight. One of the reasons I've held onto the band is that I'm afraid I'm going to lose the only family I have left. The band was the only thing of value about me to my parents. What if that's the only thing holding me and the guys together? What if I quit the band and they quit me?"

"Derek, from what I've seen, those guys are nothing like your parents," I said softly. "When you mentioned the benefit show to them, they didn't even think twice. That wasn't because of me. That was because of *you*. They love you. If you leave the band, they might be sad or even a little disappointed, but I don't believe they'll be disappointed in *you*. I think they want you to be happy."

"I hope you're right. Because I've gotta do it," he confessed. "I've gotta quit the band. I think the benefit in the spring should be my last show. It'll give them plenty of time to find my replacement."

"That's a pretty huge realization," I said. "I know it's been a long time coming, though."

"It has, and this whole thing with my parents has opened my eyes to just how much I've been shoving down my own wants and needs. It's time to do what's right for me."

I ran my fingers through his hair. "And I will support you in any way I can."

"I'm glad you said that." He tucked a piece of hair behind my ear. "Jo, I don't think I could have done this without you today. I feel like you're one of the first people who've gotten to know me—the real me—and accepted me exactly as I am. My life has started to change for the better since you came into it."

"Mine too." I smiled and placed my hand on his chest, tugging lightly at his shirt. "So, what's next for Derek Knights? The world is your oyster. Although, I actually think oysters are kind of disgusting."

"Yeah, they're pretty gross."

"How about 'the world is your chocolate cake'," I suggested.

He chuckled. "Or cheesecake."

"With cherries on top."

"Yes, that's much better. But to answer your question, I don't really know. I'm lucky to be in a position that I can take some time to really think about it." His thumb grazed my lips, and he leaned into me, pressing his lips to mine. "Whatever the future holds for me, I just know I want you in it."

My breath and my words caught in my throat. My brain was there with a flashing reminder that Derek was in an emotionally fragile place at that moment. He'd said a painful goodbye to his parents and decided he was ready to leave the band, all in one night. He was vulnerable, and I was there for him, so of course he would say something like that. But did he mean it? My heart was asking the question that my brain wasn't ready to consider. The question it was too scared to consider.

Deep down, I knew I wanted to see what Derek and I could be.

Because if the world was a cheesecake, he was, without a doubt, the cherry on top.

EIGHTEEN

Derek

THE NEXT MORNING, I woke up before Jo. We'd stayed up talking well past midnight. Even with all of the space in the king-size bed, we'd gravitated to the center, close to each other. I could see through the slits in the blinds that the sun was just beginning to rise. The light filtered in, bathing Jo in its warm glow. Her auburn hair was fanned across the pillow, and even though she didn't have on a speck of makeup, her cheeks were rosy. She was so beautiful it made my heart ache.

I hadn't even known Jo for a month, but in that time she'd helped me find strength I didn't know I had. I remembered our picnic when she'd compared our time together to a snow globe because it preserved one single, perfect moment—but to see the true magnificence of that moment, you had to shake it up first. The thing was, every second with Jo felt that magical. She'd shaken up my entire world, and the pieces showed no signs of settling. But I didn't mind.

With Jo around, it felt like anything was possible.

I heard her sigh, and I brushed her cheek with my thumb.

Her eyes fluttered open, her freckles golden in the morning light.

"Hi," I said softly as she covered my hand with hers, pressing my fingers against her cheek.

"Hi," she whispered back, glancing around. "Where's Izzy?"

"She's eating the food we put down for her in the kitchen. I can hear her crunching all the way in here," I said.

Jo grinned. "I almost don't know what to do without her hogging the bed."

"I, for one, am glad she decided she needed an early breakfast." I slid closer to her and pressed my lips to her forehead. "Because that means I get to do this." I grazed her mouth with mine. Electricity crackled between us as I held her chin in my hand. "And this." I kissed her, softly at first, savoring the way she felt, smooth and delicate as a rose petal.

My tongue parted her lips as we sank deeper into the kiss. One hand cupped her cheek, while the other tangled in her hair. She smelled sweet, like some sort of flower, but she tasted like honey.

"You taste so good," I murmured, sliding my hands beneath her shirt, her skin supple as the finest silk. I wanted to wrap myself in her. "Do you have any idea how you make me feel?"

Like I could do anything, *be* anything with her by my side. Like I was finally living. Like I was falling in love with every breath I took. The words were hanging on the tip of my tongue, but I couldn't say them. Not yet.

I couldn't tell her, but I could show her.

Her lashes tickled my skin, making the hair on the back of my neck rise.

"Derek," she whispered my name, pressing her forehead into mine as her fingers gripped my hair.

My lips found hers again. "I need you."

She nodded quickly, kissing me with the heat of a late-August sun.

I moved on top of her, helping her raise off the bed so that I could slip her shirt over her head, freeing her perfect breasts. She arched her back as I took one of them in my mouth.

"Yes," she moaned, her hands sliding down my back.

I flicked my tongue across her nipple while my hand cupped her other breast, and she wriggled beneath me.

"Fuck," I grunted, burying my face in her neck as I realized my fatal error. "I forgot to pack condoms."

"I don't care," she said between breaths.

"Are you sure?" I questioned, looking into her eyes.

She nodded. "I'm on the pill," she said between kisses. "I'm sure we're fine. I'm getting tested, you know, after everything...just to be safe."

"I'll make an appointment too," I said as her lips drifted along my neck. "Or maybe we can go together."

"Good," she whispered. "Now shut up, and take your clothes off."

She didn't have to ask me twice. I ripped my shirt over my head, tossing it to the floor. The only things separating us were her thin cotton panties and my boxers.

I leaned over her, caging her small frame between my arms. "Tell me what you want," I said in her ear.

"You," she answered.

I chuckled. "Well, that's easy." I kissed my way along her jawline. "But I want specifics."

"Kiss me," she said, biting her lip.

"Where?" I asked, moving my lips down her neck.

She sighed. "Everywhere."

I placed open-mouthed kisses down her chest until I reached her breasts. This time, I kissed around them, avoiding her already hard nipples.

"Here," she whimpered, guiding my head over until my mouth covered the center of her breast.

I obliged, teasing the rosy flesh with my tongue before gently biting down, tugging lightly.

She wriggled beneath me, and her hands found the waistband of my boxers, where my dick was already straining against fabric. I took her hands in mine and pinned them on either side of her head.

"I'm not done kissing you yet," I said softly. I scooted down the bed and took her leg in my hand, sliding my lips along her ankle, up her shin, not stopping until I found the crease where her leg ended.

"God, Derek." Her voice was breathy and soft.

I placed gentle pressure at her center, stroking her over the fabric of her panties, and she raised her hips to meet my hand. Even through the cotton, I could feel how wet she was.

"Still not done," I whispered, moving to take her other leg in my hand, repeating each step over again, this time even slower. By the time I returned to her core, her breaths were ragged.

"Please."

I stroked her again, light as a feather.

"I don't think you understand," she said. "I'm not asking." With that, she rose off the bed and gripped me by the shoulders, gently pushing me down on where she'd just been lying.

Her fingers hooked into the waistband of my boxers and greedily tugged them down. Seeing her take what she wanted, especially when what she wanted was me, was the sexiest fucking thing I'd ever witnessed.

"Fuck, Jo," I moaned as she straddled me, pressing her warmth onto my cock, her panties the only thing keeping us apart. She rocked back and forth, creating friction so intense it made me want to explode. Her breasts swayed with each movement, her hair caressing her shoulders, giving me the most spectacular view.

With her hands on either side of me, she leaned forward, grazing her lips along my jaw. She took her time kissing her way down my chest. "Now, tell me what *you* want," she said against my skin.

I reached out to her, tilting her gaze to me. "You. I want all of you." She was every fucking thing I wanted. "I want to be inside you."

She bent down and kissed my lips as I helped her shimmy out of her panties, tossing them to the floor.

She took me in her hand and stroked me slowly, before finally easing herself down my length.

I moaned, and she did the same, closing her eyes in pleasure. She ground against me, and my hands fell to her hips, helping her move up and down my shaft.

"Touch me, Derek," she panted as she guided one of my hands to her clit, pressing my thumb against her, and I used it to trace firm, tight circles. Her body immediately responded, and her breathing became shallow. "Like that. Don't stop."

"I'm so close," I said. I knew I was only seconds away from coming, her whimpers of pleasure nearly sending me over the edge.

"Me too." She moved faster, and I gritted my teeth, my pulse pounding in my ears.

"Oh my God, yes," she finally cried out, throwing her

head back as her walls trembled around me. I pushed my hips into hers as she quaked with aftershocks, and I went over the edge with her.

She sagged against me, burying her face in the pillow beside my head, and I wrapped my arms around her, kissing her shoulder. When our breathing slowed, I slipped out of her and she settled beside me as I pulled the sheet up to cover our bare skin.

I gazed into her eyes. There were a million things I wanted to say to her. So many feelings I wanted to share.

Her eyes searched mine, almost as if they were looking to uncover everything I couldn't yet say.

"Derek," she whispered my name. "I…I need to ask you…" Her hands snaked up my chest and to the back of my neck, drawing me closer. "Did you mean what you said last night?"

I kissed her softly and looked into her jade eyes, clouded with worry. "What part?"

She licked her lips as a flush crept from her neck up to her cheeks, and her gaze dropped to the sheet she was gripping with her fingers. "Um…Well, last night you said that what-ever the future held, you wanted me in it. And look, I know last night was very…heavy, and there were a lot of emotions, so if you didn't mean it, I want you to know that's really okay. Really. How many more times can I say 'really'." A nervous laugh rose out of her, and she covered her face with her hand. "And there I go again. "Wow, is it hot in here to you?" Her words spilled out of her like speed skaters going for the gold.

I smiled at her in amusement and took her hand in mine, threading my fingers through hers. "Jo, slow down. Of course I meant it." I pressed a kiss to her fingers. "And I know you got your heart broken not that long ago. So if you're not ready, I'll understand. But I'll also wait until you are. We can take this as slow as you need to."

"It's not that." Her face relaxed a little, and the worried look in her eyes faded. "It's just that...I didn't know until you said it how much I wanted it to be true." She blew out a breath. "I guess that ever since I met you I figured there had to be an expiration date on us because you had the band, and I would eventually get back into news, and honestly, now that I say it all out loud, it all sounds ridiculous." She turned her head closer to me, causing her hair to fall in her eyes.

"I care about you." I swept the hair off her face, tucking it behind her ear. "A lot."

"I care about you too," she replied.

"And I don't think it matters if we have it all figured out," I said softly. "As long as we figure it out together."

Her lips curled into a smile, and she pulled me in for a kiss. "I like the sound of that."

NINETEEN

Jo

It was the Friday evening before Thanksgiving, and I was seated at Katie's dining room table finishing a few follow up emails to some local businesses that were donating gifts for the Project NENA Christmas party. I smiled, my soul filled with a sense of purpose and belonging. I felt useful, like I was really doing something good, something that mattered.

None of it would have been possible without Katie, Derek, and all their friends. They'd donated their money and time and shared their connections with me. Once people got wind of the band's involvement, doors flew open. We were able to procure so many things that the kids needed, including laptops and internet subscriptions for their families, and Marathon Music Works even offered to donate their space for the party.

After I tapped out my last email, I closed my laptop and walked into the kitchen, glancing at the clock on the wall. It was a little after eight, and Katie would be getting home from work soon. I grabbed the kettle off the stove and filled it with water before placing it back on the burner, flipping the knob to high.

My phone rang from the dining room, and I wondered if it was Derek just getting out of his writing session with the band. I sprinted back into the room and snatched the phone off the table, my face immediately falling when I saw the name on the screen.

I sighed and answered. "Hi, Dad."

"What's the latest on the job search?" he asked without saying hello.

I groaned inwardly. "No updates," I said, which wasn't really a lie. There weren't any updates because I hadn't been looking. I'd been splitting my time between Derek's apartment and Katie's house, busying myself with planning the party for Project NENA and laying the groundwork for the benefit concert in the spring. "A lot of people are probably off for the holidays. I'm sure I'll hear something after the first of the year."

He let out a frustrated breath. "I don't understand, Jolene. You're my daughter for God's sake. Every news organization in this country should be lining up to hire you."

"I'm sure something will come up soon," I said half-heartedly.

"Well, do you need anything?" he asked. "Do you need money?"

"I'm okay," I answered. "I had a good bit saved up. But thank you."

"Alright," he said. "And how's your mother?"

"She's great," I replied, thankful for the change in topic. "She and John are going on a cruise for Thanksgiving. Actually, I wanted to talk to you about that." I took a deep breath. "I was thinking maybe I could come see you for the holiday. I could come to New York, and we could spend the weekend together."

We hadn't spent a holiday or a birthday together since I was a child. I thought spending Thanksgiving together could be a good opportunity to talk to him about my career and what I was feeling. Maybe I could even tell him about Derek.

"Ah, no can do," he said. "I'm going to be in Syria with the President visiting the troops." He cleared his throat. "Maybe you can join your mother on her cruise."

My heart deflated. "It's okay. I'll just have Thanksgiving with Katie and her friends. She's got this wonderful group of—"

"That's great, sweetie," he said, cutting me off. "Listen, I've got to run, but keep me posted on the job situation."

"Oh. Okay." I tried to keep my voice chipper, but it came out dejected. "Sure, I'll keep you posted. Love you, Dad."

My words were met with silence because he'd already ended the call. I placed the phone face down on the table and pushed my hands through my hair. Our conversation had been so short the water on the stove hadn't even had time to boil.

I heard the key turn in the lock of the back door, followed by Katie's voice.

"Hey." She flopped her purse and keys on the counter.

"Hey," I said, ambling over to the cabinet next to the stove. "I was just making some tea. You want some?"

"Sure," she replied. "Earl Grey, please."

"Splash of milk?"

"That sounds great," she answered as I pulled the tea bags and a couple of mugs from the cupboard.

"I made some lentil soup for dinner," I said, placing the sachets into the mugs. "Want me to warm some up for you?"

"Maybe in a little while," she said. "I'm too exhausted to even eat right now."

"Go sit in the living room," I insisted. "I'll bring your tea to you."

She gave a weak nod and headed for the living room.

Once the kettle had boiled and the tea had steeped, I added milk to her mug and a little honey to mine and brought them to the couch where Katie was waiting.

"Here you go," I said, handing her a mug. "Rough day?"

"The holidays are always nuts," she explained. "It gets busier every year. I love it, but my body doesn't. I feel worn down. Maybe I'm just getting old."

"You're not old," I insisted. "Because if you're old, then I'm also old, and I refuse to accept that."

She laughed. "How was your day?"

"It was good," I said. "Derek and I pretended to be tourists and took Izzy for a walk around the city."

"That sounds fun."

"It was. He brought his camera and took a bunch of photos of things he found interesting or beautiful..." I trailed off, lost in the memory. I often found myself the focus of his lens, and every time it melted me into a giant puddle of goo. Seeing the world and myself through his eyes was invigorating. Everything felt brighter, more vibrant. "Anyway, the band had a writing session tonight, so he went there, and I came home to send some emails."

Derek had decided to wait to tell the band of his plans to quit until after the holidays. He'd gotten back into therapy to help him work through everything that happened with his parents, and he already seemed lighter.

Knowing he would soon be free from his commitment to the band, Derek had actually been able to enjoy their recent writing sessions. It was amazing how removing the pressure made room for him to have fun again. It became something he enjoyed doing once he no longer felt the weight of its ball and chain.

Katie cupped the warm mug in her hands and looked over at me with a smile.

"What?" I asked.

"Nothing," she said. "It's just nice seeing you happy is all. You and Derek are so good together."

I let out a contented sigh. "It's so weird. You don't even know how much you're settling until you're with someone who doesn't ask you to…someone who sets the bar beyond your wildest expectations."

She snorted. "What's that like? I'm still stuck in Tinder dating purgatory. All the guys are just so…unappealing and immature."

Derek was the opposite of that. I thought back to the day we'd gone together to get tested after we'd gotten back from Kentucky. I wasn't going to insist that he go, but he'd done it gladly, all because he wanted me to feel comfortable.

"Anyway, it's just good to see you like this. You've even started incorporating color into your wardrobe." She gestured at the eggplant purple sweater I was wearing. "You look great."

"I feel pretty great." I took a sip of my tea. "So, I was wondering something. Do you think it would still be okay if I joined you all for Thanksgiving at Liv's? I just talked to my dad, and he's going to be out of town."

"Of course it's okay," she said. "Liv was hoping you'd make it. Everyone loves you."

I grinned. "I love them too." I thought about the planning sessions I'd had with everyone over the last couple of weeks. The guys were all excited about the benefit concert in the spring and had convinced a few more big names to get on board. Helping Project NENA was important to me, and because of that, Katie, Derek, and their friends had made it important to them. "I know I haven't known them long, but they make me feel like I matter—like I have a family again."

"That's because you do," Katie said.

I studied her face for a moment, noticing the purple circles imprinted under her eyes. "I don't mean to nag, but have you made an appointment with your doctor yet? I'm worried about you."

She shook her head. "I'll call Monday. Promise. Really, I think I'm just run down."

"Well, you know what helps that?" I asked, reaching for the remote on the coffee table. "Watching *Golden Girls* with your best friend and going to bed early."

"Wow," she said, taking a drink of her tea. "I thought you said we *weren't* old."

I pulled the throw blanket off the back of the couch and draped it across our laps. "Really, when is watching Betty White with your bestie ever the wrong choice?"

"You have a point there," she said as we nestled into the couch for a wild night in with Dorothy, Blanche, Sophia, and Rose.

THE NEXT MONTH PASSED IN A BLUR OF PUMPKIN SPICE AND twinkle lights. Thanksgiving with the group was boisterous and hilariously chaotic, especially when Ella accidentally spilled the entire bowl of sweet potatoes in Luca's lap. Naturally, she cried about it.

By the time the day of the party arrived, I was a bundle of nerves and excitement. I got up early and threw on some sweats so I could get to the venue and help set up. I gathered my things and my outfit for the evening quietly so as not to wake Katie, and I'd almost reached the back door when I heard her stirring.

"Jo?" Her voice was weak and strained.

I rushed to her room and opened the door to find a pajama-clad Katie curled into a ball with only the sheet covering her, tears leaving wet streaks down her face.

"Oh my God, Katie." I ran to her side. "What happened?"

"I...can't...go to...the party," she choked out, her shoulders shaking. "I think I have the flu or something."

I grabbed a tissue off the nightstand and dried her face. "Oh honey, I'm so sorry." I pressed my hand to her forehead. "You don't feel feverish. Let me get you some Tylenol, though, just in case."

I quickly made my way to the bathroom and retrieved the medicine from the cabinet before grabbing her some water from the kitchen.

"Here you go," I said, placing the glass on the nightstand and handing her two pills.

She raised up slightly, just enough to take the pills and chase them with a little water. I took the glass as she laid back down.

"I'm so dizzy," she cried. "It feels like the room is spinning, and my chest feels so tight."

"Are you cold?" I asked. "How about I bundle you up in your quilt?"

"It feels too heavy. It was so uncomfortable I had to get it off of me."

I studied her delicate frame. "It's the weekend so I know your doctor's office is closed, but why don't you let me take you to a walk-in clinic?"

"No, there's no sense in that," she said. "There's not much they can do for the flu anyway."

I smoothed her hair with my hand. "Katie, I'm really worried about you. What if it's not the flu? Did you ever make an appointment with the doctor?"

She shook her head, then cursed because it only made her more dizzy. "I had an appointment, but things got so busy at work that I had to cancel it. I need to reschedule."

"Yes, you do," I agreed. "You've been feeling so crappy lately. I know you love your job, but do you think you're overdoing it? Maybe you should take a little time off."

"Yeah, I'm taking off the week of Christmas, so that should help."

I pursed my lips, not satisfied with her answer. "I really think you should let me take you to a clinic today."

"I'll be fine," she attempted to assure me. "Besides, you have to be there today. You've worked so hard on this, and I just hate letting you down. I was really looking forward to seeing all the kids."

"You're not letting me down. You're sick," I said softly. "You can't help that, and I'm not going to just leave you here like this."

"You have to," she insisted. "I promise I'll be fine. I'm just going to be sleeping anyway. You've worked too hard on this party to not be there. You've got to go."

I sighed. "At least let me call someone to come hang out with you. I could call Dallas?"

"No," she said quickly. "He's so excited about the party. I don't want to spoil it for him."

"What about Ella?"

"I would feel awful if I gave whatever I have to her, especially with her being pregnant."

"Okay, here's the deal," I said firmly. "I'll go, but only if you let me call someone to be here with you today. You're dizzy. What if you need help getting up to go to the bathroom? What if you need someone to take you to the doctor later?"

"I don't need a babysitter. I'm going to be fi—" she started, but I cut her off.

"You let me call someone to come stay with you or I don't go. Period. I'm not leaving you here alone like this."

She blew out a breath. "Okay, okay. Fine. But everyone is supposed to go to the party. They've all been looking forward to it, and I know they'd be sad to miss it. Well, everyone except maybe Luca. He's not exactly great with kids. He forgets you can't cuss like a sailor in front of them."

I raised my brow at her.

"No. Hell no. Anyone but Luca."

"Grace?" I asked.

"I wouldn't want her to get sick and then get Ella sick," she answered.

I propped my hand on my hip.

"Fine," she said weakly, pointing to her phone on the nightstand. "Call Luca. But just know that if I die in his care, my blood is on your hands."

I laughed as I scrolled to Luca's contact info in Katie's phone. He wearily answered on the fifth ring, and after I told him three different times who I was and why I was calling, he promised to be at Katie's within the hour—but only if we swore not to tell anyone what he was doing.

"It's not like any of them really expected me to show up anyway," he said.

"Well, were you going to show up?" I asked.

"Probably," he said. "For a minute at least. Kids make me

uncomfortable. They're like little drunk people who always say what they're thinking. Who does that shit?"

I snorted. "You do."

He choked out a laugh. "Touché, Jo." He ended the call without so much as a goodbye.

"You need to go," Katie pressed while we waited for Luca.

"Nope," I said, gently laying on the other side of her bed so as not to jostle her. "I'm right where I need to be."

Half an hour later, Luca arrived looking like he'd just rolled out of bed. I showed him where everything was and made sure he had my number in case he needed anything. Finally, I took him to Katie's room.

He took one look at her and wrinkled his nose. "Girl, you look like shit on a stick. You're not going to puke on me, are you? I love ya and all that, but I don't do vomit."

Katie exhaled sharply and turned her head to me. "Leave before I summon up the energy to kick your butt for this."

TWENTY

Derek

I ARRIVED at Marathon Music Works to find Jo flying around the venue like an airplane in distress. Lindsey, the founder of Project NENA, was following behind her in an equally frantic state. Though Jo looked stressed, she also looked completely in her element and stunning in a long sleeve, burgundy velvet dress.

The place already looked magical, like something out of a Christmas movie. Lit garland with extravagant bows were hung on the walls. There was a photo booth on one wall with a sparkly backdrop and props just waiting for families to take pictures. A DJ was set up in one corner playing holiday tunes next to a small dance floor, and there were round tables with small Christmas tree centerpieces, fancy plates, and flatware spread throughout the venue. At the center of the room was a large green velvet chair where Santa, the star of the show, would be seated.

"What are we going to do now?" I heard Lindsey ask Jo. "We have two hundred kids expecting to see Santa. I can't believe that dipshit."

"Hey," I said as I approached. "What's going on?"

"It appears our Santa had a little too much eggnog and a few, ahem, *special* cookies at a party last night," Jo answered, pressing her palm to her forehead.

"Weed cookies. He had a whole plate of weed cookies," Lindsey added, shaking her head. "Why couldn't he just fuck an elf or something? Now we don't have a Santa."

"Oh wow." I tried my best to keep a straight face. "Was Luca your Santa? I heard from Dallas that he wasn't coming."

Jo's eyes widened, and I noticed her make a funny face. "No, it was a friend of Lindsey's. I think Luca is just under the weather or something."

I snorted. Luca had probably been at the same party as Santa.

"And since Santa is...indisposed," Jo continued, "we're screwed. We have the suit, but no Santa to go in it."

"I'm seriously going to kill him." Lindsey pressed her fingertips to her temples.

"I could do it," I said with a shrug.

"Do what?" Jo asked.

Lindsey raised her brow. "Kill him?"

I laughed. "No, I could be Santa."

Jo's eyes widened. "Really?"

"Of cou—" I began, but Lindsey cut me off with a slap on the back.

"Sold," she said cheerfully. "To our handsome friend in the leather jacket. Let's get you suited up. The kids will be here soon. "

"Thank you, thank you, thank you," I heard Jo say as Lindsey carted me away.

Half an hour later, I was dressed as the big guy in red, complete with a fluffy white beard.

"Give me a *ho, ho, ho,*" Lindsey chirped as we waited for the DJ to give us our cue.

"Ho, ho, ho," I replied, but it must not have been convincing enough because Lindsey's face wrinkled in horror.

"Oh, no, no, *no*," she said. "I need more bravado, more pomp, more circumstance. It needs to come from deep in your belly, like a bowl full of jelly or whatever that damn song says."

I cleared my throat and tried again, channeling the jolliest tone I could muster. "Ho, ho, ho!"

"Perfect." She nodded her approval as the DJ announced Santa's arrival from the North Pole.

"Well, big guy, it's showtime!"

It turned out that being Santa was a lot harder than it looked. The kids either loved Santa or were completely terrified, and there was no in between. Luckily, I'd managed to win over even some of the most fearful little ones.

A few times, I caught Jo looking on with a big smile on her face. Everyone had shown up, except Luca and Katie, who were both under the weather. While I didn't doubt that was true for Katie, I wondered about Luca. Was he really sick or had he just been over-served, like he'd been so many times before?

The line came to an end as the families found their seats and the appetizers were delivered to the tables. I was about to stand and stretch my legs when I looked up to find Jo staring down at me.

"You know, I never would have pegged myself for having

the hots for Santa, but here we are," she said, her voice low so that only I could hear her.

I chuckled. "Maybe later you can sit on my lap and tell me what you want for Christmas."

Her cheeks flushed, and she giggled. "If I do that, I'll end up on the naughty list for sure."

"One can hope." I raised my brow and laughed. "So, how's the party been going?"

"I think the kids are having a great time," she said. "Dallas really stepped up and helped McKenzie with the food. He's kind of brilliant in the kitchen."

"He is," I agreed.

"Jax and Liv have been manning the present station with Lindsey and handing out gifts," she went on. "Ella and Grace have been handling the face painting booth, and shockingly, Ella has only cried once."

"The night is young, though," I said with a laugh.

"And Cash, Antoni, and Nate have been hyping up the kiddos on the dance floor." She pointed to where the three of them stood near the DJ booth.

"That sounds about right."

She leaned down to me, close enough that I could smell her perfume. "I couldn't have done any of this without you. I wish I could kiss you right now, but I'm pretty sure that would freak out the kids."

I chuckled as a woman with dark, curly hair approached with a little boy in Christmas pajamas. He looked to be about four or five.

"Hey, Santa," she said. "My son Micha has been working up the nerve to come say hello."

"Hi, Micha," Jo greeted him, stepping aside.

"Say hi." Micha's mom smiled, and the little boy hid his face behind her leg.

I gave him the heartiest *ho, ho, ho* I could muster. "Hello there, Micha. Would you like to come tell me what you want for Christmas? I hear you've been a very good little boy this year."

"He has," his mom said. "I'm Lanna, by the way."

"Yes, of course," I said, pretending that Santa knew exactly who she was. "You were on the nice list this year."

Micha raised his head and looked at me wide-eyed, then turned back to Lanna.

"I know, bud," she said to Micha. "He knows who we are. You want to go sit on his lap?"

Micha gave me a shy glance before finally nodding.

I reached for him, and he settled onto the velvet of my suit, peeking up at me with big, enchanted eyes.

"I can't tell you how much it means to me that y'all did this," Lanna said. "This is our second year with Project NENA. I got hurt on the job last year and wasn't able to work, so y'all have been a godsend." She paused for a moment, glancing over at Jo. "Are you Jo?"

"I am," she answered.

"Lindsey told me about you." Lanna smiled. "She said you saved Christmas this year."

Jo blushed. "I can't take credit. I had a lot of help."

I felt a surge of pride for Jo as Micha curled my fluffy, white beard in his fingers.

"Now, what would you like for Christmas this year, little one?" I asked.

Micha stared up at me thoughtfully. His brown eyes were full of wonder, but there was something else there too. Something I recognized. Sadness.

"I want you to bring my daddy back home," Micha answered finally, his voice small. "You don't have to bring me no other presents. I just want my daddy back, okay?"

My chest constricted, and I locked eyes with Jo. She maintained her smile, but her eyes had glossed over.

"Micha, sweetie," his mother said, her voice wavering. "We've talked about this. Daddy can't come back."

"But, Mom," Micha objected. "Santa's magical. He can do anything. He can bring Daddy back."

Lanna crouched down and stroked the little boy's head. "Micha's dad...He's not able to be in our lives anymore. He had a lot of problems, and it became...an issue." Tears welled in her eyes, and my heart broke for them both.

"But Santa can make daddy all better and bring him back." Micha turned his hopeful eyes up to mine. "Can't you, Santa?"

"I'm so sorry, Micha," I said, my voice falling out of character. The little boy didn't seem to notice. "I can't bring your dad back for you."

His eyes brimmed with tears. "But why? All my friends have a family but not me."

"That's not true," I said gently. "I know it's hard when you see other girls and boys with their dads, and you wonder why you don't have that. But the thing is, you do have a family even if it looks a little different. I know you have a mommy who loves you very much."

"And Grandpa Rupert and Nana. And we can't forget Nugget. That's our dog," Lanna explained. "And you have so many friends that love you, sweetheart."

Micha was deflated. "But they're not my family."

"Do you know what the difference is between our family and friends?" I asked him.

Micha shook his head.

"Our friends are the family we get to choose," I said gently. "All we need to have a family is love. It doesn't matter if we're related to someone, or even if they're human."

His eyes brightened. "Like Nugget?"

"Exactly," I answered. "As long as you love each other, that's what matters. Our families are the ones who always have our backs, who love and support us."

"Like you, Santa?" he asked.

I chuckled. "That's right, Micha. Like me."

The boy threw his arms around my neck, and I had to clear my throat to keep from getting choked up.

"Thank you," Lanna mouthed to me, tears streaming down her face.

I held Micha in my arms, wishing I could somehow give him all of the love he so greatly deserved.

Jo caught my eye, and I felt a surge of gratitude for the acceptance and love she'd brought into my own life. I may not have had the love and support I deserved growing up, but in that moment, looking at Jo, I had everything I ever needed.

TWENTY-ONE

Jo

MY HEART SWELLED with joy as I glanced around the room. It was nearly nine p.m. The meal had wrapped up, and families were back on the dance floor and taking pictures in the photo booth. Everyone looked so happy, it was impossible not to feel that same energy coursing through my veins. Being there while the kids opened their gifts had been so heartwarming, made even better by the knowledge that each parent would be sent home with more clothes, shoes, winter coats, and toys for the children to receive on Christmas.

To my left, McKenzie was crouched on the floor with a young girl. She was straightening the child's tiara, a broad smile painted on her face. When the girl ran off into the crowd, McKenzie stood, and I caught her eye.

"Hey," I said as I approached her. "I wanted to thank you again for all of your help. Those hot chicken sliders you made were amazing. Everyone was talking about them."

She gave me a shy smile. "Thanks."

We stood together in silence for a moment, watching everyone enjoy the party.

"What you did tonight…" McKenzie trailed off, looking down at her feet. "You did something really special for these families. Something they'll never forget."

"It wasn't just me—" I started, but she cut me off.

"Nope," she said. "Don't downplay what you did here."

I smiled over at her. "Thank you."

Her eyes met mine, and she shoved her thumbs in her pockets. "My dad's been out of the picture since I was twelve, but up till then, my mom stayed at home with me and my older brother. After he went away, she had to work two jobs just to keep the lights on. It was because of an organization like this one that we even had a Christmas or clothes on our backs." Her gaze returned to the ground. "Those Christmases were really special to us. And being on the other side now and getting to see how all of these people came together to make these families feel loved…It's really incredible." She looked back up at me, her eyes glossy. "And you did that, Jo."

My throat tightened. "McKenzie…I—"

"Look, don't make it weird." She shook her head and grinned. "We don't have to, like, hug or anything. It's not that serious."

I returned her smile and nodded, though her eyes said it mattered a lot more than she was letting on.

"I'm not gonna lie. When you came to work with Katie the first time, I wasn't sure about you," McKenzie admitted. "You were extremely perky, and I just find that to be very unnatural."

I laughed. "I used to get up for work at three a.m. Perky was part of the job description."

McKenzie scrunched her nose. "Well, your job *sucked*."

"Yes, it did."

"But you decidedly don't. Suck, I mean." She gave me a

nod of approval, complimenting me in her own roundabout way.

"Look, McKenzie, don't make it weird," I joked. "We don't have to hug or anything."

She laughed.

"But could I interest you in a high five?" I asked.

She feigned disgust. "Now you've crossed the line."

After a moment, she rolled her eyes and smiled, holding up her hand which I clapped with my own.

"I've got to head out," McKenzie said. "Tell Katie I hope she feels better."

I thanked her, and she disappeared into the crowd. I was about to go find Lindsey when I heard someone say my name.

"Hey, Jo, have you seen Derek?"

I turned to see Dallas approaching me.

"Actually, he left about twenty minutes ago." I answered. "Some kid had a little too much punch and peed all over him. He went home to clean up."

"You're kidding." Dallas chuckled. "Damn. Where was I?"

A smile tugged at the corners of my mouth. It had been pretty hilarious, but Derek had taken it in stride. "By the way, I wanted to thank you again for all of your help today."

"Of course," he said. "I was happy to be involved. I hated that Katie couldn't be here, though."

"Me too."

Dallas crossed his arms over his broad chest. "Actually, I've been wanting to thank you too."

"Me?" I asked. "What for?"

His lips curled at the corners of his mouth. "Let's just say that before you came into the picture, Derek was struggling in the band. I don't know what was going on. He just seemed unhappy…distracted. But since you've been around, all that's changed. I feel like I've gotten my cousin back."

I swallowed, my throat suddenly dry. "Oh?"

"It's like you reignited his love for music," Dallas continued. "You must be his muse or something."

I opened my mouth, but no words came out. My stomach whirled like the disco ball above the dance floor. Dallas had no idea Derek was leaving the band, so of course he didn't know that was the reason for his cousin's renewed sense of joy in his music.

"Derek's a great guy, but he's a little impressionable. Probably a side effect of being the youngest." He squeezed my shoulder. "But you've been a good influence on him. Anyway, I just want you to know I appreciate it."

"Oh, um, thanks." I forced a smile and nodded, but his words nagged at me. Dallas obviously knew Derek better than I did. They'd grown up together, and if Derek *was* as impressionable as Dallas had said, had I unintentionally convinced him to quit the band?

"I'll be honest, I was getting a little worried about the band," Dallas said. "Because it only works with all of us, you know? Nobody's replaceable."

The disco ball inside my belly was spinning out of control. "Of course."

"But things feel…good now. Really good. Derek seems happy," Dallas went on, oblivious to how uncomfortable I was. "And, hey, I know Katie's really happy you're here too."

I sucked in a deep breath. "Yeah, I really missed her."

"What I'm trying to say is that you're alright, Jo," he said. "You're like this little ray of sunshine that came along and made everything bright again."

His smile was so genuine and kind that I instantly felt

guilty. What would Dallas think when Derek left the band and the sun fell out of the sky?

"I'm about to head out." He opened his arms to me. "Tell Katie I missed her tonight."

"I will," I replied, hugging him. "Thanks, Dallas."

He melted into the thinning crowd. I could see why Katie liked Dallas so much. He was sincere and fiercely protective of those he cared about. He'd been nothing but welcoming to me since I'd been in town, but I worried that welcome was about to run out.

"There you are." Lindsey's voice pulled me from my thoughts. "Girl, tonight has been amazing. What do you say we get a drink after everyone clears out? We could go to the art crawl over in East Nashville. My friend Juniper actually runs it."

"I'd love to," I answered. "But I really need to get home and check on Katie. She was pretty sick today."

She smiled. "Raincheck then."

"Definitely," I said.

"I couldn't have done this without you." Lindsey pulled me in for a hug. "Thank you so much."

"Hey, we're not done yet. Now we have a benefit concert to plan!"

"Yes, we do. But first, we enjoy our Christmas break," Lindsey said. "My wake up alarms are officially off until after the holidays, and I couldn't be happier. But I also can't believe Christmas is a week away. How the heck did that happen?"

I chuckled. "Very, very quickly."

We were interrupted when some of the families approached to say goodbye. The kids were all smiles and rosy cheeks as we wrapped up the party, making it that much easier to put Dallas out of my mind.

———

It was nearly eleven p.m. by the time I returned to Katie's. I quietly fit the key into the lock of the back door and gently pushed it open so as not to wake her if she was sleeping. When I opened the door, I was met with the sound of raucous laughter. I dropped my bag on the counter and padded the short distance down the hall to her bedroom.

Nothing could have prepared me for what I saw.

Luca was sitting at Katie's bedside in a chair he must have dragged in from the dining room, his feet propped on the bed. He was wearing a cloud-printed headband, a purple sheet mask, and a set of gold eye gels. The movie *Bridesmaids* was playing on the TV on top of the dresser, specifically the part where Melissa McCarthy was pooping in a sink. There were takeout containers on the nightstand along with a couple of styrofoam cups.

Katie was sitting up in bed bundled under a pile of blankets, wearing a sheet mask that looked like a watermelon, and cupping a steaming mug between her hands.

Both of them were laughing so hard they didn't hear me come in.

"Looks like somebody is feeling better," I said, causing them both to startle and Luca to jump to his feet, knocking the mask to the floor. "Am I too late for the slumber party?"

"Hey," Katie greeted me. "How'd it go?"

"It was great," I answered, trying not to laugh as Luca ripped the headband from his head, leaving his mop of dark hair standing up like Frankenstein's. "Everyone missed you. Both of you."

Luca snorted. "Trust me. Nobody missed me." He fumbled for his keys and wallet on the nightstand. "I should, uh, get going."

"Don't you want to watch the rest of the movie?" Katie asked.

"That's okay," he answered. "I should head out."

Katie's face fell slightly. For someone who hadn't wanted me to call Luca, she was sure disappointed to see him leave.

"Thanks for hanging out with me, Luca," Katie said, and he squeezed her foot through the comforter.

"Don't mention it," he mumbled and started for the door. "Literally."

"Hey, Luca, wait," I called after him, following on his heels. He stopped just short of the back door and turned to face me. "Thank you again for being here. I really appreciate you."

Luca opened his mouth to say something but changed his mind, turning back toward the door. He extended his hand toward the knob but stopped mid-reach, then faced me. "Jo?"

"Yeah?"

He narrowed his eyes. "If you tell anyone about this, I *will* deny it."

I nodded, a smile tugging at the corners of my mouth. "Of course."

"I mean it."

"Okay," I said. "But um—"

"But what?" he asked.

I cleared my throat. "You might want to uh…take care of…" I gestured my hand over the hollows of my eyes, referencing the gels he still wore.

"Ah fuck," he muttered, snatching the gold pads from beneath his eyes and storming out the door.

I smiled to myself as I locked up behind him.

"Need anything from the kitchen?" I called to Katie as I grabbed a bottle of water from the fridge.

"I'm good," she answered.

I pushed the fridge door closed with my hip, and something caught my eye on the counter where Katie kept the liquor bottles. A half empty glass filled with dark liquid and a fifth of Jack Daniels with the cap off just beside it.

My brow furrowed. I couldn't imagine Katie had felt up to drinking straight whiskey as bad as she'd felt that morning.

Luca. My heart sank. I knew from what Derek had said and the seemingly innocuous remarks from the others that Luca was known for having a wild streak. Surely he wouldn't have been drinking when he was supposed to be helping Katie…right?

I picked up the glass to put it in the sink but was caught off guard by the scent that wafted out of it. It was sweet, but not in the nauseating way that whiskey often was.

I held the tumbler to my nose and inhaled. It didn't smell like whiskey, so I brought it to my lips and took a small sip. My tongue was met with the taste of Coke and not a single drop of alcohol. I plunked the glass in the sink and instantly felt horrible for placing blame on Luca. But the whiskey *had* been opened, which I still found strange.

"Hey, Katie," I said as I padded back to her room. "I have a ques—"

"Why don't I ever make hot toddies?" she asked, before I could finish my sentence. She took a big sip from her mug. "They're so comforting. Remember when Granny used to make them?"

I smiled and sat at the foot of her bed. "Yeah, I do. Have the flu? Drink a hot toddy. Sprain your knee? Hot toddy."

"Get your heart broken?" Katie continued.

"Hot toddy," we said together and laughed.

She looked down at her mug. "I was telling Luca that I wished I had one of her hot toddies, so he went into the kitchen after dinner, dug out Granny's old recipe, and made it for me."

So Luca *had* opened the whiskey, but he'd done it to make something to help Katie feel better. Guilt clawed at my insides.

"I feel bad that I didn't want him to come at first," she said. "In all this time I've known him, I've never spent any one on one time with him, you know? I think I might have misjudged him."

I blew out a breath. "I think we all might have."

"He was so sweet, Jo." Katie looked at me, her brow furrowed. "Attentive. He didn't get weirded out when I was crying. He just reached over and grabbed my hand. He didn't even leave my side when I finally fell asleep."

"I'm not going to lie," I said. "This isn't what I expected at all."

"Right? Me either. But he took such good care of me," she continued. "I felt a bit better when I woke up, so I told him he could go home, but he wouldn't hear of it. We were watching movies, and he started playing around with my box of sheet masks just to make me laugh."

My chest squeezed. "I'll admit, I never would have pegged him for the nurturing type."

"Erratic maybe," Katie said. "Even careless at times. But today he was totally different—gentle and kind. I think we've all been wrong about him."

It occurred to me then that Derek might not be the only member of Midnight in Dallas who had secrets. Luca had come through for us when we needed him, and for that, I owed him. If he didn't want anyone to know about where he'd been or what he'd done, his secret would stay safe with me.

TWENTY-TWO

Derek

JO CALLED ONCE she got home and settled in after the party letting me know that Katie was still under the weather and asked if I would come there for the night. She told me that Katie said I could bring Izzy with the sole condition being that she got to steal her for the night. Of course, I was happy to oblige.

It was nearly midnight by the time I got there. Izzy was thrilled to climb in bed with Katie, and I was even more thrilled to climb into bed with Jo. She nestled into my arms, her fingers tracing shapes along my chest.

"You were so good with those kids tonight," she said, her voice piercing the darkness. "You handled that whole thing with Micha with such love and compassion."

I rubbed a piece of her hair between my fingers. "He deserves that. I wish I could have done more."

We laid in silence for a moment before Jo spoke again. "You'd make a good dad one day."

Her words pelted me in the chest. I knew she meant it as a compliment, but I couldn't have disagreed more. It wasn't that

I didn't like kids—I did. But liking kids and being a father were two very different things.

"Do you think you'd ever want to have children of your own?" she asked.

My breath caught in my throat. It wasn't something I'd often thought about. Why even allow myself to consider something that would likely never be anything but a hypothetical?

"I don't think so," I answered quietly. Worry gnawed at my chest. What if the truth changed how Jo felt about me? "I'm just not sure the dad thing is for me, you know?"

Because I didn't trust myself not to one day become like my own father. What if his problems were genetic? I'd suffered enough at his hand to know I couldn't risk the possibility that I would somehow end up like him. I knew what it had done to me, and I refused to explore any possibilities where I could do the same.

"What about you?" I asked, running my hand along her arm in an attempt to quiet the nerves building inside me.

"I don't think they're a part of my plan either." She sighed softly. "I guess I've always been so focused on my career that I never really stopped to think about the idea of having a family. And it didn't help that my dad was always talking about all the reasons not to. Sometimes I wonder if he regrets having me."

I tightened my arms around her.

"Maybe he feels like I held him back," she whispered.

"I don't think he could ever think that," I said. "Your dad is extremely successful."

"Yeah, but it's never been enough, you know? The more successful he became, the further the benchmark moved. He was always chasing something bigger and better." She snuggled deeper into my chest. "Let's talk about something else. Talking about my dad is kind of a downer after the great day we had."

I kissed her forehead. "You were amazing today, Jo. Totally in your element. You did something incredible, and I'm so proud of you."

I felt her smile against my chest. "Thank you," she said and blew out a breath. "I feel like this entire holiday season has flown by and I haven't really slowed down long enough to enjoy it."

"Actually, I'm glad you said that because there's something I've been wanting to talk to you about," I began, taking a shaky breath. "I completely understand if you have plans already with your mom or Katie, but if you don't, I was wondering if you'd consider spending Christmas with me? We could rent a chalet in Gatlinburg, just the two of us. And Izzy, of course, if Katie doesn't dognap her."

Jo laughed. "Now, *that* is a very real possibility." She raised up, brushing my lips with hers, her hair tickling my face. "I'd love to spend the holiday with you."

Her answer made me feel like a kid on Christmas morning. "Really?"

"Yes," she replied. "Katie is going to visit her aunt and cousins in Chattanooga. I didn't bother to ask my dad what he was doing because I already know he'll be working. Of course, I can go to my mom's, and I'd love to see her, but honestly, the idea of Christmas in Florida sounds kinda depressing. Way too warm. Now, Christmas in the mountains with you? That sounds perfect."

"I was hoping you'd say that, because I actually already rented a place," I confessed. "If you'd said no, I would have just canceled it, but I wanted to make sure everything didn't get booked up."

"When do we leave?" she asked.

"Well, technically it's ours from tomorrow through New Years," I answered. "But if that's too soon, we can leave whenever is best for you."

She kissed me again. "Tomorrow is perfect."

A Smoky Mountain getaway ended up being exactly what we needed. There was no talk of the band, and Jo was taking a break from helping Project NENA until after the new year, so we got to spend the entire time enjoying each other. We took Izzy for walks and drove around town to look at Christmas lights, and the chalet we were staying in had a breathtaking panoramic view that we enjoyed from the hot tub.

We spent the day before Christmas Eve in Dollywood, where we rode the Dollywood Express and took in the sights, snuggled close together. We drank hot chocolate and ate cinnamon bread while browsing through different shops. When Jo stepped away in search of a restroom, I came across a beautiful clothbound journal. It was vibrant and colorful, just like Jo. The clerk had been kind enough to gift wrap it for me, and I tucked it away in my coat pocket.

"What's this?" she asked when I presented it to her over dinner that night.

"Just something I saw today that made me think of you," I'd answered. "When I saw it, I knew you had to have it."

She gingerly untied the ribbon, prying the wrapping paper away from the corners until she'd uncovered the journal.

"Derek…" She ran her fingers along its spine. "It's beautiful."

"I wanted you to have that as a reminder that your voice needs to be heard," I said. "You have such a beautiful heart, Jo. And you view the world with such compassion and empathy. I know you're not reporting anymore, but I don't want you to forget that your voice matters, no matter how you choose to use it."

Her eyes were glossy when she looked up at me. "Thank you. This is…It's perfect."

When we got back to the chalet, I started a fire while Jo took Izzy out for a bathroom break. A few moments later, the two of them came bounding through the door.

"Derek!" Jo cried, causing me to nearly jump out of my skin.

I spun around to look at her. "What's wrong? Are you okay?"

"Of course I'm okay! It's snowing!" Her cheeks were rosy, and snowflakes glistened in her hair.

I chuckled. "You lived in Chicago. Didn't you see snow all the time?"

"Yes," she replied, running to me and grabbing my hand. "And it wasn't nearly enough. You have to come look."

Izzy grunted and heaved her little body onto the couch, clearly not sharing Jo's enthusiasm for frozen precipitation.

"Okay," I said, and I let her lead me to the door, only stopping long enough to throw on my coat.

Cold air burned my lungs when we stepped outside. We leaned against the rails of the balcony, peering off into the night. The snow fell, shimmering against the pitch black sky as though it were raining diamonds.

I looked over at Jo with her face turned up to the sky in childlike wonder, and I'd never seen anything more beautiful.

She sighed and turned toward me. "Isn't it amazing?"

I nodded, and my breath hitched in my throat. "We're in a snow globe."

Her smile sparkled with the snow as she circled her arms around my neck, and I wrapped mine around her waist.

"We are." She placed a kiss on my lips, and I leaned my forehead against hers, gently wiping flakes of snow from her cheeks.

"Jo?" My throat tightened as though it were locking my feelings inside. I was ready to say the words, to tell Jo how much I loved her, but I wasn't sure that she was ready to hear it.

"Yes?" She took in a breath as her eyes searched mine.

I opened my mouth but no words came out. Instead, I kissed her and pulled her close, our breath forming small clouds in the night air. We stood that way for a while as the snow fell around us like confetti. A single, perfect moment, frozen in time.

TWENTY-THREE

Jo
___

I BLINKED, and it was mid-January. A freak winter storm had blown in and dumped nearly eight inches of snow on the city, which was unheard of for Nashville. Middle Tennessee wasn't like Chicago. That much snow paralyzed the city for nearly five days, but it gave me time to really ramp up plans for the Project NENA benefit show in April. I was still snowed in at Derek's with nothing but time on my hands, so I made use of it, sending emails and making phone calls.

It was a blustery and cold afternoon, and Derek was in the other room on a virtual appointment with his therapist while I was curled up on the sofa with Izzy and my laptop when my phone rang from the coffee table. I glanced at the screen, and my heart lurched when I saw Lindsey's name. I'd reached out and asked her for a favor to help me surprise Derek. It hadn't been easy keeping it from him, but if it all went as planned, it would be well worth it.

"Hello?" I answered.

"Hey, girl," Lindsey chirped. "So, I've got good news."

I snapped my laptop shut. "Really?"

"Yep," she said. "I sent my friend, Juniper, who does the art crawl the pictures you emailed me of Derek's photos, and she *loved* them. Actually, she said something far more pretentious than that, but that was the gist of it. She's going to give him his own booth the first Saturday in February."

I laughed. "Oh my God. This is amazing. Thank you so much, Lindsey."

"Of course. I'm happy to help. And I didn't tell her anything about Derek being in Midnight in Dallas, though I doubt she knows who they are. She pretty much only listens to Willie Nelson," she said. "Oh, and while I've got you, I actually wanted to tell you something else."

"Sure, what's up?"

"I'm still processing the donations from the end of the year," she began. "There were so many it's taking me a while. And I just saw two I think you may want to hear about."

"Oh?" I asked, furrowing my brow. "Why? Is something wrong?"

"No, no," she answered quickly. "Not at all. You know how there's a notes section on the donation form?"

"Yeah…" I replied, still confused as to where this was going.

"Well, a couple of your friends sent in donations with messages attached," she explained as I heard what sounded like the clicking of a keyboard in the background. "The first one is from a Carina and Riggs. The note says, 'We are so proud of you, Jo. Miss you.'"

My heart melted. "Those are two of my friends from Chicago! That's so sweet of them."

I heard more clicking on the other end. "The other one was a sizable donation from Kimber Sutton."

I nearly choked on my own spit. "Oh, wow. Really? What does the note say?"

Lindsey cleared her throat. "It says, 'Jo, I've always admired your determination and kind heart. I'm so happy you've been able to put your energy toward such a wonderful cause that no doubt changes the lives of many. That's the news that really matters. Xoxo, Kimber.'"

My mouth fell open, and my eyes widened.

"Are you there?" she asked. "Did I lose you?"

"No, I'm here," I answered. "That's incredible. I'm just... I'm blown away."

"You did great work, Jo. You're the best volunteer I've ever had," Lindsey said. "And if what you've been sending me for this benefit show is any indication, this year is going to be life-changing for Project NENA. And *that*, my friend, is because of you."

I smiled. "I'm just glad I could help."

"Listen, I'm getting another call, but I'll reach out after this crap melts, and we'll grab a coffee," she said.

"That sounds great," I replied and ended the call.

I couldn't wait to tell Derek about his spot in the art show. But first, I needed to reach out to Kimber. I opened my laptop and toggled over to my email screen, where a new message caught my attention. It was from one of my old friends whom I'd interned with. She still worked with the station, now as an associate director, and I'd messaged her when we were looking for media coverage for Project NENA.

Subject: Part-time reporter position

My interest was piqued. I clicked the message to open it.

Hey Jo!

Not sure that you'd even be interested, but we're looking for a part-time reporter. It's mostly human interest stuff, but we do like to promote from within, so there are always opportunities to advance. Let me know if you're interested, and I'll set up an interview. It'd be great to have you back.

Warmest Regards,

Leigh Ann Hale

I chewed my bottom lip. Not working for the last couple of months had been nice, but I knew I needed some kind of income. I'd been paying for everything out of my savings, and I didn't want to completely drain it. Plus, I had to admit, the idea of getting back into a newsroom without the pressure of a full time commitment appealed to me. The market in Nashville would be different than it was in Chicago too.

I clicked *Reply* and typed out my message.

Hey Leigh Ann!

Thanks so much for thinking of me. I would definitely be interested. Let's set something up.

If nothing else, maybe this would at least buy me a few months while I figured out what I wanted to do, and it still gave me plenty of time to fulfill my commitments to Project NENA. It also had the added benefit of getting my dad off my back.

I clicked to open a new message and keyed in Kimber's name until her email address filled the recipient's box.

Subject: I'm sorry.

I pressed my lips together as I considered what to say. Finally, I began to type.

Kimber,

I wanted you to know I'm so sorry for that day in the conference room. The way I acted had nothing to do with you and everything to do with me. You were always the right person for the job. If you'd be open to it, I would like to start over, but I would also understand if you never wanted to talk to me again. I'm so sorry. I'll do anything I can to make this right.

And thank you for the donation you made to Project NENA and for the kind words. I can't begin to tell you how much that means to me.

Jo

I smiled to myself as I snapped my laptop shut. It felt as though my blood was vibrating through my veins. Maybe not having a plan would end up being the best thing that ever happened to me.

THAT NIGHT, I INSISTED ON COOKING DINNER. DEREK TENDED to enjoy doing the bulk of the cooking, but I wanted to do something special. I sent Katie a text and asked her for Granny's famous chicken pot pie recipe for the occasion. We already had most everything I needed, but I was a couple of carrots short, so I just added more potatoes.

I'd forgotten how therapeutic it was to chop vegetables and roll out a pie crust. Derek turned on a playlist that was full of singer/songwriter tunes, and I settled into a groove. He tried several times to assist with the meal, but I told him the best way to help was by hanging out with me and keeping the wine flowing. He always spoiled me, and I wanted to do the same for him.

After I assembled the pot pie and placed it in the oven, Derek leaned against the counter next to the sink.

"Will you at least let me do the dishes?" he asked as I started to load the dishwasher.

"Not a chance," I answered, standing on my tiptoes to kiss him. "I want to treat you because tonight, we're celebrating."

His eyebrows raised. "Oh? What are we celebrating? Besides the fact that we're maybe the first couple in history who can be snowed in together for days and not kill each other."

I laughed, but my insides turned to mush. "Yes. Besides that."

We still hadn't officially put any labels on our relationship, and hearing him call us a couple made me weak in the knees. My feelings for Derek had grown, filling all the open spaces in my heart. I was in love with him, and I'd nearly told him so the night before Christmas Eve when I'd dragged him out into the cold night to see the snow. There was something so magical, so pure about that moment, but when I'd opened my mouth to say the words, nothing came out.

"So, what are we celebrating?" he pressed, reaching for my waist and tickling my sides.

I jumped and let out a high-pitched squeal, nearly dropping the cutting board I was holding.

"Okay, okay," I said, placing the board in the dishwasher. I dried my hands on the towel that hung beside the sink before turning to him and snaking my arms around his neck. "We're actually celebrating two things."

"Two things?" His grin stretched across his face.

I nodded. "The first is that I got an email today about a reporter job that's available at the station I interned with here in town. My old friend is the associate director there, and we're setting up an interview."

A look I couldn't quite read flashed across Derek's face before his smile returned, albeit not as wide.

"Oh, wow," he said. "I mean, that's great, but are you sure that's what you want?"

"I don't really know yet," I admitted. My excitement slowly leaked out of me like helium from a balloon when I saw the expression on his face. "It's just part-time for now, which gives me plenty of time to devote to my volunteer work with Project NENA and to explore other options if I want to. I just...I've never done this type of job without using my dad's barometer for success. What if I find a whole new love for it on my own terms?" I shrugged, unsure if I was trying to convince him or me.

Derek nodded. "That's a great point, and I think it's smart to give it another shot without the pressure of your dad."

"And it's mostly human interest stuff. I've always loved those stories, but felt like I was less of a journalist when I covered them because my dad always said they weren't real news. Maybe with this job I'll find out that I don't miss covering philandering senators at all."

He chuckled, tightening his arms around my waist. "I think that's awesome, Jo. I really do."

"Really?" I asked.

"Absolutely." He kissed my forehead. "I just wanted to make sure that it's what you *want* to do, not what you feel you *have* to do."

"I may not even get the job, so it could all be a moot point, but it feels kind of good to be getting back out there," I said, and I realized I meant it.

"So, you said there were two things we were celebrating tonight." Derek cocked his head to the side.

"Actually, this next thing is the main reason we're celebrating," I confessed. "I have a surprise for you."

"Okay..."

"Come with me," I said, leading him to his wall of photographs in the foyer. "What if you could see your work— your amazing, beautiful pictures—in an art show?"

He licked his lips, a puzzled expression on his face. "I mean, that would be awesome, but I honestly don't know the first thing about how to make that happen. And it's really just a hobby. I don't know if they're good enough for that."

"They are," I insisted. "And I'm not the only one who thinks so."

Derek's brow creased, and his eyes narrowed.

I took his hands in mine. "I hope you won't be upset, but I took pictures of your work and shared them with Lindsey, who showed them to her friend who runs the East Nashville Art Crawl. She loved them, Derek. She wants to give you a booth at the crawl the first weekend in February."

His eyes widened as he withdrew his hand from mine, rubbing it along the stubble on his jawline. "Are you serious?"

My heart sank. Had I overstepped? Had this been a mistake? "Yes. I am."

He looked from me to his photos and then back to me. "My pictures…in an art show…"

My mouth went dry. "I'm so sorry, Derek. I didn't mean to upset you. I should have asked you first. You don't have to—"

Derek closed the distance between us, lifting me off the ground, spinning me around. "Are you kidding me? I'm not upset. This is amazing, Jo!" He set me back on my feet and cupped my face in his hands. "My work is going to be in an art show."

I nodded, giggling.

He leaned in and kissed me hard. "This is the most amazing thing anyone's ever done for me. I…I'm speechless. Thank you. Thank you so much."

I opened my mouth, those three little words dangling from the tip of my tongue. They were so close to the surface, yet just out of reach.

"You're welcome," I said softly, then I kissed him, hoping my lips could tell him what my words could not.

TWENTY-FOUR

Derek
_____

IT WAS the first Friday in February, the day before the East Nashville Art Crawl. The icy wind nearly sliced me in half as I walked out of my therapist's office that afternoon. I pulled my phone from my pocket to see if Jo had texted to let me know she was done with work. She'd just started her job at the news station and had already jumped in full steam ahead. I glanced at the screen, but there were no messages from Jo. All that waited for me was a missed call from my mom. I sighed and locked the phone as I waited for my Uber at the curb since it was too cold for me to ride my bike. It was the third time she'd called in a month without leaving a message.

After I'd left my childhood home and my relationship with my parents behind, I didn't hear from them, nor did I really want or expect to. I'd made my peace with it as best as I could, and the therapy I'd been doing in the three months since then was helping me understand how much grief I'd still been holding on to.

I'd already sent my mom enough money to cover my dad's

expenses and hopefully enough to help her get back on her feet after he was gone. When she'd started calling a few weeks before, my first thought was that he'd passed, but I knew if that had happened, Dallas would have found out from his mom and called me. Then, I'd wondered if my parents had already gone through the money, and I started to feel guilty. My therapist had quickly reminded me that I couldn't control how they used the money I'd given them. That I had to stop taking responsibility for their actions. And damn, was that freeing.

I found I was spending less of my recent therapy sessions talking about my parents and more of them talking about the band. I still hadn't told them I was quitting.

"Why do you think that is?" my therapist had asked that afternoon.

I didn't really have a reason. Not a good one, anyway. I kept saying I was waiting until the right time. Things had finally been good with Dallas and me and the guys, and telling them would be like tossing a grenade in their faces.

The black escalade I was waiting for arrived, and the driver rolled down the window. "Are you Derek?"

"That's me," I said, opening the door and sliding in the backseat.

She confirmed the address for my condo and pulled away from the curb.

My phone rang from inside my coat. I pulled it out, hoping it was Jo, but it was Ella's name that flashed back at me.

"Hey Ella," I answered. "What's up?"

"Hey," she said, and I could hear the baby crying in the background. "Sorry, can you hear me? Bettina is losing her shit."

I chuckled. "I can hear you. Bettina's a little hell-raiser, just like her mama."

"You got that right," she agreed. "Two weeks old today and this little shit nearly took my whole tit off."

I burst out laughing.

"Hang on," she said. "I'm putting you on speaker." There was a brief pause before I heard her again. "Can you hear me?"

"Loud and clear," I answered with a smile.

"Anyway," Ella continued, "Don't let the no teeth thing fool ya. She's got the jaws of a snapping turtle." She made soothing, shushing sounds at the baby. "Come on, Betty girl. Just take the boob. You know you want it."

Finally, there was quiet. "Sorry about that," Ella apologized. "I just wanted to call and wish you luck on your show tomorrow. I'm so upset we can't come. Cash and Grace had to go to LA again, and I don't feel comfortable leaving Bettina with a sitter yet."

"Thank you," I said. "And really, it's okay. You just had a baby."

"And she can't wait to see her Uncle Derek again. You and Jo should come by sometime this weekend. I think I may already have a touch of cabin fever, and with Cash gone, I am in dire need of a conversation with someone who doesn't require that I change their diapers." She chuckled. "And I miss everyone bringing me snacks."

I laughed. "Tell you what," I said. "Jo and I will swing by on Sunday, *and* we'll bring snacks."

"Yay!" she exclaimed. "Thank you! I can't wait to hear all about—"

There was a whimper on the other end, followed by the baby's piercing cry.

"Cash cannot get back here fast enough." Ella let out a sharp groan. "I'm so exhausted."

"I'm so sorry," I said.

"Shhh. It's okay, sweet girl," she cooed to an inconsolable Bettina. "Listen, I'm gonna have to run, but I'll see you Sunday!"

"Bye." I shook my head and smiled as I disconnected the call, nervous energy shooting through me.

The art crawl was everything I didn't know I wanted. I was invigorated. The more I got to be myself, the more I wanted it...the more I craved authenticity. But I had a feeling that once I got a taste of what it felt like to be recognized for something besides the band, I wouldn't be able to put off quitting Midnight in Dallas for much longer.

I GOT TO THE MARKETPLACE IN EAST NASHVILLE AT SIX P.M., fifteen minutes before the art crawl started. Jo had helped me set up my booth after she got off work the night before, so all that was left for me to do was show up. I clenched my hands and released them as I walked through the door to find my booth.

Other artists milled about, chatting amongst themselves as they found their spots, checking out the other talent. I noticed the couple in the booth next to mine, and my chest tightened. Jo was running behind because an interview she had for a segment she was doing had run long. She'd texted just before the Uber dropped me off to let me know she was leaving the station.

I felt ashamed to admit, even to myself, that I was a little envious of her job. I'd gotten so used to our time together that it felt like a bit of a shock to my system when she'd taken the position at the station. Plus, I'd thought she'd decided reporting wasn't for her. We had a bond built around living lives we didn't want, but maybe she *did* want hers after all. And I was happy for her—I was. Seeing her eyes light up like a Fourth of July sky while she told me about the stories she was covering filled me with indescribable joy. I just worried that if she settled back into her old life she wouldn't need me anymore. That I wouldn't fit into the equation.

A woman with wavy, waist-long blonde hair approached with a broad smile. "You must be Derek."

"I am," I said.

"I'm Juniper." She took my outstretched hand. "So glad you could join us tonight."

"Thank you for having me," I replied. "Seriously, this is amazing."

"Your work is so fresh...so *inspired*." She floated through the small booth, the gauzy fabric of her dress trailing behind her. "It's filled with humility...empathy...heart. It's beautiful."

"You're very kind," I said, thanking her again.

"This is your first art show?" She turned to face me.

I nodded.

"I can say with certainty it won't be your last. I'd love to have you back again." She smiled. "Well, I'll leave you to it. Jo has my contact information, so please reach out, and we'll get you back here soon."

"I'd love to," I said. "Nice to meet you."

She waved as she strolled away, stopping at another booth.

I stood back and took in all of my pictures. We'd brought most of the ones from my photo wall and a few more I'd had printed and framed just for the occasion.

My eyes settled on the photograph that I loved most. Jo on Christmas morning. She'd taken Izzy out at sunrise, and it was flurrying. I was about to join her outside when I looked out the window and saw her standing there, her cheeks pink, eyes closed, head tilted toward the sky. She wore a serene expression as the snowflakes settled on her lashes. I'd grabbed my camera and zoomed in on her angelic face through the window. The shutter clicked, her beauty forever frozen in time.

I'd given all of my pictures names for the art crawl, and I called that one 'Hope.' Because that's what she'd given me.

"I'm here! I made it." Jo's voice pulled me from my thoughts. "I cut off at least three people on I-40, and I'm pretty sure that when I die, I'm going straight to purgatory in a DMV because of it." She stepped on her tiptoes and kissed my lips softly. "Hi."

"Hi," I said, wrapping her in my arms. Holding her was like the rush of warm air that engulfed you when you first came in out of the cold.

"Sorry I'm late."

"You're not late," I replied, gesturing to the patrons that were starting to filter inside. "You're right on time."

"I'm going to go find a restroom real quick," she said, fidgeting, shifting her weight from one foot to the other, talking faster than an auctioneer. "I downed a huge coffee before I interviewed those sweet girls at the hospital—the kidney transplant I told you about? It was so incredible. They had been Instagram friends for like three years and had never even met before today. The girl donating the kidney came all the way here from Spain! Can you believe—"

God, she was so fucking cute. "Jo?"

"Yeah?"

"Go pee," I said with a chuckle. "*Then* tell me about it."

"Right." She spun on her heel, her hair twirling with her. "I'll be right back!"

I laughed as she disappeared into the crowd.

A couple of people entered my booth, studying my pictures intently, pointing to the ones they liked. I overheard someone say how much she loved the one of Jo, and my heart swelled.

"Cool setup," Dallas said as he sidled up beside me, looking around. He had on a beanie, covering up his signature shoulder-length hair, making him much harder to recognize. "Where's Jo?"

"She's here," I said. "She'll be right back."

He nodded. "Jax and Liv are coming closer to eight. I think they were able to get a sitter. They're picking up Katie on the way."

"Yeah," I said. "That's what Jo told me, and I got a text from Luca a while ago. He said he'd be here around seven thirty."

"I think Antoni and Nate are going to try to make it out too." Dallas shoved his hands in his pockets.

"Excuse me," a woman said as she approached. "Are you the artist?"

I felt Dallas tense beside me.

"I am," I answered.

"Have you ever done the art crawl?" she asked. "I don't think I've seen you here before."

I shook my head. "This is my first show."

"Ooh, well, congratulations," she said. "I'm excited to see your work."

"Thanks for coming," I said as she walked away to look at the wall of portraits.

Dallas cleared his throat, and we watched as she poured over the pictures.

"It was nice of Jo to set this up," he finally said. "I know you've always enjoyed photography."

My eyes widened as I looked at him and thought that maybe, for the first time, Dallas finally got it. Maybe he actually saw what this meant to me.

He clapped me on the back and gripped my shoulder. "Hopefully this'll help you get it out of your system for a while, though, because we have an album to finish writing."

The floor had vanished beneath my feet, and my heart sank as Dallas ambled over to the next booth, looking at their work the same way he'd looked at mine—with total indifference.

Jo bounded back to my side, pulling me out of my thoughts, and squealed when she saw the people in my space. "This is so awesome!"

I turned and kissed her temple.

She leaned in and whispered in my ear. "I'm so proud of you."

My throat tightened. She had no idea how much I needed to hear those words at that exact moment. I opened my mouth to speak, but nothing came out. Instead, I cupped her face in my hands and kissed her hard, nearly knocking her off balance.

She giggled. "What was that about?"

I smiled as I looked into her eyes—eyes that filled me with a sense of hope and belonging I'd never felt before. "Nothing."

Except it wasn't nothing. It was everything.

TWENTY-FIVE

Jo

BETWEEN LANDING the reporter job and planning the benefit concert for Project NENA, I was swamped, and the month of February passed at warp speed. What was supposed to be part time at the station had stretched into something more. I'd been able to track down some pretty impressive human interest stories with positive slants, and the viewers loved it. I loved it too.

In the last month I'd had everything from long distance friends donating kidneys to a local radio disc jockey who had organized a rally for suicide awareness in remembrance of his best friend. I'd even been able to interview Lindsey about Project NENA.

It turned out that people wanted their newscasts to end with something hopeful. So, what started as a twice a week segment became the sign off for the nightly news.

What free time I had I spent with Derek and Katie. When I was staying with Derek, I made sure I talked to Katie daily, unwilling to let our friendship fall back to once a week phone calls.

"He told me all about his new carnivore diet." Katie's words came out through fits of giggles. It was the first Thursday of March, and I had called her on my morning commute to the station to find out how her Tinder date had gone the night before. "Oh, and Pantera."

"What? Why? Isn't Panera more known for their soups and salads than their meat?" I asked.

She burst into laughter. "Not Panera. Pan*tera*. The heavy metal band. Before last night I couldn't even name one Pantera song, and now I could write a dissertation on their entire body of work."

"Oh, wow. Panera would have been much better."

"I was so mad," she said with a chuckle. "I could have been at home curled up on the couch with my heating pad watching *Gilmore Girls*. I could have ordered Panera."

I laughed. "Sounds like it's back to the drawing board."

"Anyway, so what's the latest on the benefit since the venue fell through? A couple of days ago you thought you might have found another one?"

I smiled to myself, still floored we'd been able to secure the new location. "You're never going to believe this. We got Bridgestone Arena."

"Shut *up*. That's amazing."

"It was some crazy luck, that's for sure," I said. "Carrie Underwood was supposed to be playing that night, but ended up with a scheduling conflict and had to move her show. The booking guy remembered I'd been looking for that date and called me."

"That's perfect!" she said.

"Especially now that we have Kings of Leon and Kacey Musgraves involved too. It's going to be huge."

"I'm so excited!" Katie squealed. "I love Kacey Musgraves."

"The timing couldn't have been better because the tickets need to go on sale next week." Admittedly, I'd been a little worried about that. The idea of putting tickets on sale less than a month in advance made my insides tingle with anxiety. Ella's husband Cash had assured me, though, that with a roster like Midnight in Dallas, Jax and Liv, Sam Corbyn, and now Kings of Leon and Kacey Musgraves, we'd have no problem selling out the place. In fact, he'd predicted it would happen in minutes.

"I can't believe it's only a month away. You've worked so hard on this, Jo. You should be proud."

"I just hope it helps Project NENA get ahead and takes some of the pressure off Lindsey," I said. "She does so much of this stuff on her own."

"I know it's going to help," she assured me. "By the way, I've been meaning to ask, did you ever hear back from Kimber?"

My heart warmed. "I did. We talked a few days ago. She emailed me and said she'd be glad to talk, so I called her."

"And?" she asked. "How did it go?"

"She was gracious and amazing as ever, and she said it was all water under the bridge," I said with a sigh. "I still feel absolutely horrible."

"You're too hard on yourself," Katie said gently. "Everyone makes mistakes, Jo, but not everyone learns from them, and you did. That takes a lot of humility."

"Thank you. You might be a little biased, but I love you for it." Call waiting beeped in my ear. I glanced to where my phone was clipped to the dash and groaned. "Katie, I've gotta let you go. My dad's calling me with what I'm sure is another lecture about my wasted potential."

"Don't let him get you down," she said. "You're doing awesome. I love you."

"Love you too," I replied and tapped the screen to answer the call.

"Hey, Dad. How's it going?"

"I was calling to see if you'd had any luck finding a job," he responded, his voice brusque.

I bit down on my lip to keep myself from exploding. "I already got a job, Dad," I said as calmly as I could manage. "I told you about this. At WKRN where I interned in Nashville."

He let out an exasperated sigh. "Jo, that is *not* where you need to be. I saw some of the segments you've done, and you have so much more potential. You should be reporting hard news. Not stories about some family reuniting with their lost cat after seven years, for crying out loud."

Of course that was the story he'd caught. "That's not all I've covered," I said defensively. "Did you see the one about the radio DJ?"

"You should be covering politics and international affairs. You should be the face our country sees when there's breaking news," he persisted. "You're a Kingsley, Jolene."

My pulse banged in my ears as I pulled into the station parking lot. "But, Dad, I—"

"No. Enough is enough." His voice rose. "You're acting like a spoiled child, just wasting away your future."

I blew out a breath. "How? I'm back working at a news station, I'm doing a lot of volunteer work. I'm—" I almost told him I'd met someone, but I knew that would do nothing to help my case. That was certainly no accomplishment in his eyes, which was precisely why I'd never told him.

"I'm not sure that being in Nashville has done you any favors, Jolene." Disappointment dripped from his voice. "You've got to get your head back in the game."

Tears stung my eyes. I wanted to tell him that my head had never felt *more* in the game. I was doing things I loved; things that mattered. I was proud of my accomplishments. Why couldn't he be proud of me too?

I cleared my throat, prepared to ask the question. "Dad, why can't—"

"I've got to go," he said abruptly. "I have an interview with the Vice President in ten minutes, but this conversation is *not* over. I'll talk to you soon."

The line went dead.

My jaw clenched, and I gripped the steering wheel so hard I thought my hands might melt through the rubber and bend the steel. I took a few deep breaths, trying to calm the urge to start screaming like a banshee in the parking lot.

I checked my makeup in the rearview mirror and dabbed at the corners of my eyes with my ring finger, determined not to cry. I didn't know what I'd expected. I'd been trying my whole life to get my dad to accept me.

When I was a little girl, there was nothing that my dad loved doing more than his work, so I figured if I got into broadcasting, he'd want to spend time with me too. It was the only thing we ever really bonded over and did together. But as my career took off, the bonding stopped, and I became nothing more than the next in line for the news journalism throne. And I wanted my dad to be proud that I was his daughter for reasons that had nothing to do with my job.

A lump formed in my throat. How pathetic was it that I was a grown woman in my thirties begging for her father's approval? Even as I thought about the question, I knew it wasn't only his approval I longed for. It was his love.

———

"Jo?" Adam, my cameraman at WKRN, raised an eyebrow at me.

It was late Sunday afternoon of the following week, and I was *certain* I was dying. I suddenly felt like I'd been hit by a bus—a bus that decided I wasn't dead enough, so it backed up and hit me again just to be sure. My entire body throbbed, and the back of my neck was damp with sweat. The insides of my stomach sloshed and rocked like a rickety sailboat lost at sea.

"Yes?" I replied, snapping to attention in the sparkling white foyer of a ginormous house in the heart of Green Hills, one of Nashville's most prominent neighborhoods. We were there to film our segment that would air on Monday's six o'clock news…if I could hold it together.

"Mr. Cartwright asked if you wanted some water," he said slowly, nodding toward the Ken doll looking man with gleaming white teeth. "While we wait for Mr. Holbert to get here."

"Please." Mr. Cartwright held out his hands. "Call me Landon."

I forced a smile and nodded. "Sorry. Yes, I would love some. And would it be okay if I used your restroom?"

"Sure, darlin.'" He gestured beyond the foyer to a long hallway. "First door on the left."

"Thank you," I said as he disappeared.

"Are you sure you're okay, Jo?" Adam asked once Landon was out of earshot. "You don't look so good."

"I'm okay," I answered quickly. "Er, I will be. I just need a second. I'm feeling a little flushed."

He narrowed his eyes with concern. "You're looking a little…rough."

The walls swayed as I carefully found my way to the bathroom, shutting the door behind me. My purse was clutched in my arms like a football as I leaned against the cool wooden door.

"What is happening to me?" I muttered to myself as I pushed off the door and crossed the short distance to the sink, tossing my purse on the counter. My reflection startled me. Adam hadn't been kidding. In fact, he'd put it far too nicely.

I turned on the faucet and splashed cold water on my face, then swept my hair to the side, placing my cool, wet hands on the back of my neck. I frantically dug in my purse for my makeup bag and touched up my face in an attempt to make myself look like I wasn't on the brink of death.

Once I was finished, I appraised my reflection again. If I could manage to continue to stand upright, there was a chance no one would even notice I was sick. But that was a big *if*.

I returned to the foyer where Adam was waiting for me.

"Better?" he asked.

"Yep," I lied.

He eyed me carefully before stepping closer to me, clipping my mic onto the collar of my dress. "Come on. Mr. Holbert just got here. I got everybody mic'd. We're live in three."

My eyes widened. It felt like I'd only been in the bathroom for a couple of minutes, but it had actually been more like twenty.

Landon was seated on a tufted white sofa holding an acoustic guitar with an older gentleman next to him.

"Hi, Mr. Holbert," I said, extending my hand. "Jo Kingsley."

He nodded politely. "Call me George."

I put in my ear monitor and sat across from the two men in a velvet armchair.

"You ready?" Adam asked, his face wrinkled with concern.

I took in a deep breath through my nose, releasing it slowly through my mouth, and nodded.

"We're rolling in three, two…" Adam held up one finger then nodded at me.

"Tonight I'm in the home of local songwriter, Landon Cartwright. Now, you may not have heard his name, but I'm sure you've heard his music. His songs have been performed by artists like OneRepublic, Kelly Clarkson, and even Garth Brooks." I focused my eyes on the camera. "But none have been more popular than 'Drive By,' a song performed by country up and comers Magnolia Lane. If you were watching the Grammys last month, then you already know 'Drive By' took home the 'Best Song' category. But what you might not know is that the popular song is based on a very real encounter Cartwright had that changed his life forever. Tonight, I'm here with Mr. Cartwright, and his friend and former Uber driver, George Holbert."

The two men nodded and smiled.

I focused my attention on Landon. "When you got in George's Uber back in 2016, you didn't even know how to play the guitar. Is that correct?" I asked.

Landon chuckled. "It sure is. I'd just turned twenty-one and moved to Nashville from Oklahoma. I didn't even have a home yet; I was sleeping on my buddy's couch. I'd been out at a concert one night, and called an Uber to pick me up afterward. The good Lord must have known what he was doin' cause he put me in the back of George's Honda Accord."

"Tell me about that ride," I said. "The one that changed the entire trajectory of your life."

"We were talking about music and the different stuff we liked," Landon answered. "That's when I noticed his guitar case in the front seat, and I told him I'd always wanted to learn to play. I wrote poetry a lot, and I wished I had the ability to turn those words into songs. And George here said to me, 'Well, you're my last ride of the night. You want me to show you a few things?' And I told him I'd like that. We pulled into a Walmart parking lot and sat on the hood of his car, and he taught me three chords."

"All you need to write a good song are three chords and the truth," I said with a soft chuckle. "Now, this wasn't the last time you saw each other, was it?"

"No ma'am," Landon replied. "George and I became buddies that day. He's a retired vet who was driving for Uber to make a little extra cash. I asked if I could pay him for actual guitar lessons."

"But I said no," George continued the story. "The only payment I'd accept was that we'd have a cup of coffee together afterwards. I'm almost seventy years old, never married, no kids. I don't have no family, and most of my friends ain't alive anymore. I was just happy to have some company."

"And what began as an unlikely friendship has become so much more, hasn't it?" I asked.

"It sure has," Landon said. "George has become like a father to me. I wouldn't be where I am now if it wasn't for him."

"Ah, that's not true." George beamed with pride, patting

Landon's shoulder. "You'da got there one way or another. I was just along for the ride."

"One thing's for sure, people come into our lives for a reason," Landon said. "That person you meet in an Uber, or standing in line at the grocery store or at the bar might change your whole life. Hell, they might *become* your whole life."

I found myself getting choked up. I blamed it on whatever the hell was ravaging my body, but deep down I knew it was more than that.

I dabbed at my eyes. "It really is true that every person we come across has the potential to help us write a whole new chapter of our story."

"In my case, George helped me write a whole new book," Landon said, his voice breaking. "And I got a best friend in the process."

My mind went to Derek. "Wow…That's truly beautiful. Thank you both for sharing your story with me," I said, before turning back to the camera. "In the news business, it's hard to not get a little jaded because let's face it—there's a lot of bad things happening in the world. There are a lot of broken-hearted people out there, but just as Landon and George found out, there's a lot of healing too. You never know what—or who—is just around the corner….or in your Uber. I hope tonight's story will encourage you to strike up a conversation with someone you don't know and not be afraid to shake things up a little. Because you never know when an ordinary moment will turn into something good." I smiled, and a tear slipped down my cheek. "Landon and George are going to take us out with a song. Good night, everyone."

I sat back as Landon and George began to play, and I didn't move until Adam gave me the all clear.

A wave of nausea swept over me, turning my stomach

upside down. "Excuse me," I said, quickly ripping off my mic and monitor.

"Jo?" I heard Adam say my name, but I couldn't open my mouth to respond. If I did, it wouldn't be words that came out.

I ran back in toward the bathroom, but as soon as I entered the foyer, I knew I wasn't going to make it. My eyes flashed around the room, looking for a trash can, a potted plant, *anything*. With no options in sight, I flung open the front door, nearly launching myself over the railing of the porch as I emptied the entire contents of my stomach into the bushes.

TWENTY-SIX

Derek

I WAS ABOUT thirty seconds away from being the guy who shits his pants. My hands trembled as I fumbled with my key, trying desperately to hold still so that I could fit it in the lock. I'd left our writing session early because I didn't feel right, but 'not right' had spiraled out of control. Beads of sweat formed along my hairline and on the back of my neck as I finally managed to get the key in and shove my way inside, slamming the door behind me.

Izzy wagged her tail and tilted her head up at me as I dropped my bass in the foyer and took off down the hall. She barked and followed behind, certain this was a new game we were playing.

My head was splitting, and my entire body ached. "What is happening to me?" I asked, clenching my ass cheeks together as though I was holding a marble between them.

I worked to unfasten my belt and nearly tripped over my own feet as I stumbled into the bathroom, gripping the door frame to catch myself. My hands were clammy, causing my fingers to slip on the buckle.

"Fuck," I cursed, finally free of my belt. Izzy was wide-eyed and clearly confused about the object of our new game. I kicked the door closed, wrenching my pants and boxers down, barely landing on the toilet in time.

Izzy startled and backed away toward the door, letting out a sharp bark.

"Look away, Izzy," I croaked out. "I don't want you to see me like this."

She took this as an invitation to come closer, placing her front paws on my knees.

My stomach churned, and nausea ripped through me in such a way that I knew things were about to go from bad to worse.

"Fuck, fuck, fuck," I muttered, my entire face damp with sweat. I was cold and hot at the same time, and bile burned at the back of my throat. My stomach bubbled like a cauldron, and I knew whatever was causing this wasn't going to wait for me to get off the toilet. I reached for the small trash can to the side, and hurled with the force of a monsoon.

Izzy ran to the other side of the bathroom, barking ferociously as though she could expel the demon that was clearly the source of this catastrophe from my body.

"Stop yelling at me," I groaned, pausing a few seconds before the next wave of nausea hit. "Oh God. This is it. This is how I die."

Izzy's head tilted side to side, and she eased toward me.

Once I was confident I could move again without becoming a human geyser, I got up and washed my hands, splashing my face with cold water.

My stomach gurgled as I ran a washcloth under the water and wrung it out, holding it to the back of my neck. I sank to the floor and leaned against the wall, just inches away from the toilet. My limbs felt too heavy to move, and I was afraid to be out of arm's reach of the porcelain throne.

Izzy laid next to me, resting her head on my leg, and I heard the front door slam shut.

"Derek?" Jo's voice called. I could hear her muttering to herself as her feet shuffled closer.

"I'm in here," I answered back, my voice weak.

"I'm going to quarantine myself in your spare room." Her voice was hoarse. "I think I'm sick."

"Oh God," I replied. "You've got it too?"

"Wait, what? You're sick?"

I moved the cool compress to my forehead. "Either that or I'm experiencing a demonic possession."

"If it makes you feel any better, I threw up in the bushes outside in front of God and everyone after my interview," she said.

"I almost shit my pants."

"Okay, no, you definitely win," she said with a laugh. "I ordered some stuff on Instacart. Some Gatorade, crackers—"

My insides flipped. "God, don't say crackers." It was too late. I was on my knees in front of the toilet retching at the very thought of saltines.

I heard the bathroom door click open.

"No, Jo," I choked out as I flushed the toilet, sliding back against the wall. "You can't see me like this."

"Well, I'm not going to die alone in the guest room." She gave me a weak smile as she dropped to the floor beside me, sprawling out like a jellyfish. "This feels so good." She patted the smooth tile beside her. "Here, lie down. It helps."

I slowly slipped down onto the floor. It felt like the first rush of air when you opened the fridge. "Oh wow. Yeah, this is good."

Izzy settled between us.

Jo reached over her for my hand, lacing her fingers through mine. "How did it go today?"

I was supposed to finally tell the guys I would be leaving the band. I'd put it off long enough and had decided that I'd talk to them after our session, but my stomach had other plans. "I didn't do it."

She gave my hand a squeeze. "I'd say being sick is a pretty good reason to delay that conversation."

I sighed. "Yeah, but I need to do it. I've put it off long enough. It's not going to get any easier."

"It'll happen when it happens," she assured me.

We laid there quietly for a moment, and I finally looked over at her. "Just so you know, there's no one else I'd rather be violently ill with."

She chuckled. "Me either."

I managed a smile. "I guess the romance is officially dead, huh?"

She laughed softly. "I'd still kiss you," she said. "Once we've both brushed our teeth and the room stops spinning, of course."

"Even if I'd shit my pants?" I joked.

Her shoulders shook with laughter. "Even then."

THE WORST WAS OVER WHEN WE WOKE UP WEDNESDAY morning. Our fevers had broken, and we hadn't been alternating trips to the bathroom or lying on the floor for a few hours.

We sat up in bed, drinking Gatorade as we watched Netflix with Izzy wedged between us. It was a little after eight a.m. when Jo's phone rang.

She glanced at it on the nightstand and hit the button to ignore the call. "It's work," she said. "I'll call them back."

A few seconds later, her phone trilled with a notification— then another, and another, and another, all in rapid-fire succession.

Jo groaned and snatched her phone, narrowing her eyes at the screen. Suddenly, she gasped and shot up, causing both Izzy and me to jump. "Oh my God."

I touched her arm. "What's wrong? Is everything okay?"

Her eyes were wide as she stared at her phone screen.

"Jo?"

She turned toward me, handing me her phone. "My story went viral." The inflection of her voice rose on the last word as though she were asking a question. "The one I did about the songwriter and the Uber driver."

I looked at the Twitter app on her phone and scrolled. *#SomethingGood* was trending with the video of Jo's segment, and thousands of people were sharing their own stories of the chance encounters that ended up changing their lives forever.

"Jo, this is incredible," I said as her phone pinged in my hand. I gave it back to her, and she swiped across the screen.

A smile bloomed on her face. "Work is freaking out. Apparently, they shared my story on the *Today* show!" She gasped again. "Oh my God. Hoda Kotb knows I exist." She flopped back on the bed and squealed as Izzy attacked her face with kisses. "I know, Izzy! Can you believe it?"

I laid down at Jo's side, and Izzy gave me a consolation lick. "I'm so proud of you."

Jo beamed as she went back to scrolling Twitter. "I just... all of these people sharing their stories..."

I touched her cheek. "And it all started with you. I've told you before, Jo. Your voice matters."

She looked over at me with tears shining in her eyes. "Thank you. For believing that before I did."

I pressed my lips to hers, a mixture of emotions flooding through me. I was so fucking proud of her, so happy for her. She deserved this. But I also felt a pang of something else... something that felt a lot like envy.

I didn't begrudge Jo her happiness—not at all. But the satisfaction that filled her eyes...I wanted that too. I had to tell the guys I was leaving the band. It couldn't wait any longer.

———

THE NEXT DAY, I WAS FEELING WELL ENOUGH TO GO TO OUR writing session. I'd decided I was going to tell them first thing. The benefit would be my last show since we didn't have any more scheduled performances until that summer, but I was willing to stick around for a couple more months if anything else came up before they found my replacement.

I arrived at the Hutton Place writers studio a little after three p.m., my nerves causing my pulse to pound in my ears. Luca leaned against the wall, holding a cup of coffee in one hand and scrolling on his phone with the other, while Cash was telling Jax and Antoni a story about Bettina. Dallas hadn't arrived yet.

"Hey," I said, as I placed my stuff on the floor by the wall.

"Good afternoon, sunshine," Antoni said. "We've got Starbucks over there." He pointed to a table on the other side of the room.

I nodded. "Thanks." I didn't need caffeine to make me any

more jittery than I already was, but I was anxious to have something to do with my hands. I crossed the room to the table and poured myself a cup of coffee from the box before taking a seat on the piano bench.

Dallas was grinning ear to ear. "Afternoon, gentlemen!"

"Somebody's awfully chipper today," Antoni said.

"That's because it's a good damn day," Dallas replied. "We're getting close to finishing this album which means we can finally get back into the studio and head out on tour. I don't think I've ever been so ready to hit the road."

My hands tingled, and my stomach churned. All of the color must have drained from my face because Luca looked up from his phone. "You alright, man? You're not still sick are you?"

My mouth felt chalky, and sweat formed along my brow.

"Yeah, you're looking a little pale," Cash said.

I wiped my hand down the leg of my jeans and bounced my knee.

"Dude, what's with you?" Dallas asked.

I gripped my coffee cup with both hands. "Listen, I need to talk to you guys about something."

Jax and Cash exchanged glances.

"I think you may want to sit down for this," I said, rubbing the back of my neck.

Antoni sat beside me on the bench as Jax, Cash, and Luca each pulled up chairs.

"I'm fine where I am," Dallas said, eyeing me suspiciously.

"Okay." I cleared my throat. "This band has been…Well, you guys have been my life for a long time. You've been my family, and I love you. Nothing will ever change that. But I'm not happy, and I haven't been for a long time. I'm ready to do something else, to start a new chapter in my life. I'd like the benefit show to be my last, but I'll stay on as long as you need me to until you find my replacement."

Antoni gasped, Luca was rooted to his seat, shock covering his face, while Jax and Cash exchanged a worried glance. Everyone looked shocked, as though I'd just announced I was flying to the moon. Everyone but Dallas. He was pissed.

His eyes darkened, and the vein in his neck popped to the surface. "What the fuck, Derek? Are you fucking kidding me?"

"Dallas," Cash warned.

"Shut up, Cash," he fired back, and Cash's jaw clenched.

"Look, I've tried," I said. "I've tried to pretend this is what I want, but it's not. I'm grateful for the life this band has given me, but it's not the life I want to live forever."

Dallas crossed his arms over his chest. "So, 'it's not you, it's me.' Is that it? I don't understand. You love music. You've always loved music."

I looked down at my hands. "I loved what music did for me. It got me out of my house when we were growing up. But it was always a means to an end for me."

Dallas stared at me, dumbfounded. "A means to an end? For fucks sake. What are you even talking about? You live a life thousands of people would give their fucking left nut for. Nothing about that is a means to an end."

"You don't know what you're talking about, Dallas." I pressed my lips together. "You think you know, but you don't."

A knowing look settled on his face. "Wait…is this…is this because of Jo? She comes to Nashville having some sort of identity crisis, and now you're suddenly having one too?"

"That's not what's happening," I insisted.

"Fuck, all this time I thought she was such a great influence on you, helping you get your shit together," he said, shaking his head. "But all she did was sink her fucking claws into you and convince you to do something stupid."

"No, Dallas," I said, my voice rising. "My decision has nothing to do with her and everything to do with me."

"But she encouraged you, didn't she?" he snapped.

"Jo encourages me to do what makes me happy," I said. "This doesn't have anything to do with her."

"The hell it doesn't," he shouted. "She is the *only* fucking thing that's changed in this equation. So now you're going to do what? Play house with Jo and pretend to be an artist instead of being here for this band? For your *family?* Family doesn't walk out on each other, man."

His words slapped me across the face.

"Enough!" Cash's voice boomed as he stood. "That's enough, Dallas. Look, if Derek isn't happy, we need to respect that."

Dallas looked away, shaking his head.

"Of course we want him to stay, but if this isn't what he wants then—" Dallas cut him off before Cash could finish his sentence.

"Derek doesn't know *what* he wants," Dallas seethed as Cash shot him daggers.

"It's a huge loss," Antoni said. "But y'all, we get one life, and if this ain't the way Derek wants to spend his—"

"What about *us?*" Dallas interrupted. "He's not thinking about what this is doing to *us.*"

I slammed my coffee cup on the bench beside me so hard that some of the liquid sloshed out. "I've done nothing *but* think about what this would do to you. That's the only reason

I didn't quit a long damn time ago. Because I didn't want to hurt you, any of you, after everything you've done for me."

"This is so fucked up, man." Dallas threw up his hands. "We made a commitment to this band, to each other."

"We did," Luca spoke up. "But a lot has happened since then, and I think it may be time to consider that maybe we're trying to force something that isn't working anymore."

"Fucking hell!" Dallas yelled. "Seriously? You too?"

Luca shrugged. "I don't know if this is what I want to do for the rest of my life."

"What the fuck else are you going to do, Luca?" Dallas asked. "Drink your fucking life away in a bar?"

"Dallas!" Cash scolded him.

Luca held out his hand. "No, it's alright, Cash. This has been a long time coming." He rose to his feet, raking his hands through his hair. "You know what, Dallas? *This* right here is why I'm done. I'm so fucking sick of your sanctimonious bullshit. I hate to break it to you, dude, but there's so much more to life than *this.*" He gestured around the room with his hands. "This isn't real life."

Dallas opened up his mouth to speak, but Luca cut him off.

"I'm not fucking done yet," he said, stepping closer to Dallas. "Not that it's any of your damn business, but I haven't had a goddamn drink since Thanksgiving. And frankly, I don't know why you even want me in this band since you think so fucking little of me. I know I've always been the wild card, the problem child…" He threw his hands up. "But did it ever occur to you even once that maybe I was struggling?" Luca paused and turned to address us all. "Did it occur to *any* of you? Or did you just keep throwing stones at me from your glass fucking houses?"

Nobody said a word.

My heart sank. How many times had I personally assumed the worst of Luca? Too many to count.

"Exactly," Luca said as he grabbed his guitar. "So, you know what? I'm fucking done. I officially quit. Thank you, Derek, for starting this conversation today. And Dallas?" He raised his middle finger right in front of Dallas' face. "Fuck off."

"Luca, wait—" Cash tried to stop him, but Luca shook him off and stormed out.

"Maybe we all need to take a step back," Jax said carefully. "Maybe we just need a break, some time to pursue other things."

"I don't need a break," I shot back. "I'm telling you I'm out, and I'm not sure you'll ever convince Luca to come back."

Dallas was red-faced and trembling. "Un-fucking-believeable."

Jax studied me for a moment. "You're sure? You're sure this is what you want?"

I nodded. "Yes. This is what I want."

"Okay." Jax pressed his lips together, his gaze falling to his feet. "Alright."

Dallas' mouth gaped open. "That's it? That's all you have to say?"

"Look, Dal, I know this isn't what you want to hear right now," Jax began. "But maybe this thing has run its course. I love this band, but we're not Midnight in Dallas anymore without Derek and Luca. So many bands keep going, cycling through members until they become something nobody recognizes, and then eventually disappear into the ether," Jax said. "I don't want to do that. Maybe the benefit *should* be our last show together. Why don't we go out while we're still on top?"

Dallas huffed, shaking his head in disgust. "You know what? Fuck all of you. Fuck every single one of you for not giving a shit about this band and making me out to be the asshole because I do. And now that I fucking know what you pricks think about me, I guess I'll see myself out."

"Come on, Dallas," Antoni said. "Please don't be like that. Let's talk about this."

Dallas pushed his way out the door, slamming it behind him, leaving Cash, Antoni, Jax, and me sitting in silence.

I swallowed hard, and Jax walked over to me and squeezed my shoulder.

"I'm so sorry." I raked my hands down my face.

Cash shook his head. "You have nothing to apologize for."

"Sure don't," Antoni agreed. "Don't ever apologize for living your truth."

"Dallas will never forgive me." I dropped my face into my hands. "He fucking hates me."

"Dallas will get over it," Jax said.

"What if he doesn't?" I asked.

"Then that's Dallas' problem," Cash answered. "Not yours."

I sighed. "He didn't even let me tell him everything. There's so much he doesn't…that you all don't know."

Antoni leaned closer to me, brows drawn together. "Like what?"

My throat tightened. "It's a long story."

Jax moved to sit back down. "Well, good thing we've got this place rented for another five hours."

"Okay." My mind spun like a ferris wheel out of control as it tried to find the exact right words. For the perfect way to tell them everything I'd kept hidden for so long. But there wasn't one. So I stopped searching for right or perfect and settled for real.

I told them everything.

BY THE TIME I GOT BACK TO MY CONDO THAT EVENING, I was completely drained. My limbs felt heavy, like I'd been treading water for hours. The only thing that kept me going was knowing that Jo was waiting for me inside. I wanted to hold her so badly my arms ached.

When I pushed through the front door I was met with a spicy sweet scent that would normally make my mouth water, but there was only one thing I was hungry for. Only one thing I needed.

"Hey," Jo's melodic voice called to me as I entered the kitchen. "I hope you don't mind, but I picked up some Thai food for dinner." She was unpacking a large paper sack, placing covered containers on the counter. "My eyes might have been a little bigger than my stomach. I didn't get to eat lunch today, so I'm starving."

I stood behind her, placing my hands on her shoulders, then slid them down around her waist.

"I got spring rolls *and* steamed dumplings as appetizers because I couldn't decide which one I wanted," she continued.

I moved her hair to the side and kissed her neck. Her body responded, leaning into me.

"Oh, well, hello there," she said with a giggle, turning to face me. Her face fell when she looked into my eyes. "Derek, what's wrong?"

I placed my hands on the counter on either side of her.

Her eyes searched mine. "Derek, what is it?"

"I did it," I said. "I quit the band."

She nodded and cupped my face in her hands, stroking my cheek with her thumb. "Are you okay?"

I covered her hand with mine, leaning into the warmth of her palm, her touch a salve on my wounds. "Dallas hates me, and I'm pretty sure Luca hates us all."

"I'm so sorry," she murmured. "They're just upset right now, but they're your family. They'll come around."

I shook my head, dropping my gaze to the floor. "I'm not so sure. I'm sorry, Jo. I don't know what this means for the benefit show. Things didn't exactly end on good terms." That was an understatement, but I didn't want to go into all of the details yet. In that moment, all I wanted was to wrap myself up in her.

"Hey, look at me," she said, tilting my face toward hers. "It's okay. We'll figure it out."

I blew out a breath. "You've worked so hard on it, though."

"It'll be fine" she promised. "I don't want you worrying about that, okay?"

I nodded. "Okay."

Her lips grazed mine, and my entire body thrummed with need. My hands tangled in her hair as our kiss deepened.

"I need you," I whispered, my teeth lightly grazing her bottom lip. "I just need to be close to you."

She pressed her hips against mine, her eyes flickering with desire, and I knew she could feel how much I wanted her.

"There's something I need to tell you," I said. I'd set my past life on fire by finally speaking my truth to the guys, but there was still something I was holding on to. Something equally as true that I'd been too afraid to say.

Her eyes sparkled up at me. "Okay."

My hand slipped around the back of her neck as I leaned my forehead against hers. "I love you, Jo."

I heard her breath catch, and she brought her lips to mine, kissing me tenderly. "I love you too."

The world might have been burning around me, but in that moment, nothing else mattered. I was finally free.

TWENTY-SEVEN

Jo

I woke up early Friday morning so I could get back to Katie's house by eight to pick up some notes I needed for work. I'd kissed Derek on the cheek with the promise that I'd see him later that evening, then practically floated to my car.

My smile felt like it was etched onto my face, a sign for all the world to see that love lived inside me. The night before played on a loop in my mind like a highlight reel. It had been an otherwise ordinary Thursday evening that had turned into the most special night of my life.

Derek had told me he loved me. I giggled to myself and blushed as I thought about what had happened after—Derek shoving the takeout containers aside and lifting me up onto the kitchen counter, pushing my skirt up my thighs. We'd been so overcome with desire that we hadn't even been able to make the few steps to the bedroom. Instead, we'd made love right there in the kitchen. Twice.

I cracked my window, letting in the cool, crisp March air. The sun was shining, the birds were singing, and I was so happy I thought I'd burst.

My phone rang, and my happy bubble threatened to pop when I realized it was my dad.

I sighed and answered the call, his voice filling the car.

"I'm in Nashville," he said by way of a greeting.

"*What?*" My voice raised an entire octave. "*Why?*"

"I saw your little video." He sounded almost jovial. "Well done."

"I'm glad you liked it," I said. "But…You didn't have to come to Nashville for that."

He laughed as though that was the most absurd thing he'd ever heard. "That's not why I'm in Nashville. I'm here with my friend and colleague, Brent Kirkpatrick." He paused dramatically. "And he wants to meet you."

"I'm sorry, *what*? The president of CNN wants to meet *me*?" I couldn't believe what I was hearing. Why would he want to meet *me*?

"I showed him your video, and he loved it," my dad said. "The fact that you're my daughter doesn't hurt either."

"Oh…oh my God. When? I get off work around seven—"

"We're headed back to New York after lunch," he interrupted. "You need to be at Flemings at noon sharp."

"But—"

"It's time you start thinking about moving up to the big leagues," he said, sounding exasperated. "Forget about that other job. I stuck my neck out for you because I believe you're capable of big things, Jolene."

His words hung in the air, so close I could almost touch them. My dad had clearly gone through a lot of trouble to set up this meeting, and he'd done it all for me.

"I'll be there," I said firmly.

"Good girl," he said. "I'll see you at noon."

"Okay. I love—"

He'd already hung up.

My stomach fluttered. This was good, right? I mean, it was CNN for crying out loud.

I cut the ignition and went inside. Katie was already gone for the day, so it was quiet except for Granny's old wall clock that ticked in the kitchen. I went to my room and found the notes I was looking for and caught a glimpse of my peri-winkle dress in the mirror.

"Hmm…" I smoothed my hands down the fabric before walking over to my closet and plucking out a smart black wrap dress. I hadn't worn all black since I first returned to Nashville, but I knew it was probably a better choice for CNN. I quickly pulled the dress I had on over my head and tossed it on the bed. I was in the process of wrapping myself in the new one when I heard a knock at the back door so loud it caused me to jump.

"Just a second," I yelled, securing the belt around my waist.

And then there was pounding.

I slipped on my black pumps and strode to the back door, prying back the small curtain to see Dallas standing on the porch.

A pit formed in my stomach when I opened the door and saw the anger emanating from his face. "Hey, Dallas."

"Where the fuck do you get off?" he boomed, storming past me into the house. "I hope you know this is all your fucking fault."

The hairs on the back of my neck stood on end. Derek had said that Dallas was upset, but that had clearly been an under-statement. "I'm sorry, but wha…What are you talking about?"

"Don't play dumb with me," he spat. "Don't act like you're not pleased as fucking punch that Derek left the band."

My hands started to shake, and I took an involuntary step back. "Dallas…I understand you're upset, but I promise I had nothing to do with Derek's decision."

"The fuck you didn't, Jo!" he shouted. "The only thing that's changed around here is *you*! Everything was fine until you came along!"

My voice wavered. "This was Derek's choi—"

"Bullshit! I told you at that fucking Christmas party that he was impressionable, and you used that to manipulate him!"

His words caused my fear to give way to anger, and I exploded. "God, would you listen to yourself? Do you know how absolutely insane you sound right now? Not to mention completely out of line. Seriously, Dallas. Do you really believe Derek isn't capable of thinking for himself?"

"Don't put fucking words in my mouth, Jo," he warned. "That's not what I said."

I held out my hands. "Isn't it though? Isn't that *exactly* what you're saying?"

"You don't know what the fuck you're talking about."

"Has it ever occurred to you that maybe *you* don't know what *you're* talking about?" I countered. "That maybe there are things *you* don't know about Derek?"

He folded his arms over his chest. "Like what?"

My mouth went dry. Derek's story wasn't mine to tell. He'd told me in confidence, and I wouldn't betray his trust.

"That's what I thought. You don't get to tell me about *my* cousin. I've known him his entire life!" He was yelling so hard his face turned red. "You've known him for, what? Five months? And now you've managed to alienate him from his fucking family. You're fucking selfish, Jo."

Tears burned my eyes. I hadn't done that, had I? I'd encouraged him to do what made him happy. It didn't matter to me if that was the band or something completely different. But I *had* pushed him to pursue his photography because I knew how much he loved it. Had I forced it? Should I have urged him to reconsider his choice?

"You've ruined everything. *You* are the reason our fucking band broke up."

What? Derek didn't tell me the *entire band* broke up. It felt like the wind had been knocked out of me. "I...I'm sorry," I choked out. "I had no idea. I never meant to—"

"You destroyed my family." His voice broke then, and he moved closer to me, shoving his finger in my face. "That's on you."

He pushed past me and slammed the door behind him, leaving me standing alone in the kitchen with tears streaming down my face. My entire body trembled as I sank to the floor and wept into my hands.

Was Dallas right? *Had* I caused this? When I'd first come back to Nashville, my entire life had gone up in flames. My world was burning, and Derek had ran straight into the fire to save me. And, foolishly, I'd let him.

———

"It's a new show—all current events and hard news, interviews, but with a fresh perspective," Brent Kirkpatrick explained, taking a sip of his scotch. "The anchor we had tapped for it...Well, he found himself in a bit of a scandal, so we had to part ways. But his loss is your gain."

It was just after noon, and I was seated at a table in the middle of the dining room at Flemings with my father and the president of CNN. My dad never requested private tables, though I was sure most places would have been happy to accommodate him. But he never minded when other diners craned their necks or snuck pictures of him.

After Dallas had confronted me about Derek leaving the band, I'd pulled myself together and gone to work, desperate for a distraction. When I'd told the team my dad was in town to meet me for lunch, they were happy to cover for me, excited by the fact that they were only one degree of separation away from *the* Daniel Kingsley.

I wrinkled my brow and gave a polite smile. "I'm sorry, Mr. Kirkpatrick. I...I don't think I'm understanding what this has to do with me."

"Don't be so modest, Jo." My father's voice was soft as cashmere, but when his eyes met mine, his gaze was pure steel.

Mr. Kirkpatrick chuckled, drink in hand, the ice cubes in his glass clinking together. "I want you to take his place, Jo. You have the type of on-air personality viewers respect. Sure, that story about the Uber driver and the songwriter was interesting, but it went viral because of *you*. You're relatable, and people like that. Plus, you're practically journalism royalty. And with you on deck, I think we can do so much beyond this show." He held his hand up, palm out as if he was projecting an image in the air before me. "I'm picturing the first ever father/daughter news team."

My eyes widened.

"I know, I know," Mr. Kirkpatrick said. "I'm getting ahead of myself. All in due time."

I picked up my water glass and took a sip.

"First things first. We want to get you up to New York and introduce you as the newest face at CNN."

I coughed, choking on my drink. "I'm sorry," I said,

clearing my throat. "Don't I need to interview for this? Don't you need to see my reel?"

Mr. Kirkpatrick shook his head. "Not when you're Daniel Kingsley's daughter."

My head was spinning, the room and the whole entire world knocked completely off its axis. For so long, this very scenario had been my dream. I'd played it out in my head millions of times. But that was before. Before I met Derek. Before I came back to Nashville. Before I considered that maybe my dreams were changing.

I thought about the life I'd built here—all because things hadn't gone according to plan. I liked my job at WKRN. I loved being near Katie again.

And I loved Derek. In the time I'd known him, I'd blossomed like a flower that had been kept out of the sun too long. His belief in me filled my cup. It fueled me. He was the best thing that had ever happened to me.

But was *I* what was best for *him?* And what if my dreams really hadn't changed?

Mr. Kirkpatrick leaned his elbows on the table and clasped his hands together. "So, Jo, are you ready to join the CNN family?"

"Wow," I began. "This is…a dream come true. It really is." I swallowed hard, stalling. "But it's all happening so fast. Could I have a day or two to think it over?"

Mr. Kirkpatrick looked at me as though I'd suggested we play a game of strip poker. "I'm sorry?"

My dad cleared his throat and removed the napkin from his lap, placing it on the table. "Brent, if you'll excuse me. My daughter and I need to have a word."

He stood, and I followed as he led me toward a hallway at the back of the restaurant.

"What are you doing, Jo?" he asked, placing his hands on his hips. "Do you know how many people would kill for this job?"

"Of course I do," I answered. "But this is a lot to consider. I have a life here, Dad. I'm *happy* here."

"You haven't even been back in Nashville that long," he argued. "Is this about that job you got?"

I opened my mouth to speak, but he cut me off.

"Jo, don't be ridiculous. Compared to CNN, that place is like working for the school paper."

My face fell. "It's the top news organization in the mid-state."

"We're talking about CNN here," he said. "These opportunities don't come along twice."

"That's not the only reason." I looked down at my feet. "I met someone."

My dad sighed. "Really, Jo? It can't be that serious."

The words stung almost as much as what Dallas had said that morning.

He dropped his voice. "I don't have to tell you how things ended for your mom and me. You don't want to pass up an opportunity like this for a relationship that likely won't even stick."

Tears pooled in my eyes. Once Derek realized he regretted leaving the band, that I'd been the one to drive the wedge between him and Dallas and the guys, he'd likely resent me and with good reason. Even if I hadn't consciously manipulated Derek into quitting, I'd still encouraged him. He hadn't started making these life-altering decisions until I showed up, unsure of my own path and lonely. My life had imploded, and he'd become collateral damage. If I asked him now, he'd say that wasn't true, that this was his choice. But once the regrets seeped in, he'd see me for what I was: a mistake.

"Jo…" My dad's face softened. "You've worked so hard for this. Don't throw it all away. This is the right choice." He placed a hand on my shoulder. "I'm proud of you, honey. You deserve this chance. And we'll get to see each other all the time. You heard Brent. We'll be the first father/daughter news team."

I forced a smile. I'd longed to hear those words my entire life, and here he was, finally saying them.

"So," my dad said, "are we going to go back to the table and tell Brent he has a deal?"

It felt like the universe was pushing me back toward the plan I thought I'd abandoned. Maybe this was what was supposed to happen. Derek needed his family, and with me out of the picture, he'd get them back. I would be doing what was best for him. And me. Because if I was finally earning my father's approval, I had to be doing something right.

Finally, I nodded. "Yes. Okay."

"Good girl." My dad winked at me, and he was positively beaming as we wove through the dining room back to our table.

"Jo would love to accept your offer," he said before I even had a chance to sit.

Mr. Kirkpatrick grinned and shook my dad's hand as though they'd just secured a major deal, and I'd had no part in it.

Mr. Kirkpatrick leaned toward me. "We're happy to have you on board, Jo."

"Thank you so much for the opportunity," I said. "I'll need to give notice at my job and tie up some loose ends here but—"

"Oh…" Mr. Kirkpatrick cut his eyes over to my dad, then back at me. "I'm sorry, I thought you understood that production was starting right away? I need you in New York by Sunday morning."

"As in two days from now?" I asked more sharply than I'd intended.

"Yes," my dad answered. "But that won't be a problem, will it?"

I knew there was only one acceptable answer to the question. Maybe it was better this way. No long, painful goodbyes. No time for Derek to try to change my mind. I had to push my feelings aside and stand firm in my decision. The only way to get through this would be to completely detach myself, because one false step could cause the thin armor around my heart to shatter.

He'd know, that in the end, I wouldn't be the happily ever after in his story, so I needed to close the book now, rather than prolong the inevitable heartbreak.

Even if it meant breaking my own heart.

I shook my head. "No, not a problem at all."

TWENTY-EIGHT

Derek

I DIDN'T HEAR from Jo all day, but that wasn't entirely out of the ordinary. When things were hectic at the station, it wasn't unusual for her to not call or text until she was leaving for the day. But when I hadn't heard from her at all by six p.m., I sent her a message to ask what she wanted for dinner. I took Izzy for a walk while I waited for her to reply, checking my phone every few minutes.

When she hadn't responded by the time I got back in at seven, I sent another text. The more time that passed without hearing from her, the longer each minute that ticked by stretched. Ten minutes, fifteen minutes, half an hour, all passed at a snail's pace. It wasn't like her to not respond, even if it was to say that she was running behind or would get back with me in a soon.

The closer it got to eight, the more anxious I became. Something felt very, very off. My heart raced as I tapped the phone screen to access her contact info and hit send. The call went straight to voicemail. There had to be some reasonable explanation, but even as the thought crossed my mind, I knew it wasn't right. Jo's job could be demanding, but when I reached out, she always got back to me within a few minutes.

I waited twenty more minutes and called once more, and again, voicemail. Terrifying scenarios played on a loop in my mind. What if she was hurt? What if she'd been in an accident and was in a hospital somewhere alone and confused or even unconscious?

Izzy watched as I paced the living room with my phone in hand. I checked that my ringer was on at least twenty times. By nine p.m. I was out of my mind with worry. I called Katie, but her phone went to voicemail too.

I pushed my hand through my hair then rubbed it along my jaw. A pit formed in my gut. Something was wrong, and I couldn't just stand there and wait. I hurried to the hall closet to get my jacket, then grabbed my keys off the counter.

Before I could make it to the front door, I heard a soft knock. My heart lurched, and I ran for it, flinging it open.

Relief washed over me when I saw Jo standing there. I reached for her, folding her in my arms. "Christ. Jo, I've been worried sick about you. Are you okay? I've been trying to call you."

She didn't respond. Not with her words, and not with her body. Her arms that would normally find their way around me remained at her sides.

The relief I felt was short lived once I really took her in. Her eyes were puffy and swollen, her fair skin was splotchy. If I didn't know better I'd have thought she'd been at a funeral between her all black outfit and how distraught she looked.

"Jo, what's going on? Are you hurt?" My questions came urgently as I took her face in my hands. "What's wrong?"

Her eyes wouldn't meet mine, and I took in a long, deep

breath in an attempt to slow my pounding heart. I moved my hands down to her arms.

"Come inside," I urged her. "Talk to me."

But she said nothing as silent tears streamed down her face.

"You're scaring the shit out of me, Jo." My voice shook. "What the hell is going on?"

"Derek, I'm so sorry," she finally choked out.

My brows knitted together. "What for?"

She looked at me then, and her bottom lip quivered.

Finally, she spoke. "I'm leaving. I'm going to New York in the morning."

"Okay," I said, tilting my head. "Are you going to see your dad? Is everything alright?"

She swallowed hard. "I will be seeing my dad, but that's not…That's not why I'm going."

"Oh." My tongue flicked across my lips as I attempted to process what she was saying. "So…Why are you going?"

She crossed her arms over her body as though she were trying to physically hold herself together. "I got a job there. I have to start right away."

I blinked slowly, my mind unable to keep up with what was happening. "What? When did this happen, Jo?"

"Today," she answered. "My dad came to see me, and he brought the president of CNN and…He offered me a job. I… I'm going to have my own show."

My eyes widened, and a flood of emotions coursed through me. I knew this was a huge deal, and if that was what she wanted, I was happy for her. But why hadn't she told me her dad was coming into town? Why hadn't she introduced me?

"But…wow. Okay…I just…I thought you were happy

here?" I studied her face. "That you like your job now that you're doing the news thing on your own terms?"

"I...I know," she said. "But things...changed."

"I...Well, that's great, Jo." I forced an encouraging smile. "This is good then, right?"

She nodded slowly. "Right."

"Look, I would never hold you back from doing something you want to do," I began. "But are you sure this is what you truly want?"

It didn't make sense. All these months she'd spent pushing me to do what I loved, and now she was abandoning what *she* loved.

"It's...a once in a lifetime opportunity. I have to take it."

"Okay then. I support you," I said gently. "We can do long distance for a bit. My commitment to the band is almost finished, so there's nothing stopping me from moving there to be with you. Whatever it is that I need to do to make this work, I'll do it."

She sniffed and looked at the floor. The forlorn expression on her face and her silence spoke volumes.

I pressed my lips together and took in a shallow breath. "You *do* want this to work, right?"

She didn't take her eyes off the floor. "I...I don't think it's a good idea."

My blood turned to ice, freezing me in place. "What?"

Her voice was raspy when she spoke, as though she'd been crying for hours. "I think it would be better if we ended this now. This job...It's going to be demanding, and I need to be able to put all of my energy into it."

My eyes burned. "But...I don't...I don't understand." I scrubbed my hand down my face. "I love you, Jo. And you told me you love me too. As long as we have that, we can make this work."

She squeezed her eyes shut, and tears rolled down her face, but she said nothing.

My heart thudded in my ears. "We *do* have that, right?"

Her arms tightened around her body. "I've been thinking, and I…We haven't known each other that long. Not really."

"Don't do that." I shook my head. "Don't minimize what we have here because of some arbitrary timeline that doesn't fucking matter. You know me, and I know you." I stared at her, willing her to say something, to reveal that this had all been some terrible misunderstanding or some ill-timed joke, but she didn't utter a word. "Say something, Jo."

"Maybe…Maybe you don't know me as well as you thought," she choked out.

I recoiled as if she'd slapped me across the face. "What are you even saying right now? Of course I know you."

More silence.

I gripped her shoulders with my hands. "Look at me and tell me I don't know you, Jo. Look me in the eyes."

For a moment, the only sounds I could hear were those of our shallow, ragged breathing.

Finally, she gazed up at me, and her face softened. I saw the same emotion I'd seen in her eyes the night before when she told me she loved me. But then that expression gave way to something else. Something I didn't recognize.

"You don't know me." Her voice shook. "I'm not good for you, Derek. I shouldn't have let this go on as long as it did. I…I'm sorry."

My arms fell to my sides, heavy with sadness. "What was this then? What was I to you, Jo? Just something you were trying on?"

Her lips trembled, and her silence was my answer.

I studied her face for a moment. "So, you came here to just try on a whole new life. New job, new clothes, new guy, and now you're going to pretend none of that mattered—that this didn't mean shit to you?" I shook my head and rubbed my hand along my jaw. "No. I don't believe that. That's not you, Jo."

I waited for her to tell me I was right, that she was making a big mistake, that she'd just gotten scared, that she loved me. But she didn't. She didn't say any of those things.

"I'm really sorry I led you on," she said. "I didn't mean for any of this to happen. You have to know—"

"Know what, Jo?" My words came out razor sharp. "That you completely played me? You're telling me that this entire thing, these last five months, meant *nothing* to you? I showed you parts of me that nobody in my life knew about. This was real for me. This wasn't something I was just trying on to see if it fit. I wanted you, Jo. Every fucking bit of you."

She hung her head and heaved a sob. "I'm sorry. You didn't deserve any of this."

Hot tears spilled down my cheeks. "So, that's it then? You're just going to go to New York and pretend like the last five months didn't happen?"

Once again, I was met with silence.

"Maybe you're right then," I said, my voice small. I felt numb and hollow inside. "Maybe I didn't know you after all."

She winced, and when I looked into her eyes, they were dull, lifeless. "I should go."

I took in a shaky breath before finally nodding.

Her eyes held mine for a moment, and she scanned my face as though she were memorizing every line. She reached out her hand but pulled it back quickly like she'd been burned by a hot stove.

"I'm so sorry, Derek." Her voice was barely above a whisper, and with one final look, she was gone. I stepped out into the hall and watched her leave.

Once she was out of sight, I went back inside and closed the door, leaning against it. That's when it hit me—that I'd really lost her. I sank to the ground with my back to the door, and Izzy padded over to me, crawling onto my lap. My body was wracked with sobs as reality sunk in.

Jo had walked away. Away from the life we could have had. Away from me.

TWENTY-NINE

Jo

"THIS IS A MISTAKE." Katie's voice was even as she stood in the doorway of my bedroom early the next morning before dawn, the calm at the center of the storm of emotions that was raining down on me. "Put your stuff down, and let's talk this through."

"I can't, Katie. I'm sorry." I pushed past her with the belongings I'd accumulated since arriving in Nashville stuffed into oversized totes and the weekender bag I'd taken on our holiday trip to Gatlinburg. "The job starts right away. I have to go."

"Not the job." Her voice and footsteps followed behind me as I stumbled down the hall, the bags I carried bouncing off the walls like bumper cars. "Take the job if that's what you really want, but you don't have to end things with Derek."

I swiped at the tears that spilled onto my cheeks with the back of my hand, causing me to drop one of my bags, sending an array of wrinkled and wadded up clothes spilling out onto the floor. I groaned and dropped to my knees, grabbing fists of cotton and cable-knit sweaters and shoving them back inside.

Katie knelt beside me and placed her hand on top of mine, pinning me with worried eyes. "Jo, please talk to me. There's more to this than what you're telling me. You *love* Derek. What is going on?"

I wanted to tell her everything, but each time I opened my mouth to do just that, no words came out. I couldn't let her try and talk me out of it. This was what was best for everyone. I had to keep reminding myself of that, which was easy to do anytime I pictured Dallas telling me all the ways I'd fractured his relationship with Derek. And as much as it hurt to hear it, he'd been right. I'd been hell-bent on finding a new reality, and I'd dragged Derek along with me. I may not have been the one to set his life on fire, but I'd poured gasoline all over it and handed him the match. I didn't want to ruin things with Dallas and Katie too.

She wasn't ready to admit it yet, but I knew she was in love with him, and I had a strong sense that he felt the same for her. If I told her the whole truth about what had happened, she would take my side, even if I was wrong, all because we're family. I'd be denying her a chance at real happiness, and I couldn't do that to her.

"Please," Katie begged as she helped me gather the rest of my stuff off the floor. "Just talk to me. We can figure this out together."

I shook my head. "I've already figured it out. Someone gave me some tough love, and helped me see that me being with Derek was a mistake."

"Your dad? Is that who said something to you?" she asked. "When has he ever guided you in a way that wasn't for his benefit? How can you not see that?"

I pressed the last T-shirt into the bag and rose to my feet. "It wasn't my dad, alright?"

Katie stood and shook her head, narrowing her eyes. "Then who was it?"

"It doesn't matter," I said, bumbling my way through the kitchen with her on my heels. "I've made up my mind."

"Clearly," she muttered as she followed me out the back door and to my car. She stood by as I popped the trunk and tossed my things inside. "I wish you'd talk to me. We've always told each other everything. I don't get it. Did I do something wrong?"

"What?" I asked. "No, of course not."

Katie's eyes were glassy, and she winced when I slammed the trunk shut. My chest felt like a ball of yarn. All of the months I'd spent unraveling the threads that had bound me together for so long were tied back up tight as a corset.

I closed the distance between us and threw my arms around her, holding her tight. "I promise this isn't because of you. This is all me, and I know it doesn't seem like it now, but me leaving is what's best for everybody." I sucked in a breath. "And I know my dad hasn't always been the most supportive, but he was so proud of me when I accepted this job. He and I will finally be in the same place and get to spend more time together. We'll be able to have the relationship I always wish we had."

Katie pulled back and looked me square in the eyes and nodded. "Okay, so are you going to let him get to know the real you or the person he wants you to be?"

I dropped my gaze and ground my black ballet flat into the gravel. I didn't know how to answer that. Maybe those versions of me were one and the same, and even if they weren't, did it really matter?

"That's what I thought." Katie gave me a look like my

mom used to when she'd tell me she 'wasn't mad, just disappointed'.

"I'm so sorry, Katie," I whispered, my eyes stinging. "Please don't be angry with me."

"I'm not," she said with a resigned sigh. "It just seemed like you were finally living your life for you, and you were happy, Jo. I'd never seen you so happy in all the years I've known you. I just wish it was enough for you."

It is enough…or it was.

But I couldn't continue to be pretend that what had made me so incredibly happy hadn't also hurt people. My happiness wasn't worth that. When I was years into my career at CNN and my face was on billboards in Times Square, I'd look back and know this was how it was always supposed to be. That this is what I wanted all along. It hurt in the moment, but it wouldn't hurt forever. These few months would be a small detour on the road to who I was supposed to become.

My throat was dry as a jar of cotton balls as I hugged Katie once more, squeezing my eyes shut. "Thank you," I said. *For giving me a safe place to fall apart. For loving every version of me even if I didn't always deserve it.* "Thank you for everything."

"Let me know when you get there?" she asked, finally breaking our embrace.

I nodded. "Of course."

"I still think it's a bad idea for you to try to drive straight through," she said. "You haven't had nearly enough sleep."

I shrugged. "I'm not so sure I'd be able to sleep anyway. I'll stop every few hours to stretch my legs. Besides, it will make it easier for me to hit the ground running tomorrow afternoon when I meet with the producers."

"Alright," she relented. "Drive safe."

"I will," I promised. "I love you, okay? Always."

"Always," she echoed with a sad smile.

I squeezed her arm before settling behind the wheel of my car, fastening my seatbelt. I gripped the steering wheel and started to pull out of the driveway, pausing for a moment before turning out onto the street.

I could stop here. I could go back inside and talk to Katie and try to sort through this mess.

The idea was so tempting that I could almost see Katie and me at Granny's dining table with mugs of tea hashing everything out, but then I pictured Derek and remembered why this all made sense. Dallas had been right. I *was* selfish, and the most selfless thing I could do for him now was let him go. But there was no way for me to stay in Nashville and do that, and there was no way for me to stay with Katie without ruining her relationship with Dallas. Me being out of the picture was what was best for everyone.

I eased off the brake, and the gravel crunched beneath my tires as I pulled onto the street. I waved to Katie where she still stood in the driveway as I rolled to the stop sign on the corner. With one last look at her standing outside Granny's house, I pulled away.

Away from Katie. Away from Derek. Away from the woman I'd thought I could be.

THIRTY

Derek
_____

I DIDN'T SLEEP at all the night Jo left. Izzy kept vigil in the bed next to me, her head resting on my chest. She fell asleep periodically, her cloudy brown eyes searching mine when she woke.

The night before played in my head on a torturous loop as the morning sun shimmered through the blinds. The warmth I'd found in Jo had been replaced with ice. She'd seemed removed, emotionally detached. Nothing about the Jo who showed up at my door was like the Jo I loved.

It didn't make sense...or did it?

I'd broken free of my father and the yearning for his acceptance, but Jo's relationship with her dad was altogether different. She longed for him to be proud of her, to love her for who she was—even if it meant changing who she was.

But Jo was only on the cusp of figuring out how much she'd been pushing aside her own hopes and dreams in favor of the life her father wanted her to live. What if he'd convinced her this was what was best for her? What if he'd pressured her? I knew all too well that gaining the approval of our families was a hell of a drug.

I'd put up with a lot over the years for that very reason, only to be rejected over and over and over again. Only to never be enough. But time had shown me that I wasn't the one who was lacking. I'd come to see that my parents had torn me down and tried to use my broken pieces to fill the cracks in their own hearts. But that was like putting a bandaid over a bullet hole. And the thing about wounds that deep was that if you didn't get to the source of the damage, you'd eventually bleed out.

Maybe Jo's father really would support her on this new endeavor—at least until he inevitably moved the goal post again. But why did she have to change to be worthy of his affection? Daniel Kingsley had only ever fought to turn her into someone she wasn't, but I was going to fight for her to be who she *was*. The beautiful, driven, compassionate, magical woman I'd fallen in love with. I didn't care where she lived or what job she did or didn't have. I only wanted her.

A plan started to crystalize in my mind. I would go to Katie's and catch her before she could leave. Her dad would learn to like me. Or maybe he wouldn't. I didn't really care. I would accept him because he mattered to Jo. Because that's what you did for the people you loved. You made room to let them be who they wanted and love who they wanted. And you fought like hell to keep them in your life.

"That's it," I said to Izzy, scruffing the top of her head and tossing the covers aside. "I'm bringing her back to us."

I threw on my jeans and T-shirt from the day before that laid in a crumpled heap on the floor beside my bed. Izzy sat up, ears at attention as I grabbed my keys and wallet off the dresser. She barked and pressed her front paws into the mattress, her butt in the air.

"I'll be back soon, Iz," I said, placing a quick kiss on top of her head.

I moved as quickly as I could, shoving my feet inside my sneakers and my arms through the sleeves of my leather jacket. In a matter of just a few seconds, I'd sprinted all the way down to the garage and fired up the ignition of my bike. My hand flexed against the clutch, adrenaline coursing through me as I pulled onto the main road with Jo on my mind.

If we could just talk this through, we'd be able to put the past twenty-four hours in the rearview, and it would be nothing but blue skies ahead.

"WHAT THE..." I MUTTERED TO MYSELF AS I PARKED MY BIKE in Katie's driveway and pried the helmet off my head. My heart sank when I saw that Jo's car had been replaced by Dallas', and he was standing on the back steps looking like a scolded puppy as Katie's finger drove into his chest. She was barefoot on the back porch in a pair of pink pajamas, and she was *pissed.*

"Selfish, Dallas,' she yelled. "That's what you are! This is all your fault!"

"I know, I know," Dallas said as I approached. "I'm sorry, but would you keep your voice down?"

"No, I will *not* keep my voice down," she spat. "I don't care if the entire damn neighborhood hears what an idiot you are!"

"What on earth is going on?" I asked. "Where's Jo?" I

silently prayed she'd called this whole thing off and had gone to work or literally anywhere but New York.

"She's already gone, Derek. She left about an hour ago." Katie flashed me a look of sympathy before shifting her gaze back to Dallas, her eyes turning to ice as she slapped his chest. "And it's all *his* fault."

"Ow!" Dallas recoiled, taking a step back.

"Wait...what?" My attention snapped to my cousin who pushed his hands through his hair and rubbed at the back of his neck, his movements shaky.

"I realized last night that I was wrong, so I came here first thing to try and fix it." Dallas' voice trembled slightly. "I never dreamed she would leave."

"Isn't that *exactly* what you were hoping for?" Katie fired back.

"Would somebody please tell me what the fuck is going on?" I shouted, causing both Dallas and Katie to fall silent. "What does Dallas have to do with Jo leaving?"

Katie narrowed her eyes at him. "Yeah, Dallas. Why don't you tell Derek what you did?"

I swallowed hard. "What did you do, Dal?"

Dallas blew out a breath and shifted his gaze downward, unable to meet my eyes. "I came to see Jo yesterday morning."

"Why?" I shook my head. "Why would you come see her?"

Dallas continued to focus his stare on the ground and sighed.

"Tell him." Katie hit him again.

"Alright, alright." Dallas finally looked up at me, his brow furrowed. "I was upset, okay? I was pissed about you leaving the band, and I came here and I kind of...blamed Jo."

"You did *what*?" I asked, my voice as tight as my fist.

Katie shot him an accusatory glance. "*Kind of?*"

"I *did* blame Jo. I told her that she was what had changed around here." His voice was almost inaudible. "That you leaving the band was her fault."

I pressed the heels of my palms to my forehead, attempting to stop the explosion of rage building behind my eyes. "Dammit, Dallas. Are you fucking kidding me? Why the fuck would you do that?"

"I was angry," he admitted. "I snapped."

"And what else did you say?" Katie asked with a bite in her voice that told me she already knew.

Dallas shook his head, crossing his arms across his chest as though he were putting up a wall between us. "I told her she broke up our family."

"What the actual fuck, Dallas?" I gripped him by the collar of his shirt, pressing him into the railing of the rickety stairs. "Why would you fucking say that?"

Dallas held up his hands in surrender. "I was upset, okay? I felt like I was losing everything, and I...blamed her because...because—"

"You blamed her because this was what you fucking hoped would happen. You got *exactly* what you wanted!" My fists tightened around his shirt. "We're all fucking changing, Dallas. Every damn one of us except for you! You're just pissed because you don't have anything but the fucking band. It's just too fucking much for you to accept that someone or something else might make me happy."

"Go ahead. Hit me," he said, his shoulders slumped. "I deserve it."

"Yes, you fucking do," I spat, releasing him with a shove. "But then I'd be no better than you."

Katie placed a hand on my shoulder. "I'm so sorry, Derek. I had no idea. She didn't tell me about this. I knew something more was going on, but she wouldn't tell me."

"I had no way of knowing her dad was going to come in and offer her that job," Dallas said. "I couldn't have known that. I was blowing off steam, and I took it out on her."

"You were horrible to her," Katie said through tears. "Even if you really felt that way, that wasn't the way to handle it."

"I know," Dallas said, his eyes pleading with hers. "I'm sorry. I fucked up, but I'm going to fix this. I'm going to make this right. I promise."

Dallas reached for her, but she backed away, holding her hands out to stop him from coming closer. "Don't touch me." She turned toward me and studied me for a moment. "Are you going to be okay?"

"This can't be how our story ends. It just…can't." I raked my hands down my face. "I should have tried harder to stop her from leaving. If I'd pushed harder I could have gotten to the bottom of this shit. I was just so stunned. I was so fucking hurt."

"This isn't on you." Katie cut her eyes to Dallas and then looked back at me. "I need to get ready for work, but if you need anything, let me know, okay?"

"Yeah, okay," I answered.

She gave me a quick hug before going back inside and shutting the door, ignoring Dallas completely.

Once we were alone, Dallas sighed. "I'm really sorry. I shouldn't have—"

"No, you shouldn't have." My voice bubbled like a volcano, dripping hot lava. "There's so much you don't fucking know about, Dallas."

"Derek, I—"

"I can't even fucking look at you right now, man," I said, backing away from him and moving toward my bike. "But I'll tell you one damn thing. Somebody did break up our family, and it sure as shit wasn't Jo."

With that, I pushed my helmet on and revved my bike, leaving Dallas on Katie's back steps with his head in his hands.

THIRTY-ONE

Jo

IT WAS NEARLY one a.m. Sunday when I finally checked into my suite at the Mandarin Oriental hotel in New York. CNN had booked an extended stay since I'd accepted the position on such short notice and would need time to find an apartment. Not that I was in any hurry. Nothing would feel like home the way Nashville had. Or like Derek had.

Once I was in the elevator, I finally allowed myself to look at my phone. I had silenced it for the drive, and there were several missed calls from Katie, Derek, and a number I didn't recognize. I had five new voicemails, but I couldn't bring myself to listen to them, certain that hearing Derek's voice would send me over the edge.

As I rode up to the forty-second floor, I texted Katie to let her know I'd arrived safely, then found my room through bleary eyes and slid my keycard in the door. When I heard it click, I shoved the door open. Even in the dim entryway light, I could see that the space was stunning. Silk lined the walls, and there was a small seating area with a plush sofa and a crystal chandelier off to one side. I padded into the bedroom, dropping my bags to the floor, before trudging over to the nightstand to turn on the lamp. A cozy bed that looked as fluffy as a cloud awaited me, along with a large, cellophane wrapped basket. I flipped up the attached notecard to read it.

Welcome to the CNN family, Jo! Hope you feel right at home! I'm sending a car to pick you up at nine a.m. on Sunday to meet with the production crew. Can't wait to get started!

Sincerely,

Brent Kirkpatrick

I should have been elated to receive a gift basket from CNN, and I would have been if this had happened months ago, before I ever returned to Nashville. I would've been thrilled for Brent Kirkpatrick to even know who I was. But as I slowly tugged on the ribbon holding the wrapping in place, I felt like it was me that was about to come undone.

Inside was a bottle of champagne that was worth more than my car, a box of truffles, a brand new iPhone, and gift cards to eateries with names that sounded expensive and were no doubt some of the hottest spots in the city. There was a company credit card and the number for their car service, as well as a gorgeous set of pearls with matching stud earrings. They were beautiful, classic—the kind you'd expect to see the likes of Diane Sawyer wearing. I ran my fingers along the smooth beads before moving to the window. I opened the drapes and was met with a view of the city that should have taken my breath away. And it did, but for all the wrong reasons.

My hand flew to my mouth stifling the cry that clawed its way out from the pit in my stomach as the last thread holding me together fell away. Looking out over the city lights and

Central Park, I felt an ocean away from home, from the person I'd been the last few months.

My breathing turned shallow as sobs racked my body. I backed away from the window until my legs collided with the bed, and I crawled onto it, curling into a tight ball. I only wished that I could make myself small enough to disappear.

I missed Derek. I missed Katie. I missed Granny's house and the smell of cinnamon. I missed my job and Sunday dinners. I missed Izzy. The emptiness in my chest seeped into my limbs, and I worried it might swallow me whole.

For the second time in a year, I'd lost everything. This time was different, though. This time, I'd left on my own, fleeing the scene after burning the life I loved to the ground. But it had to be done. Dallas had been right. Derek needed his family. He needed the band, and without me in the picture, he could focus on what was important.

And maybe one day, I'd be happy again too. I'd look back on all of this and realize it had been the push I needed to make my wildest dreams come true. That was the lie I told myself over and over as I cried myself to sleep.

THE NEXT MORNING, I DRESSED IN A SIMPLE BLACK BLOUSE with matching trousers and carefully dabbed concealer beneath my eyes in a fruitless attempt to hide my puffy, tear-stained skin. Looking at my reflection, I hardly recognized myself. The woman staring back at me was only vaguely familiar, like someone I used to know...someone I wasn't sure I liked anymore. Somewhere behind the sad eyes and black clothes was the colorful person I'd become after leaving

Chicago. It was as though a storm had moved in and edged the sun right out of the sky.

I turned off the bathroom light on my way out of the room and grabbed my phone off the bed, unable to face my own scrutiny any longer. My finger scrolled along the screen until I landed on Lindsey's name, and I took a deep breath as I tapped the call button. I owed her an explanation, and I was ashamed for not telling her in person before I'd left. But I knew the longer I stayed in Nashville, the harder it would have been for me to leave.

"Hey girl," Lindsey answered on the third ring. "Everything is going according to your carefully laid plans, so I don't want you stressing, okay? You really outdid yourself with this benefit show. Now all we have to do is show up and enjoy it."

"Lindsey, I...I actually have something I need to tell you." My voice wavered, and my throat constricted as I told her where I was and about my new job. "I'm so, so sorry. I should have talked to you before I left. I should have—"

"Listen, girl, what we're not going to do is apologize for taking chances to better ourselves," Lindsey said, cutting me off. "You've done so much for me and for Project NENA, and I am beyond grateful for you."

Her words wrapped themselves around my heart and squeezed, a bittersweet reminder of everything I'd walked away from.

"This is a huge opportunity for you, Jo," she continued. "I always knew you were destined for big things."

"Thank you," I said, trying not to cry.

"The main thing is that you're happy." She paused for a moment. "And you are, right? You're happy?"

"I'm still processing everything and feeling a little overwhelmed," I answered. It was the closest I could get to the truth. I'd quit on her a week before the benefit concert. The last thing I needed to do was burden her with my emotional turmoil.

"That's understandable," she said. "It's a lot of change at once. But no matter what, I know this is going to be good for you."

"I hope so," I managed.

"Well, listen, I just got to my first meeting of the day, but don't be a stranger, alright?"

"I won't," I promised. "Thank you. For everything."

"And Jo?"

"Yeah?"

She hesitated a second before speaking again. "You're not stuck if it ends up not being what you thought. Or if it just plain sucks. I mean, New York ain't nothin' like the South. Can you even get sweet tea there?" I smiled, and I could hear in her voice that she was smiling too. "All I'm trying to say is, you can always come home."

"Thanks, Lindsey." I ended the call and flopped on the bed, staring at the ceiling until the landline rang to alert me that my ride had arrived. I quickly gathered my things and headed to the lobby. When I stepped outside, I saw a gentleman with cotton-white hair waiting outside a shiny black Escalade.

"You must be Miss Kingsley," he said, smiling and extending his hand to me. "I'm Lewis, your driver. Anywhere you'd like to stop on the way to the office this morning, ma'am?"

"My driver?" I asked, shaking his hand. "This isn't…This isn't an Uber?"

Lewis chuckled. "No ma'am." He tapped the SUV with

his fist. "This here is your own personal chariot from now on."

I imagined the many conversations I'd had with my dad as he was carted between appointments and meetings. It was something I'd once thought was a perk of the job, but now that I was the one being chauffeured around, it felt strange. Especially because my driver looked like he could be my grandfather and wouldn't stop calling me—

"Ma'am? Are you alright?" Lewis asked. "You look a little pale."

"Yes, sorry," I answered. "This is all a bit different for me. I wasn't expecting to have my own driver."

He gave me a warm smile. "I understand, ma'am."

"Jo," I said. "Please, call me Jo."

"Jo," he echoed, his voice as stiff as an over-starched pair of pants. I could tell that calling people by their first names wasn't something he was used to. "Of course." He opened the back door of the car and gestured inside. "Are you ready?"

I wasn't. Not even a little bit, but I got in the car anyway, thanking Lewis as he shut the door.

"Any stops you'd like to make, ma'am? I mean, Jo," he asked again, correcting himself.

"No, thank you," I replied as my phone rang from inside my purse. Katie's picture smiled back at me.

"I'm sorry," I said, holding the phone up. "Do you mind if I take this?"

Lewis laughed and shook his head as though that were the most preposterous question he'd ever heard. "Of course not."

"Did you get my messages?" Katie blurted out before I could even say hello.

"No," I said. "I'm sorry. I saw I had voicemails last night, but I was so wiped when I got in that I didn't listen to any of them." I left out the details about crying myself into a fitful sleep.

"Dallas has been trying to get in touch with you."

"What?" I asked, almost inaudibly.

"He came here looking for you after you left yesterday morning." Her voice was full of hope. "He felt awful once he found out you'd left."

I blinked slowly, my brain trying to catch up with Katie's words. "Did he…"

"Tell me what he did? Yes, and I'm *pissed,* but that's not the point," she said impatiently. "The point is that you can come home. You can be with Derek. I know you let Dallas get inside your head, and after he told me what he said to you, nobody could blame you. But he was wrong."

I pictured Dallas, anger and anguish converging on his face as he hurled his words at me. The way he'd looked had stuck with me—the skin creased around his eyes and his mouth in a rigid line, both souvenirs of the pain I'd caused.

"I…I don't know." I chewed my lip.

"What do you mean? What's there not to know?" I could hear her sigh through the phone. "Dallas is why you left, but he knows the band breaking up isn't your fault. He told both me and Derek what happened and that he never should've blamed you."

My breath escaped my lungs as though I'd been punched in the gut. He'd told Derek? The sound of his name made my chest ache.

But did Dallas really feel that what he'd said was wrong or was he trying to save face with Katie and Derek? If I went back, the band would still be broken up, and there would still be tension between Derek and Dallas. Katie would never give Dallas a chance because with me close by, she'd feel like she was dishonoring our friendship. Going back would be selfish. It might make me happy, but it would cause nothing but problems for the people I loved.

"Katie, I'm not coming back," I said softly, as Lewis's eyes caught mine in the rearview mirror.

"But...Dallas was wrong," she insisted. "He admitted it."

"He wasn't though," I countered. "Maybe he feels bad about the way he told me, but he wasn't wrong. I just couldn't see it for myself."

"I don't understand," she pressed on. "You were so happy."

"But at what cost?" I asked. "As much as I don't want to admit it, *I* am the thing that changed. *I* am the common denominator here. I don't think Derek would have left the band if I hadn't encouraged him. We both went off script because it was something fun, something different, but he can't fight who he is anymore than I can." The words tasted sour on my tongue.

"And who is that, Jo? Who are you?" Katie asked, her voice rising. "Don't try to tell me you're like your father because we both know that's not true."

Tears stung my eyes as I considered her question, and my voice was barely a whisper when I finally answered. "I think it is."

The line was quiet for a second. "You're wrong," she said, her voice breaking. I knew then that Katie was beginning to have her doubts. That maybe the Jo who'd been living with her since last fall wasn't real. That maybe I was more like my father than either of us ever wanted to admit.

The Escalade pulled to a stop, and Lewis nodded at me in the rearview mirror, indicating that we'd arrived at our destination.

"I'm going to have to let you go. I just got to the office. I...I'm sorry." I wasn't sure if I was apologizing for needing to end the call or for letting her down...or both.

"Right," she said with a deep sigh. "Okay."

I started to apologize again, but I told her I loved her instead.

"I love you too," she replied. "Enough to tell you you're making a big mistake, Jo."

I swallowed the lump that formed in my throat. "I...I've got to go."

I squeezed my eyes shut and ended the call, clutching the phone to my chest.

"You alright, Jo?" Lewis asked softly.

I opened my eyes to see him turned around, his hand resting on the passenger seat. "No, I...I don't think I am," I admitted.

He nodded solemnly as he reached into the front pocket of his suit and handed me a white handkerchief. The simple gesture was enough to send the tears in my eyes spilling over the edge.

"We're a couple of minutes early," Lewis said. "What do you say we drive around the block before you go in?"

"Thank you." I nodded and gave him a small, grateful smile.

"Very good," he said, turning on his blinker to merge back into traffic.

I gazed out the tinted window and dabbed at my face with the soft, cotton fabric.

"I have three daughters. When they were in school and having a rough start to the day, I'd do another loop around the parking lot before dropping them off." His eyes flickered to

mine in the mirror. "Sometimes all we need is a little do over
—a second chance."

"I'm going to have Wardrobe do a focus group, but I'm
liking the image she's giving off with the all black," Mr. Kirkpatrick said from where he sat at the head of the mahogany
conference table. His attention was on a woman with a slicked
back pixie cut and perfect olive skin named Marla. I'd gathered from the meeting that she was my executive producer,
though I couldn't be certain because no one in the room had
actually addressed me directly. "I'm not sure about the red
hair, though," he continued. "Maybe we should make her
blonde."

Blonde? That wasn't part of the deal. I loved my hair and
had no desire to find out if blondes had more fun. Fun was
overrated anyway and not something I'd be having again
anytime soon. I opened my mouth to speak, but my words
caught in my throat.

Marla shook her head, appraising me in a way that let me
know my feedback wasn't needed. "Red is a power color. It
makes her stand out."

There were twelve people in the meeting, none of whom
had been formally introduced to me. A couple looked bored,
sneaking peeks at their phones while others took notes furiously, nodding in agreement with everything Marla and Mr.
Kirkpatrick said, occasionally adding their own commentary.

"Fair enough." Mr. Kirkpatrick glanced over at me and
pursed his lips before shifting his gaze back to Marla. "We
want to toe the line between approachable and commanding,

just like Daniel Kingsley. We have the heiress to the news media throne, and we want everyone to know it "

I wondered if my dad had ever felt invisible at a conference table while a dozen people talked about him like he wasn't in the room.

"Alright," Mr. Kirkpatrick said finally. "Everyone has their assignments. Let's get to work."

Only then did he give me a small, encouraging smile before leaving the room.

"You have a wardrobe appointment at two," Marla said without looking at me as she rose to her feet. "I have a meeting that won't be over till then, so I'll be a little late, but Lewis already knows where to take you."

I nodded, but she didn't see because she was already out the door.

THIRTY-TWO

Derek

"OKAY, FELLAS." Cash clapped his hands. "That'll do it for today. Same time, same place tomorrow."

I unplugged my bass, and we each packed our gear in silence.

A week passed, and I still hadn't heard from Jo. I'd texted Katie to see if she'd heard from her, and she let me know Jo had made it safely, but that was all she knew. I was slowly starting to face the reality that the damage Dallas had caused couldn't be undone.

The band was getting ready for what would be our final show together, the benefit that Jo had planned. Every rehearsal drove the knife deeper into my chest. Tension hung in the air like smog. Every breath I took polluted my body with rage. I hated that our last days as a band had come to this. I wasn't speaking to Dallas, and Luca was barely speaking to anyone. He had agreed to do this last show together before we went our separate ways. Dallas had reluctantly accepted that the band was done, and both Cash and Jax were just trying to keep some semblance of peace.

"Hey, Luca, can we—" Cash tried to catch Luca as he slung his guitar case over his shoulder, but he pushed past him and out the door. Cash sighed and pushed his hands through his hair.

"I can't believe we only have one week left as a band," Jax said as he came up beside me and placed a hand on my shoulder.

My eyes settled on Dallas, who sat behind his drum set with his head in his hands

"Right now, it can't come soon enough," I muttered, and Jax frowned. I knew it wasn't fair to him. It wasn't fair to Cash or Luca. But now, all I could see when I thought of this band was Dallas and what he'd cost me.

"Can we talk?" Jax asked. "Outside?"

I nodded and followed him out the door, down the narrow hallway and into the parking lot. Luca had just backed out of his spot when his eyes met mine. His stony expression softened for a split second before he shifted into drive and pulled away.

"What's up?" I asked as Jax sat on the curb.

He gestured with his head for me to take a seat beside him, which I did. Jax ground the toe of his black Converse into the pavement, his eyes focused on the asphalt, then turned toward me. "Listen, Derek. I know what Dallas did was shitty. He had no right. But are you really never going to talk to him again?"

I blew out a long breath, but the poison that hung in the air of the rehearsal hall still filled my lungs. "I honestly don't know. Right now, I'm so fucking angry I can't imagine being able to speak to him without thinking about what he did."

"I can understand that. It's all very fresh right now." He paused for a moment. "But he's your family, man."

"Which makes it even worse, Jax. Surely you can see that." I scrubbed my hand over my mouth. "I mean, what if this had been you and Liv? What if Dallas had sabotaged your relationship with her? You wouldn't have any of what you have right now."

Jax nodded. "You're right. I'd be pissed."

"Would you be able to let it all go and move on from that? Would you really?" I asked.

He chewed his lip and scratched a speck of dirt off the side of his shoe. "I'd like to say that I would. Because we have a history together. All of us do, but you, me, and Dal, we grew up together. So I'd like to think there's nothing we couldn't work through." He rubbed his thumb along his jaw. "But I don't know. I don't know if I could get past it."

"I know you mean well, man. I do," I said. "But this isn't so black and white. Nothing about this is simple. What Liv is to you, Jo is to me, and Dallas made her feel like she ruined my life."

He turned toward me and gripped my shoulder. "Look, if Jo is your Liv, then this isn't over. What's happening right now…it's nothing more than a pause—a brief intermission. You'll see."

"How can you be so sure?"

He gave me a small smile. "Because love will always lead you home."

I scoffed. "I'm pretty sure Jo was led to New York."

The door behind us clattered open, and Dallas spilled out of it. His shoulders were hunched over, his gaze focused on his phone screen.

"I should get going," I said, rising to my feet.

Dark circles framed Dallas' eyes when he glanced up at

me. His mouth opened as though he were about to say something, but instead he cast his eyes downward.

I looked back to Jax. "I'll see you tomorrow."

He nodded as I strode over to my bike. In my sideview mirror, I saw Dallas drop onto the curb beside Jax, wiping beneath his cheeks with his fingertips. Was he crying?

My chest constricted, and I gripped the handlebars tighter. It killed me to see Dallas like that. Regardless of how angry I was, I still cared about him. So much so that for a moment, I considered getting off my bike and talking to him, trying to find some way to bury the hatchet.

But then I pictured Jo's tearstained face the night she left me and the way her vibrant colors had faded to black. The fire in her eyes had completely burned out, coating me in the ashes of every perfect moment we'd shared, making it almost impossible for me to breathe.

With that last image of her in my mind, I pulled my helmet on and revved my bike. Even over the roar of the motor, I could hear my pulse pounding in my ears as I drove away.

THIRTY-THREE

Jo

I WAS GOING to be sick. It was the morning before the day of my first broadcast, and I was in my dressing room with Marla who was making some final notes on my script. We were about to do our last run through of the show, and I was a wreck.

My reflection in the vanity mirror was flushed. Sweat formed on the back of my neck, and my hands were clammy. Everything about my new job, New York, and my entire life felt wrong, and for the last week, my body had decided to stage a revolution against me as a result. It didn't help that all of the news outlets were reporting about the last Midnight in Dallas show—the benefit *I'd* helped to plan, that was taking place in two days. My stomach churned, the half of a bagel I'd choked down that morning sloshing around like a cup of coffee that has been filled to the brim. Any sudden movements and it would spill out over everything.

"You have *got* to work on your delivery," Marla said without looking up at me. "We want a sense of urgency. We want thought provoking. We want eggs Benedict, but you're giving us day-old biscuits from McDonald's."

She wrinkled her nose, and I stifled a snort. There was a zero percent chance Marla had ever stepped foot inside a fast food restaurant. In the time I'd known her, I hadn't seen her consume anything but Starbucks and thirty dollar salads.

"Right," I said. "Of course."

"You're Daniel Kingsley's daughter for Chrissakes," Marla continued, plucking a red pen from above her ear and scribbling something in the top corner of the notepad. "You need to act like it. Grab the viewer by the throat. Take control. Give 'em hell."

I shuddered. Why did it all have to sound so *violent*?

There was a knock on the door followed by a nasally chirp of a voice. "Ten minutes!"

Marla finally raised her head, glancing at me in the mirror as she stood and started toward the door. "You look like death warmed over," she stated simply and factually, as though she'd told me the sky was blue. "For the love of God, please do *something* that will make you look less like a corpse, or Brent will have a conniption. I'll see you out there."

The door closed behind her, and my insides lurched. Bile burned the back of my throat as I sprinted five feet to the small bathroom, barely making it there before hurling the contents of my stomach into the toilet. I snatched some tissue off the dispenser and wiped at the corners of my mouth before flushing and returning to the vanity.

Marla was right. I looked like hell. My eyes were red and watery, my skin was splotchy, and my hair had certainly seen better days. I ran a brush through it and touched up my makeup as best I could. It wasn't great, but it would have to do.

My personal phone rang from where it laid on the counter with an incoming FaceTime call from Carina. I grabbed the phone and held it for a second as I considered screening the call. I didn't want her to witness me in the state I was in, but I also knew it would be good for me to see a friendly face. I'd barely talked to Katie since I'd gotten to New York two weeks before. I'd called her a few times, but our conversations had been few and far between, and the ones we did have were short. I could feel her disappointment in me through the phone by the way her voice dipped every time she answered, and she always had to cut our talks short.

I swiped across the screen to answer the call, and Carina came into view along with half of Riggs' face.

"CNN!" Carina exclaimed. "Girl, when were you going to tell us? Harper mentioned it at the staff meeting this morning! Everybody's freaking out!"

"I'm sorry I didn't tell you," I said. "This whole thing has been a whirlwind, and I guess I'm still trying to catch my breath."

Carina let out a happy shriek. "This is amazing, Jo! You did it. You hit the big time."

"I always knew you had it in you, kid," Riggs said. "I'm proud of you."

"Thank you." I forced a smile. "It's a really great opportunity."

Carina tilted her head and narrowed her eyes. "Then why does your face look like that?"

"Like what?" I asked.

"Like you've never been more miserable in your entire life," she said. "I thought you'd be over the moon."

"I am." It was a statement, but it came out like a question.

"Uh huh." Carina pursed her lips.

"What?" I asked.

"You know I love you, right? So, when I say what I'm about to say, please remember that," she said.

Well, that didn't sound good. "Okay…"

"You look like shit," Carina deadpanned. "Like worse than the day you blew chunks all over the conference room."

"And that was pretty bad," Riggs reminded me, as though I hadn't been the one who tossed her cookies in front of God and everyone.

"What's going on?" Carina asked gently.

"I don't know." I sucked in a breath. "I pictured this in my head so many times, but it's nothing like I imagined. I don't feel how I thought I would."

Riggs leaned into the frame. "And how's that?"

"Happy," I answered. "For so long, this was the dream, but…I don't know if it was ever really *my* dream."

Polaroids fell on the floor of my mind—snapshots of Derek, Katie, and sweet Izzy. I pictured Lindsey and the kids at Project NENA and remembered the sweet story of an unlikely friendship between a young man and his Uber driver. None of these things were 'big time' to people in the news world, and certainly not to my dad, but they were everything to me.

"What does that man of yours think about all of this?" Carina asked. "Does this mean you guys are long distance?"

I dropped my gaze to my lap and shook my head.

Riggs's eyes softened. "I'm sorry, Jo."

"It's okay," I said even though it wasn't. I wasn't sure I'd ever be okay again. "I just…I wasn't good for him."

"I don't believe that's true. You were both good for each other. You were so happy. You'd even started wearing color, for crying out loud." Carina frowned. "I see you're wearing all black again."

I cleared my throat. I knew I needed to change the subject or I'd start crying, and there was no telling if I'd be able to stop. "How's Kimber?"

"She's good," Carina answered. "Honestly, I wouldn't be surprised if a big network doesn't snatch her up. Harper will have a fucking cow if that happens."

There was a knock on the door followed by Marla's voice. "Shit or get off the pot. It's time to go."

"Coming," I called, raking my hand down my face.

"Who the hell was that?" Riggs asked.

I sighed. "My producer."

Carina snorted. "Well, she sounds lovely. What's her deal?"

"I don't know, but I'm pretty sure it has to do with her hating my guts," I said. "Sorry, guys. I've got to go. We're doing our final run through."

"You'll do great," Riggs assured me. "Everything's going to be okay."

"Yeah, it will," Carina added. "You've got this, Jo."

"Thanks." I gave a faint smile, wishing more than anything I could reach through the screen and hug them both. "I'll talk to you soon."

"Bye!" Carina and Riggs waved before ending the call.

I slid my phone onto the counter and buried my head in my hands. Riggs was right. Everything would be okay in the end, even if it didn't feel like it now. It didn't matter that my old way of life fit about as well as a pair of pants that were a size too small. As long as I could contort myself enough to squeeze into them, I'd eventually lose enough of myself that they'd fit just right.

The door vibrated with the force of a pounding knock.

"Two minutes," Marla boomed.

Hot acid bubbled in my throat, and my stomach felt like it was on a carnival ride.

"Okay." I pushed out of my chair and said a silent prayer that I would make it through the next hour. That was just how it was going to be for a while. Trying to make it one hour, one minute at a time.

THIRTY-FOUR

Derek

I was leaving our final rehearsal two days before the benefit when thunder rumbled beneath my feet and the first few drops of rain dotted the asphalt of the parking lot. Dallas rushed out of the metal door behind me, calling my name, but I pretended I didn't hear.

"Come on, man," Dallas said, closing in on my heels. "Please talk to me."

I continued to ignore him.

"So you're just never going to speak to me? We're going to do this last show together, and then what? I'll never see you again?" His already hoarse voice cracked like worn paint. "I fucked up, okay? I fucked up, but we're family and—"

I turned to him, shoving my finger in his face. "And that's *exactly* why this is so messed up. We *are* family, and you fucking stabbed me in the back!" The thunder vibrated around us as though it was punctuating my every word.

"And I'm sorry," Dallas cried. "If I could take it back, I would. I've tried. I've called Jo. I've sent messages begging her to talk to me, but she won't respond."

Bitterness dripped off my tongue. "I can't fucking imagine why."

"I know," he said, raking his hands over the back of his head and down his neck. "Look, I want to fix this. What can I do to make it right?"

I shook my head in disgust. "You can stay out of my fucking business. That's what you can do." I turned and started toward my bike, flexing my fingers into my palm.

"I'm trying here, Derek. I want to make things right with you and Jo. I want to make things right with *us,"* he pleaded. "I've accepted that the band isn't what you want anymore. I don't understand why, but I've accepted it, and—"

"This band was my way out," I blurted out as I spun around to face him. "*You* were. I thought maybe we'd play through college, and then we'd eventually move on. I never wanted this to be a permanent thing." The words poured from my mouth like the rain that fell around us. "My dad hit me, Dallas. He was a goddamn drunk, and he treated me and my mom like shit my whole life. And for the last few months, I've been trying to process the fact that the bastard is dying. He's fucking dying, and you know what? He's not sorry for what he did to me. He and my mom didn't even want me. I was a fucking mistake."

The color drained from Dallas' face. "*What?* He…He *hit* you? Derek…I'm sorry. I didn't know any of this. And he's… dying? I didn't…" He took in a shaky breath, his eyes glossing over. "I'm so sorry. I had no idea. Why…Why didn't you say something?"

"I don't know, Dallas. I guess there's never really a good way to say 'my dad beats the shit out of me'," I spat. "It's not like you could have done anything about it."

"Like hell I couldn't." His voice broke. "You could have come to live with us. We could have gone to the cops."

I pushed my hands through my hair. "Nobody would have believed me."

"I would have," he said quietly. "I'm sorry you went through this. That I wasn't there for you. Why didn't you tell me back then that you didn't want to keep going with the band? I would've understood if I'd known what you were dealing with."

"You don't get it, Dallas. I shouldn't have to be going through some sort of tragedy to get your blessing to do something else with my life."

His Adam's apple bobbed as he swallowed.

"Besides, I knew how happy the band made you. I couldn't be the one to take that away from you." A bitter chuckle seeped out of my throat. "Because I actually give a shit about your happiness. I didn't want to ruin that for you. But when you were given the chance to do the same for me, you didn't hesitate to fuck up my life."

Rain pelted my skin as the clouds broke open.

"Let me make it right." He took a step closer to me. "Please."

"That ship has already fucking sailed, man." I turned away and climbed on my bike.

"What do you want me to do?" Dallas asked. "Tell me what to do, and I'll do it. I'll do anything."

"After this show is over, I want you to stay the fuck away from me. Understand? Leave me the hell alone." I shoved my helmet on, slammed the kickstand up, and drove away.

I didn't look back. I couldn't. Pain was all that remained there.

I WAS ALREADY AWAKE WHEN MY ALARM SOUNDED THE NEXT morning. I turned it off, opting instead to lay there with Izzy for a few more minutes. She snored softly as I rubbed the top of her head, running my finger along her snout. Today was our last day of press as a band, and Jo's absence was weighing heavily on me, like a winter coat with bricks in the pockets. I'd seen commercials for her new show, her face rigid and unsmiling. She looked nothing like the woman I knew, so I'd made it a point to keep my television off, and I even deleted the social media apps off my phone so I wouldn't be tempted to look. I told the guys that if they watched her show that I didn't want to know about it. It was better that way.

In a couple of hours, Jax, Luca, Dallas, and I would be set up in a room at the Omni hotel where a parade of journalists would filter in and out of the room to ask us about our last show. They'd ask us about our split, what was next for each of us, and how we felt about our futures. I'd known from the moment I'd made the decision to leave the band that this was going to be a bittersweet day for me. But now, all of the sweetness was gone. Jo was in New York, and I couldn't stand to be in the same room as Dallas. An incredibly important chapter of my life was coming to a close, but I hadn't expected it to end like this. Jo was supposed to be standing next to me, and we were supposed to walk into the next chapter of our lives together.

Up until she'd left, I'd felt hopeful about the future and all of the possibilities that came with a blank page. Now the unknown loomed over me like a dark cloud.

"I've got to get ready to go," I said to Izzy.

She blinked her eyes open and peered at me through slits.

"We've almost made it." I scratched behind her ears. "After tomorrow night, no more long rehearsals. No more Midnight in Dallas."

She cocked her head at me and let out a soft whine.

"Don't worry. There will be plenty of walks," I promised, giving her one more pat on the head before getting up.

I went through the motions of getting ready and ordered an Uber Black to take me to the hotel. As we got closer, I could see that fans had gotten wind of our destination and were lined up outside with signs and posters, hoping to catch a glimpse of us. As much as I appreciated them and their presence, I couldn't handle their expectant faces, so I had the driver pull up to the side door, and I slipped inside unnoticed.

Cash had texted me the room number we would be in, so I found the stairwell and made my ascent to the third floor, managing to avoid the media circus that had already formed in the lobby. I trekked down the hall and was about to glance down at my phone to confirm the room number when I saw Luca outside one of the doors, one foot against the wall, arms folded over his chest.

"Hey," I greeted him.

He nodded at me, and we stood in silence for a moment.

"So, this is it," I said. "Our last press junket."

"Fucking finally," he replied. "I'm so ready to be done."

I studied Luca's face. Over the years, he'd never minded being the center of attention. But I wondered if any of that had been real or if it had all been an act to hide the parts of himself he didn't want us, or anyone else, to see.

"Listen, Luca." I shoved my hands in my pockets. "I just...I want to say I'm sorry. What you said the day everything kind of blew up…You were right. I wasn't the greatest friend to you. None of us were."

He shrugged. "Well, it's not like I made it easy on you."

I shook my head. "It doesn't matter. Here I am, so pissed about Dallas not hearing me, but all this time, I never once heard you. I've been a hypocrite, man, and I owe you an apology."

His eyes dropped to the floor. "You really don't have to do this."

"Yeah. I do," I said. "I've lived with so many regrets. There are so many things I wish I'd done or said sooner. But I don't want to do that anymore."

He shifted his gaze back to me.

"I'm sorry, Luca. I'm sorry I wasn't as good of a friend to you as I should have been, but I want you to know that, if you'll let me, I'd like the chance to be a better one." I leaned against the wall beside him. "I know the band is coming to an end, but I don't want us to."

He nodded, his eyes wrinkled in concentration. After a long moment, he glanced over at me. "Look, I'm not going to hug you. I've already used up my good person quota for the year, and I do have a reputation to uphold."

The corners of my mouth tugged into a grin. "I'd expect nothing less."

Without even looking in my direction, he extended his hand to me.

I shook it without hesitation. "Thanks, man."

Before we could say anything else, Jax came out of the room, followed by Cash.

"Have either of you heard from Dallas?" Jax asked.

Luca snorted. "What the fuck do you think?"

I raised my brow. "He's not here?"

Cash shook his head. "And he's not answering any of my calls or texts."

Shit. Was this my fault? I'd come down hard on him yesterday. Not that he didn't deserve some of it, but I probably could have handled it better. Or at least tried to keep some modicum of peace.

"We kind of had words yesterday after rehearsal," I admitted. "He didn't say anything about not coming today, but I guess it's possible. I'm sorry. He's probably pissed at me."

"No. This isn't on you. Dallas has an issue with all of us right now," Luca said, steepling his fingers. "And frankly, he can be pissed all he wants. He deserved whatever tongue-lashing you gave him and then some."

Jax pushed his hands through his hair. "You don't think he'd no-show us, do you?"

Luca shrugged. "Honestly, it wouldn't surprise me if he didn't bother to show up today or for the benefit tomorrow just to prove a point."

Jo's benefit.

My heart sank. Even if we weren't together, even if she never talked to me again, I wanted that concert to be perfect for her.

"Fuck," I muttered.

Cash held his hands up. "Let's not get too ahead of ourselves. I'll keep trying him, but we have to get started. *Rolling Stone* is already in there waiting."

"They're going to ask where Dallas is." The muscles in my neck tightened. "What are we supposed to tell them?"

Cash scrubbed his hands down his face. "We tell them that he was a bit under the weather, and he's seeing a doctor to make sure he's ready for tomorrow."

Jax's jaw clenched, and he flashed me a panicked glance.

I massaged my temples, trying to ward off the headache that was setting in. "And what if he doesn't show up tomorrow?"

Cash sighed, his eyes creased with worry. "We'll cross that bridge when we get there."

THIRTY-FIVE

Jo

NOTHING WAS GOING ACCORDING to plan.

The network had arranged for the hair and makeup staff to come to my hotel room before the show, but the production team had told them the wrong location, causing them to arrive forty-five minutes late. Then, my first guest had to be changed at the last minute because the governor I was supposed to interview about the recent election fraud allegations in Arizona had a family emergency. That meant I spent the entire morning preparing for a back-up guest, the CEO of a social media platform that had recently suffered a huge security breach, resulting in millions of users' information being stolen. I'd dealt with all of this while trying to force down a few crackers to settle my nervous stomach.

The beauty team was packing up when there was a knock on my door. I excused myself to answer it, and found myself face to face with my father.

"There she is," he said with a smile, walking past me through the small entryway. "The woman of the hour. How are you feeling?"

My eyes widened. I'd hardly seen my dad since I'd arrived in New York two weeks ago. He's been busy every time I'd asked to get coffee or have dinner together, so I was more than a little surprised to see him at my door unannounced.

"Nervous," I finally answered, following behind him.

"Nonsense." He brushed me off.

The makeup artist and hairstylist rolled their kits to the door, and I thanked them as they left. My dad took a seat on the sofa in the living area.

"I heard the Robson interview is out." He relaxed into the cushion, crossing his right ankle over his left knee. "Convenient that he suddenly had to cancel."

I blinked slowly as I sat in the wingback chair opposite him. "Daddy, his wife had a heart attack, and it happened while she was getting ice cream with their kid last night. She's in the ICU."

He wasn't listening to me. "But talking to that Cliff guy will be a great jumping off point to show the viewers that you mean business. Don't take any bullshit. You're a Kingslsey. This is in your blood."

Is it? I massaged my temples. Everything felt wrong. No matter how hard I'd tried to force myself to adopt the take-no-prisoners Kingsley persona, it didn't feel right. I continued to tell myself that things would get better, but with every minute that passed, my doubts grew.

"By the end of the day, everyone's going to know who you are." He held up his hands as though he were framing my face. "Jo Kingsley: the only one you can count on to ask the hard questions."

I gave him a weak smile. "What about you?"

He waved me off. "Everyone already knows they can rely

on me, but I won't be around forever. One day, my legacy will be your torch to carry." His face softened. "And I know you're going to make me proud."

There it was—the carrot being dangled right in front of me. My father's belief in me was the only thing that could possibly make all of this pain worthwhile.

My throat tightened.

"Well, I won't keep you," he said, rising to his feet. "I'm sure you'd like a few moments to yourself."

I walked him to the door, and he turned to look at me. "You've done well, Jolene. I'll be there to cheer you on."

My chest ached. "Thanks, Dad."

"And Jo?"

"Yeah?"

He reached out his hand, and for a moment, I thought he might pull me into his arms. Instead, he placed his hand on my shoulder, giving it a gentle squeeze.

"Never forget who you are," he said. His eyes lingered on me for a moment, a wistful smile playing on his lips.

I nodded, unable to form words. Partly because I could count on one hand how many sweet, meaningful moments my father and I had shared, including this one. And partly because I could feel in my soul how far I'd strayed from the woman I'd been in Nashville. But that woman wasn't who he wanted me to remember.

He let himself out of the room, and I leaned against the door as the lock clicked into place. It was taking every ounce of strength I had to keep my body upright. Every nerve was flashing big, neon warning signs, telling me to head for the hills. The blood in my veins sloshed around like angry rapids, warning me to float away from this place.

I knew that once the cameras started to roll, things were

going to change. Once I put on that hard-nosed facade, that's who I'd have to be for the rest of my career. Maybe even the rest of my life. The very thought made my insides tense. Would this ever feel right, or was I doomed to feel like a lost soul inhabiting the wrong body?

I started back to my room to change out of my fluffy white robe and into my sharp black suit when a knock at the door stopped me in my tracks. I glanced around, wondering if one of the makeup artists had left something behind. For a fleeting second, I even wondered if it could be my dad. Maybe he could sense how off I was, how completely sad I felt. Maybe we'd finally have a real heart-to-heart for the first time in my life.

"Coming," I called, making my way to the door and flinging it open.

I blinked rapidly, unsure if what I was seeing was real. When the apparition didn't disappear, I finally spoke. "*Dallas*? What are you doing here?"

He gave me a sheepish grin. "Surprise?"

"I'll say. How did you even find me?"

"Sometimes being famous has its perks," he said with an awkward chuckle. "People are more willing to break the rules and give you information."

"So much for privacy," I muttered. "Anyway, why are you here?"

He shifted awkwardly on his feet. "You're a tough person to get a hold of."

I shrugged. "Or maybe I just didn't want to talk to you."

He nodded. "That too."

"Look, Dallas, we don't have to do this, alright?" I pushed my fingers through my hair. "You don't need to pretend to like me or make nice with me to save face with

Katie. You were right about everything you said, even though the way you said it *really* sucked. So, congratulations. You were right *and* you were a complete jerk about it. I'm sorry you wasted your time coming here for me to tell you that, but now you know. I'm on the air in an hour, and I still have to get dressed and get to the network, so if you'll excuse me." I started to shut the door, but he stopped me with his hand.

"Can we talk?" he asked, his eyes pleading with me. "I promise I won't take up much of your time."

I crossed my arms over my chest. "Look, I really—"

"Please?" he said softly. "Can I just have five minutes?"

I took a deep breath. "Fine. Five minutes." I stood to the side, waving him through the door to the sofa my dad had been seated on moments before.

"Okay, shoot," I said, taking a seat across from him.

Dallas leaned forward, his tattooed forearms resting on his knees. "I owe you an apology, and a big one at that."

I shook my head. "No, you don't. You were right."

"Let me finish. Please," he said gently. His gaze was warm when it settled on me, his eyes framed with faint purple circles. I knew those circles well because I had some of my own buried under a mountain of concealer. He looked tired and...sad.

I nodded. "Alright."

He studied me for a moment before he finally spoke. "I was wrong, Jo. What I said to you that day...You didn't deserve it. You didn't deserve any of it, and I wouldn't blame you if you hate me for what I did." He raked his teeth over his bottom lip. "Things with the band have been changing for a long time. It had nothing to do with you. I know that, and it's important that you know it too. I lashed out at you when all you're guilty of is making my cousin the happiest he's ever been."

My throat tightened at the mention of Derek.

"I didn't want to believe that everything I've ever loved and wanted, everything I've ever worked for, was coming to an end. It felt like my entire world was going up in flames, and there was nothing I could do to stop it. That band is everything to me." His eyes glistened. "I don't really know who I am without it—without *them*—and that scares the fuck out of me." He pinched the bridge of his nose. "Shit. I'm sorry. I shouldn't even be telling you this. I'm not trying to make excuses for what I did. I guess this is just the first time I've been able to put how I feel about it into words."

My chin dropped to my chest, and I felt a prickle behind my eyes. "The fire doesn't have to be a bad thing, Dallas."

"What do you mean?"

I sighed. "When I first came to Nashville, I felt a lot of what you're feeling now, and honestly, I was terrified. I felt lost, like without all of the things I used to have in my life, I wasn't me anymore. But when my world burned to the ground, it made room for a better version of myself, and I felt more like me than ever. I never would have found myself if all the brush and tired old mindsets hadn't been cleared out. In the moment it's scary and painful, but once the ashes settle, you start to rebuild and find out who you really are without all of the things you've let define you."

He ran his hands down his face. "What if I'm nothing without this band, Jo?" His voice was low: small and defeated. "What if, when you take all of that away, I'm *nothing*?"

I held his gaze. "Even if you take every bit of that away, you're not nothing, Dallas. But you're never going to figure out who you could be if you're not willing to let go of who you are now. And you have a lot of people who will stand by you and support you while you figure it out."

He shook his head. "I don't know. I don't know if they'll ever forgive me."

"They will," I said softly. "Tell them what you told me. And also, will you *please* tell Katie you're in love with her already? This is getting a little ridiculous."

Dallas turned to me with a slight smile, his cheeks tinged pink. "Please come back to Nashville with me."

My gaze fell to the floor, and I shook my head. "I can't do that."

"But everything you just said…" he trailed off. "You were happy until I went and fucked everything up. Derek needs you and Katie needs you…We *all* do. You're one of us now."

An invisible string tugged on my heart. It stretched all the way to Nashville, winding around Derek and Katie and the city I knew like the back of my hand.

"I made a commitment," I said. "I have to see this through."

"But you love Derek," he insisted. "I know you do."

"I do, very much so, but I have to stay." I dropped my gaze to my hands. "My dad got me this job, and all my life I've been trying to get him to…I don't know…*see* me. And he finally does. I can't throw that away now. I have a real shot here to have the kind of relationship I've always wanted with him. I could finally make him proud of me."

He nodded, considering what I said. "But are *you* proud of you?" There wasn't an ounce of sarcasm or snark encapsulated inside his words.

I swallowed the lump in my throat. "The jury's still out on that. I'll have to let you know."

He drew his brows together. "There's really nothing I can do to convince you to go back with me?"

I squeezed my eyes shut, holding the tears inside and shook my head. "No."

Dallas' shoulders were slumped and his forehead creased as he rubbed his thumb along his jaw. "Okay. Alright. I guess I'll go."

He rose to his feet, and I followed him to the door.

"I guess this is it then." He shoved his hands in his pockets. "I really am sorry, Jo."

I gave him a weak smile. "I know. And it's okay." I extended my hand to him. "We can even shake on it."

He looked at my hand for a moment before pushing it away and hugging me with the force of a linebacker.

"Oh, wow. Okay." I chuckled as he held on to me.

"I hope you know I mean no disrespect when I say that you deserve so much more than this." His voice was barely above a whisper.

My eyes burned. I didn't have to ask him what he meant because I already knew. More than a swanky hotel room for one. More than a job I wasn't excited about. More than trying to be someone else to make my dad love me.

I relaxed into his embrace. Then it was me clinging to him, the last thread connecting me to Nashville and the life I had there. I knew that once he was gone, so was any possibility of returning to the city, the people, and the version of myself that I loved.

He planted a kiss on top of my head. "Take care of yourself."

With one last look, he was gone.

THIRTY-SIX

Derek

WE'D DONE SO many interviews that by the end of the day I had no clue what outlet we were even talking to anymore. Cash and our security guard, Brady, ushered representatives from each publication in and out so quickly that it felt like our room had become a revolving door.

"Thanks for taking the time to speak with me today," a reporter wearing a Nashville Predators ball cap said, taking a seat in the armchair across from us. He could have been here at any point earlier in the day and come back, and I never would have been any the wiser.

"Yeah, of course." Jax was chipper, as though this were our first interview of the day, and we weren't all growing more nervous with every moment that Dallas didn't walk through the door.

The reporter introduced himself and told us which magazine he was from. I nodded at what I hoped were the appropriate moments, my eyes glazed over, a byproduct of sitting too long and being stressed out of my mind.

"So, first things first. Where's Dallas?" he asked, gesturing to the vacant spot beside me on the sofa.

"He's been under the weather," Cash answered from where he was propped on the arm of the couch. "The guys have had a pretty grueling rehearsal schedule preparing for tomorrow night, so he's getting treatment for dehydration right now. But he'll be back in fighting shape tomorrow."

"Ah, I'm sorry to hear that, but glad to know he'll be back in action, and this won't affect the show," the guy said.

We certainly hope it won't. I squirmed in my seat while the reporter asked the same questions every other journalist had asked.

How does it feel to know that in just twenty-four hours you'll be playing your final show together?

What caused the band to break up? Was there some sort of conflict?

How is the relationship between you all now?

Where are you all going from here?

Out of my mind, I wanted to answer. Because it felt like that was the only place I was going. Each question was like a hand gripping my insides and wringing them out.

Jax, Luca, and Cash looked at me stone-faced as the reporter turned his attention to me.

"I'm sorry," he said. "What was that?"

Shit. Had I actually said that out loud?

I cleared my throat and pasted on a smile. "We'll see in time."

He nodded, keeping his eyes on me. "By the way, Derek, I came to your art show a few weeks ago. You're a really talented photographer."

I shifted uncomfortably, sinking deeper into the cushion. "Thank you."

The reporter folded his hands in his lap. "Do you think you'll pursue a career in photography now that you're wrapping things up with the band?"

"Maybe," I answered. "I'm keeping my options open."

It was hard to imagine any future without Jo in it. When she left, the color had been drained from my life, along with all hope and possibility. I loved photography, but it was Jo who'd helped me realize it could be something so much more than a hobby. With her by my side, I felt like I could do anything.

The interviewer nodded before shifting gears. "So, how did you guys get connected with Project NENA?"

Jax passed me an almost imperceptible glance. "A good friend of ours started doing some volunteer work with them. She saw a need, and we were more than happy to help however we could."

Jax was telling the reporter more about Project NENA and their mission when Cash's phone pinged. He glanced down at it immediately, furrowing his brow as he quickly tapped his thumbs across the screen. He frowned before tucking the phone in his pocket and clasping his hands together. "Sorry, Jonah. That's our time. I've got to get these fellas out of here."

Jonah nodded and extended his hand to shake each of ours before Brady escorted him from the room.

Cash turned to us as soon as the door closed. "I heard from Dallas."

"What did he say? Where is he?" Jax asked all the questions that were rattling around my brain.

Cash shook his head. "He didn't say. All he said was he had to take care of a few things and that he'd be back soon."

Where the hell could he be? My mind immediately went

to my parents. But I didn't think he'd go speak to my mom and dad without my permission. Even though we hadn't talked much about it, I felt in my gut that he'd respect that unspoken boundary.

Luca snorted. "Soon? What the fuck does that mean? Soon could be today, tomorrow, a fucking week from now."

"I asked if he'd be back in time for the show." Cash crossed his arms over his chest.

"And?" I asked.

"He said yes." Cash shrugged.

"*And?*" Luca prodded.

"That's it," Cash said. "That's all he said."

"Well, that's just great." Jax pressed the heel of his hand to his forehead. "So we don't know if he'll be here tomorrow morning or five minutes before showtime."

"And he didn't say what it was he had to take care of?" I asked.

Cash shook his head.

Luca stretched back in his seat with his hands behind his head. "I think we have to consider the possibility that Dallas is fucking with us. He's pissed that the band is done and bailing on us might be his way of exacting some sort of revenge."

"No. No way." Jax leaned forward with his elbows on his knees. "He wouldn't do that to us no matter how mad he is."

"You sure about that?" Luca asked.

My stomach churned. "He may be pissed, but this band is his life. He'll be here."

"I agree," Cash spoke up, though his face looked less than confident. "There's no way he would do that to the fans."

I raked my hands over my face.

"He's gonna be here." Jax placed a hand on my shoulder

and squeezed. "No matter how upset he is, he wouldn't let us down like that."

"I can't help but feel that this is my fault. I came down on him hard." I sighed. "Maybe I should have just apologized."

Luca scoffed. "Oh, fuck that. You can't behave the way Dallas did and not expect some fucking consequences. He was a dick, and he's still being a dick." He rolled his eyes. "Shocker."

"Look, Luca, no matter how you feel about Dallas right now, he's still our brother," Jax said evenly. "He's not perfect, but neither are we. We've all had our moments over the years. But what makes us family is that we stick by each other anyway."

Luca blew out a breath and shrugged.

Jax turned back to me. "Dallas *will* be here. Because that's what family does. We show up for each other."

I leaned my head against the back of the sofa. "I hope you're right."

THIRTY-SEVEN

Jo
___

I was clasping my pearl necklace when the front desk called to let me know Lewis had arrived to pick me up just moments after Dallas left.

"Thank you," I said, before hanging up the phone. I took a deep breath, grabbed my bag, and headed for the elevator. As the floors counted down, I felt like I was descending into a pit of darkness. When the doors opened, the late afternoon sun filtered in from the floor to ceiling lobby windows, but even that wasn't enough to light me up inside.

"Big day today." Lewis greeted me with a smile as he opened the back door of the SUV.

I forced a smile. "Big day."

Once I was tucked inside, Lewis strolled around to the driver's side, got in, and fastened his seatbelt. "How are you feeling? Excited?"

I gave him a half-hearted nod. "Yeah…and scared."

"It's okay to be afraid, Jo." He eased the car away from the curb. "Growth is rarely comfortable. That's what I've always told my daughters."

"Lewis, can I ask you something?" I leaned my head against the window, watching as the sidewalks bustling with people passed me by.

"Of course."

"What would you do if one of your daughters didn't want the life you wanted for her?" I asked. "Maybe at one time she thought it was what she wanted, but now she's found something much bigger and more meaningful, even though you think it's smaller. What would you do?"

"Hmm." He drummed his fingertips lightly against the wheel. "It's hard for me to answer that, at least in the way you're asking. You see, Jo, there's no life path my daughters could take that's too small for me. Anything they want, anything that brings them happiness…Well, those are the *biggest* things in the world to me. They're everything. My oldest, Lydia, is the vice president of a fancy tech company, and she loves to travel. Then there's Maggie. She lives in Jersey with her wife Annalise, and she's a competitive ballroom dancer." He chuckled. "Remind me to show you some videos. She sure didn't get her grace from me. And my youngest, Chelsea, is a stay at home mom to my two beautiful, perfect grandchildren. She loves hosting game nights with her husband and reading and she's never stepped foot on an airplane in her life. But do you know what they all have in common?"

My chest squeezed. "They're happy."

"Exactly." He nodded. "Each of their paths are different, but they're all just as meaningful." His eyes locked with mine in the rearview mirror. "Listen, Jo, let me tell you something about parents. We don't always get it right. Now, some of us are humble and wise enough to admit it, but some aren't. That's where you have to trust in yourself. Whatever it is that brings you joy, you have to run after it. You chase it until the soles of your shoes wear out. The years are too short to live anyone else's life but yours."

I swallowed hard and blinked away the tears that had glossed over my eyes. "Thanks, Lewis."

As we drove through Times Square, I heard Lewis gasp. "Well, will you look at that."

I glanced up in the direction he was pointing to see my own face staring back at me on a billboard. "Cheese and rice," I muttered. The larger than life version of Jo was dressed in a sharp black suit, identical to the one I was wearing now. It was a photo from the press shoot I'd done on my second day in New York. My hair was ironed stick-straight, and my painted red lips were sculpted into a hard line. My arms were crossed over my chest in a serious *I-mean-business* stance.

I didn't look like me. So much so that it was almost laughable. I looked like myself in a hard-hitting journalist Halloween costume. Like that time when I was a little girl and I dressed up as Katie Couric for my project on who I wanted to be when I grew up.

"I had no idea my face was going to be on a billboard." I pushed my hands through my hair.

"Must be a sign," Lewis said.

"Of what?" I asked as we zipped past the monstrosity.

His eyes connected with mine again. "You tell me."

My heart was slamming against my chest like some sort of erratic pigeon trapped in a box, but my limbs were frozen, stuck somewhere between fight and flight.

"We're here." Lewis's voice broke through my thoughts. "Do you need me to take another lap around the block?"

It was the moment of truth. Part of me wanted to ask

Lewis to start driving, to take me anywhere but here. But I knew running wasn't the answer. I had to face this.

"No," I told him. "I think I'm ready."

"WHAT'S WITH YOUR FACE?" MARLA WRINKLED HER NOSE AS she approached me, notepad in hand, mere moments before we went live.

Being around that woman was enough to give anyone a complex.

My shoulders tensed. "What do you mean?"

I was standing off to the side near one of the cameras, staring at the oversized desk that awaited me. A dream I'd had thousands of times was happening right that very second, and it looked exactly like I'd always imagined it would. The set was perfectly lit, the CNN logo emblazoned on the shimmering granite floor. *Hard Questions with Jo Kingsley* lit up the screen behind the desk. It was everything I could have hoped for, but it all felt wrong. So completely wrong.

"You look like a possum that ran out in the middle of oncoming traffic," she said, her voice flat.

I rubbed my forehead. "I think you mean a deer in headlights."

"I said what I said." She pursed her lips as a sound tech approached, clipped a mic to my lapel, and handed me my earpiece, which I quickly put in. "Anyway, do you have any questions about the changes I sent over?"

I swallowed hard and shook my head. "No."

"Five minute warning," a stagehand called, and the commotion picked up as everyone scrambled to their places.

"Makeup!" Marla shouted before setting her sights back

on me. She propped one hand on her hip and gestured at the desk with the other. "Well, what are you waiting for? I hope you don't expect me to hold your hand."

"Of course not," I bit back. It'd be like holding hands with a shark and would probably yield the same grisly results.

I took a deep breath and stepped onto the stage, my heels clicking across the floor. The makeup team swarmed me as I sat behind the desk, fluffing my hair and touching up my face.

"More powder," Marla barked at the young woman who was sweeping a brush over my cheeks. "I can practically see my reflection on the girl's forehead."

The makeup artist's jaw clenched as she applied more powder to my skin, and I silently prayed she wouldn't let me go on live television looking like an over-floured biscuit.

"We're on in two," a voice called. "Everyone clear the set."

The makeup squad scurried away as Marla folded her arms over her chest and appraised me. "Alright then. That will have to do. Production has Cliff on standby via Zoom," she said before striding off set into the control room.

My fingers tingled as I smoothed them over the notes atop the glass desk, and there was a loud buzzing in my ears above the voices of the producers. I slipped my earpiece out for a couple of seconds in an attempt to escape the noise, but it was still there.

This is wrong. All wrong.

I glanced to the side and saw my dad standing next to Mr. Kirkpatrick. He smiled and nodded, which did nothing for the panic that snaked through my bones.

I'm not supposed to be here.

"Thirty seconds," a voice called, and the buzzing got

louder, almost like I had bumblebees lodged in my ears. The hairs on the back of my neck stood on end.

No, no, no. I'm not supposed to be here. I can't do this.

My foot bounced like it was winding me up for take off, my limbs that had previously felt frozen deciding that now was the time to fly.

I can't do this. I'm not supposed to be here. I can't do this. I'm not supposed to be here.

My heartbeat had reached hummingbird-wing speed.

"Ten seconds!"

What am I going to do?

"Nine."

I'm not supposed to be here.

"Eight."

I can't do this.

"Seven."

I have to get out of here.

"Six."

No no no no no.

Marla's voice counted down the remaining seconds in my ear. "Five."

My heart pounded as though it were trying to break free.

"Four."

I shut my eyes and prayed that when I opened them I'd be back in Nashville in Derek's bed telling him about a crazy dream I'd had.

"Three."

Try as I might, there was no waking up from this nightmare.

I have to get out of here.

"Two."

I want to go home.

"One."

The world's longest ten seconds passed, and there I was, my eyes wide, my lips frozen into what I was sure was a deranged smile. Out of the corner of my eye, I saw the faces of Mr. Kirkpatrick, my dad, and people whose names I couldn't remember crumple in horror.

"Are you insane?" Marla's voice barked in my earpiece. "Say something!"

I steeled myself and tried to focus all of my energy on the teleprompter. "Good evening. You're watching *Hard Questions with Jo Kingsley*. You might recognize my last name because it's the one I share with my father, Daniel Kingsley." I cleared my throat before continuing. "For as long as I can remember, I've watched alongside many of you as my father delivered our nation's biggest news stories. I've listened in awe as he interviewed world leaders and change-makers, asking the hard questions—the kind that can transform our lives and the way we view the world. These are the kinds of questions that help hold us accountable as a society and prevent history from repeating itself. *If,* of course, we can be wise enough to admit where we have fallen short. If we can be brave enough to be vulnerable. Today, I…"

Tears blurred my vision, and I dropped my gaze to the notes on my desk.

"Today, I begin by answering your first question," Marla snapped in my ear. "Pull it together, Kingsley!"

"Sorry." I dabbed beneath my eyes as I looked back up at the camera. "Today, I begin by answering your first question. Why should you trust me?"

My words lodged in my throat as the teleprompter continued to scroll. This was the part where I was supposed to say that, like my father, I had confidence and moxie, and I wouldn't stop until I got the answers that viewers deserved. That I would never stop seeking the truth.

"Earth to Jo!" Marla cried in my ear.

"Why should you trust me?" I repeated the question and took a deep breath. "The answer is that you shouldn't because God knows for the last two weeks I haven't trusted myself." I heard Marla's sharp gasp and removed my earpiece. "And I guess if I'm being honest, I've spent the better part of my life not really trusting myself. For so long, I wanted to be just like my dad, but I never stopped to ask myself why."

I glanced over at my father who was staring at me with wide eyes, his hand clasped over his mouth. Mr. Kirkpatrick held his hand up to gesture for someone to cut the feed, but my dad stopped him.

"My father is the best this business will ever see." I tore my gaze from my dad and focused it back on the camera. "He's devoted his life to you at home, to making sure he brings the news right into your living room every night. He's spent countless holidays with the troops, and his feet are always the first to hit the ground when our forests are on fire or when there's a threat to our country's safety. My father has been there to have the hard conversations with presidents and senators and activists and real people who have suffered real losses just like you. He's had the career of a lifetime."

"But...But at what cost?" I blinked back tears as I pictured every Thanksgiving dinner my mom and I shared with an empty seat, the school talent shows and birthday parties he'd had to miss. "That wasn't something I ever really thought about...what I'd have to give up in order to have a prolific career like his. It never occurred to me because I was building my entire world around the hope that if I could do this *thing*, if I could be this *person*, I would somehow matter more. But in reality, I never mattered less."

I let out a soft, wistful laugh. "Not that long ago, I was climbing my way up the broadcasting ladder, and you know what I was? Miserable. I barely had a life outside of the news van, and I let my ambition turn me into someone I didn't even recognize. It made me competitive and cynical and hard. But none of that is who I really am."

My eyes fell for a moment as I remembered how good it felt to laugh with Katie on the couch in Granny's old house, to feel Derek's warmth and the wind in my hair when we were riding on his bike. I remembered Lindsey and all of the kids at Project NENA and the beautiful stories I'd gotten to tell and be a part of that filled my soul. But more than that, I remembered what it felt like to be loved, to be wanted, and to be free.

"A few months ago, I lost everything. My job, my crappy apartment, and my even crappier boyfriend." Tears spilled down my cheeks. "I went home to Nashville to regroup and get my life back on track, but what happened was so much... bigger. Once I stripped away all of the things I'd used to define myself I got to see what I was really made of. No, I wasn't changing the world, and I didn't have legions of people who knew my name. But those who did mattered to me, and I mattered to them. They were my whole world, and I walked away to do this." I pointed to the screen behind me with my name on it. "To be someone I'm not."

I found my dad's eyes once again, only this time I didn't look away. "I'm sorry I can't be who you wanted me to be. The life I want may not be important enough or good enough for you, but it is *everything* to me. "

I rose from the desk, forcing myself to keep my head held

high. The click of my heels punctuated the silence as I walked off the set. I kept my eyes forward, avoiding the penetrating stares from everyone around me. The only pair of eyes I tried to find were my father's, but I only saw the back of his suit as he followed Mr. Kirkpatrick into the control room. When I finally pushed through the door that led out to the hallway, I blew out a sharp breath, and with it came the release of a hundred pound weight off my chest.

"What the fuck was that?" Marla's voice stopped me in my tracks.

I smoothed my palms down my pants to wipe away the sheen of sweat that had formed on my skin before I turned to face her.

"Look, Marla, I know you don't like me very much and for good reason. I've made a mess of everything, and I'm sorry," I said. "I know you expected more of Daniel Kingsley's daughter. That I would grab 'em by the throat or whatever. But that's not me, and I'm sorry it took me this long to say that out loud. You told me to take control, and that's exactly what I'm doing. Except what I'm taking control of isn't on the other side of a TV screen. It's my life. Or whatever's left of it."

I turned on my heel and started back down the hall when Marla called after me. "Hey, Jo?"

"Yeah?" I asked, facing her.

"Give 'em hell."

The beginnings of a question formed on my lips. "But…"

A hint of a smile played on her mouth. "I said what I said."

"For what it's worth, I'm proud of you, Jo," Lewis said as he pulled to a stop in front of my hotel. I'd just finished telling him about the spectacle I'd made of myself on live television.

"It's worth a lot." My eyes glistened as I reached across the center console to grab his hand. "I'm sad I won't get to see you anymore."

"I know," he said. "Me too. But I'll always be rooting for you. And I believe that one of these days our paths will cross again."

"I hope so." I smiled.

"So, what's next for Jo Kingsley?"

"Next, I go home to Nashville and try to piece my life back together." My heart ached as I wondered how much of the life I loved would be waiting for me, but it didn't matter. I still had to try. "I already got an email on my phone from the HR department telling me I have to check out of the hotel immediately. And speaking of HR..." I held up my company-issued phone. "Do you mind getting this to Marla? I guess I won't be needing it anymore."

He nodded. "You did good, Jo. Big things are coming down the pike for you. I can feel it."

"I hope you're right," I said, reaching for the door handle.

"Not so fast there, missy." He quickly unfastened his seat-belt, got out of the SUV, and walked around to the passenger side. With a chivalrous bow, he opened the door.

I laughed as I climbed out, and he opened his arms for a hug that I gratefully received.

"You're going to come out on the other side of this better than ever, Jo. You'll see."

"Thank you, Lewis. For everything." I pulled back so I

could look him in the eyes. "Well, I guess I better get in there and pack before they start throwing my stuff out in the hall."

"Take care, Jo," he said as I headed inside.

The televisions in the lobby were programmed to another news channel, and I could see a picture of my face on the screen with a talking head in front of it as I walked by. I couldn't read the headline, and I didn't want to. I was sure it said something to the effect of *News Anchor Has Breakdown on Camera*. The thought stung a little, though I knew the world would forget who I was when the next news story came around. But *I* wouldn't.

I stepped into the elevator, alone with only my reflection once the doors closed. For the first time since I'd been in New York, I finally recognized the woman staring back at me, and I made a silent vow to myself that I'd never forget her again.

The elevator stopped on my floor and as I started down the hall, I noticed a figure sitting on the ground near my room with their head bowed down. As I got closer, I realized that it *was* my room, and I knew exactly who it was.

"Dallas?" I said as I approached. "What are you still doing here?"

He smiled up at me. "I was waiting for you."

"Well, that much is clear," I said with a laugh. "But why? I thought you left."

He rose to his feet and leaned against the wall. "I guess I hoped you'd change your mind. And according to what I saw on TV, it sounds like you did."

I sighed as I moved to stand beside him. "You saw that, huh?"

"I did. And I thought it was pretty fucking incredible." He looked over at me. "I was actually thinking that I wish I could be more like you."

I snorted. "What? Completely crazy?"

"Brave." His voice was low. "What you did...You put yourself out there, Jo. You showed the whole world your heart. It takes a lot of fucking courage to be that vulnerable, and it made me realize how much of my life I've been living scared. Afraid to change or take any risks."

"That's the thing about risks, though," I said. "There are no guarantees. I don't know if Derek will even speak to me again. I just know I have to try."

"He will." Dallas looked me in the eyes. "Derek loves you. I know that because..." He trailed off, his gaze falling to his feet. "Well, I just know."

A smile tugged at the corner of my mouth. Maybe Dallas would finally tell Katie how he felt about her after all.

"I have to get my stuff packed and get out of here before they kick me out," I said. "I might drive a little tonight and then I'll get a hotel somewhere. When's your flight back?"

Dallas rolled his eyes as I fished my room key out of my purse. "I'm not flying home and leaving you to drive. I'll help you pack, and then what do you say we grab some dinner and hit the road? I can drive while you rest."

I pursed my lips as I considered his offer.

"It's the least I can do after how awful I was to you," he insisted.

"That's true." I smirked. "You were kind of a butthead."

A smile creased his eyes. "So, what do you say? Will you take a road trip home to Nashville with me...even if I *am* a butthead?"

A seed of hope bloomed in my chest. "I'd love to."

I woke with a jolt as Dallas drove my Ford Focus over a bump on the interstate. I didn't know exactly what time it was, but I could see that the sun was beginning to edge the darkness out of the sky.

"Good morning, sunshine," Dallas' chipper voice greeted me.

I groaned as my stomach lurched like it was being shot around a pinball machine. "Oh no. Not again."

After Dallas and I had dinner the night before, I'd settled in the passenger seat of my car and let him take the wheel. We talked for a while, mostly about how excited I was to see Derek, before the roll of tires over asphalt lulled me into a deep sleep. I'd thought that with New York in the rearview and Nashville on the horizon, the nausea I'd been experiencing over the last couple of weeks would finally subside.

"Again? Huh? Are you alright?"

"I don't feel so good," I murmured, clutching my midsection. "Can you pull over?"

"Can you wait for me to get to a rest stop?" he asked. "I think we're coming up on one in a mile or so."

I quickly shook my head, the bile already rising in my throat.

"Okay, okay," he said, turning on the blinker and slowing to a stop once he'd gotten a safe distance off the road.

I ripped my seatbelt off, flung the passenger door open, and managed to sprint six feet away from the car before I hunched over. The ground crunched beneath Dallas' shoes as he ran to my side.

"Whoa, are you okay?" he asked, gathering my hair in his hands.

My answer came in the form of a croak as my vomit splashed at our feet.

I moaned. "You can go back to the car. I might be a minute."

He didn't move, continuing to hold my hair. "Were you having a dream about being sick or something?"

"What?"

"Before we pulled over," he continued. "You said, 'oh no, not again.' But you weren't sick before. You were sleeping."

"Oh." I sniffled. "Yeah, I've had this weird nausea thing happening the last couple of weeks. Probably from all the stress of coming to New York."

"But you seemed okay yesterday afternoon and last night."

More vomit. "It's usually just the first part of the day, and then it mostly goes away," I choked out.

He paused for a moment. "Um…Jo…" he said finally. "That's…uh…That's kind of weird, isn't it?"

His words and the sounds of the cars on the interstate whirled around my already jumbled-up insides.

"What do you—" I cut myself off as I raised up with a sharp gasp and frantically began doing the math in my head. *No. I couldn't be. When was my last period? It was before New York. Before Derek and I had gotten that awful stomach flu.* "Ohhhh my God."

My brain searched for the memory of the last time Derek and I had sex. It had been the night before Dallas showed up at Katie's house, before my dad came, and I uprooted my entire life. Derek and I had barely gotten over being sick.

I'd taken my pills religiously, like I always had. There was no doubt in my mind. But had they stayed in my system when I'd emptied the contents of my stomach over and over and over again? My skin was clammy, and I wobbled on my feet.

Dallas steadied me by the shoulders and spoke softly.

"Look, I'm not trying to get all up in your business or anything. But, uh, is it possible...Do you think you could be…"

An icy chill trickled down my spine.

Dallas' eyes held mine. "Do you think you could be pregnant?"

I answered by puking on his shoes.

THIRTY-EIGHT

Derek

_____

IT WAS JUST after ten a.m. the day of the benefit show. I'd been up since before sunrise, unable to sleep, armies of emotions at war inside me. Izzy and I had gone for our morning walk while the city was still asleep, but my thoughts more than made up for the absence of sound.

The closer I got to our final show, the sadder I became. Not because the band was breaking up. I was ready for that. But what I wasn't ready for were the changes that were guaranteed to come with it. For as much as the band had held me back from doing other things, it had also held me together. Through all of my silent struggles, the guys had been my safe place, my lifelines. And as much as I wanted to pretend that didn't have to change, I knew it would. And it needed to.

If the last few months had taught me anything, it was that living uncomfortably in my truth was far better than living a happy lie. I was overcome with the kind of fear, excitement, and wonder that came with having a book full of blank pages yet to be written rather than a plot with a safe, happy ending that had already been laid out for me. But knowing that Jo wouldn't be a part of what was to come dampened that feeling. It seemed so incredibly wrong that her name would only be in a few chapters when she'd helped change the entire book.

Izzy stretched in her spot beside me on the couch, resting her head on my leg. I still had several hours to go before I had to get to the venue, so I ordered a coffee and some food from the place on the corner. I was waiting for it to be delivered when my phone rang from its spot on the coffee table. I reached for it, an unfamiliar number with a Kentucky area code flashing across the screen. I hovered my finger over the decline button, but something stopped me from hitting it.

I swiped my finger across the screen. "Hello?"

"Derek." My mother's voice said my name from the other end.

"Mom?" I asked. "Where are you calling from? What's going on? Is it dad?"

"No, your dad is still with us," she answered. "But I…I'm calling from a motel."

"Oh." I blew out a breath. There it was. She was calling to ask for more money.

"It's not what you think," she said quietly. "I promise. Derek, I know I've lost the right to ask you for anything, but I'm asking you to hear me out. Can you do that for me?"

Even through the phone, I could hear the pain in her voice, and it made my chest ache.

"Okay," I said, my voice laced with trepidation.

"I've done a lot of thinking about what you said the last time I saw you, and…God, Derek, I've made a lot of bad decisions. Ones I would give my life to go back and change."

Her voice broke. "I left your father. Not alone. I'm still helping to take care of him, but I've left him in all the ways that matter. And I know how that must look…to leave a man on his deathbed, but I couldn't let him have that one last thing. I had to be the one to make that choice, if only to know that I was strong enough to make it."

I covered my mouth with my hand as I continued to listen.

"I just…I wanted you to know that I heard you," she said. "And I'm sorry it took me so long. But I'm in therapy now. I know I have a long road ahead, but I'm committed to getting better. To *being* better. And I wanted to know if there was a chance that maybe we could start over. I'm not asking for money or anything like that. It's my responsibility to fix what I've broken. All I'm asking from you is a chance—a chance for us to try again."

Tears stung my eyes, and I cleared my throat. "Mom…" A flood of emotions rushed over me. Streams of relief, hurt, and sadness all collided in a river of hope. "Look, I'm sorry. I wasn't really expecting this. I've done a lot of work to come to a place of peace with all of this, with not having you in my life anymore." I paused for a moment, taking in a shaky breath.

"It…It's okay." Her voice cracked. "I understand. You don't need to apologize."

"I wasn't finished," I continued. "I was going to say that I've got a lot going on at the moment, so things are a little crazy right now. But I'd really like to work through this with you."

She choked on a sob. "I'd really like that."

"But there are a couple of conditions." I knew that for us to stand a chance at having any semblance of a relationship, there would need to be some boundaries in place. It wasn't something that could happen overnight.

"Anything. I'll do anything, Derek."

"You have to stay in therapy," I said. "And I think we should go to counseling together to work through some of our issues. If you're willing to do that, then I'm willing to try."

"Yes," she cried. "Of course I am. I love you, sweetheart."

My heart swelled, but a knock at the door interrupted my thoughts.

"I love you too, Mom," I said. "Listen, I've got to go, but I'll call you soon. I promise."

We said goodbye and I exhaled, scrubbing a hand down my face as I headed toward the foyer. I grabbed my wallet from my back pocket and pulled out some cash before opening the door.

"Hey." I recognized the young blonde girl who greeted me with a takeaway coffee cup and a small brown paper bag as someone who delivered in my building regularly. "The doorman told me I could come on up. Order for Knights, right?"

"Yep." I nodded as she handed me my order, and I slipped her two twenties. "Thanks."

"You're welcome. Have a good day." She smiled and waved before starting off down the hall. I closed the door and padded to the kitchen, placing the bag of food on the counter. There was no way I could even think about eating it now. My nerves were too shot. I started back the couch, my mind reeling, still trying to process the conversation I'd had with my mom, but before I could sit down, there was another knock at the door.

I wondered if there'd been a mistake with my delivery order. At that point, I didn't even care since I'd lost my appetite anyway. I strode back over to the door and flung it open, expecting to see the girl from the cafe. But it wasn't her that was standing there.

My heart slammed against the walls of my chest. "Jo... Dallas? How...What are you doing here?"

"Something I should have done a long time ago," Dallas answered, pulling me into a hug. "I'm sorry I was so selfish. I was wrong, but I hope it's not too late for me to do the right thing." He clapped me on the back. "Now, I'm going to get out of here because I think you two have some things to talk about."

I nodded, standing there stunned as Dallas embraced Jo and gave her a brotherly kiss on top of the head. "Everything is going to be alright. I promise." He squeezed her shoulder before disappearing down the hall.

"I can't believe you're here." I was almost afraid to blink, afraid that if I did, the beautiful apparition in front of me would disappear, and that this was all a dream. "I mean, *how* are you even here? I thought you started your job in New York."

Her eyes were brimmed with emotion. "Can I come in?"

"Of course." I led her inside and over to the sofa where Izzy was waiting, her tail thumping against the cushions.

"Hey, Izzy girl," Jo cried as she sat, burying her face into Izzy's fur. "I missed you so much."

Izzy whined and licked away the tears that spilled down Jo's cheeks.

"She missed you too," I said softly, sitting beside her. "We both did."

She turned her body toward me. "Derek, I'm so sorry. Walking away from you was the biggest mistake of my life."

I took her face in my hands, wiping away the dampness on her cheeks with my thumbs. "It's okay, Jo. I—"

She shook her head and covered my hands with hers, pulling them onto her lap. "Please, I need to say this."

I nodded. "Okay."

"Regardless of what Dallas said, I never should have doubted you," she began. "I let him get inside my head. But I need you to know it really wasn't ever you I doubted. It was *me*. I'd spent so long living a life that wasn't really mine, a life I'd convinced myself I wanted, that somewhere along the way, I stopped trusting in myself and what I felt, what *I* wanted. I knew that I was happy and that we loved each other, but what Dallas said made me question if all of that could actually be *real.* That maybe I didn't know what was best for my own life, which meant I also didn't know what was best for *us.*" Her gaze fell to our intertwined hands. "Then my dad showed up with the CNN job, which only made me doubt myself more. And I didn't want that to be the thing that came between you and your family. So when my dad made me an offer that would take me out of the equation and maybe even make him proud of me, I took it."

"I just wish you would have talked to me." I tilted her chin to bring her eyes up to mine. "I wish you would have told me what Dallas said."

"I felt like I'd caused enough damage, and I didn't want to make it worse. I tried to convince myself that taking that job was the right thing to do even though every fiber of my being told me otherwise. Dallas came to see me to try to bring me home, but I still didn't believe I couldn't trust myself…even though I knew he was right, and all I wanted was to come home to you. It wasn't until I was there on set that I realized I was about to make the second biggest mistake of my life. So I quit. Right there on live television."

My eyes widened. "You *quit*?"

She gave me a sheepish nod. "I guess you haven't seen the news."

"I haven't," I admitted. "I…I couldn't."

She sighed. "Well, that's a story for another day. But it ends with me knowing at that moment that even if you couldn't forgive me for what I did, I still had to try."

"Of course I forgive you." I pulled her closer, resting my forehead against hers. "But you didn't have to quit the job for me to forgive you. I would have supported you no matter what."

"I know," she said softly. "But I didn't want that job or the life that came with it. I want *you*. You showed me a kind of life and love I never knew were possible."

I let her words wash over me. Jo was here. She was back and saying everything I could have hoped for.

"I'm not going anywhere, Jo," I promised. "Not now, not ever."

"But there's something else." Her voice cracked, and she drew in a shallow breath. "There's something I found out this morning that might…change things."

"Listen to me." I pulled back so I could look her in the eyes. "*Nothing* is going to change how I feel about you. I want to be with you. You're all I want."

"I think I might be pregnant," she choked out.

The floor fell out from beneath us, and the room started to spin. "What?" I couldn't possibly have heard her correctly.

"And I know you don't want kids," she cried. "I know that was never part of your plan, and I don't want you to stay with me if that isn't what you—"

My mind was whirling out of control. *"Pregnant?"*

She nodded. "I don't know for sure. I bought a test. It's in my purse in the car, but I haven't taken it yet. I'm too scared. I didn't think a kid was ever in the cards for me, but now that it could be, I think…I *want* to do this. But now I'm scared that if I am, it means I'll lose you."

Tears pooled in my eyes. *I might be a dad?* The thought made my entire body hum with nervous energy, but mixed in with that feeling was something else. Something that felt a lot like joy.

I kissed her forehead. "No matter what that test says, we're in this together."

"But I thought—"

"I thought I didn't want kids because there's a part of me that's always been worried that if I had a kid I'd end up messing them up the way my dad did me. That somehow it was contagious, and I'd ruin that child's life." I took her hands in mine. "But I won't because I'm not my father. The cycle stops right here, Jo. It ends with you and me. We would give our baby the best life. *We* would have the best life as long as we're together."

"Really? You still want to be with me?"

I gently pressed my lips to hers. "I want to be with you whether we have zero kids or a hundred. There's no life I want to live that doesn't have you in it."

She flung her arms around me. "I love you, Derek. I'm sorry I was so stupid."

"I love you too. So much," I said in her ear. "And you weren't stupid. You were scared."

I held her in my arms, and Izzy nosed her way onto our laps, determined to be a part of the moment. Jo giggled and pulled back enough to let the pup wedge herself between us where she showered us with kisses.

I laughed as I dodged an Izzy lick right in the ear. "We're just glad you're here."

"Sorry I'm so late," she said with tears in her eyes. "I guess I took the long way home."

I placed my hand on her cheek. "What do you say we find out if Izzy's going to be a big sister?"

THIRTY-NINE

Jo

"I'M SO FREAKING proud of you, Jo, and I just want you to understand the amount of willpower it took not to call Derek and tell him everything after I saw you walk off that set." Katie chuckled and hugged me where we stood backstage at the benefit. "But I knew you'd find your way back home so you could tell him yourself. And Dallas is lucky you did because I was ready to kick his ass."

I grinned. "Oh, I think he knows, but don't hold it against him, okay? We had a long talk, and things are good now. I think Dallas and I understand each other in a lot of ways, actually. We even drove from New York to Nashville together and didn't kill each other, so that's got to count for something, right?"

The band was moments away from taking the stage for the last time to a sold-out crowd at Bridgestone Arena for the Project NENA benefit show, and the energy was electric. One of the other acts, Sam Corbyn, was playing, and the audience was singing along.

"I'm just glad you're back," she said, her eyes traveling

over to where Dallas stood talking to Derek nearby. "It feels like the universe is righting itself."

I followed her gaze and saw the exact moment Derek told Dallas our news. He pulled Derek into a bear hug, and my heart exploded into a cloud of confetti.

Dallas bounded over to us, nearly knocking me over as he threw his arms around me. "It's a good day, Jo." He kissed me hard on the cheek, and I could see he had tears in his eyes.

I laughed as he hugged my best friend, lifting her off the ground for a moment before placing her back on her feet. Derek caught my eye and gave me a knowing smile.

"A damn good day." Dallas squeezed my shoulder before sauntering back over to Derek where Jax and Luca had joined him.

Katie giggled. "What on earth was that about?"

My stomach fluttered. Derek and I had agreed that Katie and Dallas were the only people we'd share our news with for now.

I shifted on my feet. "Actually, there's something I need to tell you."

Katie's gaze shifted to a space somewhere behind me. "Well, it might have to wait."

"What? Why?"

Her eyes grew wide. "Because your dad's here."

"What?" I turned around, and sure enough, there he was, standing amidst the throng of people that had gathered back-stage. Our eyes met, and he raised his hand in a small wave.

"Go," Katie said, giving me a gentle shove in his direc-tion. "I'll catch up with you later."

I wove through the crowd to get to him. "Dad?" I shook my head with confusion as I approached. "What are you doing here?"

"I tried to catch you before you left New York, but you were already gone," he answered. "I wanted to talk to you."

"You came after me?" I asked, my brain still trying to catch up with reality. "I mean, you could have just called."

He shook his head. "Not for this. This needed to be said in person."

Here it comes. I held my breath, bracing myself for a fight, for him to demand that I return to New York, to call me out in front of God and everyone in the arena for making a mockery of him.

His green eyes—the ones that matched my own—turned glassy. "I'm so sorry, Jolene. I'm sorry that I ever made you feel anything less than the spectacular young woman that you are."

My mouth fell open. "What?"

"I realize now that I haven't really listened to you in a long time. But I did yesterday. I heard you when you said you were sorry you couldn't be who I wanted you to be, that you weren't enough for me. I heard you when you were naming off my accomplishments, but didn't think that it was you that was the greatest of them all." His eyes fell. "Though, I don't really know how much I had to do with it. I wasn't exactly father of the year."

I blinked slowly, unable to believe what I was hearing. "Daddy…"

He looked at me intently. "You are my world, Jo. I love my career, but *you* are what matters most to me, and I'm sorry. I'm so sorry I ever made you doubt that for even a second. I got caught up in this idea of you following in my footsteps because it was a way I could bond with you and relate to you, but that was selfish of me. I should have met you exactly where you were."

My face softened. "You're not upset that I embarrassed you on live TV?"

"Embarrassed? I'm *proud* of you." He placed his hands on my shoulders. "If I had half the courage you did, well, maybe I wouldn't be where I am now."

"What do you mean? You're one of the greatest journalists in history."

"But at what cost?" he asked, echoing my own words from the day before. "Your mother was the love of my life, and I lost her. I haven't been there for you. Somewhere along the way, I lost myself, and it cost me years with you that I'll never be able to get back."

For the first time, I saw what was buried beneath the confidence and expensive suits. *Loneliness.*

His voice broke. "I know I can't change the past, but will you give me a chance to change the future…to be the father you deserve?"

I wrapped my arms around him. "Of course I will."

"You're everything to me, Jo." He smoothed his hand over my hair. "Things are going to change. *I'm* going to change. In fact, I've already put in for a leave of absence at work."

I leaned back, my eyes widening.

"I was thinking it might be nice to spend some time in Nashville with my daughter."

"I'd really like that." I beamed up at him. "So, I guess Mr. Kirkpatrick is pretty upset, huh?"

"Don't you worry about him," he said. "He'll be fine. I already promised to help him find someone else for the job."

A lightbulb went off inside my head. "Actually, I think I may know someone who'd be perfect. Kimber Sutton. She's the one that got the anchor job back in Chicago."

His interest was piqued. "You think she'd be good?"

"She'd be amazing," I answered. "And I kind of owe her."

"Okay. Put me in contact with her, and I'll set up a meeting."

I saw Derek look over at me out of the corner of my eye, so I motioned for him to join us. "Daddy, I have someone I want you to meet."

"OUR LAST ACT NEEDS NO INTRODUCTION," CASH'S VOICE echoed over the cheering fans. "With their help and yours, we've raised over one hundred thousand dollars to benefit Middle Tennessee's youth!"

The crowd roared in response, and Derek squeezed my arm from where we all stood together off stage.

"I'm so proud of you," he whispered in my ear.

I kissed him softly. "I couldn't have done it without you."

He pulled me into his arms, and I was overcome with gratitude for him and the sweet secret that was nestled safely between us. And I was thankful for the new family of friends I'd found that surrounded us.

"It's been my distinct honor to work with Midnight in Dallas," Cash said, "first as their manager and now as the head of their record label. I've been blessed to have a front row seat as these four talented fellas became one of the best bands in the world and four of the greatest friends I could have ever asked for." He paused for a moment and looked to his right where we all stood. "Tonight's performance closes the book on the story of Midnight in Dallas, but it's also the first page of four stories that have yet to be written. And I, for one, can't wait to see how they turn out."

Screams and applause filled the arena as Jax, Luca,

Dallas, and Derek came together, four men who were so different, but also the same. Jax hugged Derek while Dallas extended a hand to Luca and they exchanged a quick look, some sort of secret code that only brothers could understand.

"Nashville, it is my privilege to introduce for one, final time, Jaxon Slade, Dallas Stone, Derek Knights, and Luca Sterling." Cash beamed at the crowd. "Give it up for Midnight in Dallas!"

The guys took the stage to ear-splitting cheers and cameras flashing like a disco ball. They took in the sea of people for a moment before Dallas counted them off, and they dove in together to ride the waves.

"So, does this mean you're ready to help me plan the next benefit?" Lindsey materialized next to me wearing a broad grin.

"Heck yeah," I answered. "I'm ready when you are."

"It's good to have you back, Jo," she said before one of the media outlets covering the event approached us and swept her up in a flurry of questions.

"Jolene Kingsley?" The question came from somewhere beside me causing me to jump. I turned to see a dark-haired woman I didn't recognize.

I nodded. "Yes, I'm Jo."

She held out her hand to shake mine. "I'm Kelsey Hewitt, a producer on the *Today Show*. I'd like to talk to you about bringing your voice to our program."

"*What?*" The word came out in high-pitched squeak.

"You've been on my radar ever since that story you did about the Uber driver went viral," she continued. "Congrats on that, by the way. But when I saw what you did on CNN, I knew we had to have you."

I snorted. "You mean for showing my crazy to literally the entire world?"

"You call it crazy, but I call it vulnerable," she said. "The things you said resonated with people. Everyone's talking about you." She pulled her phone out of her purse and opened her Twitter feed, turning the screen so I could see.

My mouth fell open when I saw the words in front of me.

That was the most refreshing thing I've ever seen on TV. #JoKingsleyForPresident

YES!!! We need more Jo Kingsley's in the world.

That Jo Kingsley chick has heart. Did you see the story she did about the Uber driver?

A quick scroll showed that there were hundreds more comments just like those.

I shook my head in disbelief. "I…I can't believe it."

"You've struck a chord, Jo." Kelsey stuffed her phone back inside her bag. "You've been in the business a long time, so I don't have to tell you that bad news is rampant. It's the world we live in, but people are begging for some hope. A reminder amidst all of the hardship and sadness that there is still some good left in the world. And that's where you come in."

"What do you mean?" I asked.

"We'd like to take the segment you were doing for your local news and bring it to a much larger audience," she answered. "The *Today Show* audience. We were thinking we could call it *Tell Us Something Good* and once a week, you bring our viewers a positive, uplifting human interest story."

I pressed my palm to my forehead. "What? Are you serious?"

"But that's not all," she added. "I don't think a once-a-week segment is enough. We need a place our audience can go anytime they need a boost, so we want *Tell Us Something Good* to have its very own place on our website where we'll have daily webisodes and more feel-good written content. And viewers will be able to send in leads and share their own inspiring stories with us on our message boards."

"This is...*Wow*. This is a lot," I admitted. It sounded like a dream come true, but it also sounded like the kind of opportunity that would require a huge time commitment—one I wasn't sure I wanted to make right now. "I'm flattered. Really, I am. But I don't know if I want to get back into the grind that working with the *Today Show* would entail. I've got some pretty big life changes happening, and I want to put my focus on my family and living life. And my life is here in Nashville."

"You would be in the driver's seat," Kelsey said quickly. "You'd have a whole team of people helping you, and you wouldn't have to relocate. You could travel to cover some stories and do some remotely. You'd have a crew that could go when you can't or don't want to travel. You could even batch content and take weeks off at a time." She looked me in the eyes. "We believe in you and this idea, Jo, and we're prepared to do whatever it takes to make this offer work for you."

I couldn't believe it. This woman I'd just met was basically offering me my dream job on a silver platter, but I wondered how serious she was about sweetening the deal. "You said I'd have my own team. Would I be able to pick these people?"

She nodded. "Absolutely."

My eyes shifted to where Derek was playing on stage, my mind whirling with possibilities. This could be a place where he could showcase his work, capturing the best parts of humanity—if that was something he wanted to do. This could be something that wasn't just mine, but *ours*.

"Can I have some time to think about this?" I asked finally.

"Of course." She handed me her business card. "Give me a call next week, and we'll set up a meeting."

I smiled. "I'd like that. Thank you. It was so nice meeting you."

"You too," she said before weaving her way through the swarm of people.

I didn't have a second to consider her offer before Katie was back was at my side, her arm wrapped around me.

"So, are you going to tell me what Dallas was going on about earlier?" she asked. "Do you have some wild and crazy plans that I need to know about?"

I leaned into my best friend, our heads pressed together.

"I do, but not yet." I closed my eyes, my heart filled with love and pride and hope for what was to come. "I just want to enjoy this moment a little while longer."

Epilogue

Derek
September

"DEREK, we're going to be late for dinner," Jo called from downstairs.

It was early September, and we were due over at Jax and Liv's for our first Sunday dinner in three months. Life had been hectic between work, Jo's dad visiting, and me spending some time with my mom. My father had lost his battle with cirrhosis soon after our last show, and my mom and I had started counseling together. We still had a long way to go, but it was a start.

Izzy perked her head up from the giant furry donut beside my desk in what would soon be mine and Jo's shared office. That was, of course, if we ever got it unpacked.

A photo I'd taken of a sixty-eight year old grandmother filled my computer screen. It was a picture of her with two brides at their recent wedding. The woman, known to many as Granny Love, traveled to every wedding, birthday, and graduation she was invited to in order to be a stand-in granny for anyone who didn't have family to celebrate their special day. I clicked to save the edits I'd been working on and snapped my laptop shut.

"We'll be back soon, girl." I reached down and scratched the top of Izzy's head before weaving my way around the towers of boxes. "Coming!" I yelled, bounding down the hall and toward the stairs.

With the baby on the way, Jo and I had decided we wanted a bigger place, somewhere quieter with a yard, where we could eventually have a treehouse or a tire swing. We'd been in our two-story house in the suburbs of Nashville for a little over six weeks and were slowly making it feel like home. Between traveling for *Tell Us Something Good,* getting ready for my third art show, and preparing the nursery for the arrival of our daughter, setting up the office had fallen to the back burner.

"Sorry," I said when I reached the bottom of the stairs. "I lost track of time."

Jo beamed at me, her smile making me weak in the knees.

"I know," she said. "By the way, Carina called. They wrapped up the story about that teacher in Memphis and are headed back to Nashville. We'll have time to finish up everything before we drive up to New York to meet with Marla on Tuesday."

"Ugh. Marla." I groaned, not exactly thrilled about seeing the stone-faced executive producer Jo had hired. She was fine, I supposed, but she was about as nice as a lion before it pounced on a gazelle.

When Jo signed on with the *Today Show*, one of her stipulations was that she get to bring on her own crew of people. It hadn't been hard for her to convince Carina or Riggs, especially once they found out they would still be able to call Chicago home. When we traveled, we often did so in the bus the network provided, allowing us to work on the go and giving Jo the ability to bring her friend Lewis into the fold as our driver.

Jo laughed. "She'll grow on you. I promise." She grabbed her purse from the console table in the foyer. "You ready to go?"

"Actually, I just remembered I forgot to do something." I hit my head as though a lightbulb had gone off.

"Babe! We're already late." She furrowed her brow. "What did you forget?"

I stepped closer, drinking her in. Her cheeks had a glow to them, a permanent shade of rosy pink, and her eyes sparkled. She wore a blue cotton dress that hugged her baby bump, and I couldn't think of a time when she'd been more beautiful than she was at that moment.

"This," I said, leaning in and placing a soft kiss on her lips.

She grinned up at me as I rested my hands on either side of her belly, my whole world nestled right there between my palms.

"Oh." She pressed her lips to mine. "Well, there's always time for that."

AFTER DINNER WAS OVER AND THE DISHES WERE CLEARED, WE remained at Jax and Liv's dining table, catching up on what had been happening in our lives. Grace and Sam kept Chloe and Jonathan busy by helping them paint pictures at the kids' table, while Antoni bounced baby Bettina.

"An-to-ni." He enunciated each syllable, causing Bettina to dissolve into peals of laughter. "An-to-ni."

"Listen here, An-to-ni," Ella quipped. "If that little twerp says your name before she says 'mama', you and I are going to have words."

"She means it." Cash winked at Antoni. "She didn't speak to me for a week when it *sounded* like Bettina said 'dada'."

Ella crossed her arms over her chest. "Oh, she said it alright."

Cash laughed. "She was just babbling."

"Then it'll have to be our little secret, won't it, Betty Boop?" Antoni cooed and the baby gurgled her reply. "Won't be long and we'll have another precious, smooshie baby around here."

"Speaking of." Ella turned to me and Jo. "Have you guys decided on a name for Bettina's future bestie?"

"You could name her after her Auntie Katie," Katie piped up.

Dallas shrugged. "I think Dallas is a good name, and it could work for a girl."

"I vote for Katie," Luca said. "The last thing this world needs is another Dallas. A Luca maybe, but not a Dallas."

It was good to see Luca and Dallas messing with each other again. I knew their relationship was far from perfect, but it appeared they'd made some sort of peace with each other.

Dallas narrowed his eyes. "Or what about Brandi?"

"With an i," Liv added, and everyone burst into laughter.

Luca shook his head. "You guys are really never going to let me live that down, are you?"

I grinned. "Not a chance."

Jo wrinkled her brow. "I think I'm missing something."

I promised to fill her in later, much to Luca's chagrin.

"We don't have a name yet," I said. "But I don't think Brandi will make the cut."

Dallas' lip quirked. "That's a shame."

"Oh, and I think this goes without saying, but please don't bring Brandi with an i to our wedding next weekend." Ella raised her brow at Luca. "Or anyone else whose name you do not know."

Luca crossed his arms and leaned back in his chair. "I'll have you know I'm going stag. This wild buck can't be tamed."

Ella stuck her finger in her mouth and made a gagging sound.

"What about you, Katie?" Liv asked. "Are you bringing a date?"

Katie's cheeks flushed, and she chewed her bottom lip. "Well…it's…*new.*"

My eyes met Jo's, and she grinned at me.

Liv squealed. "Who is it? How did you meet?"

Everyone except Jo and I searched Katie's face for answers, but her eyes were locked on Dallas who was making it a point not to look at anyone.

"Katie, girl, don't do this to me," Antoni pleaded. "You know my heart can't handle suspense."

"It's true," Nate added. "He'll only start shows that have all the episodes available."

"That's absolutely right. I binge watch my TV shows the way God intended." Antoni turned his attention back to Katie. "Now, spill!"

Dallas raised his eyes to meet Katie's. They exchanged a knowing glance, and Ella noticed immediately.

She covered her mouth with her hands. "Oh my God!"

"What?" Liv asked, still not catching on.

Luca wrinkled his forehead. "Am I missing something?"

Everyone looked from Katie to Dallas then back to Katie.

Antoni scrunched up his nose. "Why are you looking at Dal—" He gasped. "*Shut up.*"

"Am I just an idiot or what?" Luca asked. "What's going on? Who's Katie's date to the wedding?"

"Me." Dallas cleared his throat and smiled, not taking his eyes off of Katie. "She's going with me."

About Project NENA

Project NENA (North East Nashville Alliance) was founded in 2015 by my dear friend, Lindsey Langley. It's an organization close to my heart, and I have participated in their gift-giving program many times. But Project NENA's reach goes well beyond the holidays. They help provide school supplies to children in the community, assist families being displaced due to gentrification, and connect them with the help they need in a variety of areas including mental healthcare, substance abuse counseling, and so much more

Like many, Project NENA was hit hard during the pandemic, and they had to make the difficult decision to suspend services until they could safely meet the needs of the community. As of the publication of this book, this wonderful organization is back in action. However, there is no Jo Kingsley to help save the day, no Midnight in Dallas to put on a benefit concert. Project NENA is relying on real life rockstars like you to make sure the families in North East Nashville have their own happily ever after. I hope you'll join me in making a donation to this phenomenal organization. To learn more about Project NENA and their mission or to make a donation, visit www.ProjectNENA.org.

Acknowledgments

I could dedicate every book I ever write to Jennifer Bottoms and Kate Oscarson, but truly, it wouldn't be near enough to acknowledge how vital they are to my writing process. Both of these women have helped me to grow as a writer, encouraging me on the days when the job feels impossibly hard and cheering me on when the words start flowing. I'm blessed to have you both on this journey with me, and I am so grateful for your friendship.

Kate, thank you for asking me the tough questions that truly breathe life into my characters and make them that much more relatable. You always help me see things from a new perspective. Love you tons.

And Jen, thank you for being my editor and sounding board. Thank you for encouraging me to trust my instincts and for lifting me up. We make a hell of a team, and I am so fucking proud knowing that soon the world will be reading *your* book about Captain Geech and The Shrimp Shack Shooters. I love you times a million shrimp emojis.

Thank you to my husband. Life with you and our fur babies is my favorite. Love you more than anything. Let's go to Target?!

Special thanks to:

My mom and dad, whom I hope will never actually read these books, and if they do, I hope they never tell me.

Nicole, my SSMATBMDBFFAATE.

Kia, my partner in crime and mezcal adventures.

Lauren H. Mae, my awesome critique partner.

Eve Kasey, one of my favorite authors and friends.

Jen Malone, who is a literary rockstar.

Elle Maxwell, the amazing artist who brings my characters to life.

Lindsey Langley, a real-life superhero. I'm so thankful you're here.

Ali, Brooke, Dee, Sydney, Gaby, and Jena.

My cousins, Erin and Sam.

Mrs. Ross, who will always be my favorite teacher.

The Bookstagram Community who has given me so much love. Especially Allie, Kelsey, Ali, Leigh Ann, McKenzie, Morgan, Kaley, Lindsey, Sarah, Anna, Crystal, and Kerry. Y'all have been some of my biggest champions, and even though I've only gotten to meet two of you in person, I feel lucky to be able to call you friends. I hope one day I can meet you all for a Sunday dinner.

Every single person who has ever read my work or jumped into my DMs to tell me why a certain character or story I wrote meant something to them. To every reader who has left a review or recommended my books to a friend. Y'all are the reason I get to wake up and do what I love, and I'm forever grateful for each and every one of you.

Melissa Grace is a freelance writer whose work has been featured in publications like *Medium, Thought Catalog,* and *The Mighty*. She resides just outside of Nashville, Tennessee with her husband and many fur children. This is her third novel.

Learn more and stay in the loop about Melissa's future projects at: www.melissagracewrites.com. Find her on social media:

facebook.com/heymelissagrace

twitter.com/heymelissagrace

instagram.com/heymelissagrace

goodreads.com/melissagrace

bookbub.com/authors/melissa-grace

TRAITOR

Printed in the United States of America: First Printing, 2022.
ISBN 978-1-7378376-8-8 (eBook)
ISBN 978-1-7378376-9-5 (paperback)

www.huckleberryrahrauthor.wordpress.com

Copy/Line Editor: Wes Imrisek
Developmental Editor: Angela Grimes
Cover Art: Getcovers.com
Formatting: R. L. Davennor

CHAPTER 1

"Jade, you're my last hope!"

Pebble's tender voice floated up to me, soft and from far away.

Muscles tense, I crouched on a tree limb. In panther form, my balance let me focus on my goal and not on falling. The scent of burning embers reached me on a light breeze. I hunched down, raising my tail into the air to gauge wind speed. My target was roughly twenty feet away, outside my normal range, but with a bit of a run on this sturdy branch, I could make it. I had to make it. My sister counted on me. This was for Pebble.

I straightened my legs a bit, then took a few warm-up steps in place with my back legs. With two feet of branch in front of me, I took a running start before leaping into the air to fly towards my goal. As soon as I launched myself into the air, I knew I had done it. I would reach my target. Everything in me sang as I flew.

Eyes on the prize, my body angled down, hitting the ground exactly where I had planned. At first, I froze. I couldn't believe I had made the leap. A twenty-foot flight. I glanced over my shoulder; the branch seemed like a twig dangling from the tree I'd perched in merely seconds before. My heart pounded like a bass drum in my ears. Focusing on my breathing, I tried to bring my heartbeat to a normal speed.

Suddenly, someone tackled me from the side and went flying. Golden fur flashed past my eyes as I rolled across the grass. I growled low in my throat, continuing the roll until I was on top, pinning the large cat below me.

"Jade! That was amazing!"

Backing away from Owen, I turned as Bevin ran up to me. "I can't believe that leap. It was majestic. I got it on video so you can watch it as well. You landed smack in the center of the fifty-point ring. You won!"

Slowly, I became aware of the pounding of other feet and the cheers of the rest of the two packs. The wolves were coming to congratulate me.

Sarah beat them to me, bowling me over in a tackle much like Owen's, but I was braced and ready for her. Her force met the wall of my will. She lowered her head and butted me one more time.

As part of today's training, Dad had set up a competition for me, Sarah, and Owen, to see who could collect the most points leaping from a tree branch to land in a hula-hoop. Pebble made cloth centers for the hoops. Each hoop was worth points based on how far it was placed from the tree and the diameter of the hoop. The wolves laid bets before the competition began. The three of us had been close in points until this final jump.

Dad's voice rang out over the field. "Everyone back. Panthers, change. It's time for dinner."

As I approached the picnic area, the scent of the outdoor buffet reached me and my stomach growled. The meats and cheese smelled heavenly. I could also smell fruit and— breathing deeply—was that some sweets? This was the last day of the pack's training at this location, and we were having a big meal with enough food to feed the two packs.

I found my clothes and let my humanity back out. I dressed quickly in jeans and a shirt that read, 'There are two types of people in the world, those that can extrapolate information from missing information.' As hungry as I was, I found the rest of my small pack before eating.

Two years ago, it became obvious that José and Bevin were too dominant to not have their own pack. They may have been able to stay in my parent's pack, but it probably would have caused issues down the road. José still ran with the pack because he had been born into it, but I knew it was getting stressful for everyone.

During that time, I must have subconsciously agreed with José and Bevin becoming alphas because I went to them with most of my issues. My parents, my wolf alphas, had noticed. The decision was made to form a sixth North American wolf pack. I learned later that the decision hadn't been made lightly. A call had gone out amongst the alphas of the five packs that had made up the North American wolf packs, and the leaders had debated. They'd come up with a plan of attack as well.

When the pack was formed, the boys got more than just me, they also got my brother, Owen, and Brooke, a submissive wolf who was not my favorite person in the world.

Over the last two years, José and Bevin had traveled to the other five packs to both meet the other alphas and learn from them. This was part of that plan. The boys met all the other alphas, they met the boys, and all the alphas knew each other. Since all us pack members were in college, the pack training had mostly been done during the summer. José and Bevin had just returned from their last training in Colorado.

"Heya, chica, nice moves out there." José drew me into a huge hug. "I've missed you. Between you going to school out in Cali, and me being away all summer, it's been too long."

We walked towards the buffet, and I relaxed, being near my alpha. "How were the Rocky Mountains?"

"Colorado was great. Each pack is run so differently, yet so similar. Bevin and I have done a lot of talking about what we want for our pack."

"Do the rest of us get a say?" I grabbed a plate and started filling it with cheese, crackers, and grapes. Pebble stood down at the other end by Aunt Allison and Uncle Jackson. They were helping her fill a plate. I happily watched them for a few seconds.

"Nope. I mean, it isn't a complete situation of 'our way or the highway,' but too many cooks spoil the cake."

I narrowed my eyes at him. "That made no sense."

"Sure it did." He waggled his eyebrows at me. Then he pointed with his chin. "Look, cake."

I moaned as we headed for the desserts. My food plate was already dangerously full. "How is traveling with Bevin? Have you two ever spent so much time together before? Are you sick of each other yet?"

José gazed off with a blissful smile. "It's been good. The two of you going off to college together sucked. I can't believe you guys didn't stay local."

I shrugged. "What can I say, the tour sold me. It wasn't hard convincing Bevin. But I have a month to hang out with you before we head back west."

We each carried out two-plates' worth of goodies to a blanket spread on the lawn. José shrugged as he carefully lowered his plates. "Maybe, maybe not."

Turning to him sharply, I asked, "What do you mean?"

"Let's wait until we have everyone to talk about this. It's a bit of a long story, and I only want to cover the details once."

"Alphas," I mumbled, before digging in to eat.

Between bites, José gave me a penetrating stare. I could feel him reaching into me in that alpha way. "How has it been with Piper this summer?"

I rolled my eyes. "You don't need to go all alpha on me. It's been fine…good. We've lived in two different states for two years, no one is surprised our relationship dropped to friend status."

"But…"

"But she has a new girlfriend, who is great, I'm sure. Again, don't worry. We're teenagers, in college. Most of us don't find our forever mates like you and Bevin. I mean, if I had a Bevin…" I smiled.

He gently touched my shoulder. "You haven't met Julez?"

As much as his touch helped, I tensed. "No." I knew he could sense my heart beating faster, but I tried to maintain a neutral face. Piper had moved on. That had been our agreement. When I'd moved to California for college and Piper had stayed in Wisconsin, we knew our relationship would be hard to maintain. Our friendship was important to both of us, but we agreed that opening ourselves up to new relationships at our age should be considered as well. We were young, and if our futures were destined to be together, we'd find ourselves together again one day.

He opened his mouth to continue, but I shook my head.

I tucked into my food when Owen, Sarah, and Bevin settled down around us. Brooke found a spot close by. Then my mom and dad joined us on their own adjacent blanket, along with Violet and Luke, two other members of their pack. I searched, expecting Pebble to find me, but she stayed with my aunt and uncle.

José surveyed everyone sitting around eating and then looked at Bevin. They seemed to have a silent conversation. Each summer their connection grew.

Bevin gave him a half smile and nodded, as if to say, 'yep, now is the proper time.'

José put down his plate. "Okay, as you all know, Bevin and I have been going pack to pack, meeting all the different alphas and other wolves around the country. What most of you don't know is, they completely support our new pack; are excited about it. The West Coast has been in need of a new pack for some time."

Owen held up his right hand in a stop signal and then shook it. He grabbed his soda to clear his mouth. "Wait, what? West Coast. When was this decided? Did I know that the pack was moving out west?"

I slapped his hand down. "I mean, why not? You already look like a surfer."

He rolled his eyes at me and shoved the rest of his bratwurst into his mouth.

Shaking his head, José continued. "Each of the other five packs have been established for years, generations.

Because of this, they have made investments and are financially stable. To support us and our efforts to form a new pack, each of the five established packs have made a financial gift to help us start out on our own. Despite our age and small numbers, we won't be destitute. Brooke, who happens to be a financial genius, is handling the money."

Brooke froze in the act of raising a bratwurst to her mouth. "Yeah, that's what happens when you're kicked out at fourteen and forced to figure out how to survive on your own." Her words sounded flippant, but she blushed and her nutty jasmine scent told me she was embarrassed, yet proud.

I cocked my head and stared at her. "So *that's* why you were always so anti-family."

"Well, duh. When you have an abusive one that kicks you out, you learn to think of family as a bad word." She turned from me to face José. "Anyway, each pack was generous, and I've been investing the money, making sure the pack will be financially stable. I've been consulting with Clare; she's been extremely helpful. We'll have enough to do what we need and not put too much of a dent in our reserves."

Clare, José's mom, was the financial officer for my parents' pack. She'd been running the pack since she'd moved up from Florida with my mom, when she'd first become a werewolf. If Brooke had Clare's seal of approval, she was really good.

Bevin's eyes widened. "Really?"

Brooke nodded. "Yep. You heard your mate." She

tapped her forehead. "*Genius.*"

I snorted as Brooke's face morphed into a mask of superiority.

José nodded. "Right. So, besides money, each pack will be sending us one or two wolves so that our pack is large enough to grow."

My gaze snapped to my parents.

Mom smiled back at me. "Violet and Luke both want to jump ship and join you. They don't have families, so the move will be easy, and they both have jobs that can transfer to California. Andy and Chris wanted to join your lot as well, but we needed to keep some of our wolves."

"They did?" Shock surged through me at the idea so many people trusted us. We were so young, and my parents' pack was amazing.

"Yes, but uprooting their family wouldn't have been easy. Or moving their jobs." Mom's face softened.

Dad snorted at my reaction.

I quickly checked my pack connections and found links to Violet and Luke. Not only *were* they joining our pack, they already had. I turned to José, gaping.

He laughed. "Checked out the connections, did you? About time, chica."

I nodded.

His smile lit up his face. "We need a Pack House. We need land. And we need it right away. Jade and Bevin are going to school in California so I figure if we set up near their school, they could move in once the house is ready.

That way, we can establish the pack right away. Violet and Luke can relocate out there with us and live there too. School starts in four weeks. I figure we should head out in the next week and start our search."

I flopped back and stared up at the clouds. "Who is 'we'?"

"Great question. You, Bevin, Violet, Luke…" He paused as if considering his next words. "I'm transferring colleges."

My stomach muscles groaned as I sat up and stared at him.

Owen beat me to the question. "Whoa, bro, what?"

"My acceptance to Arcoíris University came in last month. I'll spend my senior year there with Jade and Bevin. That way, I can help set up the new Pack House. *My* Pack House."

Bevin quietly said, "Our Pack House."

José's face softened as he leaned back and gave Bevin a quick kiss on the cheek. "Our Pack House."

"What about me? And Brooke?" Owen sounded hurt.

José sighed. "The Pack House will be your home. If you want, you can come there during winter break. It's what I want…we want." Bevin nodded in agreement, slipping his hand in José's. "Spend New Years with us. There *are* smaller colleges in California if you want to transfer, but I don't think that that's necessary; you and Brooke are both seniors. Finish off this year, then come home to us."

Owen nodded as he followed along. His scent had morphed from a minty frustration to a mellower chamomile acceptance.

I shifted my gaze from José to my mom and back. "Do you know how many wolves each of the other four packs are sending?"

José shook his head. "It hasn't been decided and no one will be sent until we have an established pack territory."

Sarah turned to Luke and Violet. "Will it be hard for you to find a job in California?"

Luke huffed out a laugh, dragging his fingers through his light brown curls. "Nah, my job has a branch out in the area. I requested a transfer. It came with a pay raise, since the price of living is so much higher out there."

Violet shrugged. Her blue eyes, so dark they almost looked purple, moved to take us all in. Her brown hair—cut in a pixie style and dyed blue at the ends—swayed in the wind. As she studied the group, I realized she looked a bit uncomfortable. Her shoulders were hunched, and she kept studying her plate of food. I wasn't sure if it was being outside or in such a big crowd. "I do digital art. All my work is on the computer. Since I work from home, it doesn't matter where I'm located."

Owen looked around the group, eyes wide. "But can anyone in this group cook?"

CHAPTER 2

The next morning, I woke up in my old bedroom. The room was plastered in geese; bed quilt, pillow case, plush toys, and other decorations—all because of a run-in I'd had years ago.

Last night Piper texted she wanted to stop by to talk. We hadn't seen each other much over the summer, and she wanted to say goodbye before I left. Sarah would be coming over later as well.

Opening my door, I found Pebble waiting for me in the hall. "Can I run with you this morning?"

I yawned and stretched as I considered her request. "I

wasn't going to run, but sure. Where do you want to run, trail or gym?"

"Trail."

I went to change into running clothes.

The two of us headed out through the back yard. Though Pebble looked like a miniature of me with dark curls and green eyes, she had been adopted. Three years prior, a lone wolf killed her family. The authorities found her standing by the car on the side of I80, left to fend for herself. She ended up with us. In some dark part of her past, a werewolf had bitten her before she came to us at the age of five. She didn't remember it. It happened long before her parents were killed.

Young kids didn't often survive becoming a werewolf, but we were doing what we could to help her adjust and thrive. We wanted her to grow up as innocently as possible for a girl who shifted into a predator once a month. When she first came to us, she didn't run with the pack; the idea of killing her furry friends upset her. She still didn't go out on the full moon night runs, but instead shifted early to play. She spent those nights in the treehouse in the backyard, and the kids of the pack members kept her company. So far, this arrangement had worked out well.

We reached the trail, and she took off. I hit a few buttons on my watch to track our progress and ran to catch up with her.

"Alright squirt, are we just running, or did you want

to talk?"

Instantly, her breathing quickened as she pushed our pace. "Both...I...guess." She slowed down with the words. I could smell the nutty apprehension on her as our feet pounded on the pavement of the path. Finally, she blurted out, "Can I come to California with you guys? Can I join your pack?"

I almost missed a step, but caught myself. We ran for a bit before I could align my thoughts enough to answer her. "I'm going to start off with saying a simple 'no.' But I want to qualify it."

Disappointment flooded the area. It was thick enough the cinnamon scent almost smelled like snickerdoodles. For a minute it was hard to breathe, and I stumbled, but somehow kept my feet under me. Once I caught my breath, I lifted my eyes to her face. The tear rolling down her cheek felt like a knife stabbing into my heart.

"Listen love, we'll be living in apartments and dorms for a while. Bevin, José, and I will be in classes. Luke and Violet will be at work. That will be it for the pack, five of us. No one else will be around. No kids to play with. I don't even know if we'll have a safe place for you to hang out while we run."

"I can hang out with Brooke. She doesn't like to go out on the runs either."

I huffed out a sigh. "Brooke won't be living with us until next summer. She's still in school in Las Vegas. I know you want to be in the new pack, but staying here is best. This pack can raise you until you are old enough to control that beasty inside you."

She growled. "I can control the wolf. Probably better than most people in the pack. I don't remember not having the wolf so it's just me, unlike everyone else who remembers a before time…I don't."

We ran for a bit longer. "Jade, do you remember that book Mom gave you?"

"Yep. I was going to bring it to California but couldn't find it. I was thinking my little sister may have snatched it from my room."

A quick peek let me see her cheeks redden more than the running accounted for. "I've learned a lot. I knew about the gods from what you and Owen had told me, but the book taught me more."

"What have you learned?"

She kicked up her speed so her sentences came out choppy. "The twin gods. Sonnara and Mondara. Sonnara is the sun god. They are the gods who help us face our trials of staying human as we fight our beast's urges. When we turn rogue and hunt our fellow human, we lose our battle to Sonnara and our path becomes dark. This battle between the sun and the moon helps to guide us. It is the reason we know how and why our humanity is important."

We ran in silence for a few minutes. Her inclusion of fighting the urge to become a rogue wolf worried me. Before I could ask her about it, she continued.

"We honor Mondara as we sing to the moon every month. The moon brings us strength and healing, connection, and pack. It is our connection to our gods that brings us the community that I love so much."

This side of Mondara soothed something in me. Her feelings were much more heartening.

"It went on to talk about intuition, something our wolf has. But Jade…I think I feel that, even in human form. I just know when things are going to happen. I've been working with Dad some. It will become my first real training program. We'll start it in the fall or winter, but we started building it last spring."

I snorted. Dad and his training programs were legendary. He was getting more and more creative in how he set them up. The idea that Pebble was intuitive or had some sort of precognition ability and he could figure a way to train it blew my mind. He was probably in training heaven.

We got to our turn-around point and headed back home.

"I hope you understand why joining our pack right now wouldn't work. You're in school, you have your training, and you have your friends. Maybe when you get older it will work. That said, we can figure out a way that we can talk more often. I do miss you."

"I miss you too, sis. I would like to talk with you…I think…it may be important."

It was the first time she had called me that and again I almost fell. This time I avoided the fall by stopping. She did, too, and turned to me. I dropped to my knees and wrapped her in a big hug.

When we got home, everyone else was up. José and Bevin sat at the table making plans. In José's last two years of college he'd gotten an apartment off campus, and the two of them were living there over the summer.

José handed me a glass of water and a banana. "I found a flight with five seats available on Thursday."

I almost dropped the glass. "But that's in two days. I thought you said a week."

He sighed. "The sooner we find a house, a den—maybe even land—the better off we'll be."

I was about to challenge him when Pebble's fingers gently touched my wrist. My focus snapped to her. "He's right, sis. This is the best time for your group to go. Don't miss your window."

I just gaped at her. Dad chuckled at the table.

When I got my mind together enough to move my limbs, I gazed at him, and he gave me a bright smile. "That's our girl!"

After eating a quick breakfast, I ran off to shower and put on clean clothes. When I got back, Bevin and José were sitting in the kitchen with a PB&J on a plate and a mug of coffee waiting for me. I sat and dug in.

As I ate, they filled me in on our plans. "Okay, chica. We need a Pack House big enough for all of us to live in, so at least, what? Ten rooms?"

I mused for a minute, taking a sip of my coffee. "Bedrooms?" José nodded.

I started ticking off numbers on my fingers. "I would think at least that. You two, me, Violet, Luke, Brooke, Owen, and if the other four packs send one wolf each, that puts us at ten. I mean, assuming you two *want* to share a room." I raised an eyebrow at them.

Bevin blushed and looked down at his hands as José laughed from his gut.

A warmth blossomed from between them that spread happiness throughout the kitchen. I sighed and finished off my sandwich. I was still hungry, so I jumped up and put a bagel in the toaster.

While my bagel toasted, I leaned on the counter. I ticked items off on my fingers again. "I want a library, an exercise room, a sauna, a hot tub, a hidden room, a secret escape path, and a command center. Then we need the regular living room, dining room, kitchen, and basement/hang-out room. Finally, we need a private pack room for meetings."

As I spoke, Bevin's eyes widened and José's narrowed. "Chica, you've been planning."

I nodded. "I have, I put a lot of thought into this during some of my more boring classes."

Bevin's scent became spicy and he glared at me. "Is *that* what you were doodling? I asked but you wouldn't ever share. I'm your alpha, too!" And he sounded like it. *Yikes!*

"No, not in classes we had together. It was in that Art in

Society class I had. I had to do some sort of art, and architecture counted. The challenge became, what would you add into your fantasy home. I also added a pool and a rollercoaster, but you know, it was all about over-the-top crazy."

Bevin's ire turned into a vanilla amusement. "What did you earn on the assignment?"

I tried to keep my face flat as I admitted, "A 'B.' Apparently, my vision wasn't realistic."

Both boys snorted.

The sound of the toaster popping made me jump. As I prepared the bagel, I heard someone drive up to the house. With a mumble, José stood. "I'll get it."

The cream cheese tasted good, but I debated adding jelly. As I finished my bagel at the table, José returned with Piper. My ex-girlfriend wasn't a werewolf...yet. We broke up on good terms, knowing distance made dating hard, but not friendship. Despite what I told myself, I knew a part of my heart still belonged to her.

I stood and was about to hug her when I saw another woman follow her in. I didn't recognize her.

Piper walked up to me and gave me a hug. "Hi Jade, this is Julez. She ended up having today off from work and I thought she could tag along. That's okay, right?"

The girlfriend. I froze, barely able to breathe as she entered. Six feet tall, blond, blue-eyed, beautiful, and approaching me with her hand out. I had avoided meeting the girlfriend, and that had been the one good thing about leaving in two days. Taking a deep breath, I tried to get my feet moving, but nothing happened. Hand up to shake? Nope. I opened my mouth to speak, and again, nothing happened. I thought I was okay with this, but I was frozen.

José placed his hands on my shoulders. He said softly, for my ears only, "You got this."

Alpha. Pack. I closed my eyes and finally could breathe. I nodded slightly. He kissed my forehead and moved to stand next to me.

Smiling as naturally as I could, I took a step toward Julez and held out my hand. "Hi, I'm Jade, nice to meet you." Her hand was smooth as butter, and her shake was firm and commanding.

She gave me a dazzling smile. I could feel it to my toes. *Was anything wrong with this woman?* "Oh! I've heard so much about you. It's so great to finally meet you. I was hoping I'd get to meet you before you headed back to California. When are you going? Piper talks about you— well, all of you—and I was really hoping to get to connect with you." She took in a sharp breath and stepped back, ending with another brilliant smile. "I'm so sorry. I babble when I'm nervous."

I could see Bevin out of the corner of my eye trying to hold in a snort. He stood and introduced himself to Julez. Her eyes got even wider. "Oh, wow! I get to meet so many of Piper's friends. I had no idea you would be here, too!"

Julez turned to Piper and grabbed her hand. When

they touched, a small wave of love that connected them. It punched me in the gut.

I tried to swallow, but could feel my systems closing down. "Um…I need to check on Pebble. She's…um… room." I dashed down the hall and closed myself into my bedroom, sitting on my bed.

I placed my head in my hands and tried to slow my heart. My room felt small and I knew running hadn't been the right answer, but I had to escape all those emotions. Over the last two years I hadn't met anyone worth calling a girlfriend…I hadn't replaced Piper. I had focused mainly on classes. But in her first year at college, Piper had found Julez. I guess I wasn't as prepared to face it as I'd thought.

I heard a knock on my door. I sniffed. "Enter."

José came in, shutting the door behind himself. He sat down next to me and rubbed my back. "Weren't ready to meet her, were you?"

I kept my head in my hands focused on the carpet. "I'm fine."

He snorted. "Want to try that again?"

I flopped onto my back, landing on one of the stuffed toy geese. Pulling it out from under me I stared at it. "Really, José, I'm fine." It almost sounded like the truth that time.

He sat cross-legged on my bed. "Chica, you just freaked out."

I groaned, covering my face with the goose. "How obvious was it?"

He chuckled. "Probably pretty obvious, but you'll have to ask Bevin to be certain. I have a front row seat to the inside emotions, so to me it was plain as day."

"She's just so tall, and perfect. Piper really did an upgrade, didn't she?"

"I don't know. You'd be hard to replace. We don't know her, and that's the point. Ready to face the Amazon, yet?"

"No, but I can't hide out in here for two days, can I?" José's mouth twitched as he stood, reaching out to pull me up with him. "You may want to leave the goose."

I dropped my gaze to the stuffed animal I still clutched in my hands. Sighing, I dropped it on my pillow.

Arm in arm, we made it back to the living room where we found the others sitting and talking.

"...and then I couldn't help but ask her out. I mean, how could I not?" Julez finished up a story while gazing at Piper, her heart in her eyes. She and Piper were sitting on the love seat, and their scents...matched.

I paused for a second, but José dragged me to the couch where he pushed me down to sit between him and Bevin. Piper's brow dropped in concern. She knew that I would only sit between them if something was wrong. The double touch of pack helped to ground me. She was about to ask, but Julez continued her story.

Julez had turned to face the three of us. "I was so nervous she wouldn't want to date me, but she said yes!"

I smiled at them. "Seems I missed a great story."

Piper blushed. "It's mostly the one I emailed you last year. The one from the library."

My smile turned genuine. From Piper's point of view, the story went a bit differently. She had been studying when the bold, confident beauty approached her. She had wanted to make sure I was really okay with it before things had gotten too far along with them.

Just then, the door opened, and Sarah came in yelling, "Honey, I'm home!"

I was about to jump up, but two hands from two different people held me down.

She came in like a hurricane of motion. "Hiya, all. I was going to join you at Devil's Lake later, but," she looked at me and her smile faltered for a second before she turned to Piper and Julez, "I thought one fewer car would be smart." She approached the loveseat and fist-bumped the two of them. "Piper, Julez, it's been a while. Hey, would you mind showing Julez the basement and backyard? I need to talk business with Jade and the boys."

Piper's brow knit as she seemed to work through a few things, but then she nodded. "Sure. I'll show her around." Then the two of them headed off.

Sarah came over to the couch and spoke to José. "She's going to need more food after this, just so you know."

My eyes got big. "Now? But what about Julez? What if I faint?"

"Honey, you sent a calling-card I heard from home.

I came rushing fast enough; I'm glad we're in the same town. I know you're better, but I'm guessing this setup," she waved her hands at the pillars of my alphas holding me up, "is the reason."

"Can't a girl freak out without three alphas bullying her?" I grumbled.

A chorus of, 'No's' answered my complaint.

Sarah grabbed my hand and used Soul Sharing to apply my own calming technique against me, powering it with my own energy. Suddenly, I was floating on clouds without a worry in the world.

I was also hungry. My stomach growled. I had not eaten enough for this, and my vision grew dim as I slumped onto Bevin's lap.

Both José and Sarah relaxed with an audible sigh. Bevin's sigh was his usual one of exasperation at having to put up with me. I tried to move, but he held me down.

Sarah put a hand on my forehead. "She isn't unconscious. Do you want us to dig you out?"

Bevin gently wrapped his arms around me. "No. I'm not connected to her like the two of you, but she needs to feel *pack* right now. You two find her food and I'll stay with her."

With those words, I relaxed a bit more. I didn't want to be left alone. Despite the calm, I still felt anxious and alone, like when I'd come home from Florida and wasn't sure of my place in the world.

After what felt like a second, Bevin moved so that I was

sitting against his chest. His arms were wrapped around my waist like a seatbelt so I couldn't slip off the couch. Sarah and José had returned with enough food to feed an army. I gaped at the plate full of mini pancakes, sausage, sandwiches cut into quarters, fruit, yogurt, cheese, crackers, and other sundry finger-foods.

I snorted. "Who all's coming over for lunch?"

José gave me an alpha stare. "Eat."

I ate.

Once I'd finally gotten enough food in my system, things seemed less stressful. Piper and Julez returned from the tour, and I was back to sitting against the couch, all evidence of my near black-out and feeding frenzy gone.

Piper stared at me for a full minute, no doubt gauging if I was recovered. I smiled brightly and nodded. She seemed to like what she saw, because she finally sat back down next to Julez. "So, when do you and Bevin head back to California?"

It hit me. She didn't know any of the news. "José is dragging us back on Thursday."

Julez cocked her head. "Why would he be dragging the two of you anywhere? I mean, I guess they're dating, right? But why you?"

I flopped back on the couch, rubbing my eyes in disgust at myself.

José patted one of my crossed legs as he chuckled. "It isn't so much a force, as a request. I put in a transfer to their college for my senior year and want to spend a few weeks finding a place for the three of us to live and getting to know the city."

Julez's cumin scent shifted from skepticism to vanilla interest as Piper's ginger scent of shock punched me. "What? When did all this happen?"

I zoned out as José and Piper caught up on the news. He assured her it was only him who was relocating; the rest of her friends were staying in state until they graduated. During the end of the talk, I sat up to follow the conversation more closely. Julez was interested but smelled confused at how invested Piper seemed in everyone's movements.

Piper pulled her phone from her pocket. She kept darting looks at me. "My parents are throwing a celebration for…um…in October…Jade, you know."

I closed my eyes to think of any reason her parents would be throwing a celebration in October. Nothing was coming to mind.

Piper's eyes were getting wild, and she finally popped up and came over to me. "Jade, you know…it will be around Halloween…" I stared at her blankly. She reached down and took my hand. "Don't you remember? October." My panther sniffed and whispered: *wolf, three months*, before padding away.

I sat up straight as she backed up. "Oh. October. *That* celebration."

Piper started nodding quickly. "Are you coming

back to help celebrate with them? Us? Me?" Julez's scent went from confused to annoyed. I hoped her emotions would stabilize. The cinnamon was nice, but I was ready for a calm conversation. "What are you two talking about? I've heard of couples having a private language, but this is ridiculous. Does anyone know what just happened?"

Bevin, who had been watching us, turned to Julez. "I'm sure you know Piper's past. This is the first home her parents have owned where they didn't move every few months. Are they doing a Halloween celebration this year?"

Eyes wide and standing in the center of the living room, Piper slowly nodded.

Julez's eyes narrowed. "But why act so weird about it?"

Piper sighed and dropped down next to her. "Jade was my first friend. I'm asking her to fly back to Wisconsin mid-semester for something so silly. It's hard for me to ask. That's all."

Julez's whole demeanor softened as she wrapped herself around Piper to give her comfort.

Sarah took the opportunity and leapt to her feet, clapping her hands. "So, Devil's Lake anyone?"

Julez's eyes widened as she stood. "I love it there. Does anyone else like to rock-climb?"

And with that, we were off for a day of adventuring. We did get to rock-climb, and Julez was surprisingly good. After twenty minutes, Sarah and I headed off for a trail hike. One last hike together. The separation from the main group helped me relax even more.

Once we were alone, Sarah's shoulders dropped as she visibly relaxed. "Jade, you need to find a new girlfriend."

My ire started to rise. "Can we just walk?"

"Or a pet?"

"Sarah!"

"I know you are—mostly—over Piper. But you haven't fully moved on. You focus so much on school and the pack that you've given up being a teenage girl. Just promise me you'll think about it?"

We hiked in silence for a bit. "I'm not that bad."

"You know I talk with Bevin."

I grumbled. "I don't just study and hang out with Bevin. I have other friends. But…" I stopped her before she could say more. "I'll try to socialize more this year. I promise. I know that finding a pack den will be a lot, but there is more to life than books and pack."

After a few hours, we all headed home, tired yet satisfied with our day.

Two days later Bevin, José, Violet, Luke, and I boarded a plane for California.

CHAPTER 3

The plane landed in San Francisco, and we rented a minivan.

José sat behind me as I drove. "You said this drive takes a half-hour?"

Bevin snorted. "That depends on traffic and time of day. Arcoíris is a small community between Half Moon Bay and San Mateo. Traffic south of San Francisco is crazy compared to Wisconsin."

Trying to navigate said traffic, I just grunted. The city we were heading to had grown up around the college over the last century. Being a month out from the start of the semester, the city was quiet. There was only one hotel. We reserved a suite with two bedrooms—each with a pair of queen beds—a sitting area with couches and a TV, a small dining area, and an even smaller kitchen. It was a long-term rental.

After checking in, Bevin and I took José, Violet, and Luke on a tour of the city we'd called home for two years. Downtown had a few restaurants, including a local Mexican restaurant with a mole buffet. They served four to seven types of moles, depending on the night, and I had been dreaming about it since I'd left for the summer. Bevin and I kept a running tab with a pizza joint we both loved. And then, there were the Asian restaurants: Thai, Chinese, Japanese. A small New Orleans-inspired eatery had the best Po' Boy sandwiches and jambalaya this side of the Rockies. My favorite waiter, Kenny, was a local who worked year-round.

Beyond the food, we visited the different shopping centers and ended up at a park we used for our monthly runs. There were hiking trails and a fairly open area that was safe from prying eyes.

When we returned to the hotel, we set up our computers and began our search for land or an already existing building that could serve as the pack house. The boys were on the couch, Luke in a comfy chair, and I sat with Violet on kitchen stools. Though I knew that finding property was a high priority, I quickly logged onto the school's site to select the last of my classes. I had to choose an elective and had been dreading it.

Between my Junior and Senior years, I'd toured some campuses. Because a lot of the schools in California were crowded, Arcoíris University had a program in place that allowed incoming freshmen to double up their first-year classes as high school requirements. They had contacted Stolzburg High and made sure it would be okay for me to join this program. I had been allowed to start college with Bevin, finishing high school while starting college.

"Bevin, have you selected your elective for this semester?"

José continued to type as he spoke. "I'm in town; take an I.T. class. Did your dad tell you he's opening up a branch of Stone Security here in California? Once it's established, I'll be working there."

José had worked his way up from an intern at Stone Security. I knew that he was doing well at my dad's company. But I hadn't realized the company had grown large enough to support a second location.

"So, like a programming class or something like data structures?" I was browsing the class listings.

José thought for a minute before coming to look over my shoulder. "Take that one." He pointed to *Introduction to Information Security and Network Administration.*

I groaned. My mind wanted to switch off just imagining sitting through that class.

He patted my shoulder. "It will be good for you to

understand some of the basics."

I clicked the course and added it to my class cart, choosing the lecture and T.A. section that fit in my schedule.

Violet poked her head up from behind her laptop. "If José gets busy, I can help you, too. I'm going to help build the network security in our new Pack House, make sure it's safe and tight."

I tilted my head. "I thought you were a graphic designer."

She ducked behind her computer. "That too. I work for your dad in my free time. I'll be helping in the new branch. José's alpha of the pack, but I'm his boss at Stone Security… for now."

Bevin and I both snorted.

Violet gave one decisive nod and returned to her computer.

Luke squinted and leaned into his screen. "I found a few potential spots. Are we looking for a building or land to build on?"

José released a huff of air. "Ideally we'd find the perfect building, but we'll do what we need to do."

I froze for a second, then swiveled on my stool at the breakfast bar to face him and Bevin who lounged together on one of the couches. "We can afford to build?"

José was staring out the window towards the park in the distance. He nodded slowly. "Yes and no. I don't want to use up all the money we have, but we need a safe home for the pack. It's a priority." He turned away from the window and focused on each of us in turn. "I'm not going to take on the responsibility of a pack and not establish a den." He took Bevin's hand and gazed into his eyes. Then he turned back to the rest of us. "It was the one lesson that all the other packs completely agreed on. There has to be a central den. This is important."

The weight of his words wrapped around me like a cloak. Facing my computer, I got back to work. In the end, we compiled a list of locations to check out.

We spent our first week looking at the different buildings and plots. Nothing was right. There were some older Victorian homes, some old farmhouses, and some open parcels of land, but nothing quite worked.

During the second week, Luke started his new job. Violet continued to work remotely. Bevin and I returned to the University to get José fully oriented, registered, and signed up for classes. The University offered tours, but he passed on those, figuring anything the tour offered we could provide.

After José was set, we headed to my favorite coffee house just off campus. We each got coffee and I also purchased a chocolate chip muffin.

Bevin sat; the nutty scent of nerves flowed from him as he sipped his coffee. His knee bounced as his focus shifted from me to José.

With a sigh, I placed my hands over his. "For the love of a good coffee, what is wrong with you?"

He huffed out a laugh. "Sorry, I've been thinking about

something, and I don't want you to be disappointed."

My eyes narrowed. "Talk, alpha boy."

His shoulders dropped. "Okay, well, after this, I'm heading back onto campus and I'm breaking my contract with the dorms. I think you should, too. We're a pack now…and I don't want to be away from José."

"Well, I don't mind sleeping apart from José, and need a quiet place to study."

José chuckled.

I took a bite of my muffin, the chocolatey goodness melting in my mouth. "Moreover, until we have a den, I think it will be easier with one less body to house."

Bevin's nose scrunched up. "Are you sure? I get what you're saying, but having our full pack together also seems important."

José's arm slid around Bevin's waist. "Don't worry, Bev. I think we'll have a lot going on, and studying is also important. Jade will be close and," he stared at me, his alpha mantle slipping, "always a call away."

"Righty-o, boss!"

By the end of the second week, everyone felt comfortable navigating Arcoíris. Luke bought a used car to get to work. Bevin and José each owned cars back in Wisconsin which would be driven to California eventually. Bevin's wouldn't come before next summer, but Owen and Sarah would drive José's in the next week to visit and check our progress before flying back home for the start of their school year. We returned the rental car as the city was easily navigated without it.

At the start of the third week, Owen and Sarah arrived. They didn't come alone. Brooke was with them.

She entered the hotel room like a queen, marching right up to José. "You can't stay here."

He raised an eyebrow.

"I know what's in our bank account, but this is ridiculous. This place worked for a week, two tops, but this is not a long-term solution. If you can't find a pack den in the next week, you have to find another living situation as a band-aid. This is too expensive."

José dropped back into the couch where he had been sitting. "I was afraid of that. I just hadn't crunched the numbers."

Brooke rolled her eyes. "Of course you hadn't."

I shook my head at the disdain that dripped from her words. I snapped at her. "We'll figure it out. We've got it."

Brooke ignored me, focusing only on José. "I can send an email if you want, breaking it down. I have a spreadsheet. It's fairly straight-forward. I'll provide exact dates and amounts."

José's face looked pained as he closed his eyes, then rubbed down his full face with both hands. "Yeah. That would be great."

He must have been really overworked if he wanted Brooke to do such simple calculations for him. I was a bit taken aback by his quick acceptance; though, we had all been busy, what with looking for a den, school, and, of course, the new city.

Brooke just nodded and found a seat in the dining area.

Sarah, who had quietly watched the full scene, stood behind Owen. She put her hands on his shoulders and began to bounce. "Give us a tour of…well, everything!"

After the tour, I steered everyone to the Mexican mole restaurant.

The next morning, Owen and I took a walk in the park. "So, why did you want to separate me from the others, bro? Issues with Sarah? Or is it Brooke?"

He snorted. "Neither. Just haven't been able to talk with you in a long time."

I narrowed my eyes but continued to enjoy the cool morning. The path we were on cut through the park. We were surrounded by grassy hills. You could barely tell we were in a city. To the left, if you looked far enough, you could see downtown Arcoíris. To the right, over a hill, was the beginning of a wooded area. "What specifically did you want to talk about?"

"I heard you finally met Julez"

I groaned. "It's fine. I'm fine. I don't want to talk about it."

"I heard that, too." He wrapped an arm around my shoulders. "Now, unlike your alphas, I'm your brother. They may be in your head, but I know *you* better."

I closed my eyes and let him guide me for several steps. I took a deep breath and let my voice drop. "Owen, I'm fine."

When he didn't respond, I looked up at him. A smile stretched across his face and a bounce in his step matched the sparkle in his eye. This was a great way to introduce him to his new pack land, and I could see he enjoyed the walk as we continued down the path, not a care in the world.

With a huff, I stopped walking. I dropped my shoulders and turned off the path towards the trees. After a few minutes of trudging through the thick tangled weeds, I reached the treeline and followed it. The sounds of the birds singing peacefully in the shade calmed me.

I yelled over my shoulder, "Why doesn't anyone believe me that I'm fine?"

He caught up and walked next to me. "Talk to me, Jade."

I turned towards the trees to search the shadows for answers and found none. I growled low, but finally gave in. "I knew we were over. That isn't it. But no one warned me about their connection. When they touch, it's almost as intense as José and Bevin. When I met Julez, it was like a punch…so completely replaced." I thought I whispered that last low enough to not be heard.

Owen took my hand and gave it three distinct squeezes. This had been a family thing our whole life. One squeeze for each word, *I love you.* I faced the woods as a tear spilled down my cheek. After a few measured breaths to get my emotions under control, I gently wiped it away.

We walked in silence for a few minutes, Owen still holding my hand. "You know your early graduation was hard on her, right?"

I nodded. "That first semester, we were on the phone almost every night. I also talked with Sarah every couple nights. I know the two of them weren't ever very close."

Owen stayed silent as we walked, so I kept talking. "She ended up spending most of her time with Luke in the glass-blowing studio. Then, when I came home for winter break, she gave me a glass bouquet she'd made. I still have it in my room. After that, she told me she thought we should just be friends."

It still felt like I was being kicked in the stomach by a horse whenever I thought about it. It had made sense at the time. We were separated by so many miles and living such different experiences, but it still wasn't easy.

"I always wondered who initiated the breakup. I should have guessed. You both did it for the other one, and neither of you really wanted to do it. She was numb until college, never really engaging with any of us. You had Bevin to distract you."

"Bevin and I never really talked about it. He was too happy with José. I didn't want to give him more than the logic of the breakup."

"So, being your stoic self, you haven't let anyone know how you really felt about it until now."

I laughed. I couldn't help it. It just bubbled out of me. All this tension was because I had built up barriers instead of just leaning on the people around me…friends and family who loved me.

Owen squeezed me in a half-hug. "Better."

I wrapped my arm around him, as well. "Is this what you're learning in college?"

"This…and how to set up torture systems like Dad's. But I've learned most of how to train people *from* Dad."

"Why are we in the same pack? Being here I haven't had to deal with the daily routines. It's been so refreshing."

"About that…"

"No!"

He chuckled.

I wiped my face one more time and surveyed our surroundings. Up ahead, a structure peeked out of the trees. It appeared to be an old dormitory. The building was once painted fire-house red, but the paint had mostly peeled off. The building took up a large amount of space. I jogged towards it as if tugged on by an invisible leash.

Owen trotted after me.

The large structure sagged in several areas, dilapidated from years of wear and tear. The front door hung from its hinges. One tug and the thing fell off with a crash. I leapt back to avoid getting hit.

"Jade, don't go in, it isn't safe."

"But Owen, look at it. It could be perfect." My heart pounded and excitement boiled in my belly. We'd been searching for days…weeks, and here I stood, gazing at the potential future home of our pack.

"It looks like a death-trap." Not even Owen's droll comment could cut through my building joy.

Gingerly, I stepped inside. It was dark, but the sun broke through some of the grime from the windows, spearing rays of light into the building. Most of the interior was rotted, leaving a shell of a building. I stood at the threshold of the door and envisioned what it could be. Tears ran down my face as I turned to Owen. "It's our new home!"

CHAPTER 4

My campus schedule had me moving into the dorms during the last week in August. While I moved in, José and Bevin went out to check the building Owen and I had found. The former owners were old and willing to sell, as long as we agreed to keep at least seventy percent of the land wild for at least ten years. It was written into the contract. I laughed at that part, thinking, if they only knew!

The couple also wanted to remain in their small house with a small bit of yard, which was also on the property. They didn't care what we did with the rest of the land, as long as we agreed to those two conditions.

Before we made any decisions, we asked if we could camp out on the land over the weekend. There was a full moon, and it would be the first time our small pack could run together. Dad and Tanner flew out to check out the building earmarked for the new Stone Securities, so they would be running with us. We decided to get their opinions on the land as well.

We drove up to the dilapidated building and parked off to the side. While everyone fanned out and checked out the space, I grabbed the tent bags and started setting them up. Violet joined me.

"You don't want to help in scouting out the area? Determine if this is a good spot?" I asked her.

"Not really. I checked it out on satellite already. We need to get our camp set up, food made, and then we can run." Her eyes glazed by the end.

I quirked a smile. "Like the run, do ya?"

She nodded. "Getting attacked when I was young was terrifying. Your parents finding and helping me was also terrifying. I was just a hacker back then. Your dad offered me a job and a place in the pack. I had always been a loner, ya know."

I didn't know. I didn't really know much about Violet. "What about your family?"

She seemed to ignore me, focused on finishing up the first tent with me instead, before we moved to putting up the second. I didn't think she would answer. Finally, once we had the basic structure up, she stared in my direction, but not at me. "I was living in Oklahoma, it's where I grew up. My mom died young and my dad didn't understand me. He worked all the time and kept food in the house, but I never really saw him. After high school, he told me I was on my own, kicked me out. As far as I'm concerned, this pack is my family." She shrugged as we finished up the second tent.

I knew opening up to me was hard. I stepped up to her slowly, giving her time to signal no. When she was close, I engulfed her in a hug. "I'm glad you became part of our family." I moved away, and we continued setting up.

Each tent would comfortably fit four, and there were only seven of us. In all likelihood we wouldn't even use them if the weather stayed nice.

We moved on to starting a fire. Once we dug a pit and surrounded it with rocks, we built up the tinder and got the flame going. "There was this lone wolf who was attacking people down south. Anyway, I was out one night, digging for food, ya know, behind a restaurant, when this guy approached me."

As she told her story, we searched the area for logs to drag over to use as benches around the fire. They were heavy, but being wereanimals we had the strength to move them.

Once we'd moved the first log, she continued. "He said there was a better place to find free food. Being an idiot, I followed him."

"A lone wolf in human form with that much of a plan?"

"No. I mean, a plan, yes, but he wasn't the wolf. He was the wolf's bestie."

My brow knit as we dropped a second log down and headed out for a third. "Bestie? Really?"

She nodded. "Yeah. He lured me to an ally with an open door, then pushed me down a flight of stairs. At the bottom was the wolf. I fought and ran. I was shocked when the door wasn't locked, and I got away. I guess they didn't expect their targets to be scrappy enough to need to secure the door, but there I was. But the wolf had bitten me."

We dropped the third log into place to form a triangle around the fire. Sweat dripped down my back. I grabbed a water bottle from the bag and handed it to Violet. She took it and I grabbed a second one for myself. We both sat down and drank deeply.

After satiating our thirst, she continued. "A few days later, your dad found me. I guess there were several dead bodies that left a trail. Your parents came down to investigate and clean up. They found me in an alley, shaking and scared. He offered me a home and a job." A small smile played across her face as she took another drink of water.

"I'm surprised you left their pack after all that."

Violet groaned. "Snow. I hate the snow. And the cold. I know I don't leave the house often; I'm a bit of a hermit. But I'm from the south, and Wisconsin is just too darned cold. Every pack is from a snow area, except Florida, and they have alligators, and apparently panthers." She smirked at me.

I snorted at that.

The others came over to join us.

Dad was talking with José and Bevin. "I think this will work, though the structure is a death-trap."

Owen ran up. "That's what I said!"

I rolled my eyes.

José shot a glance over his shoulder at the building. "I don't know; the structure seems to have good bones. I think we can have an engineer come out and look it over, then decide if it's a total tear-down or if we can work with it."

Luke studied his phone. "According to this, the original building was a boarding school. The main building had fifteen classrooms, a kitchen, a dining room, and headmistress's office, a medical suite, and a gym. There was a second and third floor that had dorm rooms and a library.'

Everyone stared at the structure. I gazed off, imagining kids running amok throughout the area. "How small were the rooms? Or, how many students lived here?"

Luke returned to his phone, swiping and tapping. "There were, on average, two hundred students in residence here. Oh, hey! There was another building for the staff, but it hasn't survived—save for the foundation. We can probably build that up into a gym."

After dinner, we went on our monthly run to honor Mondara, the moon god, and investigated the new land. We found a coyote trail and followed it to its source. After that, we ran through the trees determining the boundaries of the land as best we could. There was a crevice with a deep pit that was hidden in the far back. At the widest point, it was about two-and-a-half feet wide. We would have to be careful running around it.

As the night wore on, I grew tired and signaled José that I was heading back to camp. I curled up near the fire to sleep. A few minutes later, Violet and Luke joined me.

I woke up early and dressed. Then I coaxed the fire back to life. I boiled some water for coffee but didn't try to make any food. I knew my limitations.

Dad shocked me by being the next up. I handed him a metal camp mug. "So, when do you and Tanner fly back home?"

"So quick to get rid of us?"

"No. Just checking if I can utilize you two to help move my stuff into the dorms this weekend."

He groaned as he drank some coffee. "We'll be here at least a week. The new site has been located, but I want to go over all of the specs with the new team and make sure everything is going in the direction I want it to go. This working from another state kind of sucks…we hope to be up and running by April."

"Who will be leading the company here?"

"No one you know. Though, if José keeps up with the trajectory he's on, he may be running the company in a few years. He's smart."

"What about Violet?"

"Oh, she's good, but she isn't a people person. I think she'd quit if I tried to put her in charge."

A voice floated out from behind one of the logs. "I would. Don't even think of it."

Chuckles chorused from the group. Slowly, everyone started to rise, dress, and make their way to the coffee.

When Bevin rose, he searched for any other offerings. "I don't know if I should complain or thank you for not making any food."

José came up behind him and gave him a quick hug and kiss on the cheek. "Thank her, mi amor, definitely thank her." Their affection always filled me with warmth. It was a nice way to wake up.

We broke down camp and headed out to find breakfast. Over eggs, sausage, and pancakes at a local diner, we discussed what we wanted in a Pack House. I had my list, and the group mostly agreed with it.

Violet read over everything I had included. "Why a secret escape tunnel?"

I shrugged. "I was watching a scary movie. I thought it sounded cool. If we're building from the ground up, why not. And look," I pointed at the list, "a command center for all the computer surveillance. It will be your favorite room.

You and José."

Her mouth twitched and she continued to scan the list. "You know that building is big enough that it could be set up with rooms like dorm rooms upstairs. We could have two or three floors. I don't think we need room for two hundred, but if the rooms were spacious, maybe twenty per floor. Some could be guest rooms, some could be game rooms, a few bathrooms, a library, study rooms…it could really be a place for people to live and visit."

Bevin's smile kept getting bigger. "A real pack den, with a place for everyone. We don't have a neighborhood, and the pack is so young and living out here is so expensive. Pack members could get their own places, of course, but the den would be big enough with room to grow."

Tanner looked at the list then each of us. "You'll have to give a reason for all of you to be living in the same place. Give it an apartment name, or country club name. Otherwise, it will catch attention. You don't want people to think it's a cult."

I started thinking of names.

Luke looked up from his phone. "How about Lupine Lounge?"

My dad and Tanner both started coughing. My dad cleared his throat first. "Only if you want to be mistaken for a seventies lounge."

Bevin played with his food. "Something with canine?"

José added. "Or just wolf? There's a Coyote Point nearby."

We were all silent as we thought and ate. After a few minutes, a few thoughts coalesced my mind. "We want this to be a safe haven for werewolves and our pack's den. It needs to be named so that on a map it looks like a living apartment building…legitimate. What about after Sonnara? Sonnaris Estates?"

José nodded. "That or Mondaris Estates. Do we want to name our den for the sun or the moon? Either way, I love the idea."

Dad stared off into space. "The big question becomes, when you finally build a grand gate over the driveway, do you want to engrave it with a sun or a moon?"

Bevin's face lit up and I knew he imagined this grand entrance. "A moon. Then we can have wolves and trees in the artwork along the side. People may not even see the wolves if they don't look closely. It could be spectacular."

We all just stared at him.

He shrugged. "What? It could be. Use your imagination." He grumbled and went back to eating.

After breakfast, I moved into the dorms, preparing to get into the headspace for my third year of college. I had unpacked some of my knickknacks first, hanging up pictures of my friends and setting up the glass bouquet Piper had made for me when she had been working with

Luke in the glass-blowing studio.

As I made my bed, I noticed a goose pillow and groaned, tucking it under my other pillows. When I spun to search for Dad to yell at him for bringing it, he was already gone.

I had a new roommate whom I hadn't met. The paperwork said she was a junior like me. That was rare. Most dorm dwellers were freshmen and sophomores. By a student's third and fourth year, they usually found better accommodations, but who was I to judge?

Bevin was helping me get my books in order when an average-looking blond girl came bounding in with a suitcase. She dropped it on the bare mattress. "Hi, I'm Alexandra, but you can call me Alex. I'm new to the school, a transfer, and super excited to meet you." Her words tumbled out of her mouth almost too fast to follow. She turned and saw Bevin and her gray-blue eyes got wide. "Oh! You're not supposed to have boys in here. This isn't going to be a problem, is it?"

I glanced at Bevin's plaid shirt with his rainbow pin on the collar and shook my head.

Bevin spun on his heel towards me with a sparkle in his sapphire eyes. Grinning mischievously, he leaned over and kissed my cheek. "Guess we'll have to wait until later, love." And with that, he completed his spin and sauntered out of the room.

I closed my eyes, trying to hold back something between a growl and a laugh. I moved to finish arranging the books he'd left on my desk. Once done, I dropped into my chair and faced my new roommate. "Hi Alexandra. I'm Jade, nice to meet you." I sounded mostly sincere.

Her friendly, bubbly demeanor was gone as she pulled items out of her suitcase. It looked like she put them away randomly. After about half her stuff was shoved into drawers, she snapped, "Is *he* going to be an issue?"

I tilted my head at the still open door. "Who? Bevin? Depends on what you mean. He and I share about half of our classes together and study together a lot. So, you'll see him around. But, you'll probably see his boyfriend, too. That said, if you think I'm going to go the year without dating, think again." And with that, Sarah had won her argument…dating was back on the table.

Her mouth dropped open as she spun and sat on the bed. "Boyfriend?"

I nodded. "Yep. Bev and I are good friends; he's like a brother. You just jumped to a big conclusion based on him putting books on a shelf. He could have been my brother, friend, boyfriend, just about anything. Instead of just being pleasant, you assumed. Is him having a boyfriend going to be a problem?"

Her face scrunched up. "Well…I don't think so."

"You've known other gay people, right?"

"Not that I know about."

I raised an eyebrow.

She sighed. "I'm from a small town in Iowa, with a

graduating class of forty-three students. A quarter of the class married another quarter…and several of them were pregnant before graduation…or marriage. I was just happy to avoid that."

I just sat, watching her. I wanted to live in the dorm for simplicity, and so far, this was not simple.

She sat on the edge of her bed, looking at her shoes. "After high school, I helped my family at home with my youngest brother. I did an online school with a vet sciences program for two years, but decided I wanted to switch to an in-person school. When I was accepted here, I asked for a roommate who was a junior." She got up and started looking over my stuff. "Do you know how few juniors live in the dorms?"

I flopped down on my bed, wondering why I hadn't just thrown my hat in with the pack. "Yep. I figured I would end up with a younger student."

"You sound disappointed."

"Nope. Just surprised."

Alexandra continued to look over my pictures and books. "Is this your schedule?"

I had my schedule front and center, on the wall, behind my desk. I didn't want to lose track of where I had to be on any given day.

"Mm-hmm."

"You are going to be very busy. Your classes look impossible." She leaned in closer. "Wow, I think we're even in a couple of classes together. Are you double majoring in vet sciences with pre-med?"

I groaned, throwing my arm over my eyes. This was not going to be simpler at all!

CHAPTER 5

Part of my early admittance to Arcoíris University was agreeing to join the track team. Practice began at six a.m. with strength training. Seven was the run. By nine I was sitting in the school's cafeteria eating breakfast, having showered and changed. I had a huge plate of food in front of me and was digging into it when Alexandra dropped down in a seat next to me.

Her voice was a combination of awe and horror as she said, "Wow, that looks like a plate of food my brother would eat, and he's a farm kid."

I slid my gaze to her then returned my attention to

my breakfast.

She slowly took a bite of her food. "So, you left the room early this morning."

I grunted.

Alexandra ate a few more bites of her oatmeal and a banana. "I get the feeling I didn't make the best first impression. Any chance we can start over?"

I dropped my chin to my chest and sighed. Before I could answer, Bevin and José joined us.

She gazed at them and a small, "Oh!" escaped her. "I see it now." She probably thought it was too quiet for us to hear, but we all heard it and, glancing at the boys, I saw we were all going to ignore it.

Bevin snatched one of my sausage links. "What's your first class? We don't have math together until three."

I glared at him. "I had weight training and had to run this morning. Are you *sure* you want to steal my food?"

His eyes almost glowed at the question. "Oh, yeah! I live for the challenges life offers."

José chuckled. "Do you have to stay on the team for all four years?"

I made a pitiful sound before taking a big bite of my breakfast sandwich. "It was part of the small print. The coach loves me. He contacted Coach Nelson my first year and together they came up with a plan." I threw my hands in the air at that last word, shimmying them. "It sucks."

Bevin snorted. "She's been complaining about it

ever since."

I punched his arm and faced José. "Now you get to hear all about it, too. Aren't you glad you transferred?"

Alexandra perked up at that word. "You're a transfer student, too? Are you two juniors as well? Hi! I'm Alexandra, by the way, but you can call me Alex. Jade's roommate."

She didn't put out a hand to shake. She looked a bit nervous, biting her lower lip as her eyes darted around. *Does she think the boys have something catching?* She smelled nervous, too, nutty, like almonds from the carnival. Now I wanted to visit a carnival…sigh, but all I had were classes to attend. There was something more to her scent, but my mind wasn't ready to suss it out; it was too evasive. I needed more caffeine to deal with this.

Bevin's amusement poured out of him and his eyes sparkled as he gazed at Alexandra. He threw an arm over my shoulder. "No longer worried about anything nefarious happening between me and Jade? I mean, we could put a sock on the door handle as a warning if it'd help."

I just shook my head and went back to eating.

José's eyes narrowed. "I'm José and this is Bevin. If you spend much time around Jade, you'll see the two of us. We're a package deal. If Bevin and I make you uncomfortable, you need to figure that out now." With that, he got to eating his breakfast.

Bevin kissed my cheek again. "I guess that means the two of us are over." Sighing, he took his arm back and tucked into his meal.

Alexandra ducked her head and finished her breakfast, saying, "Of course it's fine, it's fine, you're fine." She blushed, then mumbled, again to herself, but not too low for wereanimals, "I knew college would be different, but not quite this soon."

Once my plate was empty, I agreed to meet Bevin in math, and headed off to my ten a.m. class. Half-way there, Alexandra caught up with me.

"Jade, I'm sorry. Can we walk to class together?"

"What are you sorry for?"

"I don't know. For assuming things, I guess. For making your friends uncomfortable."

"They aren't. They're perfectly happy with who and what they are."

"Oh! Well, that's good. It's just.... It's new for me, that's all."

I slid a quick glance to her before making my way into the building. "You moved to California, to a college town. Did you not expect to meet anyone who was gay or lesbian, or different from yourself?"

She sighed. "I did, I just...I don't know. I guess not on the first day."

Irritation surged through me. "I don't get it. You were upset at the idea of your roommate...a junior you requested, having a boyfriend. Now, you're uncomfortable with him having a boyfriend. I don't really know what you expected.

You need to reevaluate what you thought you'd find here at a university, because me and my friends are pretty tame."

I made my way to the classroom and found a seat. Alexandra sat next to me. *Of course.*

Before anything more could be said, the professor started reading over the syllabus and telling us what to expect for the semester.

The two classes I had with Alexandra were back-to-back, so she followed me to the next class. We had fifteen minutes between classes, and she wanted to talk…again.

"How long have you known Bevin?"

I debated my answers, then realized I had to live with her for the next year, might as well explain a few things right away. "All my life. His mom and my aunt were best friends in college and our families brought their kids up together."

Her eyes widened. "Oh. So, you understand my upbringing where everyone knows everyone, and people marry the people they grew up with."

"I'm not marrying Bevin."

She snorted. "I picked that up. I may be slow, but even I can learn." Her eyes narrowed. "How long have you known José?"

I slowed as we neared our next classroom. "How could you tell?"

"None of you need to say much. It's almost like you read each other's minds."

If she only knew!

"Yeah, I should have said, Bevin's mom, José's mom,

and my aunt were best friends in college, and we were all brought up together."

Her smile turned triumphant. "Did they always know they'd end up as a couple?"

I snorted. I was glad I wasn't drinking, or I'd have liquid coming out my nose. "No. That didn't happen until about two years ago. It's a long story and it isn't mine to tell."

"Did you ever want to date either of them?"

She was *so* full of questions. "Do you ever stop asking questions? You should think about becoming a detective… or a journalist. And no. Neither of them is my type."

She nodded. "Because they like guys."

I nodded. "Yep, and because they *are* guys."

She froze, her mouth forming a perfect "O".

I waggled my eyebrows at her and spun, slipping through the door into our classroom. I sat and was a bit surprised when she plopped down next to me again. Her voice quavered a bit as she got out her notebook. "You're not *interested* in me, are you?"

My I.T. class was at two o'clock in one of the older buildings on campus. The lecture hall accommodated over two hundred students and had auditorium-style seating with sliding trays that flipped over to form a small desktop. They were obnoxious. To get to your seat, early arrivals had to sit near the center, or late arrivals had to navigate legs and bags.

Everything about the lecture hall made me question the I.T. class José had convinced me to take. As the heat in the room soaked into my skin, I regretted it more and more. The freshmen surrounding me weren't helping. I chose a spot near the center and near the back, away from most of the other students. I'd had enough socialization for one day. A couple minutes before class started, loud laughter startled me from my misery as two students walked in—a male and a female—who looked similar enough to be siblings. They were both tall, tan-skinned, with sandy hair, looking as if they had come from the beach, not that there were any nearby. No one else in the room made much noise, so their boisterous entrance caught everyone's attention.

After that brief distraction, I went back to deciding whether this class was worth it. The lecture was two days a week, with two days on the computer in a smaller classroom setting. That would probably be with one of the T.A.s. Would the teaching assistance be any good?

I was just about to pull up the desk when the wonder twins entered my row. I eyed them, debating if I'd have to move. With the desktop out, they couldn't pass me. Sighing, I waited.

They slowly made their way down the empty row—empty, save for me. When they reached me, the female scooted past, but the male dropped down in the seat right next to me. I closed my eyes and counted to five, confused and frustrated that my solitude was being invaded by this guy when I realized the female had taken the seat to my right. *Grrr.*

I huffed out a sigh and grabbed the desktop. I pulled it the wrong way and it locked in place. I yanked and nothing happened. I yanked again, growling low in my throat. Still nothing. Defeated, I flopped back.

The guy chuckled. "Need help? I'm Quinn, and that's my sister Greta."

I forced a smile. "No, I think I can manage it." I tried again, more slowly, and managed to get the desktop out. I then turned to smile at Greta and for a second lost the ability to think as my breath hitched. When they had come in, I'd noticed that they were attractive, but up close it was even more apparent. She was gorgeous. For a moment, time stopped. I was lost in her hazel eyes.

She gave me half a smile before turning to the front of the room and easily pulled out her own desktop.

With an effort, I shook myself, got my notebook out, and swallowed. *What is wrong with you, Jade? Get yourself together!*

Class started and once the professor began speaking, he didn't stop. He just jumped right into teaching without going through the syllabus. By the end, I had pages full of notes scribbled throughout class, most of which I didn't understand.

As I was packing up, Greta rubbed my forearm. "You wouldn't want to form a study group with me and Quinn would you?"

My pulse jumped at her touch. I couldn't remember the last time I'd had such a reaction to a person. I took a calming breath. "I don't know if I'd be of any use to you—was any of that in English?" I laughed nervously. "But yeah, I'd welcome the help." I gazed into her mesmerizing eyes. I knew I was staring, but couldn't stop.

Her lips curved into a satisfied smile as she stared back at me.

After a minute, Quinn cleared his throat. "So, which T.A. group are you in?"

I jumped at his voice, breaking out of my trance. I finished packing up my stuff and shook my head to clear it. "Um, T.A.? Oh! I only had this time free, so two o'clock tomorrow." I pulled out my phone and checked the lock screen where I'd saved my schedule. "Room nine."

Greta's face broke into a huge smile, then said, "Nice, we're in that one, too."

We all stood and shuffled out. At the edge of the seats, Quinn said, "See you tomorrow…never did get a name."

"Oh! Yeah, hi, I'm Jade."

"Nice to meet you…Jade." Quinn shook my hand as we neared the door.

Outside the room, Greta shook my hand, too. As she did, she pressed a piece of paper into my palm. "Later." She sauntered after her brother.

As they walked away, she held her hand out and he put a ten-dollar bill into it. I had a feeling I didn't want to know what that was about. Taking a quick peek, I saw numbers. I stuffed the paper in my pocket and I checked my phone again to see where my next class was.

Bevin awaited me in math class and I happily collapsed next to him.

"Rough day?"

"You have no idea."

I told him about all my adventures, though I left out mention of the twins. He told me what he'd learned about the building we were looking into and his day of classes.

I groaned when I heard the bad news. "They can't keep any of the structure? It's a total tear down?"

"Nope. But there's electricity out there and we found a caretaker's house on the property. It was in the other direction from where we ran. It has two bedrooms, a bathroom, a living room, and a small kitchen. It's small, but it's ours. There's a basement that's habitable, at least enough for guests and short-term visits. Violet and Luke said they don't mind sharing a room for a bit. We're giving them the bigger room."

"That's amazing. So, now we need to hire an architect."

"Yeah. The ones we've spoken with were so bloody expensive. We need quality at a good price. It's a big project though, so that makes it harder to find. The quotes are coming in high."

"Have you considered…"

I was cut off by the sounds of the professor clearing

their throat and then launching straight into the lecture. Like in the I.T. class, this professor didn't believe in reading to us what we could read for ourselves.

We were leaving class when my phone rang. I answered it. "Hey, Team Kid, any chance you're free?"

Zack, a lone wolf from Wisconsin, liked to call me and Bevin "Team Kid." We'd helped him out a few times with medical emergencies. I hadn't spoken to him in years.

"Zack, I don't know how to break it to you, but, I'm in California."

"I know. Did your powerhouse partner join you?"

I shifted my gaze to Bevin who chuckled softly, hearing the conversation probably as well as I could. "You're in California?"

"I'll send you my location. It isn't a huge rush, but the quicker you can get out here, the better."

I hung up. A few minutes later, a location near a beach in Half Moon Bay popped up in my text messages. Bevin texted José as we headed out to the parking lot.

José met us. "Look, I have to stay on campus." He tossed me the keys. "Be safe."

Bevin glared. "I'm not a bad driver!"

We both just stared at him. José leaned in, giving him a kiss. "You know I love you. You're great at school, brilliant at math. Your cooking is delightful. You just aren't the best driver. Let Jade have this one. She's a great driver. She has the instincts of a cat."

Bevin grumbled as he got into the passenger seat. We followed the GPS on my phone. After parking and then another ten minutes on foot, we found Zack. He stood on a rocky beach, his muscles tight, but with no obvious injury.

The scent of the water and the salt was overpowering, but there was also the scent of blood. I started to jog. "Zack, are you okay?"

"Yeah, I'm good, but since I'm going to be in the area for a bit, why don't you start calling me Zee. It's what my friends call me."

Bevin's eyes narrowed and he stood a bit taller. He assumed his alpha mantle and almost seemed ageless. "You're going to be in the area for a while? Is this your official check-in?"

"Later. Let's start with him." Zee pointed at a mangled body by his feet. A kid, maybe a year or two older than me, who looked like he'd been mauled by a wild animal. *Is he dead?* I could smell a werewolf, but I didn't recognize the wolf's scent.

I squatted down, but didn't touch. As I got closer, I could hear a faint heartbeat. My heart hammered, and I swallowed back bile as a shiver wracked my body. "What do you know?"

"Not much. I just moved to the area. I was thinking of joining the local pack." Both Bevin and I jerked at that, and Zee chucked. "I thought I would come to the water to help me make up my mind, when I found this." He pointed at the kid. "He smells of werewolf."

I leaned down, but I had already smelled the wolf on him. I gazed up over my shoulder at Bevin. "Your call, alpha-man."

He continued to radiate alpha. His face hard, he stared through me. "Have you had enough to eat?"

"Probably not."

Zee threw an energy bar at me. I opened it up and bit off a large chunk.

Bevin nodded. "Triage. Let me know his prognosis."

I tried to separate my feelings. I knew this had to be hard on Bevin too, but he had his walls up. "This is easier when the connection is direct; less energy loss."

Zee's brow dropped as his mouth scrunched up. "What's easier?"

I shook my head. "Later."

Surveying the body, I found a small piece of unmangled skin. I gently put my fingers on it and closed my eyes. I felt Bevin put his hand on my shoulder. As an epsilon, I had the ability to communicate mind-to-mind with my packmates, either through touch or through my mental pack connections. It took less of my energy if a pack member was touching me.

Panther came forward and began searching the body. It was a wreck. Everything was damaged—bones, organs, skin, everything.

Bevin, are you getting the full report?

"Yes."

Should we heal him?

"Is there a wolf or a seed of a wolf?"

We searched. After what felt like hours, but was probably five to ten minutes, Panther reported: *no wolf seed, no wolf*. This person was not a werewolf.

"Back out, Jade. Do not heal him."

I did as instructed.

Zee watched us. "Are you going to fix him?" I faced my alpha. I tried to hold my hands still at my side. Though I agreed with him, it hurt to let someone die, and I knew it hurt him, too. Swallowing past the lump in my throat I held myself tight, letting my alpha take the lead.

Bevin turned to Zee. "No. He's not a werewolf. He can't be our responsibility. There was a small town near where we parked. We'll say we saw something on the beach, put in an anonymous report. The police will come and help." Despite the coldness in his words, I could see the pain behind his eyes. We couldn't risk our pack's safety.

Zee turned on Bevin. "What if he shifts at the next full moon?"

Bevin shook his head. "Not going to happen. That's part of what Jade was checking out."

"Wait," Zee's eyes got wide. "You can tell the potential of a werewolf?"

"I can also talk to your wolf." I gave him a small smile as I took another bite of his energy bar. My hand shook as

Bevin pulled me up. I felt a bit nauseous. He slipped his arm around my waist.

"You did great. I know you wanted to heal the kid, but it isn't worth risking the pack."

We invited Zee to dinner, and he accepted. He had his own car and followed us back to Arcoíris where Bevin and I picked up José.

On the way to the restaurant we discussed the dead boy. José gazed out the window. "I had hoped we would have an established den, maybe a bigger pack, had graduated college—you know, easy things—before we had to deal with a rogue wolf. I know Half-Moon Bay isn't exactly in our territory, but we're going to have to start doing sweeps."

I saw Bevin in the backseat bite his lip and nod. "I agree. A wolf attack is major business. If we can find this upstart and deal with him, that would be for the best." He paused, staring towards José. "Our first test as alphas."

It was cute playing chauffeur to this conversation. I knew I'd be part of the solution, but I wasn't an alpha, and I was glad I didn't have to make these big decisions.

We ended up meeting Zee at the New Orleans restaurant. I needed the soul-filling food the place offered. We sat in the back corner.

José leaned back after cleaning his plate off, twice.

Amateur. "I always knew you as a lone wolf. Why join a pack now?"

Zee answered between bites of his etouffee. "I never *wanted* to be a lone wolf; I just didn't want to join the Midwest pack."

My plate had a shrimp Po' Boy and gumbo. Deciding which to sample next almost distracted me more than his words, but his statement won out. "That's what I heard. Though, it never made sense to me. Switching packs isn't common, but it's done."

Zee scent shifted to a deep confusion. His lips pushed together, and his eyes got hard. "That's not what I've been told." His gaze took in each of us. "Then again, you were all part of the Wisconsin pack, and now you're here."

Bevin gently placed his hand on Zee's arm. "Who told you it was a one-and-done permanent thing?" As Bevin's hand rested on Zee, the other man's whole body relaxed. The soothing power of an alpha, a connection to pack, letting a wolf know they belonged. Any wolf could do it, but it was more intense with the alpha.

Zee looked at the hand and shut his eyes as if trying to figure out what was going on. "Another lone wolf I ran with. I told him I wanted to find a pack and he told me to be wary of them. After a few months we split, and he migrated south. He created me, ya know. I haven't heard from him again. Don't know if he even survived."

"Well," I said. "You're welcome to join a pack. You can

leave the pack. You can join a new one. I, for one, would be happy for you to join ours. It would be easier for me to track you. Bevin, too, if the alphas are smart about the joining."

José gave me a piercing glare. "Jade!"

"What? You know I'm right. We'll be off chasing him every few months anyway. It'll be easier this way."

Bevin bit his lips to try to keep a straight face. After a bit of a struggle he finally said, "She's not wrong. If he gets lost where there isn't cell phone reception, we'd find him more easily this way."

Zee's eyes narrowed. "What the hell are you two talking about?"

José sighed. "Jade, you aren't an alpha. There are things you don't know. It's complicated."

I heard a knocking inside my head. I scrunched up my face but 'opened the door.' José was accessing my mental epsilon communication; it always sounded like someone at the door. It often led to a headache on my end, but that could have been psychosomatic because the ability was discovered by Brooke. It still irked me that she'd figured it out. Despite the pain, it was something we taught Violet and Luke right away and would teach each new member of our pack. It was too valuable a tool not to use it.

José, what's up?

"*One of the things we learned from the packs was that even though either alpha could take in the pack members, ideally one took in the majority. Right now, Bevin just has Brooke. In your parents' pack, your dad only has Tanner and Jackson."*

I nodded and dropped the connection, rubbing my temples.

Zee sniffed the air and then sniffed José. "What did you just do? You smelled like Team Kid for a minute."

I huffed. "Wait, *I'm* Team Kid, not both of us?" I waved my hand between me and Bevin.

"Whichever one of you I'm talking about is Team Kid, kid."

I tried to sneer, then laughed. Then I continued to eat, my hunger growing after the brain games José had played with me.

José sighed. "Let's do this." He stared at Bevin for a full minute. They seemed to have a conversation, though they sat like statues. Finally, José nodded. "And, as much as I don't like it, I agree that Bevin should take the reins on this one."

Bevin closed his eyes and let out the breath he was holding. His normally sparkling eyes hardened as he opened them. He placed the heel of his left hand on Zee's forehead, letting his fingers drape over Zee's head like a cap. "Zack Mallory, welcome to our pack."

Zee's eyes widened at the use of his full name, and Bevin slumped. He shook his head as if trying to get all of the extra information to settle. Then he nodded and shook his head again; this time it traveled down his full body, like a dog shaking himself.

I closed my eyes, saw the connection, and then gazed over at Bevin, who seemed to have figured everything out.

"You okay?"

He smiled weakly. "It's a lot. I forgot."

Zee watched us. "What just happened? I don't feel any different."

I grabbed his hand. "You're part of the pack. You have two alphas...who are amazing, I might add. You have me, which is a story unto itself. Basically, having an alpha means whenever you experience really sharp emotions, the alpha feels them along with you. You're connected, you have a family. There's more, we'll help you get adjusted. Since you always called on me and Bev, Bevin took on that responsibility."

"Wait, he can read my mind?" Zee started to scoot back.

I tightened my grip. "No, just strong emotions."

Zee was starting to spiral into a freak out. "I don't want anyone in my mind. I have secrets. This isn't what I thought it would be. What the hell?"

Before he could cause a scene, I found my center and released my calm. I had been practicing, and instead of blanketing the full restaurant, I focused it on just our table. Zee's eyes widened. He slumped back in his chair. His breathing evened out and he focused on me in awe.

"Better?"

He nodded.

Our waiter Kenny, who'd been serving Bevin and me since we started college, sashayed to the table. "How is everything, my favorite customers?"

In my experience, everyone who came in were his

favorites, but he was an excellent waiter who made each of his customers feel welcome and special. He brought the flavor of New Orleans to us. He'd relocated here from there several years back, and we loved hearing his stories.

José smiled up into his umber face, framed by dreadlocks held down by a bandana. "A plate of beignets for the table."

Kenny's smile widened. "The perfect end to any meal." He spun on his heel and was off to the kitchen.

Zee's eyes widened, and he started to freak out again. His sweet scent of fear was growing. I sighed. "No one can read your mind. I promise. That's not a superpower anyone wants, trust me. But this way we can more easily help when you fall off a mountain. We can find you even without the phone *if you want us to.*" He had to understand it was always his choice. "It isn't fool proof, but it's a start. So, now that you're pack, where are you living?"

His breathing began to even out, and his eyes lost a bit of their wildness. "Nowhere, yet."

José groaned. "The house on the property is pretty full, but if you don't mind a crappy basement or roughing it outdoors, you can live on pack territory."

Zee's eyes gleamed. "I love living on the land. And with access to some indoor plumbing, it sounds like heaven!"

I tilted my head, thinking. "Zee, what do you do for a living, by the way? I don't think I've ever asked."

"Me? I'm an architect."

CHAPTER 6

At two o'clock the next day I found room nine. I arrived a few minutes early. There were twenty computers in the room in four rows of five. The first two rows were full. I sat in the center of the third row.

After the excitement of dinner the night before, José had dropped me off at the dorms to do homework. There was an incredible amount for the first night, and I really didn't want to fall behind. While trudging up the stairs, I slipped my hands in my pockets and found a piece of paper. It took a few seconds to remember the siblings I'd met earlier and the paper the sister had given me.

I took it out and read *Greta* and a phone number. A smile spread across my face as tingles spread through my body.

My heart began to pound in my chest, and not from the stairs. I gently folded the paper and tucked it in my pocket. Despite my decision to follow Sarah's advice to date, I wasn't sure I was ready for this.

I carefully added Greta's contact information to my phone once I returned to the dorms. After deliberating for way too long, I decided I wasn't going to call or text. I could...I just didn't. Not yet. My first priority had to be getting my work done.

My roommate asked questions about my night, about homework we both had, and then told me about her day. I tried to ignore everything but the homework. Dorms were supposed to be easier. That's what I had told Bevin and José. That's what I had told myself. I groaned as she droned on...

I sighed, returning to the present. At least I only shared classes with my roommate every other day. On every other day, I had my morning classes with Bevin. Except for this class, I had a full day with him.

Notebook out, I surveyed the room. I didn't recognize anyone in the T.A. session of the I.T. class. Then again, I hadn't really paid attention to the other students during the lecture yesterday. Sitting so far back, all I'd really seen were the backs of everyone's heads. The only other students I'd met were the brother and sister. Beyond them and their weird act, I'd just focused on taking notes. Right before class began, Quinn and Greta ran in. They spotted me, smiled conspiratorially at each other with a smirk, and took up their seats on either side of me again.

They were late enough that we couldn't talk. There was a fifteen-minute lecture on practical applications, and then a thirty-minute lab on the computer. I looked over what we needed to do and knew it could be done in less time if the computer user wasn't an idiot, and I knew I wasn't an idiot. I started working and was through the lab in eighteen minutes. Once finished, I checked out Quinn and Greta. They lounged back in their seats, watching me finish up. Great, so much for not being the idiot. Looking around my seat, I searched for my dunce cap.

"So, you two are computer people?"

They leaned forward so we were all hidden behind the computer monitors. Talking was allowed, but once done I feared what tasks the T.A. would assign us next.

Quinn smiled, and it made him look even more handsome. "It's what I'm here to study. I asked if I could just test out of this class, but they insisted everyone in my program had to take it."

Greta chimed in. "I'm here studying graphic design, but when your twin never shuts up about all things I.T., you pick up on a thing or two."

I felt my eyes pop at that. "Twin?"

They both chuckled, but Greta answered. "Yep. And for some reason we ended up at the same college."

Quinn slid his hand into mine. "Can you clear up a bet for us?"

I didn't like the sound of this. "Not if I don't have to."

Greta's laugh flowed around me like silk, sending a thrill through me. She leaned back, smirking at Quinn. "I like her, Quinn. And you know I'm right."

He sighed.

Greta turned to me. "Are you busy after class? Would you want to have coffee with me? Just me, not him."

Mind going blank, I swallowed. "I have a class after this. But maybe after that?"

She gave a half-smile of triumph before nodding. "Sounds great. Do you have my number?"

I nodded and pulled out my phone. I sent her a text with the name of my favorite coffee shop and a time.

She checked her phone and smiled, fingers dancing over her screen. "Perfect."

Just before three, I slipped into my seat next to Bevin. He sniffed, brows lowering. "Jade? You're keeping something from me."

"I just sat down. How can I be hiding something?"

One of his brows slowly rose.

"I don't like you very much right now."

"You love me, now talk."

I groaned. "Fine." I slid down low in my seat and told him about the twins. First the big lecture, the money they exchanged, and then our conversation in the lab.

"We were in the car together for over an hour yesterday, and you forgot to tell me about this?"

"Well." I sank a bit lower.

"You know their bet was about you. Which of the two could win a date with you. And the sister won."

I rubbed my temples with my fingers, and said, "I *don't* know that and neither do you."

"Yes, yes I do, and so do you. Now, sit up, class is going to start. We'll discuss this over dinner. You have to get Zee caught up on your tricks before he slips off on his next adventure or slips off his next cliff."

Snorting, I sat up and dug out my notebook.

After class, Bevin wished me luck as I ran off to the coffee house. I got there early, grabbed a coffee and a chocolate chip muffin, and found a table in the back corner. I pulled out my phone, and found a text from Sarah.

`Don't know what's going on, but calm down, it's going to be okay. Call when you're out of classes.`

I chuckled, sipped my coffee, and waited. It wasn't like I didn't talk to Sarah most days, the distance between our colleges was no barrier to our bond.

A few minutes later, Greta slid into the chair across from me with a coffee of her own.

I could smell her interest in me, the vanilla scent added to the coffee and muffin I ate, and I was emboldened by Bevin's words. Tired of being hurt over a relationship that was long over, I smiled up at her. "Hi, beautiful."

Her eyes widened, sparkling at me. "Afternoon." She sat back as her heart rate increased.

My smile got bigger. I mirrored her position, leaning back and crossing my legs. "Are you new to town?"

"I am. My brother and I moved here from San Mateo."

"Have you two always been close?"

"Sort of. I mean, we fight, but we're also friends. We share interests. Like the same books, movies, types of girls…you know, interests."

I snorted, then covered my mouth as my eyes got wide in embarrassment at the sound. "But not the same degree? You don't have all the same classes."

"No, just the freshmen ones that everyone has. You're not a freshman, are you?"

"Junior."

She nodded. "So, dinner Friday night?"

I laughed, glad I didn't have coffee in my mouth. "You're not shy are you?…or slow."

"So, that's a yes? I'm hoping you know of a good place for us to go."

I rubbed the back of my neck, thinking, my grin widening. "Friday night."

The world around us disappeared as we got to know

one another. By the end, we were leaning in over the table mere inches apart, and at some point, our hands overlapped. I'm not sure when that happened, but everything about the time at the coffee house felt natural and comfortable. After an hour, I had to head out to meet up with the pack, so I said goodbye.

Before I left, she gave me a kiss. It was light and gentle, but it seared me to my toes. My breath stopped for a few seconds as she pulled away. Then a smile slowly spread across her face. We sat there staring at each other for an eternity before she finally said, "I'll see you tomorrow in class." She grabbed her bag and walked out of the café.

Once the door had closed, I gathered my stuff, and headed out. I had walked a block towards our Pack House in a daze before a car's honk made me jump a foot into the air. I dropped my bag and almost fell on my face. Whirling, I saw Bevin laughing in the passenger seat of José's car. I grabbed my bag and stomped over. My face burning, I slipped into the back seat and belted myself in.

Bevin turned in his seat so he had a view of both me and José. "Have a nice date?"

My face burning, I bit my lip before I said, "It wasn't a date."

"You were floating on a cloud, unaware of anything around you. Want to try that again?"

I huffed and crossed my arms, sinking into the seat.

José shot a quick peek in the rear-view mirror.

"What's wrong?"

"I don't know. It was nice, really nice. I just want…I don't know, my friends back, just for a day. Right now you're my alphas. I don't know if that makes sense. How about this: I'll go out on my date with Greta on Friday, and on Saturday we'll hang out and gossip like the old days. I'll come over and we'll do homework and catch up."

José watched the traffic. "I don't know if it makes sense to me, but I didn't grow up with parents who were alphas."

Bevin's eyes sparkled brightly. "Date on Friday?"

I smiled back at him and nodded. "Yeah. I have to figure out where. But Saturday?"

They both nodded as we pulled up to the new Pack House.

Inside, José made a beeline for the kitchen. Bevin and I headed to the living room where we found Luke and Zee playing cards.

I flopped down on the couch next to Zee. "Hey. How goes it? Anyone read your mind lately?"

He slid his eyes to me for a minute before playing a card. "Ha, ha! Now, don't distract me."

I snorted and waited for them to finish their game. Once they were done, I could smell something good coming from the kitchen. "José, want help?"

"Yes, chica, but not you."

"I can help, I just can't lead."

"Mm-hm. Bevin?"

"Coming." He stood and made his way into the tiny kitchen.

"Well, while they cook, let's talk. One of the things I can do is reach out and talk to the members of the pack." I closed my eyes, found the connection to Zee and said, *Hi!*

He leapt up and his eyes bugged out. He took a few steps away from me. "Holy hell, what was that? You said you *couldn't* read minds!"

I sighed, "I can't read your mind. I'm epsilon. It's a rare type of werewolf. It's why I can heal you, but it also lets me talk to you—just communicate, not read thoughts."

He panted and smelled of wolf. He backed up to the wall and his eyes were wild.

I closed my eyes and released calm. "I can also do that."

He slumped, landing on his butt on the floor. He shook his head to clear it. "Okay, I think I'm better. So, you can just talk into my head whenever you want?"

"Mostly, but it gives me a headache, and I pretty much never want to do it."

"That's good."

"And you can do it back to me." I waggled my brows.

"Does it give *me* a headache then?"

"Oh, no, always me. I get *all* the headaches."

He snorted. "How can I reach out to give you the headache?"

"Well, I think if you focus on me and call…you know, in your head."

Luke, who chuckled softly at our conversation, said, "I imagine a door with a large letter J on it. I then knock on it like, *bam, bam, bam*." He rapped his knuckles against the tabletop to add action to his words. Apparently, he actively did the action in his mind as well because I could feel the knocking in my mind. Instantly, my head began to throb.

I put my right hand to my temple. "Not so aggressively, please."

Zee closed his eyes and started to nod to a beat only he could hear. A few seconds later, I could feel his knocking. It wasn't as hard as Luke's had been.

Hi, Zee.

"*Can you hear me?*" It was soft, almost a whisper.

I smiled at how gentle his voice came across. *I can.*

"*How far can this connection reach?*"

I don't know, but I've used it to span several miles, so you can reach me on your adventures across California.

He disengaged. Luke sniffed. "Good, you're done."

Zee's eyes widened. "This's why José smelled like you the other day."

I nodded.

Zee's head tilted. "One question."

"Yeah."

"Why don't any of you smell like wereanimals? All I can smell is your forest smell. Nothing of your animals."

"We get special soap and shampoo from the werebears. I was going to bring that up next, anyway. You should start using it for safety reasons. It's protection for all of us."

Just before winter break of my junior year of high school, I learned that my gym teacher was more than he seemed; he was a werebear. Growing up, Owen and I had always been told there were only werewolves. Then I went to Florida and was bitten by a werepanther. I was pretty sure the werebear was the last of the list, but at this point, nothing would surprise me.

As it turns out, the sleuth of werebears in Wisconsin are very protective of their privacy. The reason we never knew about them was their ingenuity. They'd created a line of toiletries that covered wereanimal scents. It allowed them—and now, us—to move around safely.

Zee's eyes darted between me and Luke. "I'm sorry, there are werebears?"

CHAPTER 7

The first week of classes felt longer than the average first week. If this was indicative of the year, I wasn't sure I would survive. In I.T. class on Friday, the T.A. stated he wanted to put us into groups. "Throughout the semester you will be creating a blueprint for a network, a security system, and implementing it in a sandbox created for you in a playground I'll be setting up for each group."

The T.A. scanned the room to make sure we all paid attention to his important announcement. "Each group will be made up of five members, and each member will be assigned a role: administrator, reporter, writer, timekeeper, and organizer. I have cards with the duties for each role.

There is a quiz on the class portal where you can let me know if there are people in the class you feel you would like to work with, but I will be assigning the groups next class. You have until Sunday midnight to fill out the quiz with your group requests."

He started handing out the papers with the descriptions of the roles and the basic outline of the assignments the groups would be working on. "There will be more details on the assignments, but the groups will be responsible for midterm and final projects."

After that he handed out the assignment for the day and we all got to work. Before I logged in, Quinn grabbed my arm. "Do you want to request to be in a group with me and Greta?"

I eyed him wearily. "Why would you want to be in a group with me? You do know I know nothing about any of this, right? I'll bring you two down."

He gave me a devastating smile. "But I could do this in my sleep. This is about socialization, my dear. I hear you and my sister are going out on a date tonight."

My face started to heat. "Okay, yeah, I'd like to be in your group. Do you know anyone else in class?"

He made a show of looking up and down our empty row. "Nope."

After that, we focused on finishing up the assignment well within the time allotted. Once I was done, I logged into the class portal and found the quiz. It had a few basic questions, including class section, and classmates I would like to be in a group with, classmates I wouldn't like to be in a group with, and special learning accommodations I may need. I started to enter the twins in the former and then realized I didn't know their last name.

I asked over my shoulder. "Last name?"

Greta put her hand on my shoulder and leaned in, watching what I was doing. "Verater. Yours?"

"Stone."

It took only a moment to enter their names in the spot for who I wanted to work with. I left the next two sections blank before I saved the quiz and logged out. Greta continued to lean into me, observing me type. It was a bit distracting.

I sat back when I finished. Greta shifted from leaning into me to resting her hand on my knee. Her focus was on her phone, not me, so despite my heart skipping a beat, I tried to play it off like it was nothing. Unsurprisingly, Quinn also played on his phone.

That night, Greta and I met in front of the main campus administrative building. I wore a simple black dress with a green sparkly shawl that matched my eyes. She wore a turquoise shirt I didn't quite understand that wrapped around her and a black mini skirt. As I approached, my breath hitched. *Wow!*

She gave me a big smile and my steps faltered. "Don't you look wonderful?"

My mouth instantly dried. I tried to swallow. Closing my eyes, I took a calming breath and finally got my voice back. "So do you."

She beamed at me and slipped her arm in mine. We started walking down the street. "Where are we heading?"

"There's this amazing Thai restaurant a few blocks away. Do you like Thai?"

She moaned deep in her throat and I almost tripped. Her arm in mine was the only thing keeping me up.

She laughed and said, "Yes, Thai is perfect. I know it's only been a week, but I'm tired of campus dorm food. Real food sounds amazing, and Thai…. God, that sounds amazing."

After that we focused on getting to the restaurant. Arm in arm we laughed as we walked the streets, avoiding other people and listing what we'd get at the restaurants we passed.

It didn't take us long to get seated and we ordered right away. Focusing on food helped me to get my thoughts straightened out. "Do you have other siblings?"

She hesitated before she answered. "Well, no. Quinn is my only sibling, but I grew up with a bunch of kids around me, so it *feels* like I have other brothers and sisters."

I chuckled. "I get that. Why so many kids?"

"Oh, my mom wanted to raise her kids with her sisters'

kids. She is one of three sisters. I was brought up with my cousins. We all live on the same block. When Quinn got obnoxious, I'd just go sleep at a cousin's house."

"That sounds great. Do you have a lot of cousins?"

"Enough. I ended up on babysitting duty a lot. For some reason, Quinn got out of most of it."

"And are your parents okay with this?" I waved my hand back and forth between us.

She shrugged. "What they don't know..."

Disappointment filled me. "Really? You and your brother seem so free."

"Well, Quinn knows. He figured it out last year. He promised not to say anything. I don't know that the—well, my parents wouldn't be okay with it. They are *very* traditional."

"Do any of the cousins know?"

Her eyes grew distant as she thought about it for a minute. She looked over my shoulder staring off into space. "No. I can't see telling them. It would make them all uncomfortable. Do your parents know?"

"Yeah. When I told them, they said they had a bet going on as to when I'd come out.... Mom won."

Greta snorted. "Do all your friends know, too?"

I huffed out a laugh. "Yep. I have a pretty diverse friend group. It isn't an issue. Maybe you'll meet the ones who are in town."

She reached over and squeezed my hand. "I'd like that. I'd really like to be in a group where I didn't have to pretend.

I just can't imagine it."

"You had to pretend even with your friends? In all your world of people, only your brother knows?"

She bit her lip and nodded.

I scooted my chair so that I was next to her instead of across from her and slipped my arm around her. She gave me a slow smile.

The next morning, I woke up early and took a run around campus before making my way back to the dorm for a shower. I took a screen capture of my watch and logged it with the track coach. Once I'd finished my running duties, I quickly dressed, grabbed my bag, and found Bevin waiting for me in José's car.

I poked my head in the window. "Any chance I can drive?"

"Just get in," he growled.

I did, chuckling.

When we got to Pack House, José had just finished preparing a breakfast feast. "So, chica, did you survive your first week of classes?"

"I guess. Each year gets exponentially harder. I thought freshman year was hard, but I would love to go back to that level of difficulty."

"Can you imagine what I'm going through?"

"Considering my one I.T. class, I would rather not."

He chuckled as we each filled a plate of food. "José, how did I not realize how good of a cook you were? You never cooked for the pack back in Wisconsin."

"No one ever asked. Whenever my family was assigned the job, my dad just took on the responsibility."

"But you may be better than him."

Bevin took a sip of his coffee. "She's not wrong. I love your dad's cooking, but this is spectacular. Having this to look forward to every day gives me the chills."

José's eyelids lowered. "Is that the *only* thing that gives you the chills?"

I covered my ears. "No! Na-na-na. Not at breakfast."

They both shook with laughter, so I uncovered my ears and glared at each of them. "You two are like my parents now. None of that. Not until we are in the study period of the day and you're like friends again. Separation. I'm not kidding."

Bevin sighed. "Fine. Am I at least a friend when we're in class?"

I leaned my head on his arm. "Yep."

After breakfast was cleared away, we moved to the living room and got our books out. "Okay, before gossip—José, have you taken this math class? Can you help with this damn question? It's a review, I don't know why I can't get it."

Bevin stared at me, head askew, brows knit. "How do you not know?"

"Know what?"

He turned to José. "How does she not know?"

José bit his lips, then took a long breath. "I don't advertise it and she was two years behind me in school."

"Advertise what? What am I missing?" My gaze shifted back and forth between them, finally I threw my arms out to the side in bafflement. "What?"

José sighed. "Chica, I'm not good at math."

My face scrunched up in confusion. "But you're graduating as an I.T. engineer."

"That doesn't make me good at math."

"But how is that possible?"

Bevin slid my hand in his. "Jade, let it go. José is amazing at a lot of things; math just isn't one of them. Let me check out the problem so that we can move on to your date from last night." He waggled his brows with a smile.

While he studied my notebook, I buried my head in my arms. It took him a few seconds to find where I'd made my mistake. After that, we moved on to other topics.

I filled them in on my date. I told them about the twins, getting coffee with Greta, and my dinner date with her. I wasn't sure if meeting for coffee counted.

José sat close to me on the couch, arm slung over my shoulder, smirk on his face. "Oh, it counts. And I am happy for you. For too long, you've focused only on school, track, and pack. You're in college; you need to have some fun!"

I hit my head against his shoulder but his words filled me with warmth.

Bevin returned from the kitchen with sodas. "I missed

that embarrassed smile from you."

I groaned, hiding behind my hands. "Really?"

He chuckled, sitting in a chair on the other side of the table. "So, when do we get to meet this mystery woman who has you turning all the shades of red?"

My head dropped down. "Never?"

"Not good enough, chica. Are you embarrassed by us?"

When I elbowed him in his gut, he had the decency to pretend it affected him. "Of course not. I'm embarrassed by me. Fine, maybe next Friday—if Greta is available. I'll ask her, but no promises."

José beamed, and his arm tightened in a side hug.

Bevin leaned back, amusement clear in his demeanor. "So, was staying in the dorms the right choice?" Now that he'd gotten his way, it seemed he was willing to change the subject.

I shook my head. "Don't know. This place is busting at the seams, but Alexandra…" I opened up my soda. "She's so confused. She's never left the farm before this. I'm trying to figure her out, but I don't think she's figured *herself* out yet."

Bevin's eyes narrowed. "Maybe we should try harder with her. Mold her into a more open-minded small-town person."

José groaned. "You two can have the side project if you want, but count me out. I have enough to worry about. But let's talk next week. We have a reservation at a steakhouse on Van Ness in San Fran for your birthday."

My stomach growled as I imagined the good food. "You remembered!"

Bevin threw a pillow at me. "Of course we remembered!"

"I don't know if…" I heard a knocking in my head before I could finish. It was Violet.

What's up?

"*Come quick. They're cleaning it up.*"

She disengaged before I could get more. Closing my eyes, I found my connection to her and mentally followed it to a coffee shop on the other side of town, maybe ten miles away. I leapt up and filled the guys in as I ran.

José grabbed his keys, and I collected my stuff. Bevin ran to the kitchen, returned with a dark green bag, and we all piled into the car. Once we were on a main road, I poked Bevin's shoulder. "What's in the bag?"

Amusement boiled out of the front seat from both alphas. I got wary.

"What is it?"

Bevin tossed the bag to me. "Open it."

The bag was rectangular in shape and canvas. It looked like an oversized food bag. When I opened it, I saw that that was exactly what it was. It was full of energy bars, nuts, and drinks. I selected a chocolate milk, zipped up the bag, and handed it to Bevin.

"That's all you want?"

"Violet said it was getting cleaned up. Sounds like norms are there. Don't think I'll be doing much, but her knocking hurt my head. Chocolate milk sounds heavenly right now. Too bad it isn't one of Tanner's magic concoctions. José, can you figure out *that* recipe?"

A grunt was all the response I received.

When we arrived, the police were there and a crowd surrounded a man lying on the ground. We parked and got out. Instantly, the scent of werewolf slammed into me. Taking a deep breath and closing my eyes, I sorted through my memory. I grabbed Bevin's arm.

He put his hand on top of mine. "I know."

I looked over at José, who asked, "Is it the same one who mauled the boy Zee found?"

Both Bevin and I nodded slightly.

José pinched the bridge of his nose, like his head pounded. "We have a rogue in town, and they are getting closer."

CHAPTER 8

There wasn't anything we could do with the crowd present. The person was dead, so there was no concern about a new werewolf rising. José texted Violet that we were there. Her reply came quick; she followed some of the action, but she was leaving and would catch up with him once she got home.

The three of us each took a direction to see if we could find the werewolf's trail, but the scent was drowned out by the sheer number of people in the area. By the time we left, my head was swimming with all the scents.

I decided I had had enough excitement and asked José

to drop me off at the dorms. I trudged up to my room and collapsed face-first on my bed.

Several moments later, Alexandra came barging in. I heard her skid to a stop. I glanced over my shoulder. She stood there, staring at me with wide eyes. "Jade, I didn't know you were here. Did you hear about the guy who was killed downtown by the wild animal? Isn't it awful? I wonder if the person is from around here or had any kids? I remember when some of my friends...anyway...I wonder how the animal got into the city unseen and where it's from? I wonder if they'll discuss this in one of our classes. It would be interesting, don't you agree?"

I rolled over and rubbed my eyes, sighing. *So many questions.* "Hi, Alexandra."

"You know, you can call me Alex. My friends call me Alex. Did I tell you that already? Maybe I did on that first day. I don't really remember, but yeah, you can call me Alex if you want." She spoke so fast, I wasn't sure how all the words came out so clearly or in the correct order.

I groaned.

Alexandra came over to my bed and put her hand on my shoulder. "Are you feeling okay? Have you had dinner? Do you want to head down to the cafeteria? The food isn't the best, but college food, am I right? Or we could order pizza. I haven't had pizza in forever!"

I was at a loss, but the thought of pizza had my stomach rumbling. I sat up and eyed her. "What do you like on your pizza?" If she was a vegetarian I was going to move out.

She paused, looking uncertain. "Anything really, as long as there's meat."

The breath whooshed out of me that I didn't know I was holding. Finally, something we saw eye-to-eye on. I grabbed the phone and dialed the number I had memorized after living in dorms for the last two years. Alexandra's eyes widened as I ordered three large pizzas for the two of us and paid with the card I had on record with them. After ordering, I flopped back down and rested my arm over my eyes.

When the phone buzzed, she ran down to grab the pizza. I yelled after her to leave a good tip. I didn't want to get on the bad side of the best pizza parlor in town. Bevin would kill me.

We sat on the floor with the pizzas between us. I started in on the sausage and black olive; she took the supreme.

As we ate, I gazed at her stuff. She didn't have much up on her side of the room. "Why don't you have any pictures or posters?"

She wrung her hands as she swallowed a bite of pizza. She was still on her first slice, while I had already scarfed down several slices. "I don't know. I don't really get along with my family and was kind of a loner at school." She shrugged. "I don't know what picture to put up."

"There are some shops downtown. You could go and look around. Maybe find something that speaks to you."

She nodded with a slight smile. "Maybe. I don't know.

I wouldn't even know where to start."

She smelled nervous and confused. The only time she seemed secure in herself was when she talked about animals.

Suddenly, pain shot through my head. I clutched at it with shaking hands. Something was crushing my chest. I tried to get air in, but I couldn't. I thought I heard someone call my name as the room shifted. My head hit the floor.

Everything went black.

The next thing I knew, I was lying on my bed. My head felt like a kid was pounding on it like a new drum set. I had a throbbing headache. Cracking open an eye, I saw a blurry head hanging over me. As my vision cleared it became Bevin's concerned face. "What the heck?" I croaked out.

José rubbed my shoulder. "That's what I want to know. We were having dinner when…well, what happened?"

Bevin turned from me. "Alexandra, would you mind getting Jade a cup of water, and maybe coffee. I see there's pizza, so we have food."

Her voice sounded soft but strained. "Yeah, sure. Liquids." I heard the door open and then close.

The bed drooped. José squeezed my arm. "Chica, we were eating, and I felt your stab of pain. And then you passed out. What were you doing?"

I tried to sit up, but failed. "Please help me. I don't want to face the ceiling." Bevin worked his way behind me so I was leaning against his chest. "Alexandra and I were eating pizza. We were actually having a nice conversation. I wasn't *doing* anything. There was a stabbing pain in my head, and…well, then you two were here."

The door opened and Alexandra returned. I took the water with a grateful smile. "How did you two end up here?"

"Chica, we called your phone. After the third time, Alexandra answered. She said you just passed out and she was ready to call emergency services. We convinced her to wait for us to come, and that we could help."

Bevin started to rub my arms, and between the two of them, my breathing evened out. Bevin said, "And you were just eating pizza? Not doing anything…more?"

Alexandra smiled. "I was telling her about back home. There really isn't anything exciting about that or my life in general."

Bevin's phone rang. It took a bit of wiggling, but he got the phone out of his pocket. "Yeah? Okay, yep, got it. Nope. Yep. Call her tomorrow. Bye."

As the call ended he tensed, which caused me to tense. "What?"

"Apparently, your brother was in a training session at your parents' house. He got hurt. Sarah freaked out and, well, used the training you've given her to try to help. He'll be okay now, and she was calling to check in on you. I texted her that you passed out."

I slid my eyes to check on Alex, who looked confused. Personally, I was happy to understand the situation.

I let out a huff of laughter and relaxed, leaning back

against Bevin. Sarah had pulled on my healing ability to heal Owen. It was an ability called "Soul Sharing" that an alpha panther could initiate with her packmates. In this case it was healing, and I paid the price. Not being prepared, I passed out. We tried training the different types of Soul Sharing but determined for the most part healing was too extreme, especially without warning. Dad, our trainer, decided we should stick with my calming ability. She must have been really afraid to have used it.

José leaned down and picked up one of the pizza boxes. He placed it on my lap. Pineapple and ham...Hawaiian, yum. He recoiled. "Are those pieces of pineapple on the pizza?"

Laughing at his scandalized expression, Bevin and I both snatched a slice. The two of us dug in.

The following Tuesday, I found out I was in an I.T. study group with Quinn, Greta, and two other people, Maryanne and Elroy. Our T.A. session consisted of meeting our group and assigning roles. I was assigned the role of organizer. I wasn't thrilled with this, but I wasn't sure I wanted any of the other roles, either. Maranne took on researcher, Elroy time keeper, Quinn was the administrator and Greta took the role of the presenter.

That night, the pack took me out for dinner. Turning nineteen had never tasted so good.

Friday night, I introduced Greta to Bevin and José at our favorite sushi joint. Something about our double date gave me warm fuzzies. I'd started off worried, but as we got closer to the dinner, I was just happy the people I thought about most would all know each other.

When Greta and I arrived, Bevin and José were already seated at the table. Before we could sit, they both stood.

Bevin's hand shot out first. "Hi, I'm Bevin, and this is José. I'm sure Jade has told you this, but the three of us grew up together, so you have to pass the test."

I punched him in the shoulder before sitting down across from José.

Greta nodded with a serious look, but her eyes danced. "Good to know." She shook both boys' hands before taking a seat across from Bevin. As she sat, so did they.

After perusing the menu and ordering we all sat back. Greta's eyes narrowed. "Has Jade always been so…"

She faltered before finishing her sentence.

I gave both boys a look of death, letting them know they better not answer.

For their part, they had kept neutral faces. José had always been good at doing this, but I wasn't sure how Bevin was maintaining the look. Bevin slowly crossed his arms over his chest and leaned forward. Then his lips began to twitch, and I knew I was in trouble. "So nerdy? So oblivious to everything around her but school and classes? Are you wondering how she never got kidnapped with how she never seems to know what's going on around her?"

I dropped my head into my hand, moaning while both José and Greta started to laugh. Bevin, for his part, held his mostly neutral face for a few more seconds.

I sighed, leaning back in my seat. "This is being my friend? This is supporting me?"

That broke him. His smile lit up his face and his eyes sparkled. The transformation, as always, was magic.

Greta's scent morphed with his glee at annoying me. "Wow, you're beautiful. Too bad you're a guy and I'm gay."

I snorted and started laughing. Her confusion rolled over me, making me laugh more. Bevin's amusement rolled off him as well, but he just smiled.

José reached across the table and grabbed my hand. "Calm." It filled me. I breathed and relaxed.

Lifting my head, I said, "Thanks."

Greta's brows came together as she watched us. "What just happened?"

I leaned over and kissed her. "You know when people have known each other too long. Well, that's what happened."

When I pulled away, the look of approval from the boys was almost too much. I covered my face with my hands.

Bevin laughed. "Oh, no, you just did that in front of us." He turned to Greta. "She's usually *very* private. You are doing good things for our young Jade."

"Bevin!"

"Because of that," he continued, "I'll tell you what set her off." He went on to explain his past. When he got done Greta blanched, the curry scent of embarrassment filling the air.

Bevin reached across the table and took her hand. "Do *not* be embarrassed. The compliment you gave was well taken. I don't think I've ever really presented as a girl, even when I was little." He turned to me and José. We each shook our heads.

"He's always just been Bevin. I mean, he chose the name in, what, sixth grade—fifth for me—but even before that, you always dressed the same way."

Greta just stared at the three of us, mouth open. After a minute or so she shook her head. "I can't imagine living in a family, a group of families, so accepting. I can't even tell my family about myself. The only person who knows is my brother Quinn. That's just amazing."

The waiter came with our food, and we ate. Conversation shifted to classes and what we wanted to study. Ironically, Quinn and José were in similar study programs, but one was starting and the other was graduating.

The next few weeks flew by, proving the first week didn't always equate to how the whole semester would go. Classes became a routine. I figured out a pattern with Alexandra. My study group regularly entertained me. Zee created a working blueprint for the new Pack House and construction began. And I had another date with Greta.

In our math class, Bevin groaned as a review sheet was passed down the row. "This midterm exam is going to be painful. Did we really learn all of this?"

I perused all the concepts. "This professor is magical. I mean, how else could this list be so long?" I felt dizzy just imagining the following week's exam.

"Sunday?"

"Sunday."

We started to pack up. As I got everything tucked into my bag, I asked, "Any more leads on the rogue?"

Bevin shook his head. "It's like he just disappeared. No one has caught sight or scent of him. And it's been weeks. I don't know if we should be thankful or nervous."

I shrugged. "No idea. Well, I have to meet with my study group. Have fun tonight."

He gave me a quick hug. "You know, I miss living in the dorms with you. I see you in class and a bit on the weekends. This really sucks. Move into Pack House…now! Alpha law!"

"How about 'no.' That place is full to capacity. It was too full before Zee, now it's just ridiculous."

"Well, construction has started. They think that it will be livable in January. You could relocate for the spring semester."

"Livable, but not done. I don't know if I want to live in a construction zone. Maybe I'll just stick with where I'm living now."

We were walking out of the building, and he had his arm wrapped around me tightly as if he weren't going to let me go. "Can you agree to come over more? Dinner once a week and over the weekend?"

"Yes, Mom. I'll come home more often."

He smiled and waggled his brows at me. "That's all I'm asking for." Then he kissed the top of my head before slipping off to find José.

I spun on my heel and made my way to the cafeteria to meet up with my study group. The first part of our big project was due Friday, and we had to put the final touches on our presentation. We had gotten into the habit of working over dinner. When I arrived at the cafeteria, I saw Elroy eating at one of the large tables. He was tall and elegantly dressed in tan slacks, an off white button down, and a green tie. Somehow, he always looked presentable. His dark eyes found me, and he waved as I got into one of the lines for food.

By the time I sat down, Maryanne and Greta were at the table as well. It only took a couple minutes for Quinn to join us, as well.

Maryanne was small and mousey with brown curly hair and gray-blue eyes. She wore bright, colorful dresses that would have stood out in the sixties. She was always transfixed by my meals. She gazed at my tray of food, then at me, then at my tray again. "Where do you put it? I see you eat a mountain of food every time we study together, but I never know where the food ends up."

I shrugged. "Track. I wake up early and train most days. Running causes this." I waved my hands over the mounds of food on my tray.

Elroy squinted at me. "You're on the track team?"

"It's been weeks; I've told you this." I wasn't sure I had. It was such a part of my routine, I never thought about it.

"Nope, you haven't."

Greta cocked her head to the side. "I don't think you have. You said you run a lot, but never a reason why."

"Really? Huh? Well, there you have it. The coach likes to torture me with early morning drills. So, I make up for it with late-night eating. It's my own version of yin and yang."

Quinn shook his head. "I really don't think it works like that."

I ate a bite of my grilled cheese. "Greta, are you ready to amaze the class with all of our work?"

She flung her hands out, palms out, as if to present herself. "Of course."

Quinn rolled his eyes. "I'll finalize the computer side of the presentation so all our hard work will look slick. Greta can make a paper bag seem magical when she talks fast enough. I think this midterm project is in the bag." He laughed at his own joke. "Get it?"

Maryanne shot him a pained look. "A magical paper bag?"

After the presentations were done, we all agreed to celebrate.

The following week, I had midterms in the remainder of my classes. All of them. I thought my head was going to explode. It wasn't finals week, but the exams would be hard, and the classes were relentless. Because of this, I didn't stay out celebrating late.

Friday night after my I.T. group celebrated, I returned to the dorm room to hit the books. I was sitting on my bed organizing for the week ahead when Alexandra came in and flopped onto her bed.

"Jade, do you drink?"

I continued to stare at the calendar I was working on. "Something wrong?"

"Sucky week. Sucky life. I don't know. Do you drink?"

I swung around until I could see her. "Come again?"

"I see you leave early to run track. You study all of the time. You're never here. I don't really know much about you. But I did bring some moonshine with me, and thought this would be a good time to break it out."

I didn't drink. I wasn't sure with two wereanimals if alcohol would affect my system. But the week had been stressful. "Moonshine?"

"My uncle makes it in his cellar."

I slowly closed my books and moved them to my desk. "Moonshine."

"It's good. It doesn't even taste alcoholic."

"Yeah, right. Sure."

"Should I grab two cups? Or should we drink from the jar?"

In for a penny... "Let's just drink from the jar. Nothing to clean up."

Her face split into a smile and she scrambled out of bed dragging a chair to her closet. She climbed up and rummaged around on the top shelf until she came back with a bell jar full of a golden liquid. She came over to my bed and stopped near me.

In for a pound. Closing my eyes, I patted the bed by my thigh. She bounced happily before landing next to me and crossing her legs. She opened the jar and took a sip then handed it to me.

I carefully took a sip. It tasted like apple pie. Nothing like I'd expected. I shot her a questioning look before I took a second sip.

"Isn't it good? It's flavored like the fall, which it is. Fall moonshine!"

We continued to take sips passing the jar back and forth. The drink was tasty, but I wasn't sure what we were supposed to get out of it. When the jar was about half gone, Alexandra carefully spun the top on it and handed it to me. "Can you put this on my desk?"

"Sure." I scooted to the edge of the bed, and that's when I knew something was wrong. Everything in the room swayed to a dangerous angle. I grasped the edge of the bed with my free hand and tried to steady myself, but I wasn't actually moving.

Gently, I placed the jar on a desk—my desk, close enough—and scooted back against the wall as the room began to move erratically.

"Jade?"

Slowly, I turned my head to face Alexandra. "Yeah?"

"Why don't you like me?"

I scrunched up my forehead, trying to think. Her question didn't quite make sense. I knew each of the words, but together as a sentence I couldn't work it out. "Huh?"

"You don't like me. Why?"

"Why do you say that?"

"You won't call me Alex."

I groaned. Her voice was getting louder, and it felt like it was jabbing into my head. I tried to take short, staccato breaths, but it wasn't helping.

"Um, well, I just... I don't know. I guess we're just roommates."

"We *are* roommates. I'm glad we're roommates."

"Okay."

"Jade?"

"Yeah."

"Can I ask you a question?"

"Sure."

"Have you ever felt weird in your skin, like you were wrong?"

I sat up trying to focus, but my head throbbed, and the walls spun. I leaned back against the wall again, trying to pin it down before it escaped. "What do you mean?"

"You know, like one day you're a girl, then the next, you're just a person...I don't know. I tried to explain it to a friend one day, and then everyone at school teased me."

"Is this why you want me to call you Alex?"

"Sort of. Isn't it a great name? It's so... I don't know... neutral, I guess. No one knows anything about me when I'm Alex."

I massaged my forehead with my fingers and thumb. I had to clear my head. I was so much better than this. I needed Bevin here. He was good with this stuff.

"Alex..."

"You called me Alex! Does this mean we're friends now?" Her voice bubbled out of her like a stream, bright and chipper.

I groaned. "Alex, do you like when people call you 'she'?"

"Umm, I don't know. I never thought about it. I mean, I am a she, even when it doesn't seem right, right?...Jade, I'm tired. Can I sleep here?"

"No, let's get you on your own bed."

A snore came from her.

CHAPTER 9

The next morning, I went to breakfast in the cafeteria. I had slept in, but since I normally woke up early, sleeping in meant still up before seven. I filled a big plate with scrambled eggs, bacon, and a waffle. I followed it with a travel mug of coffee. My head pounded, it felt full of cotton, and I hoped the coffee would be my salvation. I had a big schedule of studying to do, and I had to wake up first.

I started in on my food when Elroy joined me, looking dapper as ever. "Hey, Jade, you're up early."

I lifted my head to focus on Elroy. I managed a grunt.

"Wow. You don't look good." He plopped down

with his tray.

"That's not nice."

"No, but it's honest. Rough night?"

We spent the next few minutes comparing notes on how we were preparing for midterms.

He eyed me. "You know, you need something better than cafeteria coffee. Wanna head to the café downtown?"

I weighed the three-block walk against decent coffee. The idea of liquid ambrosia won out. I slowly nodded and Elroy snickered. We returned our trays and moved out.

We exited the cafeteria onto the empty streets of Arcoíris. This early in the morning on a college campus there was barely a soul to be seen. There was a short cut to the café through an alley between school buildings and local businesses. I probably could have walked this route in my sleep, which was pretty much what I was doing.

We were a block from the café when I realized the air was still. I hadn't been listening to my instincts because of my headache. Elroy had gotten about a half block ahead of me. My heart pounded. "Elroy, wait up." My voice croaked, and my voice came out at barely a whisper.

Despite my cry, Elroy kept walking with his usual swagger. I picked up my pace, starting to jog. Barely three steps into my stumbling run, the rogue werewolf shot out from behind a bush and leapt on Elroy's back, biting down on his neck. I sprinted. I wrapped my arm around its neck and stuffed my hand into its mouth to stop it's biting Elroy. As I yanked back,

I screamed down the connections for my alphas.

Rogue, café, help!

The werewolf flipped around, clearing my hand from its mouth, and snapped at my neck. I had its head in both my hands, but it flipping around shifted my center of balance and I fell on my back.

The wolf broke free, biting down on my left hand. I wrapped my legs around his abdomen, stopping him from lunging at my neck. The wolf scratched with his front paws, digging into my chest. I moaned.

Using all my strength, I yanked my hand from its mouth, wrapped my hands round its head, again, and this time rotated the head as hard as I could. Bones snapped. The paws stopped digging. The wolf dropped on top of me, heavy enough to drive the air from my lungs.

As I gasped for breath, the scent of the werewolf hit me and I knew it was the same rogue as before.

I shook my head to try to think, I knew I couldn't stay there. This was a thoroughfare and someone would come along soon. I rolled to my side, dumping the wolf off me. Its claw was stuck in my gut. I groaned. I grabbed the leg and slid the claw out. A squeak of pain escaped me. I lay there panting for a moment.

Move Jade!

Groaning, I rolled up to my hands and knees. I saw blood drip from my belly to the pavement. I shut my eyes and tried to ignore the pain. I needed to hide the evidence.

I pushed back so that I was sitting on my heels. The pain washed through me, almost overwhelming me. In a rush, I closed my eyes and found my animals.

Panther? Wolf?

Panther trotted up to me. *"We are fixing you."*

My hands shook as I breathed through the pain for another minute, and then I knew I had to move. I dragged the wolf to the bush it had been hiding in. If it transformed into a person here, and someone stumbled upon us, there would be too many questions. Every yank on the wolf wracked my body with more agony. It took too much time; everything I did was taking too much time. Finally, the wolf lay hidden in the foliage. I tried to use my senses to make sure I was still alone, I changed position to crawl away from the dead creature and quickly came to the end of my energy.

Trembling, I tried to stay on my hands and knees. I wanted to check on Elroy and see if I could help him, but my body gave out on me. I collapsed. In a last ditch effort, I rolled as I fell, to save my face from hitting the sidewalk but my vision wavered. Footsteps…people were coming. That was bad…I had failed.

I let my head drop. What more could I do? I had done the best I could, hadn't I? My head wouldn't stop pounding. So much pain. I hurt everywhere. Pounding on the pavement, in my head, in my chest, it echoed everywhere.

My eyes found where Elroy had fallen. He wasn't

moving. Tears burned down my face. My failure…and he was probably dead. It was hard to tell with the relentless hammer in my head causing my vision to blur.

It occurred to me that there were two different types of pounding coming closer.

Bevin?

"Jade. Thank the gods."

I hurt.

"Talk to me, sister. What happened?"

Pain.

I sent my wolf to his wolf to explain. I didn't know if it would work but I was too tired to do anything more.

"Jade! Do not *leave me."*

Bevin? I hear people coming. They'll find me. I don't want to be found…not like this.

"It's me and José, don't worry."

I moaned in pain and lost the connection. The next thing I knew, there was a hand on my forehead. I opened my eyes and saw two blue stars. "Are you real?"

Bevin slipped his arms under me, picking me up. My head rested on his chest. I croaked out, "The rogue?"

"José is collecting the wolf. He's transformed, so we have two people to carry out.

"Elroy?"

Bevin shook his head. "We'll dial 911 once we get you out. We'll let the officials handle him."

Tears continued to flood my eyes. "My blood?"

"Jade, rest. Do you realize we're back at Pack House? You keep passing out between questions. Let me and your animals patch you up."

I rolled over and allowed the darkness to take over. When I woke up, I was on one of the living room couches. I felt better. I scooted to a sitting position and my head spun as my vision darkened. "Water?" I whispered. I was in a house of werewolves, loud wasn't needed.

A minute later José came in with a mug and handed it to me. I started to reach with my left hand, but realized it was bandaged. I eyed it suspiciously.

"Just drink."

I sneered at him, but I drank the concoction. He slipped in behind me so that I was leaning against his chest. I let my head fall back against his shoulder. I sighed and relaxed into the touch of Pack. He slipped his arm around my waist but hesitated near my stomach.

"The wolf attacked my chest, not my gut, you're good."

"I'm sorry we didn't get there faster."

"I don't think there's such a thing as fast enough. I'm just glad this wolf didn't kill me. Dad will be proud."

I could smell José's pride. "He will be. So am I, chica. You did good."

"Not good enough. Elroy…" Tears burned my eyes again. I hadn't known the other victims, but I had known Elroy.

"Yeah, not your fault."

I couldn't respond. I knew he was right, but I felt I was to blame. Tears traced their way down my cheeks. "My parents and Tanner made this look so easy. Holding land, clearing out rogue wolves, running a pack, none of this is easy."

José let my sadness fill the room as he spoke. "So, that rogue had a ring on him."

"A ring?"

"Yeah. It was on a necklace around his neck. The ring looks like a club ring or a school ring. It has a large V in the center."

I spent the rest of the afternoon healing and eating. My need for Pack meant I was never alone. Someone sat with me on the couch, lending me Pack comfort and support, at all times.

After dinner I wanted to head back to the dorm so I could sleep in an actual bed.

Bevin helped me up the stairs, even though I told him it wasn't necessary; I was feeling fine. When I got to my room, Alex sat on her bed, reading. She didn't look up. "Jade, can you forget everything I said last night? You know, about me, my name, everything?"

I paused in the doorway. "Um, no."

She jerked her head up. "Why not?" Her focus dropped to my hand. "And what happened to you?"

I sighed, dragging Bevin in with me as I dropped

onto my bed. I had showered at Pack House and put on some of Violet's clothes, mine having been destroyed. The clothes were not my style and Alex looked at me, smelling confused, doubtless trying to figure out what was different, beyond a bandaged hand.

My hand decided to throb with her question and I turned it palm up to look at it. "I just tripped up the stairs at Bevin's place. One of these days I'll let him tell you some of my gym stories from high school." He snorted next to me as we finally arrived at the bed.

When I sat on the bed, Bevin came with me. He rubbed my back, bringing us back to Alex's question about her name. "What you said was important. You said you wanted to be called Alex, not because it is a nickname, but because it has a larger meaning for you. I don't know how much, you know. You may be cisgender, but you may be more, or different. You could be nonbinary or something else."

She blushed and looked at Bevin. I, too, looked at Bevin. He returned my gaze.

I smiled at both of them. "Don't worry about Bev, he'll understand better than anyone I know."

He stared at his hands for a minute before investigating everything Alex had put up on her side of the room. "I wasn't born Bevin. When I was born, I was assigned female at birth. A lot of my family's friends had boys—José, Jade's brother Owen—so when they handed down clothes, no one really noticed that I didn't dress like a girl." His breathing got a bit slower, more focused. "When I started elementary school, my parents took me shopping for new clothes. They tried to steer me to the dresses—you know, the girl's department, but when I refused, they turned to the boy's section without comment."

Being werewolves, Bevin's parents could probably smell the horror and disgust on their young child and weren't willing to push the issue. One benefit of having parents who can smell your emotions was it cut through a lot of discussion and confusion when you were young.

Bevin leaned into me for support. "When we're young, girls tend to play with girls, and boys with boys, but every now and then, the nerds just play together, and thankfully I fit that category. In fourth grade, my teacher, Ms. Siljones, called my parents in for a meeting near the end of the school year. She explained to them that she thought I was really a boy and pointed them towards resources. She encouraged them to let me find my own name, one that suited me better."

Bevin searched my face. I stared back. I'd never heard this part of the story. He was gauging whether I was hurt, but I was more curious. Though, I would be lying if I said I wasn't at all jealous of the secrets never shared.

I bumped his shoulder, asking him to continue.

He gave a small nod. "Over that summer, I finally decided I like the name Bevin, because it felt right."

Alex sat on her bed, entranced. "Where did the name

come from?"

Bevin laughed, slipping his arm around my waist. "Jade used to make up stories to tell my sisters to get them to sleep when they were at her house. That summer, she had a series of stories where the hero was named Bevin. I fell in love with the hero, and the name."

My mouth fell open, stunned. I remembered making up stories, but not a lot of the particulars. I made up a new adventure every couple of weeks. The kiddos would demand it of me. "Really?"

He stared directly into my eyes, all mirth gone. "Really." He turned back to Alex. "I didn't tell anyone about the name until I started school in fifth grade. Then, I only told my parents, my teacher, and my best friend at school."

"Phillip," I mumbled.

"Phillip," Bevin confirmed. "It took him a few weeks to adjust, but then that was that. I decided I really felt much better as Bevin. In sixth grade I told everyone…and everyone seemed okay with it: students, teachers, friends. It was going great. That is, until eighth grade. There were a few teachers at the school who were nuts. They were convinced that I couldn't be a boy and couldn't be called Bevin."

I squeezed him. I knew this part of the story. We were close by then and those teachers had been awful.

"I almost failed English and social studies because I would only use the name Bevin, and they would not. Finally, at the semester change, I was transferred to different classes with more accepting teachers. My parents got my birth certificate changed so that my name was officially Bevin. I started taking testosterone, I moved to high school, things got better. I'm lucky my town is pretty accepting and that my friends are amazing."

Alex gazed at Bevin trying to figure him out. "So, I'm not just a weird creature that everyone hates?"

Bevin and I looked at each other and then at her. "No. At least, not because of this." I flashed her a smile. "Look, you need to figure this out. I'm not the best with this. Bev, here, is better." He shrugged. "But there are clubs on campus that can help even more, some off campus as well. Organizations. You just need to tell me what name to call you and pronouns to use and we'll be all good."

The room started spinning and I grabbed Bevin's hand to steady myself. I was close to passing out. My body was still trying to heal itself. He handed me the bottle of water he'd brought along, and I drank deeply. Once the bottle was empty, my body felt heavy.

Bevin mumbled, "Better." He laid me down, pulled off my shoes, and tucked me in. He kissed my forehead. "Sleep. Call me when you wake up."

"Yes, Mommy." My words were getting slurred. "Did you drug me?"

"That's Doctor Mommy to you. And yes, you need to heal."

I laughed. I may have been upset later, but my head was

too stuffy right then to do much more than lie there.

Alex peeked around his arm. "Is she okay?"

Bevin sighed. "Mostly. She pushed herself too hard this week. It happens. She needs sleep. She doesn't listen to many people; I am one of the few she will. If you don't mind, let her sleep as late as possible. I know she'll probably be up before you, but you never know, maybe she'll actually sleep in."

I snorted, rolled over, and let sleep win the battle.

CHAPTER 10

Body heavy and head still tender, I woke up mid-morning on Sunday. The sun sliced in through the curtains to light up the room. Moaning, I rolled over, turning my back to the light.

The door shut and I sniffed. Alex had just left the room. Not wanting to think about anything, including why, I pulled the covers over my shoulders and took stock of my condition. A stab of pain reminded me I shouldn't be using my left hand. I rubbed my torso, but everything there felt healed. I closed my eyes to find my animals.

Panther? Wolf?

"We are here."

Am I still healing?

"Only your hand. There was much trauma in your gut, hand, and legs."

Legs?

"Yes. Did you not feel the scrapes and muscle loss there?"

I hadn't. No wonder Bevin drugged me. I was about to ask another question when I heard the door open, and the scent of coffee wound its way around me. I poked my head out from under the covers.

"Bevin asked that I get you coffee at the first sign of life. He also asked that I call him."

I rolled over as she'd put the coffee on my desk. I propped myself up on my elbow and took a sip. A bit sweeter and creamier than I usually took it. "You added sugar and cream?"

"Yeah, Bevin said that's how you liked it."

I moaned in pleasure and took another drink. "Have you called him yet?"

She ducked her head, looking sheepish. "On the way down to get the coffee. I hope you aren't mad."

I sat up fully, crossing my legs on the bed. "No, not mad. He'll be here soon with José. They're worried about me. Has news come out about Elroy yet?"

Her eyes widened. "How did you know? I didn't want to give you more bad news, but yeah. The school email came out this morning letting everyone know that he passed. They'll be holding a memorial service Tuesday night."

"Did they say what happened to him?"

"Just that he died Saturday morning."

My head dropped into my left hand before I remembered the bandages. Pain radiated up my arm. With a sigh, I dropped my hand into my lap and leaned back against the wall. Going for another sip of coffee, I realized it was gone and I set the empty mug on my desk as I huffed out a breath.

"Do you want more?"

"Almost always."

She snorted before taking the mug and heading out.

I grabbed my phone and saw I had a text from Greta. Did you hear about Elroy?

Yeah. I'm broken up. Do you know what happened?

I watched the text indicator for a few minutes. I didn't know if she was typing a book, or debating what to type, but I sat there, frozen. This was my generation's version of sitting by the phone waiting for it to ring. After a few minutes the indicator stopped.

I gaped at my phone, annoyed. Then I shook it, as if that would get her response to appear. Finally, I tossed my phone down and collapsed back on my pillow.

Alex appeared with another mug of coffee. I tried to muster the energy to sit up, but I didn't have it in me. I gazed into space and mumbled, "Thanks."

A few minutes later, I heard the door open and shut. Sniffing, I caught the scent of Bevin and José. I burrowed into my bed. José came over and picked me up to sit next to me; Bevin took up a spot on the other side. I refused to sit up, so I flopped over, leaning on José. He wrapped his arm around me as he grabbed my coffee and handed it to me.

Grunting, I took the coffee and lifted my head enough to drink. José gave me a squeeze. "Can we go for a walk?"

"I don't want to walk; my bed is my friend."

Alex sat on her bed. "You okay?"

I lifted my head, then finally sat up. "Yeah. Just upset about Elroy."

Alex nodded. "I had a friend die in high school. They competed in an impromptu bull fight and the bull won. He got gutted. I tried to convince him to walk away, but he refused. He had been my only real friend in school. Three kids didn't make it past that event." A tear slipped down her face as she told her tale.

Bevin moved over to her bed and squeezed her hand. "Why did you stay in that town so long?"

"Family. My parents needed me to watch my kid brother until he started school. As soon as he did, I came here."

"Are you planning on going back?"

"I always had that thought, but the longer I'm here, the more I feel myself. I think I was playing a role there. I don't think I want to go back."

Bevin squeezed her hand again. "You don't have to. It

doesn't sound good for you."

My phone buzzed. I picked it up. I had a text from Greta. `Quinn said Elroy was attacked by a homeless person.`

My head was spinning. I texted back. `What?`

`He was near the café.`

`Are there homeless in Arcoíris? I don't remember seeing them.` My head pounded from this new idea.

`Apparently. Quinn hacked into the police record. Are you with your local family?`

Quinn was a hacker? `Yes.`

`Good.`

I turned off my phone and leaned on José again. My stomach made itself known.

Alex chuckled. "I've never known anyone who could eat as much as you."

Bevin and José both smiled at her comment. I grumbled. "Fine, we can take a walk. Are we heading to get food?"

José rubbed my back. "We can find food. Bevin, can you check out her hand first?"

Bevin came over and knelt in front of me. He gently unwrapped my hand. Once the bandage was off, he massaged my hand, and I winced. He rubbed the scars and investigated the wounds. "Why isn't this healed?"

"Did you know I had injuries on my leg?"

"Oh, yeah, both legs. You lost some muscle tissue."

I made a pitiful sound. "Why didn't you fill me in on all of my injuries?"

"Because you were out of it and healing. But your hand should be healed. Is there still foreign matter in there?" He continued to rub, getting deeper into the muscles with each pass, slowing down his motions as he focused near my fingers.

"Not from what I can tell, but do you feel anything?"

"Not yet." He started honing in on one spot near the base of my pinky and ring finger. He laced his finger through mine to open up the bone structure and slowly rubbed in a circle. "I think I feel something here."

"What do you want me to do?"

Bevin turned to José but focused on Alex, who had been listening to us. "You need *them* to find the object."

I nodded. Closing my eyes, I found my animals.

Panther, can you find the debris in my hand?

Panther and Wolf both ran off. Bevin continued to rub my hand as well as connect to me to monitor what my animals were doing. His wolf was somehow helping out.

After a few minutes, I whispered, "You need to cut my hand open. It's deep, you'll need to stitch it up afterwards." I groaned and opened my eyes.

Bevin shivered and opened his eyes, too.

José was still holding me. "Not here."

Bevin stood and pulled me up with him.

Alex sat on her bed, eyes wide. "What the hell did you

two just do?"

I rubbed my forehead with my right hand. "Bevin and I are pre-med. He just did a check up on my left hand. That's all."

Alex shook her head. "No, it was more than that. I'm vet sciences. I may not know people medicine, but I know medicine. I grew up on a farm. Your hand wasn't bandaged yesterday morning. And you mentioned your leg. So, let's try this again, what's going on?"

I spun to José and raised an eyebrow. He just stared at me. My eyes widened and my arms shot out. "What?"

"You two are idiots." He snarled the words.

I snorted and turned to Alex. "I don't know what to tell you. I did get hurt yesterday. I heal fast. I always have. Bevin really does need to get the debris out of my hand."

Alex eyes just went flat. "Fine. I get secrets. I'll see you later." I could smell the frustration and defeat on her, it was earthy and minty and made me think of tea. Despite that, my gut clenched. I felt like one more person in a line of people who treated her poorly.

I turned to grab clean clothes when three pack members knocked on my mental doors at the same time. The knocking was hard enough that it made my eyes cross, and I tripped on bare carpet. I fell, landing on my hands and knees. Pain lanced from my hand to my head. I lowered myself onto my elbows, grabbing my head with my hands as I opened communication.

What?

I heard *"Break in at Pack House"* from three separate voices.

Groaning, I flopped to my side, shaking in pain.

Bevin and José were by me, rolling me onto my back. Bevin sat cross legged and pulled me onto his lap. José cupped my face in his hands "What happened?"

"Break in…house."

Bevin picked me up. Standing in one smooth motion, he carried me out of the room.

"I can walk."

"Yep."

"Put me down."

"Okay."

I could feel him running down the stairs. "Bevin!"

"Yes?"

"You're still carrying me."

"Huh? You don't say."

I growled deep in my throat. "Bevin! Put me down!"

He grunted and set me on my feet. Turning, I bumped into José's car. I whipped around and pounded both my fists into his chest. "Jerk!"

He snorted, getting into the car.

I slipped into the back seat, and struggled into my seatbelt using only my right hand.

CHAPTER 11

We circled Pack House as wolves. The scent of the burglar was thin, but I could follow it. He was male and related to the werewolf I had killed the day before—a brother or father, maybe a cousin. By some miracle, he hadn't actually gotten into the house. All the noise he'd made in getting the door open had woken Luke and Violet from their late morning slumber. Zee saw the car fishtail down the driveway as the intruder fled.

No one had gotten a good look at the rogue or the car. They noted he drove a small blue car, and the man had dark hair, but that was it. Despite his quick getaway, we wanted to gather as much information as we could in case we ran into him in town, thus the search in animal form.

After circling the house one last time, I sneezed, found my pajamas, and shifted by them. I still hadn't eaten and felt horrible. Once I'd dressed, I flopped down in the grass and waited for the others to finish with their investigations. I don't know if I fell asleep or passed out, but I woke up with Bevin picking me up...again.

I tried to push his hands away, but he was stronger than me, at least at this moment. I rolled away, got to my hands and knees, and pushed myself up to my feet. "Bev, I can walk."

The world tilted a bit, but I was determined to get inside on my own two feet.

"Jade, you have no color, and I found you passed out on the grass. I don't know when you last ate, and you were attacked by a rogue yesterday. Please let me help. I still need to cut into your hand, and I'm not very happy about that."

My shoulders drooped and my chin hit my chest. He came over and wrapped his arm around me. We walked into the house together. I didn't want to admit how much I needed his support.

He deposited me in a recliner and José handed me a plate with leftover pizza. It was cold and delicious, and, before I knew it, gone. "More?" Violet brought a second plate as Bevin came over with a shallow bucket and medical supplies.

"We really don't have a medical room set up yet. Since you're so comfy looking, why don't I work on your hand here?"

"We need to do more of a search inside the house. Again, I feel like my parents made this look so simple. Tanner should've held classes, or one of the other wolves on the police force. They stinted our education by protecting us from this."

"You're not wrong, but we're doing our best. But right now I want to get you fixed up so you're strong and healthy for the next time we need to battle this wolf."

Sliding my left hand to him, I shook my head as I slumped. A wave of dizziness hit me and my stomach grumbled, letting me know I'd pushed myself too far, so I continued to eat. While Bevin probed my hand, I tried to ignore his ministrations. He cleaned my wound with warm water and iodine, then used a topical numbing agent, but it still hurt. Whatever was stuck in my hand was deep. He sliced my hand and dug around with tweezers. I closed my eyes and used my connection to him and my animals to help guide him, so he didn't have to dig for long.

Despite my help, every prod sent shocks of pain shooting up my arm. It took everything in me to hold still. I bit back a groan, not wanting to distract him or know how much it hurt.

As he worked, he said, "José has been talking with your dad and Tanner, discussing ways to handle this situation. I know it feels a bit out of our wheelhouse, but we're trying to get caught up. Tanner offered to come out, but right now we feel we can take care of our own."

Once Bevin had the debris pulled out, I leaned back and closed my eyes, focusing on my breathing. Bevin rinsed out my wound and wrapped it in a bandage with suture tape. His motions were quick and efficient. Once the procedure was finished, he held my hand and soothed me using the power of alpha and his pack connection.

"Thank you."

He leaned in and kissed my cheek. "Glad to do it, hon." He grabbed the equipment and disappeared into another room to clean up.

Once fixed up, I ate my fill and convinced José to take me back to the dorms so I could get some studying done. Bevin followed to make sure I was okay, and so we could finally study math. The dorm group room was mostly empty, and we eventually felt we may pass the midterm exam.

Tuesday night, I met up with Greta, Quinn, and Maryanne for the memorial service. We all sat together near the back to pay our respect. The article that came out in the newspaper didn't give any details on how Elroy had died, it only said it was an ongoing investigation.

In class, the T.A. asked if we needed a new group member or more time. We said we didn't. We felt that we could manage to finish, though Elroy had definitely pulled his weight.

Thursday, I sat in the dorm TV room on one of the

couches, zoning out. I had one more exam on Friday, but I was burnt out from studying. There was a trio playing a card game, a group playing a board game at another table, and two people watching TV at the other end. I debated being productive but relaxing felt good.

The door swung open, and Greta strutted in. I noticed the others in the room gaze at her for a moment before going back to their activities. She walked right up and straddled me. Her hair flowed down like a curtain when she leaned down to kiss me.

I rested my hands on her hips and kissed her, rubbing my hands up her back. What a perfect way to avoid studying for my last exam.

She moaned, then pulled away and pushed her hair back, while remaining on my lap.

I stared up into her eyes. "Hi." I gave her a mischievous smile.

Her own smile grew. "I missed you."

I snorted. "You saw me in class."

"Class doesn't count. You've been studying for a week. You won't go out with me. I had to take matters into my own hands."

I continued to rub her back. "Well, tomorrow is my last exam."

"Is this how you've been studying?"

"No, I'm just really tired of studying. I was trying to decide what to do for a bit of a study break."

"I have some ideas."

"I'm sure you do, but I was thinking ten minutes."

She pouted, then scooted in closer. "Fine, but I'm not moving until your study break is over." Then, she bent down and brushed her lips against mine.

I laughed. "Fair enough."

"Two weeks from now is Halloween. My brother is putting together a huge costume party. Let's go together in matching outfits. Let's be *those* people."

I ran my hands up her arms to her neck and pulled her down for another kiss. After releasing her, I sighed. "I can't. I have to go home to Wisconsin that weekend."

"What? Why?" Her voice was loud enough to turn heads for a moment, before people went back to their own distractions.

I closed my eyes, scrunching up my face. "I have a friend who needs me. She asked me to come back that weekend last July. Bevin and José are heading back, too."

"Wow! Your friend group is tight."

Laughing, I wiggled. "I'm here now."

"Can I have more than ten minutes?"

I closed my eyes, considering all I had to do before the exam. "I need to be back in my dorm room at nine at the latest."

She grabbed my wrist to check my watch. Her eyes widened. She leapt up, dragging me with her as she started to plan what we'd do with the time I'd given her.

We were leaving on a Wednesday. The full moon was on a Thursday and Halloween was on Sunday. Our plan was to fly back on Halloween. I had spoken with all my teachers about missing three days of classes. I had collected the work I would miss and had taken one quiz.

When we landed in the Madison Regional Airport the day before the full moon, over six feet tall of dark menacing danger waited for us with a car. He wore tight black pants, a black button down, and black shades, and leaned against a black SUV. Tanner's day job as a bounty hunter had worn off on his duties as my dad's right-hand man, and he scared the other people leaving the airport.

Despite his scary look—and the fact that he was scary—he was my favorite person to poke fun at. The trunk popped open and he got into the driver's seat as we approached. Bevin grabbed our bags to stash in the back.

As I slid into the front seat, I leaned over and kissed his cheek. "How did you get the short straw for having to pick us up? We're not even Pack anymore."

"But you're still the alphas' daughter."

I leaned over and kissed his cheek. "Thanks, Tanner."

He grumbled as he drove us to my parents' home. Bevin's and José's parents lived in town, but there was more space at my parent's house, the pack den, especially if Bevin and José wanted to stay in the same location. When we arrived, most of the pack was there to greet us with a warm welcome and lots of food. I was looking for one person in particular: Pebble.

My adopted sister came barreling up to me and engulfed me in a big hug. "Hey, sis, how goes Wisconsin?"

She bounced. "I get to start public school in January!"

I found my mom in the crowd. She just nodded in confirmation. "That's great! I'm so excited for you!"

When Pebble first came to us, we weren't sure she could keep the secret of werewolves. There was also the question of not biting other kids. My parents decided homeschooling her was safer. An added benefit was she met each of the adults, people important to the pack—werewolf or otherwise—in one-on-one scenarios. She would be in third grade if she were attending public school. Hanging out with adults was not as much fun as kids her own age. I wasn't surprised by her excitement.

I took my bags to my room while Bevin and José claimed one of the guestrooms in the basement during our stay. The evening was full of warm welcomes and lots of food. This was the pack that raised us, and although we were off on our own now, we'd always be pack kids to them.

The next morning, I woke up early. There was a sheet of

paper tacked onto the coffee maker with a list of exercises my dad expected me to do. I just gaped at it. There was a schedule for Thursday, Friday, and Saturday. The one consolation was that Dad had made schedules for Bevin and José as well. *His obsession with exercise programs is getting worse!*

I took mine and headed to the gym. Once there, I put my schedule on the bulletin board and got to work. I was just finishing when the boys arrived.

Bevin put his paper next to mine. "Your dad is insane."

"Yes, yes, he is."

"How close to done are you?"

"This is it. I'm off to shower and coffee. I can wake you up tomorrow if you want to endure torture together."

He came over and dropped his head onto my shoulder, yawning. "Ask me again when I'm awake."

José came over and pulled him off me. "No, the answer is *I* don't want you waking us up. You get up too early."

"Amateurs!" I raced off to get ready for the day.

After I showered and dressed, I found Mom in the kitchen with coffee and breakfast made. So much better than college fare. I happily took what she offered and joined her.

"Piper's going to want to join your pack."

I drank deeply of my liquid ambrosia and thought about that. I had Greta in my life, but did I want Piper joining us in California? After debating the pros and cons…for *several* seconds, I said, "I don't think it's a good idea."

"Why?"

"Her family is here, her girlfriend is here, her life is here."

"Most of that could be said about you, and most of that is moveable. Is there more of a reason? Do you still…"

"No." I stopped her before the question was fully formed. "Mom, just no. I'm happy for her and Julez. I have a new girlfriend, too."

Mom's brows went up. "I hadn't heard. Tell me about her."

So I did.

As I finished, Pebble came out to join us for breakfast. After taking a few bites she looked towards me, but not at me. "You're right, you know. It's a bad idea for Piper to be part of your pack at this time; it will lead to bad connections."

"What?"

She shook her head. "Sorry, that was nothing. Or maybe it was something. I don't know."

I swiveled to face Mom. "Any idea?"

"No, and I'm not sure what connections Piper even brings to a pack. It also may not be about Piper. It could be about a wolf who's going to join in a month. That's the problem with intuitive predictions."

I tapped my forehead, trying to restart my brain, then resorted to the coffee.

After breakfast, the boys and I went into the basement to hang out and play games. It felt like old times, and I relaxed more than I had in months.

"Chica, you needed this. You even smell relaxed. But *my* head needed it, too…it's about time."

"I never want to be an alpha; I can't even imagine."

He smiled. "No, you can't, but it does become background noise…mostly. You're loud."

I threw a pillow at him. I was about to say more when I heard the door upstairs. Sniffing, I recognized Piper. A minute later, she skipped down to the basement.

"Hi, everyone!"

I leapt up to give her a hug. "Hi, Piper!" The hug was enough to tell me what I needed to know. We had time, but not much; her shift was imminent. I moved back and sat on the couch.

After hugs and greeting, she sat down next to me.

"So, how is Julez?"

"Good! Really good." She looked down at her hands, made fists and then shook them out. "I'm sorry for springing her on you last time. That was insensitive."

"Don't worry about it, really."

"Are you sure?"

José placed his hand on hers. "Don't worry, Jade is fine."

Piper's shoulders dropped as she let out the breath she was holding and quirked a tiny smile. "Okay, yeah. I bet you are."

Bevin turned to me. "I remember what happened with me…but what do we do next with Piper?"

"Well, that's the question. I think she should be part of my parents' pack." Piper started to protest but I held up my hand to stop her. "Listen. Your family is here. Your school is here. Your girlfriend is here. Your *life* is here. We recently told a lone wolf that switching packs, though not common, can be done. While you are here, this is who you'll be running with."

I didn't mention Pebble's prediction because I didn't know if it pertained to her, and it would scare her. I had also forgotten to mention it to the boys earlier and now wasn't the right time.

"What about Owen? He's part of your pack."

I sighed. "That's true. The pack was made at a time when no one knew what was going on. It isn't easy having the pack strung out across the country. That's why Owen and Brooke are coming to California for winter break, not here. They've never lived in California, but that's now their home."

"What about Sarah?"

I shrugged. "I don't know. We've talked a bit, but she has another year of school. She'll finish that up and then decide."

Piper's eyes were getting misty. "But I want to be in your pack. I don't want to be left out."

José, who was holding one of Piper's hands, took the other. "We don't want to leave you out. What Jade says makes sense. Stay here until you graduate. You can switch then. I've run with a pack that wasn't mine; it isn't as comfortable. You don't have the sense of belonging. You deserve that, especially as a new wolf."

Piper searched José's face, then Bevin's. "You'll let me

come to you later?"

Bevin moved over and wrapped her in a hug. "Of course."

She dropped her head into his chest. "You two feel like home. Not this pack. But I'll follow your lead if this is really what you think is right."

They both froze and stared at each other, having one of their silent conversations. I closed my eyes, collapsing back on the couch. I knew what was about to happen. I should've told them about Pebble's warning.

José confirmed with me that Piper's wolf could be brought out a bit early. Biting my tongue about how bad of an idea I thought all of this was, I took her hand and confirmed she was good to go. After that, we brought Piper out into the backyard and told her to prepare for the shift. Mom was at work and Dad stayed inside to make sure Piper's wolf connected to José as alpha.

José knelt next to Piper, who was on her hands and knees. José put his hand on her forehead, but nothing happened.

Bevin put his hand on my shoulder and focused on the tableau in front of him. "I don't know that he knows what to do. Has he ever pulled a wolf out before?"

"What?" It took me a second to realize what Bevin meant. The two of them were so confident as alphas despite their age, I forgot that they hadn't grown up with my parents.

I sat down on one of the porch couches and closed my eyes. I found my connection to José. *Do you know what to do?*

"*Not really, chica. I haven't done this.*"

Look her in the eyes, deeply. See her wolf, and command it to come out. Say 'Out!'

"*Okay, hang on.*"

I opened my eyes, but the connection remained as he followed my instructions. I felt the intent, but the two were far enough away, I barely heard the word he spoke to her.

The shock as the shift began flooded the backyard.

José dropped her chin and stood, backing away. He watched, staying close, as her body contorted. Coarse hair shot out, her face elongated, her hands shrunk down into paws, and after several minutes, a red wolf stood where Piper had been.

A stabbing pain cut through my head. I moaned, grabbing my head with both my hands as I slipped off the couch and landed on the patio.

I panted. The pain wouldn't stop. It pulsated. It shifted. It was a whirlwind of chaos and spikes. I pushed the base of my hands into my eyes, but the agony in my brain persisted. I moaned.

I heard voices. They didn't make sense. Too much pain.

Then one word penetrated: "Connection."

Gasping, I focused on the center of my pain, located the hot, throbbing center, and sure enough, it was my connection to José. *End.* Nothing. *End.* Nothing. *End!*

There was a snap, and I was floating on a cloud.

I felt my heart beating. It raced, pounding in my chest. But I could breathe. When I opened my eyes, I found myself on Bevin's lap. I gazed into his glowing blue eyes, his alpha was showing. "We have got to stop meeting like this."

CHAPTER 12

Piper whined and danced in the yard. Her ears and tail were lowered, and her eyes wide. I could feel her confusion, and that worried me. Leaning on Bevin, my body shook, I felt bewildered.

José sat in the yard, glancing back and forth between me and Piper, his lower lip caught between his teeth. "Why are you both freaking out, chica? What went wrong?"

Sarah and Owen came crashing through the back door.

Sarah took one look at me, eyes narrowed. "What the hell have you been doing to yourself?"

Barely able to move, I shrugged a bit and waved my

fingers in a vaguely questioning manner.

José smelled relieved. "Owen, Piper just shifted and needs to run. Can you take her out?"

Owen just looked at the tense situation and his whole demeanor relaxed. He may not be a submissive wolf, but he knew how to defuse tension. "Absolutely." He ran to the yard, stripped, shifted, and reached the woods in a flash. Piper followed him.

José sauntered up to the porch. "Okay, first question. That snap was audible to me. Did you damage your brain?"

With a groan, I squeezed my eyes shut and checked out what I could see. My head didn't hurt, which was shocking. A small push of effort, and I found the pack connections. I reviewed them and they all seemed fine, even the one to José. But, there was a weird echo of Piper. As I watched, her right front paw started to throb.

My eyes snapped open. "What the hell did you do to me, José?"

"What do you mean?"

"Can you read Piper?"

"Yes, don't you have a connection to her?"

"José, I mean it. Can you sense her, like you sense me?"

"No one is like you, but yes. She's out with your brother. She stubbed her right front paw. She'll be fine. Why?"

"Because, I knew about her paw, too. I have her in my head, too. And this is *not* okay."

Sarah bit her lip.

Bevin squeezed me tighter.

José sighed. "You and your complications. Can't you just have a week of normalcy? Are you sure?"

"We'll have to see, but yeah. I don't want her in my head. You said you can feel my emotions, right? You knew when I…with Greta…when we started liking each other. And…. There is no way I'm having Piper in my head." I could feel myself beginning to spiral, but I couldn't stop it. This was too much.

José blanched. "We need to talk to your mom."

I tried to stand and collapsed into Bevin. I let my head fall back onto his chest. "Why? I just want to stand up." My face heated with my frustration.

Bevin whispered, "I can always carry you."

"I swear I'll beat you up."

"You aren't as scary as you think."

Sarah squatted down. "How about I get food and your parents?"

Smiling, I said, "How about I love you best?"

She stood and spun, heading into the house.

Bevin snorted in my ear. "You don't love me anymore?"

"Nope."

"Well, no more José cooking then."

I laughed. "That *is* a fate worse than death."

My dad came out. "I don't miss this." He squatted down beside me with an energy drink.

I drank it and he pulled me to my feet. The world tilted

149

on its side, and he went to grab me, but Bevin was still there with his arms around me. Dad shifted his hands so that I had Bevin on one side and Dad on the other. They led me into the living room.

I kept my eyes down, almost closed, because everything spun around me. When we got to the couch, they stopped.

Bevin gave me a squeeze. "How do you want to do this?"

I just pushed against him.

Without separating, he situated himself on the couch with me sitting between his legs, my back against his chest. Dad sat on the coffee table, continuing to hold my hand, massaging it. José lifted our legs and slipped in on the other end of the couch.

Dad's hand stopped moving. "That's incredible. Is it always like that?"

José patted my leg. "Pretty much. We figured it out last summer."

I was trying to figure out what they were talking about as Sarah handed me a plate with peanut butter toast and I took a few bites. "Figured what out?"

Bevin placed his chin on my head. "You can't tell?"

"What are you talking about?"

Dad's brow scrunched up as he gazed at each of us. "Pumpkin, these two are acting like power rods for you. When was the last time you passed out?"

The toast stopped halfway to my mouth as I paused to think. "Well, maybe after the rogue attack, but besides that,

I don't really know."

Bevin's chin rubbed against my head. "You passed out because you spent all night healing, didn't eat, then shifted to catch the scent of whomever broke into Pack House. That was just stupidity on all our parts. You were lying on the ground and may have just fallen asleep, too."

"Fair. Is this why you two always bookend me?"

José smirked. "I thought we had been so subtle." He turned to my dad. "Is Hazel around? We have a few things we need to talk about. Your daughter keeps doing things. Amazing things, magical things, but stupid things." He rolled his eyes. "And to think; I wanted a simple life."

Dad barked out a laugh as he pulled out his phone. He glanced at the screen and said, "She'll be here in ten minutes. She finished her last class and canceled her office hours."

I handed my dad my empty plate, grabbed the blanket from the back of the couch, and curled up against Bevin's chest.

Dad poked my shoulder. "None of that. Tell me about school."

Sarah, who was sitting behind him on one of the chairs, piped up. "And Greta."

"Can I receive coffee in trade?"

Dad agreed to coffee.

As he made the coffee, I got Sarah caught up on my new girlfriend. She knew most of it from our weekly, and sometimes daily, calls. After the coffee, I sat up, but kept myself cocooned in the blanket. The boys, my alphas, stayed close. I felt much more secure that way.

"Dad, do you think you and Mom could have done this energy thing with me as well?"

"Maybe. Parents don't tend to be as close to prickly teens as their friends, though. You really should think about writing a book. If there ever is another epsilon, it would be helpful."

"Sure, I'll just add it to my list of things to do. It's pretty short." My sarcasm was lost on no one.

Mom came in and joined us in the living room. "So, what trouble have you gotten into this time, sweetheart?"

I explained about helping José, and how we both had Piper in our heads.

"I do *not* want someone else's wolf in my head. I have enough to worry about."

Sarah made a sympathetic sound. "It really doesn't help that she's your ex."

I took a long breath. "No, that doesn't help."

Mom nodded. "We'll work on that tomorrow. Try to get her out of your 'Pack.'" She used air quotes for that last word.

She was about to get up when Bevin cleared his throat. "There's more."

Mom slowly lowered herself to the love seat she and Dad were occupying.

Bevin squeezed my hand. "We had a rogue wolf attack and kill a friend of Jade's. She was with that friend, and she dispatched the wolf."

My parents knew this—I'd called them afterwards to talk to them—yet they looked at me with pride. It warmed me.

Bevin shot me a glance. "When I was trying to heal her, she was half out of it. She…gods, I'm not sure how to even describe this. She sent her wolf to my wolf to explain her injuries. It helped me to get her patched up more quickly."

Everyone in the room just stared at us, including José. José's head tilted. "You never told me that."

"I know. It took me a while to process it all. I knew we were coming here, and I figured we'd all work through it together."

I shrugged. "I wasn't up to getting the words out. It seemed…I donno…easier? I didn't know if it'd work. Didn't know it did til now."

"A book," Dad insisted. "You need to figure this all out and write a book." He searched each of our faces. "So… should I come up with a training plan or do you want to wait until Owen has moved out there?"

CHAPTER 13

The end of our trip to Wisconsin aligned with the full moon. I wanted to run as a panther with Sarah, but she decided to sit this run out and stay home with Pebble and the kiddos. Too many dominant wereanimals.

Like old times, we ran with my parents' pack. I smelled a deer. It had been a while since we had found a deer, even on the few runs from the previous summer. Though my alphas ran with this pack tonight, in this group, they weren't the leaders. According to pack protocol, José and Bevin were guest alphas and followed the lead of the hosting alphas who invited them to join the run.

After finding the scent trail, I whined softly. Mom came over and, signaling the pack, we followed the scent trail.

I loped with the grace and stealth of a wolf. We were off a path, cutting our way through the forest, each on our own journey to a common end. I felt alive with my connection to this land and sensed my own small pack nearby.

I bunched my hind legs to leap over a downed tree, tall and thick with age. As I leaped, a scream pierced through my head, and I faltered, stunting my take-off.

I tried rotating mid-flight so that my shoulder slammed into the tree instead of my snout. I bounced off the tree and crumpled to the ground. Panting, I closed my eyes and saw the ghostly image of Piper. She was close to my location, but cowering. With my eyes half-closed so I could see both her and the ground, I rolled to my feet and limped in her direction. As I drew near, the sweet candy scent of her fear filled the area.

Piper hid in the crevice of a hollowed-out tree. A pack of coyotes surrounded her, four strong. I growled low in my throat and felt Bevin and José converge on either side of me.

The coyotes attacked, splitting up their attack on us, two each. One dove toward the leg I favored. He clamped on before I could back away. I bit down on the back of his neck and jerked my head. I heard the snap of his neck as well as felt it beneath my teeth. Pain lanced through my injured leg. Whining, I fell with my attacker

A second coyote came in low. My body ignored my

commands to move. I tried to defend myself. As worry blossomed in my head, Owen barreled in from the side, taking my would-be attacker down. I let my head drop, shaking from the pain in my front right leg.

When the shock of the pain ebbed, I sought out the other coyotes. Relief flooded me when I realized my pack had dispatched the remaining attackers.

José's nose prodded my cheek as he sniffed me, and then I heard the knocking.

I'm fine.

"*You are* not *fine.*"

I growled low in my gut. *I can make it home.*

"*Is that wise?*"

Do we have a choice?

"*Yes, you can be carried. I can think of three volunteers.*" His voice came out laced with alpha command.

I wanted to scream. I rolled up to my feet—well, three of my paws—and I hobbled. *See, I'm fine. We aren't that far.*

"*Jade, it's at least two miles.*" All amusement faded from his mental lashing.

I made some incomprehensible noises and continued my trek. Step, limp, step, limp, step, limp. It was going pretty good, if I don't say so myself. I was focused on my movement and the sounds around me…mostly.

José's grumble came through the connection. "*Jade, chica, you're going to permanently injure yourself.*" He sounded more like a friend this time, trying to break through my wall of mule-headed stubbornness.

I snuffled. *This is going well. I have a rhythm. You need to help your newest pack member. She's freaked out.*

I could feel it, see it, sense it. Her emotions were trying to take over my body, and if José didn't do something about it, I would be fighting more than just the pain in my leg.

I dropped the connection. The conversation wasn't going anywhere anyway. Step, limp, step, limp. My breathing came out choppy, which sounded strange in a wolf, but that had a pattern as well.

Several minutes into my trek, I heard human footsteps behind me. I let my head fall and panted harder. Hands picked me up. I reached out and connected with my brother.

Why? I said I could make it.

"Not to me, sis. And even if you did, you think I'd listen?" Owen started to jog as if my weight were nothing.

His motions were fluid as he moved quickly towards the house. His natural athleticism meant he moved smoothly, keeping me from jostling against him. Having grown up in this forest, he knew it well, and could probably have gotten me home blindfolded.

I don't need to be babied.

"This isn't being babied. I'm helping a packmate and my sister. Your leg is probably broken and you're an idiot. At the rate you were limping, it would take you hours to get back to the house. Bevin went to find Aunt Allison. Suck it up."

I was getting tired, so I dropped the connection and

gave up. A few minutes later Owen reached the backyard.

"Can you shift?

I whined.

"Okay, wait here." He ran into the house and came back faster than should've been possible…had I lost time? He had on jeans and carried a plate with some steaks from the fridge.

I growled at them, feeling my lips peel away from my teeth. The smell of dead meat turned my stomach.

Owen squatted down. "It's this or shift and have chocolate cake."

I immediately stopped growling and eyed him suspiciously.

"Would I kid about that?"

I closed my eyes and focused. It took longer than normal, and with a broken arm it *hurt*, but I eventually found my humanity. I lay on the ground, face down, panting and groaning.

"Do you need me to carry you in?"

"I hate you right now, Owen."

He laughed, throwing a blanket on me. I sat up awkwardly and he helped me wrap up. Sarah came out with the cake, a double layer chocolate cake with cookies and cream filling and a mocha buttercream. My eyes rolled back at the first bite.

"Okay, maybe I don't hate you. But it's cold." I took a few bites. "I can make it inside. Are there clothes close by?

I don't see mine."

Sarah tossed me a shirt and jeans. I looked at my arm and made a pitiful sound.

Owen grabbed the plate. "I'll fill this up and add some ice cream. Maybe marshmallows. Meet you two in the kitchen." He turned and headed into the house.

Sarah helped me to dress.

Once inside, I told her where to find a brace to steady my arm while I dug into the food. My plate was nearly empty when Bevin and Aunt Allison came in.

She did a field assessment at the table, knowing I needed the calories and wouldn't want to leave my desserts. "From what I can see, you've done what you can. We'd need an x-ray—or your animals—for a more complete assessment."

"They're working on it; I can feel they've already set the bone in the right position. That's why I asked for the brace. I didn't want to knock it out of alignment again."

Everyone nodded. We finished eating and headed to bed. Sleep would allow for the most concentrated healing.

The next morning, my arm was still tender, but I felt better. Piper was excited but freaking out. New wolf jitters. She was also presented with a training schedule.

Dad placed it on the table next to her as we all dug into breakfast. "You're off at college, but there are still facilities there where you can train. I expect you to follow this. I know you couldn't have taken down a family of four coyotes alone, but you do need to know how to fight. I also expect you here for each full moon; that is, until you relocate to California."

Her eyes widened. "Oh. I hadn't thought about that. I'll have to move." She turned to me and then José. "Do I have to fly out there for winter break?" She dropped her head in her arms. "I had plans with Julez. I really didn't think this through."

Bevin rubbed her back. "Ideally, if you are part of our pack, you'd come out over winter break. If you want to be part of the pack, you'll need to relocate after you graduate. That part isn't an option. This is what Jade was warning you about. You can still switch to Hazel and River's pack. It's more established, and they won't demand as much attendance." She lifted her head and her face hardened. "I know you're right. It just feels like I'm being kicked out of the gang."

José leaned back. "Our pack isn't going anywhere. You're young. We're young. Stay here and figure things out. Don't rush."

Mom, who had stayed out of the conversation, nodded from the kitchen. "Okay, about you taking up residence in multiple heads, let's get that fixed. Is it decided you're switching over to me?"

Piper nodded slightly. The earthy scent of sadness surrounded her as her eyes slid down to her clenched hands. I ached for her. This wasn't what she wanted despite it being the right thing to do.

Mom beckoned to me. "Jade, let's start with you. Come here and place your hand on my head. Focus on pushing Piper out and into me. Say her name—with finality." I followed her directions, but nothing happened. The ghost stayed. I tried a few different times, but it didn't work. My animals helped, but her echo wasn't tangible to them.

Mom grabbed my wrist. "Enough. José, maybe it's her connection to you."

José came over and repeated the action. It only took him one try and Piper moved over to my parents' pack. Mom and José turned in unison to me, but I slumped. Piper was still there, a ghost in my head.

CHAPTER 14

We spent the rest of the weekend reminding Piper of the hell we had gone through when we had first shifted. She took a small notebook out of her purse and rattled off some of her favorite memories of our struggles as new wereanimals in high school. She'd always said she wanted to be prepared.

Before any of the rest of us had become wereanimals, my mom had taught us how to take things that stressed us out and put them in mental boxes in our mind to evaluate later. It was to prepare us for the overwhelming amount of information a wereanimal picks up from their senses.

Reminding Piper of this and of Owen's method of building a moat around his emotions gave Piper several approaches.

We took her to a mall to help her adapt, and let her test out the different strategies, though we knew it would be rough for her. She didn't have any werewolves in school with her.

Pebble offered to join her for a week. It sounded weird, but since she was home schooled, it made a bit of sense. In the end, Piper decided to try it on her own.

Bevin, José, and I flew back to California on Halloween. On Monday morning, bright and early, track practice started up. My first warm-up was a five-mile run. Traveling west meant seven in the morning California time, nine Wisconsin time, wasn't as bad as when I headed home. The start of the run felt good, stretching my muscles after a day of spooky, Halloween, airport travel. Suddenly, Piper's emotions spiked and swept over my body. She was elated, her heart beating rapidly. My heart beat faster with her. Heat flooded my body as I grew excited.

I stopped running and grabbed my head in both hands. I connected with José. *Help me!*

I started to pant and fell to my knees. Her emotions were becoming my emotions, taking over my body. I didn't know where she stopped, and I began. I moaned, rocking back and forth.

José, help me!

"*Chica, what is it?*" He sounded groggy, but worried.

I can't stop her emotions. They're taking me over. I tried to gulp in some air. *Oh, gods! José, what do I do?*

"Piper?"

I think she's with Julez; make it stop!

"Oh, Sonnara save you. Put up a wall."

My body started to shake. I couldn't take in a full breath. *José.*

"*Put up a wall, Jade. Think of Pack House, with your pack in it. Imagine sitting between me and Bevin. She isn't in the house. Don't let her in. Don't let her emotions in. She isn't you, only you are you.*"

Don't let her in. Wall. Pack House. My knees hurt and I shook, rocking on the sidewalk, but I tried. I saw my wolf and panther sitting in my mental landscape, a place I'd set up years ago. A campsite with a house, a firepit, and a lake out back. The house had never been tangible, just a prop to make the woodsy area homier. With a push, the door opened and Wolf, Panther, and I fell inside the building, landing on the wood floor of the small cabin. Another push encapsulated Piper's ghost in an igloo-like structure. Laying on my side, quivering, I kicked the door shut.

Her emotions faded.

"*Chica, talk to me.*" Worry laced José's voice.

It's better. She's still there, but it's less overwhelming.

"*Good. Can you make it back to the dorms?*"

I opened my eyes and realized I lay on the ground in a fetal position, shaking, and crying. *When did I fall over?* I moaned.

I think so. I have to check in with Coach or he'll call the police.

"Bevin and I will meet you in your room."

I disconnected and rolled to my feet. Taking a breath, I began running. My heart rate was up, and I could still feel Piper in every cell of my body, but I fought it. I would win this battle. I had to be victorious; it was my mind and body. I checked my time and stepped up my speed so Coach wouldn't notice my delay.

When I got to my room, Bevin and José were already there, waiting in the hall. I collapsed into their arms, and they dragged me to the bed.

"I need to get to class."

Bevin held my hand. "You need food, and a shower. Are you better?"

I managed to sit up and nod.

José eyed me. "I'll get some food. You shower and change. Bevin will stay here in case you need help or if your roommate returns with questions."

While we ate, we discussed how to manage Piper in my head. José and Bevin had been living with others in their heads and it hadn't overwhelmed them. I wasn't sure if it was harder for me because I wasn't an alpha or because I had my ex, but by the end of the meal I felt better prepared.

Two weeks later, Greta and I studied in the library, trying to stay on top of classes while spending some time together. I read a book for one of my vet science classes while holding her hand under the table. She studied for an English class.

I finished up one class and was about to get out another textbook, when her phone buzzed. She put down her book and pulled her phone out of her pocket. She unlocked it and read the text. Her hand holding mine tightened and then started to shake.

I looked down at our hands then up at her phone where she typed quickly. A nutty and earthy scent rolled off her, nervous and sad. Her thumb paused and I shifted my attention to her face. I saw tears streaming down her cheeks. Despite her squeezing my hand, her focus was completely on her phone and the messages coming in.

I rubbed the back of her hand with my thumb as her scent morphed to a gingery shock mixed with her earthy sadness. Her feelings were as deep as the ocean.

She closed her eyes and put her phone away. She crumpled into me and trembled, crying quietly. I just held her and let her release her emotions, holding her, rubbing her back.

"I'm here," I whispered. A world of hurt had seeped from her phone, and though I didn't know the details, I knew that my being here was important.

After a few minutes, her ragged breathing evened out and she lifted her head. "I'm sorry." She sniffled and dug in

166

her bag for a tissue.

"For what?"

"I don't know. I just…one of my cousins died."

I froze. "Oh, no. I'm so sorry. What happened?"

"No one knows. He goes off into the mountains camping. He was supposed to check in, but didn't."

"Is your family sure? I don't know how to ask this, but…are they sure?"

She nodded quickly. "I don't think there's a body, or anything like that, but they're sure. He would've checked in by now. They found his last camping site with all his stuff."

I slumped in my seat. "Oh, Greta, I'm so sorry."

"Have you ever lost anyone?"

I stiffened. I don't know what she saw in my face, but she knew. A softening told me she could read my own pain. Her eyes widened as her head tilted.

I had lost too many people and several of them I couldn't even begin to explain to her. She pulled me into a tight embrace and we consoled each other letting the tears flow. The shared knowledge of having lost people brought us closer.

It was the week before Thanksgiving and Quinn and Greta were heading home. They would return after the short Thanksgiving break, missing a full week of classes. I asked if

Greta wanted me to come visit at all during this time, but she said no. Her family was large and there wouldn't be time. They also wouldn't understand or approve of our relationship.

I could understand the lack of time. For now, I would respect her wish to remain in the closet.

Alex decided to stay in the dorms for the break, but I planned to stay at Pack House. I needed some time alone, and as cramped as the house was, there was room for me in the basement.

I pulled a few mattresses onto the floor and covered them with blankets and pillows. It reminded me of the way the basement would be set up growing up with Bevin, José, and Owen. We'd stay up all night, talking, without a care in the world. A small pang of sadness went through me, remembering the past and missing how simple life was back then.

I grabbed the latest book by A. R. Grimes and started reading. Halfway through the first chapter, I was engrossed and ignoring everything around me. Suddenly, the mattress bounced as Bevin and José plopped down next to me with bowls of ice cream. They handed me one. In addition to ice cream, the bowl also contained hot fudge and mini marshmallows.

Sitting up, I sighed in pleasure. "Okay, what did I do to deserve this?"

Bevin winked at me. "Finally decided to spend some time with us."

I rolled my eyes. "I always want to spend time with you, but school is insane for all of us."

Bevin waved his hand around the basement. "Just think about what you could do with all this space. Why not move in down here?"

My gaze slid to José. He shrugged. "I agree. I'd prefer you living here to the dorms, but I'm not going to push the issue. I'm letting Bevin take point on this project." He smirked.

"What project? I'm a project? Project Jade?" I rolled my eyes at the ceiling. "Gods above, tell me I'm not a project." After taking a bite of sugary goodness, I pointed my spoon back and forth between them.

Bevin nodded. "Yep. Project 'get Jade back into the pack proper.'"

"You two were in the pack proper in Wisconsin without living in the pack den. What gives?"

They both slumped. Bevin looked at me, eyes pleading. "We're a smaller pack. Until we are established…"

"I'll move in when the big place is finished. Look, I know you didn't like the dorms, but they don't frustrate me. They're close to everything, I can get to track practice easily, not to mention my classes. Despite a few roommate issues, everything else is really convenient. Please don't be mad."

Bevin leaned into me. "Did Alex go home for Thanksgiving?"

"Nope, she is still back in the dorms."

Even José winced at that.

I didn't want anything to bring down the mood. I

changed the subject. "Now…movie, popcorn, games?"

Big smiles spread across both their faces as they flopped down on my makeshift bed and we began a slumber party ala our childhood.

The next morning, I woke up with both of them still in the basement with me. It felt so much like home and our childhood, I shut my eyes and let the warmth flow through me for a minute. They both relaxed a bit with my release of contentment, picking up on my state of mind even in their sleep.

Carefully, I rose and ran to the bathroom to wash and change my clothes. I grabbed a bagel for breakfast and headed outside to walk around the land. The house was too small for my morning energy. I hadn't made it fifteen feet when my phone rang.

"Hi, Sarah. How goes it?"

"Good, you're up. Fill me in on all of the doings in your area." The two hour difference meant even my early morning rising wasn't that early for her.

As always, hearing her voice, and spending time talking with her, made me happy. We'd spent time together over Halloween, but we hadn't spoken in the previous two weeks.

"Wow! Her cousin died? Rough. Things here have been quiet. Owen and I have the week off and are back in

Stolzburg. Then we have a couple of weeks before finals, and then we fly out to you. I don't know where we'll stay."

"You two will take the basement. I slept there last night; it's fine."

"Where will you stay over winter break?"

"I petitioned to remain in the dorms. We'll bring another mattress down to the basement for a few nights and some nights I'll camp in the wilderness with Zee."

We both snorted at that.

"What about Brooke? You know, she's planning on coming, too."

I groaned at that. "No idea. Maybe we should rent an RV. I'll stay there and let the rest of you figure out arrangements in Pack House."

"I can't wait to meet Greta and decide if she's good enough for you. We also need to compare notes on schools; it's really ramping up, getting rough."

As I walked further towards the woods, I caught a scent. "It is, but it isn't anything you can't handle."

"True enough."

The smell swirled through the trees and headed towards the edge of our property. "Any class you're worried about in particular?"

Sarah started talking about each of her classes as I followed the scent. It led deeper into the woods but stayed on our property. It was like the person—the werewolf—had a copy of our land deed and had walked the property line. I followed the trail, calling on my wolf to help keep my steps silent. Alone, I was a klutz, but with my animal guiding my steps, I could manage a bit of stealth.

As I followed the trail, it wound in a sentry pattern, much like what Dad set up at home, though the scent wasn't very fresh. I didn't rush as I walked, focusing more on deciphering the trail than speed. *Why would a person be casing our property?*

Finally, I found a campsite. The firepit was cold, and the site itself had been cleaned up. The firepit was covered in dirt but there were signs that the person who had used this site might be coming back. A blanket hung from a branch. A food box sat near the firepit. Tidy, but not broken down. I backed up and surveyed the site from behind a tree.

I crouched and cursed myself for a fool. I hadn't brought food or eaten before coming out here. I couldn't safely use any of my epsilon tools without risking myself. Sarah was still talking. I took a deep sniff and couldn't smell anything. I slowly turned and didn't see anyone. As quietly as I could, I made my way back to Pack House.

When there was a pause in Sarah's descriptions of classes, I told her I had to go, but I'd talk with her soon. Once my phone was tucked away in my pocket, I ran at top speed back to Pack House. I burst through the door to find the house still and quiet, everyone still fast asleep. The door had been unlocked. I sniffed, and I could still smell the werewolf from the woods.

My heart began beating faster than the run home warranted and my hands trembled. *Was the werewolf here while I was at his site? Is everyone here safe? Is he still here?*

I prowled, following the smell through the house and into Bevin and José's room. It had been ransacked. *This must've been done in the few minutes I was out talking with Sarah.* I ran downstairs and woke Bevin and José up. We searched the room and then the house. Nothing obvious had been taken.

José made breakfast while Bevin, Luke, and Zee joined me in an outdoor search for the wolf. We found the trail, but it ended a few hundred feet from the house. The person must have gotten into a car and driven off.

After our failure, I felt sick; we'd been violated. We returned to eat and discuss everything that had happened that morning and the werewolf who'd invaded our territory. Suddenly, José's eyes widened. He leapt up and ran into his room. After a few minutes and a lot of muttering he stomped back into the dining room, his expression bleak. "They took the ring."

It took me a second to realize what he meant. "The ring from the rogue that killed Elroy?"

He nodded, "Yep, that's the one. Our rogue has friends."

CHAPTER 15

The break-in made us realize we needed to start setting up better security. The pack had felt safe. We were small and unknown, but now we felt exposed and violated. These rogue wolves not only invaded our territory, they snuck into our sanctum. There were high levels of security being built into the new Pack House; it just hadn't occurred to anyone that we may need it for the small house being used in the interim.

Bevin and I walked over to the construction site to survey the new build. Excitement zinged through me to see progress, quickly followed by depression at how much more needed completion. Off to the side and out of the way of the work crews, we set up a picnic lunch.

My shoulders dropped as I surveyed what they'd finished. I thought about the minimum requirements to make our new pack den liveable and I didn't see them completed. "You were wrong. It won't be ready by January."

Bevin squinted, leaning a bit to the side as if it would make the den look more finished. "You may be right. There are a lot of items on our list of must-haves. *Your* list of must-haves."

Eyes wide, I slapped a palm against my chest. "My list?"

"You were the idealistic one, remember."

"You didn't really take my musings seriously, did you?"

"Not all of them, but when José and I sat down with Zee, we had your list in hand." He waggled his eyebrows at me.

"That's insane."

His wide smile was infectious. "But exciting."

I nodded. "But exciting. Do you ever think about how much we're doing? Like, we're way too young to be doing all of this."

"Do you regret any of it?"

"No. Well…maybe the bit with Piper in my head, but besides that, no."

He laughed. "That is all sorts of hilarious and messed up. Do you get as much as we do?"

"No idea. I try to ignore it. High emotions are hard to ignore." I gave him my deadliest look. "I don't like knowing when she's feeling emotional."

"Did you ever tell her about it?"

I choked. "No! Gods, can you imagine? She'd freak. She'd become a hermit. It'll be better when Greta's back and I have my own distraction, and school. School's a good distraction. I can put her in a head space and ignore it." I grinned. "Maybe incinerate it!"

"I don't think it works that way."

I huffed. "Probably not."

We finished off our lunch and headed back to the small house. We were halfway there when Violet came running up. "Hurry, there's been another death."

We ran. As we arrived, José was already getting into the car. Bevin and I piled in after him, and he sped off. José parked by the campus, and we jogged towards downtown. A tourist had been attacked leaving the same alley where the rogue werewolf had killed Elroy. He was found in the same position—face down with a broken neck. Unlike our attack, part of his torso was chewed on.

There was no covering this up as a human-on-human attack. No reporting this as a homeless person in an area without homeless people. This was obviously an animal attack. We all stopped behind the police tape. We couldn't get closer, but I closed my eyes, and blocked the background noise out as best I could. I took a few deep breaths. I sorted through the scents of all the people around. Luckily, it was Thanksgiving weekend, and most of the people were away.

For a better read on the situation, I needed to get closer. I needed to get into the alley. I backed up a few steps, then squeezed between the people behind us. I didn't think about the others as I ran around the block and to the head of the alley on the school side. No one was there. Keeping in the shadows, I slunk down the alley until I reached the end of the alley where the body had been found. It was blocked off on this side, but there weren't people nearby.

Again, I closed my eyes. I squatted, leaned against the building, and breathed deeply. There, mixed in with the plant life, was the same scent as the wolf who had broken into our house. Squatting lower, I took in a larger breath, trying to track his scent, but there were too many other odors covering it up. It was as if he'd... I opened my eyes and looked up.

It took a minute to find what I searched for, but there, halfway between me and where the rest of my pack waited, was a ladder on the side of the building. With a frustrated growl low in my throat, I realized we wouldn't be able to investigate until later, maybe not even until tomorrow. Reluctantly, I stood and made my way back to the main street.

As I squeezed between the people in the crowd, Bevin searched the faces around him. When he saw me, his eyes narrowed and his hand shot out, dragging me the last few feet. He lowered his mouth to my ear. "Where did you go?"

I pointed with my head down the lane.

"Why?" A growl in his voice told me he was barely

holding in his frustration.

"I couldn't get a good scent marker here."

His hold didn't loosen. "And did it work?"

"Yes. Why are you holding me so tightly?"

"Jade, there's a rogue loose in the area. You disappeared without telling any of us. Not even a gesture. Don't do that."

My head landed on his arm. "Yes, mom."

He rested his head on mine and his hand loosened a bit. "Okay, tell me, us, what you figured out."

"I think he used the ladder to drop in and then escape. We'll have to come back to investigate the roof later."

José placed a finger under my chin and raised it so that I was staring at him. The stress of the situation had his hold on his alpha mantle slipping. A bit of power flowed out, blanketing over me. "Was it the same wolf?"

"Yeah. The one from the campsite; the one who broke in and took the ring."

"Zee has been doing regular sweeps of the area and Violet and I have set up a few remote cameras. No one has returned to the area. We haven't touched the campsite. We will keep vigilant."

My body stiffened. These attacks angered and appalled me. Frustration oozed through my gut at my inability to find the werewolves killing and trespassing in our territory. "Good."

There wasn't anything else we could do with all the people milling around, so we returned home. Zee and Luke were going to check out the roof with José.

I spent the rest of the night with the pack. We played games and discussed how to button down the house. We decided on more cameras around the outside of the building and a more secure door. Violet showed the link to each of the cameras on her computer, how she could rotate the views, and if she wanted, have a two-way conversation through several of them. As for the door, it had a key code to get in and would always be locked. No more accidental visitors.

I went back to the dorms on Saturday.

Greta had returned, and we met for dinner in the cafeteria. She was decked out in her stylish clothes, but a look of determination replaced her carefree smile.

I sat down and embraced her. I felt her melt into me with a sniffle. "You okay?"

"Yeah." She held on. "Going home was hard. A lot of push-back about me going to college. My mom went to school here and really liked it. She wanted me to come here and experience life away from…well, away from our big family all living close together." She laughed dryly.

Holding her tight, the minty scent of her frustration perfumed the air. "I get living in a big family."

"I know you think you do, but Jade, my family is…it's really big. My dad and his brothers didn't want Quinn and me to go to college here. I don't know why. I just spent a week hearing about how bad a choice we made. It really sucked."

I pulled away so that I could see her face. "Do you think you made a bad choice?"

She started shaking her head. "No! And neither does Quinn. We love it here."

I smiled and kissed her. She kissed me back, holding onto me like I was a lifeline. I pulled back. "'Here' is rather fond of you, too."

She visibly relaxed as her shoulders dropped. Sighing, she rotated towards the table and began to eat.

I rubbed her back and turned to my food, as well. "Besides the guilt, how was the rest of the trip?"

"Good. My aunts and their kids were great. I wanted to tell them about you, but I've told you about that."

"It's okay. I get it." A knot in my gut belied what I said, but not being a werewolf, she couldn't smell my lie.

Before we could continue our conversation, Quinn dropped into a seat across from us. "Don't mind if I join you, do you?"

Greta's face turned hard again, but I smiled. "How are *you* doing?"

"I'm surviving. We didn't know our cousin that well. Enduring the guilt of the uncles was horrible. But we're back here now."

"Just in time. Two weeks until finals."

He threw a napkin at me. "You're a barrel of fun, Jade, aren't you?"

"Absolutely. At least the project was almost done before you guys left."

His mouth turned up in a smug smile. "Fact. When you

have a ringer on your team, projects are not a problem."

Greta's eyes narrowed. "Quinn, don't pretend you did it all alone."

He winked. "Fine. It was a group effort." He pulled out his phone and logged in. "Did you two hear about the tourist?"

Greta's eyes widened and her heart rate sped up. "What happened?"

"Another attack. Same spot as Elroy." Quinn's voice had dropped and he stared at Greta. Though we all sat at the same table, he only spoke to her.

She met his gaze. "Another one? Same spot? Same M.O.?"

Quinn did one quick shake of his head. "There were a few bites out of the torso…according to the article. This had to have been a wild animal…not a homeless man… you know, like last time."

Greta shivered and grabbed my hand. Closing her eyes, she slumped. "God, Quinn. Jeff and Lonny are going to have a fit."

I asked, "Jeff and Lonny?"

Greta looked over to me. "Two of our uncles who've been adamant that coming here for college was a bad idea."

Quinn snorted. "I know, expect more emails. Maybe you *should* tell them about Jade."

CHAPTER 16

After finals week and winter graduation, the city emptied out. I applied for and received a letter saying I could stay in the dorms over winter break. Alex received one, too. It wasn't until the dorm was all but empty of everyone but the two of us that I realized she had sent in a request to stay. When I asked her about it, she told me that she wanted to spend more time thinking about her future away from her family and town.

Greta and Quinn headed home, but Greta told me she planned on a visit in January to meet Sarah and Owen. We did have a quick visit to Wisconsin for Christmas but were back before New Year's Eve.

I sat by the campfire outside Pack House roasting marshmallows with Zee when I heard a sound like nails on a chalkboard and I doubled over, covering my ears. It took me a second to realize it was trees scraping against metal. After the sound stopped and the shivers dissipated, I slowly straightened to see the charred remains of my sweet dessert fall into the fire.

Grumbling, I grabbed another marshmallow out of the bag.

Zee scooted a bit away from me. "Someone's going to get killed if they ruin another one of those for you. If that happens, I'm outta here."

I snorted. "I'm not that scary."

"Riiiight." He winked but didn't move back.

A building sat in the driveway, rectangular, with what looked like aluminum siding—*pink* aluminum siding. The tiny pink house was attached to a matching pink truck. It had a few high windows and a door halfway down one side of the structure. I was so distracted by the Pepto Bismol color of the building, it took me a couple minutes to notice who was driving the monstrosity of a vehicle.

I spun my marshmallow and smashed it between two graham crackers and a piece of chocolate. I took a messy, gooey bite, getting sticky marshmallow and chocolate on my face as a perfectly put-together Brooke stepped out of the driver's side of the pink behemoth.

"Lovely, Jade. You have something…well," she held her hand up like a stop sign, palm out towards me and made a circle encompassing my whole body, "everywhere." I didn't think it was fair since I was pretty sure I didn't have marshmallow everywhere. I looked down and saw white goo on my stomach…oh. *How did I do that?*

"Want some?"

"Never." Her lifelong disdain in me and everything I represented came out in that one word.

"Your loss."

She swept past me into the house. The door was locked. That was the new policy, the door was always locked. After two tries to turn the handle, she glared at me.

I shrugged.

Someone inside apparently had taken notice of her on the cameras because the door opened. After one more haughty glare at me, she sauntered inside.

Oh, yeah, I loved having her as part of the pack.

Zee grabbed a marshmallow from the bag and started to roast it. "Wow, she is in total awe of you."

"I know, right? It's always been that way."

"Did you kill her pet or something?"

"No, I was Owen's sister."

"That's it?"

"That was all I could figure. Then I became her teacher of all things werewolf. Her wolf likes me. But to me, that's so weird, I try not to think about it."

"Her wolf is submissive, right?"

"Yep. It was how she convinced us she should be in our pack."

"Makes sense. She is just so…" Zee's hands flopped around as he tried to come up with a word.

"Oh, I know."

Bevin came out and joined us at the fire. I handed him a stick and a marshmallow.

He took them and started to create his own masterpiece. "That's her solution?" He squinted at the bright eyesore.

"Yep."

"Not very subtle. Think she'll let me paint it?"

"Nope."

He rolled his head as if trying to dispel stress.

I bumped him with my shoulder. "School's out for a few weeks. You aren't supposed to be feeling stress right now."

He cut his eyes to me. "The full pack is going to be here. For the first time, we have our own pack territory. Tomorrow night's the full moon. I'm a bit stressed. I'll be better after we cross over into the new year. Five more days."

"What's so special about the new year?"

"It's just a goal."

"You just want to survive everyone getting here, the run, and the party?"

He groaned. "How about I move into your dorm, and you run everything here for the next week?"

I wrapped an arm around him. "You and José will be brilliant. No, you two *are* brilliant!" I kissed his cheek. "Now, don't burn your marshmallow or Zee says I have to hurt you."

José slipped out of the house. "Sarah and Owen land in an hour."

I leapt up. "On it."

His eyes narrowed. "You need a bath."

Smiling, I ran up the stairs. "Just a rinse. But I'll go get them." I ran into the house and found a free sink. I got the remnants of my s'mores off my face and grabbed the car keys on my way out.

When I reached the car, Bevin trotted up, arriving at the same time I did. At my raised brow, he said, "You need company."

"I do, huh?"

"Yes." He sounded very sure about this.

"Good to know."

We got into the car, and I drove towards the airport. Bevin asked, "How is your ghost of girlfriends past?"

"Is this what we're talking about?"

"It's been a while. Have you gotten it figured out? You don't have the distraction of classes or Greta. I'm just checking in."

I rolled my eyes. "Did you and José draw straws on who

would have to deal with me?"

He reached over and put a hand on my leg. "No. And if we had it wouldn't have been in the way you're meaning. We both want to be here talking to you. There are just too many people around and this was the only time I could think to talk to you. José would have come, too, but Brooke came early and wants to discuss pack finances with him. He really doesn't want to do it alone, but she's so much nicer when it's just the two of them."

I couldn't imagine her ever being nice, but I had to believe him. "Fine. I'm sorry. I've been really defensive with you, and I don't know why. You haven't ever treated me differently." I took a calming breath, and then another one.

"It's because you're living in the dorms."

"Not this again."

"Listen to me. You've always lived with a pack. Even the last two years I was in the dorms with you. Maybe not the same room, but close, and we spent a lot of time together. This is the first time you've spent this much time away from another packmate. My guess, having Sarah stay with you in the dorm room will calm your beasts. You'll be less prickly."

Sighing, I got back to his question from before. "I keep Piper's ghost image in a cave in my head. It started off as an igloo, but that was too open; the cave is a better mental shield. It mutes her emotions. I still feel them, but not as intensely. I don't know what else to do. Do you struggle with Brooke or Zee?"

"I feel them, but it's more of a background noise. It's something I hear, but nothing I experience. That day in early November, you said Piper's emotions were taking over your body?"

"Yeah."

"That's never happened to me. I can sense them, kind of like reading a book. But I don't experience them."

"So, I'm broken?"

"No, hon; just unique."

We pulled into the cell phone waiting area. I texted Sarah to let her know to text when she was off the plane. "I sometimes hate being different. I know it comes with perks, but there are no explanations."

He patted my leg. "I know. But never forget we're here for you. José and I want to help, even when we tease you… especially when we razz you about all of it."

I rested my head on his shoulder. "I know."

It took about twenty minutes for the text to come in from Sarah that she and Owen had their luggage. I drove up to the gate she'd indicated, and they jumped into the back seat after throwing their bags into the trunk.

Bevin sat sideways so that he could face all three of us. "How was the flight?"

Sarah made a painful sound. "I hate flying."

Owen swung his arm over her shoulder. "Don't listen to her. It was fine. Smooth sailing all the way."

She leaned into him. "Let's talk about literally anything else, please."

I merged into traffic and pointed us towards Pack House. "Brooke showed up in a whale of a tiny house. Bright pink in color."

I heard Sarah laugh. "Really? Subtle, she is not. Did you see inside?"

"No, I was eating s'mores when she arrived, and you can guess her reaction to that. If I'd asked, she'd have raked me over the coals, probably literally. And then we left right after to come pick you two up."

Sarah's eyes got wide. "You walked away from s'mores for us?" She fanned her face. "I'm verklempt. I just don't know if I know what to say."

I snorted and Bevin chuckled.

Owen said, "So, this was her great solution to tight quarters. Did it even occur to her to try to blend in?"

A warmth infused me. I had missed this: chit-chatting with my friends. I relaxed and drove. "I think, to her, pink *is* blending in."

Sarah laughed. "Okay, before we get to the full group...Have you got rid of your ghost, and when do I get to meet Greta?"

Owen interrupted. "We. When do *we* get to meet Greta?"

"Ghost. No." I quickly filled her in on what I'd told Bevin.

Sarah nodded as I spoke. "We'll talk more about this. Maybe with José. I don't know, but if the three of us connect, then maybe we can fortify your cave—if that makes sense. There are some things a girl does *not* need to experience."

I agreed with her full heartedly. "As for Greta, she said she'd come back for the weekend. She's working over winter break, but plans to take next weekend off."

Sarah rubbed her hands together. "Perfect."

When we pulled up to Pack House, Sarah busted out laughing at the pink monstrosity parked in the trees. "That is the ugliest tiny house I have ever seen. There's a place that sells them between Whitewater and home, so I see them all the time, and gods above, that is ugly!"

Gods, I missed having everyone together.

The next night we took a full moon run. Sarah decided to stay back to monitor the cameras. There was a three-monitor system in the corner of the basement with the feeds from all the cameras, including the ones around the house and in the woods. This meant she could track some of our run if she desired.

If she caught anything fishy, she could easily contact me and let me know.

Our group spread out to run but stayed within visual range of one another. The woods were ours. It was our first run as a pack and learning to take signals from the alphas was important. There was no large prey to take down tonight, but the quick signals and small catches became a game for most of the pack, and we all had fun.

I stretched my muscles and ran with a small gray wolf in my wake. Despite the distaste Brooke had for me day to day, as a wolf she was glued to my side. Ever since she'd first been bitten, her wolf showed a different side than the prickly porcupine of a woman. The small gray female had a warm pleasant personality shared by many submissive wolves, which helped them act as the glue holding the pack together.

I had eaten a large dinner and wouldn't hunt tonight. Brooke wasn't a vegetarian, but for some reason her wolf was. It was probably the idea of raw meat that ruined it for her more than anything. When we headed out as a pack in Wisconsin, her wolf ran earlier in the evening and avoided the night run, opting to remain with Pebble and the kids. Since the pack was small, José and Bevin wanted everyone to run together to help the pack bonds grow, and I agreed to stick with her.

As the group prowled the darker areas of the woods, I took her on a tour circling the property. We investigated the boundaries noting where pack land ended and city property began. We'd put up a few 'No Trespassing' signs near trails and where the woods were thick, and we tied bright red nylon tags every few hundred feet to help us navigate.

On the far end of the property there was a steep hill. If you climbed it, it overlooked all our woods and the city. From there, you normally couldn't see much of Pack House, but tonight a slight glow of pink came from Brooke's monstrosity of a tiny house. I could also see a few of the taller campus buildings.

A wretched stench hit my nose and Brooke whined. Snuffling the ground, we followed the scent trail. We were nearing the edge of our territory when we found them— three people, all dead. Two adults and a child, maybe ten or eleven. A family. They had been killed at least a week earlier. Their throats were torn out and guts scavenged.

I could smell our werewolf on them. Anger surged through me at the audacity of the rogue, quickly followed by sorrow and horror at more deaths. Not only had the werewolf killed, but a child.

A mental knocking brought me out of my musings. I then heard Brooke's whine and saw her tail between her legs, as she backed up.

I spoke softly. *What?*

"*I can't.*"

I know. Do you want to just back up or try to make your way back to Pack House?

"*I'll stay. You shouldn't be alone.*"

I dropped her connection and found José.

Find me.

After that I dropped down and waited.

Once everyone gathered, Luke joined Brooke and me as we

followed one of the scent trails; it was old, but I could find it. Having the most sensitive nose, I led, with Brooke staying close behind me. Luke took rear. The path ran true—no twists or turns—through the back of our lands towards the walking trails of the park adjacent to the property.

The first deviation from a direct path came when the wolf would've had to cross where people hiked. I lead my group around the paths through some densely packed woods. Despite the option the wolf could've taken to confuse his trail, it led straight to a campsite.

The three of us broke apart and sniffed. The scents were old, from what I could tell— probably a week old or more. For the first time in a while, I felt like I was doing some good in cataloging information.

I reached out to José. *Are we going to discuss this tonight?*

"No, chica, it's late and we're all tired. I don't know where the other teams are, but when we get back to Pack House, we'll sleep, and discuss in the morning when we're all awake. Is there something important you want to share now?"

No, it can wait.

CHAPTER 17

The next morning, we ate breakfast sitting around the campfire. Breakfast came from the kitchen, but there was more room to eat outdoors.

Luke waved his fork with a sausage link on it. "The wolf is targeting us. Testing us. Seeing how responsive we are and how aware we are of it."

Violet sat hunched over her food and didn't look up. "Should we put up more cameras?"

José shook his head. "No. We'll do more sweeps. We'll set up a more aggressive schedule for patrols, especially over winter break while we have the full pack here." He seemed to settle into himself, and a sense of peace and joy rolled off him as he said the words, 'full pack.'

I finished my coffee. "I've been thinking. We're all using the products from the bears. Nothing out here smells of werewolf except for what the rogue left. None of the trails we followed were hidden or obscured from us. Maybe the rogue isn't sure what we are."

Everyone nodded, some with sparks of realization shining in their eyes, others as if this idea wasn't new.

Bevin put down his mug. "I'd been thinking the same thing. All three trails led directly to a destination, no twists or turns."

I leaned forward, holding my warm mug of coffee. "Like Luke said, it's like the person is trying to test how aware we are of them and see what we'll do. They know we hid the last body; they don't know where or why. Will we hide these three bodies or call in the proper authorities? They're trying to figure us out."

José pinched the bridge of his nose. "I think you're right. We have to play this straight. At least for now. We'll call the police, let them clean up the mess. They already have a case file for a wild animal."

Bevin was shaking his head. "Do we want them on our land searching for the animal? Is that really something we want to entertain?"

José groaned. "They'll end up here eventually anyway. Gods, we need someone on the force."

I thought before asking, "Before the other packs send members out to us, can you put in that kind of request?"

"No, we get whoever wants to move west. At least the bodies are all out on the far corner of the property."

After breakfast, José called in the discovery. We weren't in the biggest hurry since the deaths were old.

I took Sarah back to the dorms to get settled. Though the original idea was her staying in the basement with Owen, she decided I needed her more.

"Wow, I think all dorm rooms are basically the same. I could be back in my room in Whitewater. How are we going to do this? Your roommate is around, right?"

"I don't know; we'll figure that out later. Let's just relax."

We both sat on the bed, leaning on each other.

"I can't believe you aren't tired of my brother yet."

"In all honesty, I'm kind of surprised, too. Before we started dating, there were a few times when he was particularly annoying. You told me that if I gave him a chance, I'd see that most of what he presented at school was an act, that he really did have a good soul. At the time I didn't believe you."

I flopped back on my pillow. "This isn't what I meant by giving him a chance."

She laughed, landing beside me. It was a tight squeeze, but we managed. "I have an idea about Piper."

"The person, or the ghost of her living in my head?"

"The ghost."

"She had fun running last night, by the way," I told her warily. Piper's excitement had almost shattered the small confinement I'd placed her ghost in. The battle seemed to be constant, and I wasn't sure how much longer I would be on the winning side.

"Good to know…but not really."

"What's your great idea?"

"Go find your cave and connect to me."

I found my mental landscape. The campsite I'd created gave me peace and a home for my animals. The logs around the campfire had shifted to appear more like what was outside Pack House, and I realized how much this place had become my home. Off to one side was the small dirt hill encapsulating Piper's ghost.

My wolf and panther were sitting back, as confused by the cave and ghost as I was. They could interact with the cave, but not the ghost. When we tried, Piper didn't seem to notice. After a moment, Sarah appeared.

"Whoa, this place is…whoa."

"I created it a few years ago…it helps me to focus. Though, it's not as easy anymore."

She turned in a circle, taking it all in. "It's pretty fantastic, to be honest." Looking down, we watched our panthers nosing each other. "Nice! Okay, about this cave; let me see what I can do."

As I watched, the cave, which looked like a dirt covered mound, developed a stone exterior. Then bars shimmered in place in front of the entrance.

Tension I didn't know I carried eased. I gasped at the cessation of an undercurrent of information my body had been processing. It wasn't all gone but the level had dropped. In the real world, I slumped into my pillow and against Sarah.

I disconnected from Sarah, but left my eyes closed, rejoicing in the peace and quiet in my body. I felt her move away from me, and then a blanket settling over me. I let out a pleased sound as I curled up. My chair squeaked as Sarah said, "Five minutes, then we talk."

I didn't get the full five minutes because the door opened.

"Oh! Hi! I'm Alex, are you Jade's friend Sarah? I recognize you from the pictures. It's really nice to meet you. Is Jade asleep? Is she okay?"

I grunted and rolled up into a sitting position.

"Hi, Alex, I'm Sarah. Yes, I'm Jade's friend." She pointedly looked at me. "And nope, she isn't asleep. As for being okay, I've been asking myself that for years."

I laughed and threw my goose pillow at her.

Alex dropped onto her bed. "Well, I spoke with the girl in the room next door before she left for break; she gave me her key. I'll stay there for the rest of winter break. You can use my bed so neither of you needs to sleep on the floor or on one of the dorm's spare mattresses."

I gaped at her. "Really? You didn't have to do that."

"I know. I just thought it would be easier. Most of the dorm is empty, and I thought three of us in one room was crazy. It probably wouldn't be approved, but who said we're going to ask anyone?"

I smiled at that. "Well, thank you. That's great. And don't think we don't expect you in here during the day. It's still your room. But having a place for Sarah to sleep will be one less thing to worry about."

"You won't mind?"

Sarah shook her head. "Nah. We welcome all the weirdos. Like you said, there aren't many people around. We won't be here that often, but when we are, hang out with us."

It looked like she stopped breathing as her eyes got wide. Then she shook herself. "Thanks. I'm not even sure why I petitioned to stay. I don't know many people here; it's just now that I've gotten out of my small hometown…"

Sarah watched her, waiting. Finally, she threw her hands out to the side. "What?"

Alex's cheeks reddened. "I don't know if I want to go back." She ducked her head. "Is that awful of me? My whole family is there, but I don't know, even being here and not knowing anyone I feel less trapped than at home."

Sarah smiled brightly. "Then I'm glad you stayed."

I tilted my head. "Did you ever find any local resources?"

"No, I was too…I dunno, scared maybe. A little embarrassed. I don't know if I even belong to those groups."

I moved over to her bed and sat down next to her. "Look, even if you don't, they aren't going to be mean.

They'll help you figure things out. How about tomorrow we see if any are open? We can go together, either the two of us, or three. Sarah is the odd one out, but she's always up for an adventure."

Sarah jiggled her shoulders in a small dance. "I'm in."

Alex froze. "Would you really do that?"

I suddenly felt horrible for not doing this earlier. I knew she needed an ally, a friend, someone who would hold her hand. "Yes, we'll all go together."

Unfortunately, the city had closed down for New Year's—even the Youth Outreach Center. It opened back up after the weekend, so we decided to go then.

The weekend after New Year's, Greta came to visit. She came up Saturday morning and planned to spend the night. Her brother, for once, didn't join her, not having a place to sleep. We arranged to meet at a burger joint in town. Sarah and I got there early. We would be a large group: Sarah, Owen, José, Bevin, me, and Greta.

Greta was the next to arrive. When she walked up, I stood and gave her a big hug and kiss. It felt strangely like coming home. It had only been two weeks, but I missed her. I held her for a minute, resting my forehead against hers and just breathing in her scent. She didn't try to pull away, taking the time to rest her head against mine.

After a spell, we separated and I smiled up to her, then spun to Sarah. "Sarah, this is Greta, Greta, this is Sarah."

Sarah smiled. "I hope it's Greta, otherwise this display would need a *lot* of explaining. Hi, Greta."

Greta held out her hand, but Sarah shook her head and wrapped Greta in a hug. "Nice to meet you. It's good to see someone make my friend so happy."

The three of us took our seats. Greta sat next to me, scooting her chair close enough that we touched along our sides. "Have you known Jade as long as Bevin and José?"

Sarah harrumphed. "No, but in some ways, I know her better. We met in kindergarten. I didn't have the family 'in,' but we've always been besties. Once we were in high school, first Bevin joined our group and then José, not the other way around. It's because we're the best.'

Greta chuckled. "Oh, I like you."

"Honey, everyone likes me." Sarah waggled her brows.

The crew from Pack House came into the restaurant. I was happy to see everyone, until I noticed Brooke. My jaw dropped. Sauntering up to the table, she sneered, "What, you thought I was going to stay out in the woods? I want some real food, a real city, and real people."

"It's the same people. And how are the people out there not real?" I wanted to bang my head against a wall.

She looked down her nose at me. "You know what I mean." She sat in one of the seats, forcing Owen to grab a chair from one of the other tables.

I closed my eyes, and counted to ten, trying to find my calm. After a couple of breaths, I turned to Greta. "Greta, you know Bevin and José, this is Brooke, and this is Owen, my brother."

Greta shook their hands.

Once we all had burgers and fries, Brooke turned to Greta. "So, what do you see in our little Jade here? Is it her quiet stoic charm, or has she been tutoring you and you've been using her for that?"

My head snapped to Brooke, but before I could answer Sarah put her hand on my shoulder. Greta grabbed my hand and gave Brooke a huge smile, batting her eyes. "Why, Brooke, how did you know that I targeted her for her ability to guide me through my classes, ensuring I would pass?"

Brooke's eyes narrowed. But before she could say more, José's voice snapped out, "Brooke, don't."

Brooke slowly faced him and gazed at him because he hadn't said it as a friend, but as her alpha.

Finally, I found my voice. "For the record—"

José cut in. "Jade…"

"No, let me say this, in case there's any question." I knew the frustration was oozing out of me. All my focus was on Brooke. "We met in an I.T. class. I probably passed with an A because of Greta and her brother, not the other way around. Her degree is computer-based. Oh, and *that* is the only class we've discussed. She doesn't even know which other classes I'm taking, or will take. Though she does know I'm pre-med."

I took a calming breath, stopping myself before I pulled dominance from José. It was one of my epsilon abilities, and if I did it to embarrass Brooke it would *not* be acceptable. "If you have an issue with me, *why did you come?*"

She glared at me before turning away with a, "Whatever."

Owen put down his soda glass. "How has training been going?"

I turned my glare on him. "Really?"

He laughed, as did most of the table.

I fell back in my chair.

Greta, still holding my hand, whispered, "Training?"

My shoulders dropped. "First my dad, and now Owen, *love* to set up training programs to keep everyone in the family fit."

Owen gave Greta one of his most charming smiles. "Since Jade is in track, and it won't start up again for a bit, I'll be setting up a program for her to keep her in tip-top shape. I was just checking to see if she's been doing anything in the meantime."

I hit my head on the back of my chair, twice. I couldn't put it off any longer.

He chuckled. "I'll take that as a no. Maybe we can take a run tomorrow. I know Sarah's in, since she roped you into track in the first place."

Sarah started bouncing in her seat. "Hell yeah!"

Greta was watching everyone. "I think that's cool. You all really care about each other. You act like a unit, not just teens hanging out for a few weeks. There's something...I don't know, something more with you. It's kind of amazing."

Bevin shrugged. "It's probably just a continuation of how we were brought up. Except for Sarah and Brooke, we were brought up together, and Sarah was always around."

Brooke snapped, "Yeah, remind me again how I'm not really part of your group. I'm an outsider. I just love being reminded of that all the time."

We all stiffened and turned to her.

Sarah snapped back, "It wouldn't come up if you weren't so nasty all the time. But you aren't, are you. It's mainly one person, isn't it. You're fine to everyone, except to *one* person. Why is that, Brooke?"

My head jerked to Sarah at that, but she shrugged. I never realized it was just me. In high school, when she dated Owen, it had to do with her opposition to family and Owen and me being close. I figured it was just a carry over from that.

She glared at Sarah, crossed her arms, and settled back in her chair.

After lunch, we went out for a hike. Despite my hopes, Brooke wanted to join us there as well. The path was wide enough for two people to walk next to each other. It was a public path, but it passed close to our property.

Greta pointed at a tree. "Do you see those signs on the trees?"

I read one of our property signs and nodded.

"Can you imagine living this close to the park? It would be amazing."

Though Greta and I had been dating, Bevin and José and I decided we wanted to keep everything about Pack House private for now. We were a new pack, and security was an issue. She knew that Bevin and José lived off campus, but nothing more.

I just smiled and continued down the path. It looped around and part way into our walk. A police line blocked part of the path. We could make it past, but it was a distraction.

Greta's scent became minty with confusion. "What is this?"

Brooke snuck up behind us. "Didn't you hear? A family was attacked by some wild animal. Their bodies were dragged and left on the property you fantasize about owning."

"How do you know that?"

"I may look ditzy, but I read the news."

I had had enough. "José, Bevin, I'm heading home. You can enjoy..." I didn't even know what to say. "You can just enjoy. Sarah, you can stay and join me later, or come with. Owen, we'll hang out later. I just *can't* anymore."

I spun on my heel and went back to the head of the trail. Greta followed me. I could hear the others talking behind me, but I didn't care. We hadn't gotten far on the path, so it only took a few minutes to get back to the parking lot.

When we got there, I faced Greta. "Can you make it back on foot?"

She leaned down, kissing me deeply. "I'll follow you anywhere."

CHAPTER 18

Sunday morning, I woke early to take a run with Sarah. Outside, we found Owen leaning against the doors of José's car.

Sarah sauntered up to him and gave him a hug and kiss. "Morning, love."

"Eeew." I mock-shivered at the sight. In reality, the two looked good together. They made a lovely picture—my brother's surfer vibe, with his light brown hair and blue eyes, and Sarah's dark skin and almost black hair.

They both turned to me, smiling.

"Okay, are we going to run?" I asked.

We walked to the running path. Owen threw his arm over my shoulder. "Greta…I like her, though Brooke doesn't."

I scoffed. "Really? You don't say."

"She said Greta didn't smell right."

I rested my head on Owen's shoulder. "I can't believe she's in this pack. I still say send her to Florida."

Sarah came up behind us. "Are you picking Florida because it's as far as you can get from California?"

"She doesn't like snow; I'm just thinking of her."

"Riiiight." Sarah chuckled, "Always thinking of Brooke."

We got to the running path, and I dropped my arm from Owen's waist. He snatched my hand. "When was the last time you let yourself go on a run?"

I thought back. "I was going to take a real run at Halloween, but that was when I picked up Piper's ghost. So, last summer. I don't have as much opportunity here— too many runners on the trail during the school year."

Owen nodded. "I want you to take a thirty-minute run and try to beat your last distance. I don't think you can since you haven't been training for speed. We'll try to keep up, and fail, of course, but we'll all return in fifteen minutes."

"You really are taking on the role of our pack trainer?"

He smiled softly. "It speaks to me, sis."

I gave him a hug. "Fine."

I stretched and set my watch, then I took off. It had been over six months since I'd stretched my muscles and just ran. It felt good to let myself go, mind and body free.

My legs pumped and my arms swung, every movement pushing me farther and faster. The idea I could beat my old time, like Owen had said, wasn't possible, but he was right that I needed this run. Thinking about Brooke… as much as we didn't get along, she probably needed a run like this as well. She couldn't keep up with me either, but she could come closer than just about anyone else in the pack.

Thirty minutes later, we met back at the top of the trail. My breathing was rough. During track, I imitated this type of deep, side-aching, body-trembling pain from a run, but today I genuinely achieved it.

Owen's smile bloomed as he checked my watch. "That was excellent. Can you find a way to do that once or twice a month?"

"I doubt it. There really are too many people on this path when classes are in session. There's no way to do it and not be obvious, even early in the morning."

Sarah patted his back. "You'll figure something out when we're living here."

His eyes lit up. "We?"

She smirked. "I think so. You're a mess without me."

He sighed. "It's true."

I rolled my eyes. "Gods, I missed you two, even though you're both dorks. Let's find coffee."

As we passed in front of the dorms, Alex and Greta popped out of the doors.

Alex was bouncing. "Hi, I'm Alex, you must be Jade's

brother, Owen. I was looking out the window, welcoming the morning, when I saw you three returning from the running trail. I figured, knowing Jade's love of coffee, you'd probably make your way right to the café. Since Greta wasn't with you, I checked if she was awake, and well… here we all are."

Owen's eyes got bigger and bigger as Alex spoke. When she finished, he said, "Wow! Did you even take a breath in all that?"

Alex blushed. "I'm sorry, when I'm nervous, I babble. I'm not used to being with this many people. Back home, I'm usually alone. I'm from a town where everyone knows everyone, and, well, I had two friends, and they were more friends of convenience. I guess I'm just not sure what to do, and when I'm not sure, I…sorry, I'm doing it again." Her face went from pink to tomato red.

Owen doubled over, laughing. "Jade, she's great. You should put *her* in a room with Brooke."

Alex's steps faltered for a second. "Who's Brooke?"

When we got to the alley near the café, Sarah and Owen stopped. Our mood shifted and discussion of Brooke was dropped.

Sarah put her hand on my shoulder. "Is this…?"

I nodded.

The three of us stepped into the alley as far as the ladder.

Greta came up behind me. "Did you tell your friends about Elroy?"

I nodded, leaning back against her. She slipped her arms around me. "I miss him."

"I do, too."

We all headed back towards the café. As we walked, Owen knocked on my mental door.

Yeah?

"The werewolf scent isn't that old."

I know.

"There were two werewolf scents in that alleyway."

I know.

"Did you see the security cameras?"

I tripped on the flat surface and would have fallen if Owen's hand hadn't shot out to catch me. He chuckled.

Right after lunch, Greta had to leave. She had to work on Monday and had only planned on coming for a short visit.

Monday morning, Sarah and I took Alex to the Youth Outreach Center. It was an organization with programs, counselors, and drop-in help available in the center of downtown Arcoíris. As we approached, Alex hesitated about whether she thought it was a good idea. There was a bench across the street, and the three of us sat in silence for twenty minutes watching the windows.

At last, she stood up and grabbed my hand, dragging me through the doors. Sarah followed. The entryway had fliers for programs and events around town for all sorts of LGBTQ+ populations. I realized that I had missed out on a great resource all these years. I must have drooped in disappointment because Sarah rubbed my shoulders in sympathy.

Turning a corner there was a reception desk. Behind it was a person with a pin that said 'they/them.' Their hair was short, straight, and black, and they wore a tight black t-shirt that matched their dark eyes. They were an excellent gatekeeper for this place.

I took an extra moment to take in the person who represented this place and had a momentary flashback to Sarah telling me to date more. Then I remembered Greta and laughed at myself.

Sarah leaned in close and whispered softly, "Down, girl."

I glared at her over my shoulder.

The person behind the table looked up at us and smiled. "Hi, my name is Milo. Welcome to the Youth Outreach Center. Are you new here? How can I help?"

Alex froze. I gave her a nudge and she took a few shuffling steps forward. "Hi. Um. Hi. Well. Um. Hi. Um. My name is. Um. It's Alex." Her hands clenched and she turned to me. "Jade, I don't know if I can do this."

"It's okay. No one is going to bite. Just tell Milo what you're looking for. They'll help."

Alex unclenched her hands and covered her face. With her face covered she seemed to relax, at least enough to get her story out. Once done, she dropped her hands and looked at me in desperation.

Milo tapped a few pamphlets they held in one hand in the palm of their other hand. Alex spun around. Milo smiled. "Thank you for sharing. I know how confusing this all is. When I first started realizing I wasn't the same as my friends, I didn't know what to do. I didn't have anyone who would come down here with me. Coming through that door, alone or with friends, is an amazing first step. I'm proud of you."

Alex's shoulders finally loosened, and the sweet smell of terror started to dissipate. "You are?"

"I am. There's someone here who I think you'd get along with great, but I'd like you to talk to them without your friends, if that's okay?"

Terror returned. I put my hand on Alex's shoulder. "Hey, Alex, why don't Sarah and I go to the café? It isn't far, and we'll wait for you there. When you're done, find us. Then you can tell us about everything. I think this will be amazing."

"You're going to leave me here? Alone?" Her heart started beating a staccato so loud I was shocked Milo couldn't hear it.

Milo came around the table. "Can I put my arm around you?"

Alex looked at them, eyes wild. "Um, yeah. Sure."

Milo winked before doing it. "Now you aren't alone. I'm here."

Alex froze, looking shocked, and then relaxed.

Before we left, I reminded her she had my number. Sarah and I went to the café and talked over coffee and chocolate chip muffins. Alex texted she was leaving the Center an hour later. I texted back asking if she wanted coffee. She said no. Sarah and I picked up and headed out.

Outside the café, we were just in time to see the werewolf dragging Alex into the alley.

CHAPTER 19

As Alex's leg's disappeared down the alleyway, we dashed towards her. I was on the wolf before Alex cleared the sidewalk. My fist struck the werewolf's head. He dropped Alex and lunged at me.

"Jade, get Alex, I have the wolf!" Sarah ran around me, tackling him.

Alex's throat was bitten, torn, and bleeding, but her eyes were open and wild. As I tore off my t-shirt—heedless of what I was wearing underneath—to press against the wound on her neck, I connected to Sarah.

There are security cameras in the alleyway!

I disconnected, needing to focus on saving my roommate…and friend.

Kneeling, I placed my hands on her forehead and chest just below her neck, and let my panther in to investigate, to heal her. Once inside Alex, I noted it was only her neck that was damaged. Sarah and I got out of the coffee shop too quickly for the wolf to do more. Panther and I repaired the windpipe, and I heard Alex gasp for air.

I tried to stay with Panther, but I mumbled, "Please stay silent."

For some miracle of a reason, Alex did. I sunk deeper into the repairs. I opened a connection to José.

"Chica?"

Alley. Werewolf. Alex bitten. Healing. Security cameras.

I dropped the connection to focus on healing. There was a mess in her neck, and though she could breathe, that wasn't a guarantee of survival. Time passed as Panther and I continued to do what we could.

The noises in the alley changed. A hand settled on my shoulder. Energy flowed into me. Someone knocked on my mental door.

What?

It was Bevin. *"Is she stable enough for transport? We'd like to get out of here."* He sounded weaker than usual.

I performed basic triage; everything was sealed. I just needed more time to finish my repairs. She needed more healing. As I did my triage, I heard it. *Oh, no! It can't be, but it makes sense. I can't see anything and I'm not ready to face her…that right now.* I didn't want to face this new reality, so I backed out.

I started to fall and caught myself, putting a hand on the ground. "We can go."

Bevin raised an eyebrow. "We can't…not just yet, hon."

I huffed in frustration. "Why not? And how is Sarah?"

"In the car; we'll discuss everything there."

"Then let's go." I started to push up.

"You're forgetting something." He waved his hand.

I dropped my gaze down to see a lacy black bra and jeans. I blushed. Then I let my face fall into my free hand with a slap. Bevin peeled off his shirt and handed it to me. I put it on. He then carefully picked up Alex and carried her to the car. Slowly, I managed to get to my feet. The three of us crawled into the backseat of the car and José took off.

I leaned my head back, my vision spotty. "Did you get the wolf?"

Sarah sounded tired. "I did. The body is in the trunk. I'm really glad that no one is around this town over winter break. I mean, they parked the car in the alleys between the buildings on the school side, not the street side, but still, it's empty around here."

"So, a second werewolf body to dispose of?"

José grunted. "Yep."

"Was there a ring?"

"Yep."

"So, we're dealing with something bigger."

"Probably."

"Are you making me work really hard, or waiting for me to pass out?"

He snorted. "Is Alex a wolf, now?"

I groaned. "Can I tell you I don't know and have a few minutes of peace?"

"Would that be the truth?"

"I didn't *see* a wolf in her."

"Now who's making who work hard? Did you sense one or hear one?"

"Passing out now."

Bevin and Sarah both laughed.

I didn't pass out, but I dozed before we reached Pack House. I woke up to Owen carrying me. I smacked his chest. "Put me down."

"Wow, you're scary when you have no energy."

"Why aren't you putting me down?"

"I will; give me a sec." He dropped me onto one of the living room couches.

I shut my eyes in frustration. "You could have just woken me up. I can walk. I was asleep, not passed out!"

"I do as my alpha commands."

"I tell ya, I'm jumping ship. I'm going to go to the beach, and none of you will see me again."

Bevin came into the living room with a plate of food. My stomach growled loud enough for everyone to hear.

"Can I scoot in behind you?"

"Whatever."

He handed Owen the plate. I sat up enough for him to take up position as my back rest. My head spun. Then Owen handed me my plate. "See, I sat up all by myself. I'm fine."

"I watched your eyes, sis. You almost blacked out. It was fun to watch."

I gave up and just collapsed against Bevin, eating my burrito, which was heavenly. I may have moaned in pleasure. Sarah came in with a plate and sat under my legs. I growled.

"I feel like I'm being managed."

She just smiled at me. "You are being cared for so that you can continue to care for us. Give us this."

Since as soon as she sat, the room stopped spinning, I stopped complaining.

Owen knelt in front of Sarah. "What is your secret with my sister? I want the power of getting through to her that you have."

I threw a pillow at him. It was that or my burrito, and there was no way I was giving up my food.

After eating two burritos, I felt more grounded. "I'm going to go back to heal Alex. We're safe here, so I'll use both animals." I rotated my head until I could see Bevin's eyes. "If I go over three hours, let me know."

I went into Bevin and José's room and found Alex on their bed. Bevin had given her a sedative and had properly cleaned and bandaged her neck.

I sat on a chair by their bed and went back to work healing her. I sat there for what felt like a few minutes, but when I opened my eyes again, a couple of hours had passed and her neck was almost fully healed.

When I healed other people, I needed one of my animals to stay in me and pull energy from others. Since both my animals were going to be healing Alex, no one tried to feed me energy. When I opened my eyes there were nuts, protein bars, and cheese on a plate next to me.

I ate some of the nuts right away, then started in on the rest of the food.

"Jade?" Alex's voice was rough. I wasn't sure it would come back the same as it had been before. My animals and I had healed her throat, but I wasn't sure we'd put it back together perfectly.

"Hi, Alex."

"What happened?"

I connected to José to tell him Alex was up.

"You were attacked by a wolf."

"Like, the one that killed Elroy?"

"No, I killed that one."

She sat up, then grabbed her head. I was by her side supporting her before she slammed back down onto the bed. "You okay?"

She looked at me with wild eyes. "You killed a wolf?"

"Sorry, I should probably wait to explain things. I'm really tired."

José came in. "I don't know how to do this the right way. My guess is, blurting things out isn't the right way. Maybe we should talk with Violet or Zee."

I shook my head. "She doesn't know them. One thing I do know is that knowing the people helps."

Alex was panicking. "What are you talking about and where am I? Why aren't I in a hospital? Or dead?"

I sat down next to her on the bed. As soon as I got close to her, she relaxed a bit. "This isn't an easy story to tell you. But I don't have a choice. You were attacked by a werewolf."

She just stared at me. "That isn't funny."

"I'm not trying to be funny. Your neck was bitten, part of it torn out. I healed it."

"That wasn't a dream? The bite? Not being able to breathe? You in my head?"

"No. None of it was a dream. I wouldn't be telling this to you, but you've probably seen the movies, and know what happens if you get bitten by a werewolf and survive."

Her eyes got huge. "Will I start attacking people?"

"Have I ever attacked you?"

"Wait, you're a werewolf?" She looked at the room, eyes wide and mouth dropping open. You could almost hear the pieces falling into place. "That's why you heal so fast. And run so fast. And *think* so fast."

José laughed. "No, that last she's always done. Even before she turned furry."

"Isn't the running part cheating?"

221

I shrugged. "Maybe, but I don't actually run my fastest in track. That's what we were doing Sunday morning. Owen was forcing me to get an actual run in."

Owen stuck his head through the door. "And your run was crap. You need to stretch your legs out more often."

Alex gazed at him. "How fast *did* she run?"

Owen sniffed. "She ran just over seven miles in thirty minutes. Her record is closer to fifteen miles in an hour. She's out of shape."

Alex gaped at us.

I threw out my hands. "Really, I tell you you're a werewolf, and *that's* what stuns you? My running speed is the part that's unrealistic? I tell you; the youth of today have grown too jaded."

She laughed. "Am I really going to turn into a wolf one day?"

I took her hand to double check what I already knew from earlier. *Wolf.* "Yes, and there is a lot for you to learn, and a lot of decisions to make. But, as it goes, I'll help you with most of it."

José smiled at her. "She is one of the best pack trainers in the country. I stole her from her last pack, which is impressive since the last pack's alphas were her parents, and they are amazing."

"You stole both of her parents' kids away from them?"

Sarah came to the door. "Oh, no, they said they could only take Jade if he promised to take Owen as well."

Alex looked scandalized.

I leaned in. "It's a joke."

She relaxed with a slight smile.

"Anyway, the next full moon isn't until the end of the month, after school starts. Your wolf probably won't be ready to come out until then. I can go in and check, but it really would be pointless."

"You can do what now?" Her heart began to race as if she were running her own marathon.

I rubbed my head, feeling the headache start.

José reached over Alex to touch my hand. "You really are at the end of your resources, chica." He turned to Alex. "Jade is a one-of-a-kind wolf. She can do things no one else can do. So, yes, she can figure out your wolf early. She can do a dozen other things. I'll let her fill you in. It will give the two of you things to talk about in that tiny dorm room of yours. That is, until the new Pack House is built, and you both move in and give up that ridiculous building." He shivered.

Alex stopped breathing for a second, then gulped in a huge breath. "You want me to move into what now?"

I glared at José. "Now who's going too fast? I'll give you all the information, but maybe not in this bedroom, this second. Can we get more food? Isn't it dinner time? I think that would be a great time to discuss basic Pack decisions…"

We grabbed hot dogs, buns, and the fixings that went along with them, and headed out to the fire-pit. The rest of the pack was already out there.

Brooke took one look at Alex and rolled her eyes. "Another stray?"

Alex tilted her head. "Oh, my god, I see it!" She ran over to Brooke, whispered something in her ear so quietly none of us could hear it, then slowly made her way back to me. Brooke's eyes got wide—it looked like her head was going to explode—she whipped around, and stormed back into her pink behemoth.

As we sat, I leaned over and asked, "What did you say to her?"

"Oh, when I was in high school, I always knew who liked who, and why people were jerks. It was my one skill, understanding people's motivations. I just went and whispered her darkest secret to her."

Narrowing my eyes, I considered our newest addition to the pack…so full of secrets.

We sat around the fire eating hot dogs. Eventually, Brooke's hunger won out and she came back out to join us. The full pack sitting around the fire, eating.

As we ate, Violet looked up at José. "Tell us a story."

His rich voice filled the circle, tinged with his slightly Mexican accent. "What do you want to know?"

Violet ducked her head and shrugged. She'd apparently used up her words and social interactions for the day.

Brooke narrowed her eyes. "When did you come out as gay? Like, how did you know?"

José leaned back, considering. "When I was in seventh

grade, I wanted to learn more about my Mexican heritage. It's ironic, since my dad grew up in Mexico and I could've just talked with him, but who wants to talk with their dad, right?" He let his head fall back, watching the clouds blow by. "I joined up with this group, this gang of middle and high school kids. The leader, this kid called Marcus, said I could hang with them."

He shook his head remembering something. Sitting forward, he crossed his legs on the log and grabbed Bevin's hand. "We were sitting on the grass at the skate park watching some of the high school kids do tricks. There was this kid, man he was…well, we skated in shorts which showed his muscles, that's it…and I watched. The others watched for the tricks. It didn't take me long to realize that that wasn't what interested me."

His eyes slid to Bevin, but Bevin was as wrapped up in the story as the rest of us. "Anyway, a group of three high school girls all dressed in short skirts or shorter shorts and cropped tops sauntered over. The group I was hanging with went wild. Marcus decided this would be the perfect test for his newest member. He told me to go chat the girls up. I froze. Not only were they older, I was completely uninterested. Before I could adjust where I was staring, one of the guys in the group noticed me gaping at the skateboarder."

José shivered and squeezed Bevin's hand. He closed his eyes for a second. Concern bubbled out of Bevin. "You don't need to continue."

José smiled. "It's okay, I just…It's okay." He shook his head, as if to shake off his memory. "The group started asking if I was gay and chanting 'you must be gay.' I debated denying it."

Me, Bevin, and Owen all snorted.

Alex whispered, "What?"

Owen said, "José was never smart enough to lie to save his butt. I can see seventh grade José sitting there deciding what he felt, deciding he did in fact like boys and just raising an imperious eyebrow at Marcus and shrugging."

I snorted.

José sighed. "Not quite, but you aren't that far off. I ended up running away as fast as I could, but I was one of the youngest and smallest in the group. They chased me down."

Owen froze. "It was *that* day?"

José nodded. "Marcus said they couldn't touch my face, or the adults would find out. Then they caught me. They punched and kicked my chest, back, and arms. I swear they broke a rib or two, but…no, I'm jumping ahead. They ran off and I didn't know what to do. A few minutes later, Owen found me. He said he was going to get his Aunt Allison, a healer. But Marcus made it clear to me that if I told any adults he would not only hurt me, he'd hurt my sister, Estrella, as well."

I started to think back. Bevin and I stared at each other across the fire, eyes wide in realization.

José huffed out a laugh as he caught our scent. "I see

that the other players are figuring this out as well. So, Owen, not knowing what to do, called the only healer he knew who wasn't an adult…his sister."

Alex smelled confused and Brooke…Brooke's cinnamony annoyance erupted out over the group.

I shared a smile with Bevin, remembering that day. "I was in fifth grade. I wasn't allowed to walk to the park alone, so Bevin had to take me. He held my hand the whole way to keep me safe. When I got there, I rubbed down your torso… and yes, I heard the tell-tale cracking in my head, and felt dizzy afterwards. We had had a pizza party that day and I'd eaten a lot. My dad always thought that our abilities, like my epsilon one, manifested before the wolf appeared."

I rubbed my face, trying to recall everything. "After the popping in my head, you cried out, then said it didn't hurt as much. Then Bevin and me patched you up."

Bevin cleared his throat. "Yep, exactly that."

José was gazing at Bevin intently, but Bevin was focused on the fire. He seemed embarrassed. His breathing was off. After a minute he pulled at his hand, but José held tight. Then José leaned in close, almost touching, but not quite and sniffed, just behind Bevin's ear. He closed his eyes and rested his forehead against Bevin's head. I heard a soft apology.

There was a tiny gasp from Alex who seemed to follow on a level no new wolf should.

Sarah turned to me. "Do you understand what

just happened?"

"Maybe, but I'm not one hundred percent."

José sighed, closing his eyes. "Did you know then?"

Bevin shook his head. "I just knew that I loved you back then."

Owen snapped, "What are you two talking about?"

Bevin had a sad smile, eyes watching the fire. "That was the day the mating bond happened between us. I couldn't resist it. I tried, but," he shrugged, "look at him."

José sighed. "I had just realized I was gay, I liked boys, and the first person my heart wanted was a person who had seemed to be a girl my whole life. Bevin had just come out to the group as trans. I'd just taken a beating for liking boys. I was confused. I spent the next several years dating boys and thinking about Bevin—fantasizing if I'm honest. It was…well, *confusing* doesn't even begin to describe it. My seventh-grade brain didn't know how to put all the pieces together."

Alex's eyes were getting misty. "Are you two going to get married?"

It felt like everyone around the fire stopped breathing.

Bevin's sad smile returned. "We haven't talked about it. We're both young. We should probably talk about it alone before we discuss it with our pack, but maybe one day." The hope and sadness coming from Bevin were going to make me sneeze.

José scanned his rapt audience. The seemingly simple,

yet personal, question delved much deeper into his past than even he could've predicted. He leaned over and kissed Bevin's cheek. Then, before anyone knew what was happening, he slid off the log and onto his knees in front of Bevin.

"Bevin Green, I don't know when my love for you began, I just know I have always loved you. I do know that my love for you is never-ending. When I think of any point in my future, I can't imagine not sharing my life with you. In front of our friends and pack, will you do me the honor of becoming my husband?"

Suddenly, a ring pop flew through the air. I searched the faces of the pack until I saw a guilty look on Violet. The pop had landed between the boys.

Laughing quietly, José unwrapped the green pop and held it up to Bevin, love and hope pouring from him.

CHAPTER 20

Training Alex was simpler than training Brooke had been, because she didn't fight the concept—or me— as much as Brooke had. In reality, she seemed to like the idea of having a group that accepted her and wanted her to be part of them.

Sarah and I spent the next two weeks teaching her the basics of what it meant to be a wereanimal and part of a pack. We started with the different packs and her options. She decided she did want to start with our pack since she went to college in Arcoíris; it made sense.

We brought her to Pack House and showed her what

a shift entailed. She met my wolf, as well as José's and Bevin's. At first, she was terrified, but she came to realize the animal was just us in wolf form. Her terror smelled sweet as candy and at first was hard to resist, so it was good when she grew accustomed to our beasts.

Owen sat at the firepit, leaning back, amusement flowing from him. Alex, Sarah, and I were debating walking around the land, doing a visual sweep.

"Hey sis, why not show Alex the panthers? They've acclimated to wolves, let Alex see the real beauty in the pack."

We stopped and Sarah bounced. "It would be fun, I'll stay human, control my minions as we search the woods."

Alex's face scrunched up. "I do like cats."

"You do know they're bigger than the wolves, right?" I couldn't believe the vanilla interest coming from her. No fear. "We aren't talking cats that roam around your farm, we're talking panthers."

"Oh, I know. I think it sounds great."

With a sigh, I headed to my brother, and we started our change. As soon as we found our panthers, Alex squealed and skipped over to pet us.

We didn't find anything on our sweep, but Alex did learn the path and Sarah explained what we were looking for.

Throughout training, she spent time with everyone in the pack, including Brooke, who seemed to give her a bit of begrudging respect.

During one of her training hikes with Sarah and Owen, I sat on a campfire log and waited for them to return. Zee, Violet, and Luke were all at work, and Bevin and José were out on a date. I don't think the two of them got out to relax much alone. We all forced them to go.

The fire was out, and the day was cool, but I was so rarely alone; it was lovely. I debated starting up a full meditation when I heard Brooke's door open. I had somehow forgotten about her.

She came over and sat across the firepit from me.

"Hi, Brooke." My voice sounded flat and dead, even to me. I shut my eyes and centered myself. I didn't want to fight. I had to do better.

"I'm not here to fight, just talk." Her comment echoed my thoughts.

"Okay… what about?"

"Will you listen to me without assuming I'm being rude?" *Calming breath*. "Sure."

"You need to be careful around Greta."

"Why?"

"You just do. She didn't…I donno, Jade, she didn't smell

right, or feel right. You're better at these wolf things. I just know that when I met her, my wolf said 'no.'"

"Your wolf?"

"I can't explain it."

"Your wolf talks to you."

She shrugged. "I know it sounds weird. I don't talk about it with all of you, but yeah, sometimes. She gives me direction."

"Words?"

"This isn't about me, Jade."

I rubbed my eyes. "Sorry, you're only the third person I know who could communicate with her wolf. To me, that's interesting. So, she doesn't like Greta either?"

"Are we done here?" She got up and walked away before I could answer.

Mid-January, right before Owen and Sarah had to leave, we celebrated Owen's birthday with a large pizza party at Pack House followed by s'mores and a big cake.

Over s'mores, Owen turned to José. "You know, I've been thinking. Once the new place is built, this shack will be renovated too. This place is Pack House. So, we'll need a way to discuss the new structure. Our *actual* home."

José's eyes narrowed. "It will become Pack House. This will be the guest cottage."

Owen smirked. "Nah. We're more than a pack of werewolves, it should be our *Were* House."

There was a chorus of groans and giggles.

A low growl emanated from José, he even pulled out his alpha voice. "No."

Bevin placed his hand on José's arm. "I don't think you could stop it at this point. It's going to be called the Were House."

A few days later, Sarah, Owen, and Brooke had to head back to their schools.

Right before leaving, Owen presented Alex with a package.

Alex's eyes got wide. "You got me a gift."

Sarah and I immediately shook our heads. Sarah beat me to the punch. "Never get excited when a Stone man surprises you with a present."

Despite the warning, Alex bounced as she opened it up. Inside was a training notebook that would take her through to the summer when Owen was planning on moving here permanently. "Is this what I think it is?"

Owen stood proud. "Your first training manual. Usually, we wait until after your first run as a wolf, but since I won't be here for that, I wanted to give it to you early."

"How much time did you spend on this?" Alex sounded awed.

He shrugged. "I dunno."

Sarah busted him. "A lot of time. Hours. First, he evaluated you when you weren't paying attention. Then he put the program together based on what he observed hoping it would build with you…hours."

Her eyes misted over as she stood there for a second, then she ran to him and gave him a huge hug.

He smirked over her head as he returned the hug. "This is how you two should greet a new training program."

When Alex and I returned to our dorm room, I had two gifts on my bed.

Alex started to bounce. "Open them!"

I slid my eyes to her. "I could not, and pretend I never saw them."

"But they're presents, it's so exciting."

"I'm going to strangle Sarah the next time I see her." But I opened them up anyway. The first held my training program. Since I was in track, my schedule was sparse. The other, a stuffed goose with a note that read, *"Noticed you were missing most of your friends from home, Sarah."*

"What's that all about? I saw you had that one pillow and I've been wondering all semester."

Groaning, I told her the story. When I started to run, I found a family of geese on the bike path near my parents' house…their pack den. They had taken up residence on the path after I had passed the spot on my way out. When I tried to pass them in human form, they attacked me. I transformed to my panther, and they attacked that form as well. I even roared. It hadn't impressed them. They were mean. It took leaping into a tree to get away.

Ever since, I had been finding goose-themed items everywhere I turned.

She fell on her bed, laughing. I feared I would soon receive more geese from another source.

There was a week before classes started and Alex and I spent some of that time at Pack House, and some of it in the dorms.

"So, José is the main alpha?" Alex's face scrunched up as she tried to piece it all together.

"José and Bevin are both the alphas."

"Why do you go to José first all the time?"

"I don't. I just do for the splashier things. When you join the pack, one of the alphas has a closer connection with you mentally; for me, that's José."

"That's really weird, because if you were to ask me, I'd say you were closer friends with Bevin."

"As in friends, maybe. We've been hanging out longer. José is two years older than me, and in school and growing up, that mattered."

"Two years? But you and Bevin are juniors?"

"I spent my senior year of high school here in a transfer program they have so my senior year and freshman year were meshed together."

"Ah. Okay, so one of the alphas connects with us and is

closer somehow."

"José does that with the pack members."

"So, what does Bevin do?"

"The connecting is only part of it. Running a pack is creating a group dynamic. They want a pack that runs like a family. Most of us are young, so it will take even more work, especially if we get older members. Bevin will be good at that part."

"I can see that."

"Are you going to tell me Brooke's dark secret?"

"Nope."

"It was worth a shot. Have any more of that moonshine?"

"Yep, and that won't get me to spill the beans, so it isn't worth it. Let's save it."

We spent the rest of the evening discussing what it meant to be epsilon. I hadn't explained that to her yet because there was so much else to learn.

"So, you're, like, the only one who can heal. If you hadn't been there, I probably would have... died?"

"Yeah. You can see why Elroy was so hard on me. I couldn't get to him. I may have been able to save him if I had."

"You can't blame yourself that he died, Jade."

"Well, no, but it's frustrating." I needed to change the subject. "When's your next session at the Youth Outreach Center?"

Her eyes lit up. "I've been going a couple times a week. I'll probably continue about once a week once school starts. Milo, you know, the person who greeted us, they've been really helpful. Their friend has also been helping me a lot. Thanks for dragging me there."

"Can I ask, what have you figured out?"

"A lot, and nothing. I may ask you, and the pack, to use they/them pronouns with me, just to see how it feels. I don't know if I'm ready to face the world with that decision yet."

"I am definitely okay with that, and you know the pack will support you. Is that what you want?"

Alex smiled and nodded. "It's so different from where I'm from. I just…I don't know how to describe it. It's still like I'm in a dream."

José picked me up the Thursday before the spring semester began. We headed down to the police station to see if we could figure out if the security cameras in the alley were privately owned or if they belonged to the police.

As we drove, I noticed a new ring shining on his finger. It was a silver band, simple yet elegant.

"Nice ring," I said.

José's pleasure radiated throughout the car. He glanced down at his hand before focusing on the road. "Bevin has a matching one, white gold. I want to get them engraved."

"Have you picked a date?"

He tensed for a second. "I think over the summer. That way everyone can fly out here. Pack House—"

"Were House."

He grumbled, "Were House…will be complete and we'll have places to put people up."

"Whose name are you going with? Cortez? Green? Oooo, how about 'green' in Spanish? Verde? Oh, no… Bevin Verde is horrible, or…"

"Jade! Stop."

I turned to him, broken out of my musings. The scent of cinnamon filling the car as his annoyance with me grew. I smiled brightly, then made a show of biting my lips shut.

"How about Bevin and I discuss our name, and you focus on anything else."

A grin split my face. "Sooo, no coming up with a new name for you two?"

"No." He continued to glare for a few seconds, then took a long breath and smiled. His scent slowly shifted from annoyed to amused. "I'm glad you are so excited for us."

I laughed. "So, can I help in other ways? Help pick out the dress?"

We both shivered at that thought. José's hands tightened on the wheel. "Gods, I hadn't thought about the shopping involved with a wedding."

"Don't worry, Sarah will be here by then. She'll manage most of it."

José visibly relaxed. "That is a huge item off a list I hadn't started. Gods, a wedding. I'm guessing it can't be small, can it?"

"You two are the alphas, so I'm going to go with 'no.'"

We pulled into the parking lot, ending our conversation. We got out and walked into the station. The building was old with beautiful wood and tinted glass old enough it had bubbles in it. I made my way to the reception desk.

"Hi, my purse was stolen, and I saw the thief run up that alley next to the café downtown. When I got to the alley, I noticed that there were security cameras and was wondering if they were yours and if we could find the guy and my purse on the film?"

The woman behind the desk just stared at me. Then, after a minute she picked up the phone next to her and asked for Donald. A few minutes later, a heavy-set man in a police uniform came up and led us to an interview office. I repeated my story, and he took notes.

"I'm sorry, ma'am, there are no cameras in that alley. I'm not sure what you're referring to. Do you want to report your purse stolen?"

"Do you think you can do anything about it?"

He sighed. A wave of annoyance and depression rolled off him. "Ms. Stone, if your personal property was stolen, it is our civic duty to do our best to find it. However, in my opinion, it is gone. The person probably took out any valuables and trashed the rest. I am more than willing to do—"he visibly shivered, "—the paperwork. It is completely up to you."

His voice and face remained professional and neutral

throughout. I was mildly impressed.

"That's okay. I agree that my purse is a lost cause."

"I hope you've contacted all credit card agencies and your bank and informed them that the cards were stolen. You should replace all pieces of identification, yadda yadda yadda. We have some paperwork that can walk you through proper procedure, if you want."

I shook my head. He brightened once he realized I wasn't going to put him through paperwork hell.

"No, thank you. My dad works in security. I know the steps."

His eyes widened then narrowed. "Ms. Stone, as in Stone Security? The new business opening up in a few months?"

I slumped in my seat as I realized I made a mistake. My anonymity was gone. "Yes."

He pursed his lips. "Interesting." He pushed his chair back. "Good to know."

I was about to get up to leave when a tall Asian man entered the room. An officer, judging by his uniform, with short dark hair and dark eyes. He held a sheet of paper, reading it, as he opened the door. I heard him sniff. I peeked over my shoulder and saw José shrug. The scent of werewolf hit me, and I saw José's brow rise at the same time. My heart stopped as I slowly turned to face this new werewolf officer.

CHAPTER 21

The new officer stood in the door, holding it open. He came around the corner and gave me a bright smile that lit up his whole face. His name tag read Wang.

"Captain, can I speak with these two?"

"Wang, they were just about to leave. You can walk them out."

"Great." He actually sounded chipper. Wonderful.

When we got to the front foyer, Officer Wang, the werewolf, turned to us, blocking the way out. "So, Ms. Stone, right?"

My eyes hardened. "Can we go now?"

He looked over my shoulder. "And you're…Mr. Cortez? Right?"

When we came into the police station, we had only given my name, not José's. My face flattened. "Can we please leave?"

"Wait, please. Can we talk, Ms. Stone? I may be able to help you. There's a coffee shop across the street."

José placed his hand on my shoulder as he stood behind me and gave it a squeeze. His reassurance flowed through the pack connection, calming my nervousness, but his voice carried the full weight of his alpha presence as he spoke. "Officer Wang, please let us leave."

Officer Wang's eyes dropped, and he trembled. He quickly opened the door and we walked out. We hadn't made it to the car before he caught up. "Please. Five minutes."

José froze. "What do you want, Officer Wang?"

Officer Wang spoke to our backs. "Ms. Stone, Jade, I met your dad when he was in town. I met his…friend, too. Tanner. They said I should find you if I needed anything. Five minutes, please." His scent was a mixture of sweetness—he was scared—and nutty—he was nervous. My nose tickled.

My shoulders dropped as frustration flowed through me. This officer's desires were closed off to me and I didn't know what he wanted. Meeting a lone wolf while we were still trying to establish our territory was one more item on a long list of to dos. It was also frustrating that this Officer Wang knew we were establishing a pack, but never checked in with us. If he'd met my dad, he should've done at least that. That said, I had to follow through on a promise my dad made.

José growled low. "Where is the coffee house?"

We walked across the street to the coffee shop. I ordered a coffee, a ham and swiss sandwich, and a small salad. José ordered a coffee, a club sandwich, and chips. We found a table in the back corner and sat before the police officer ordered. It was early enough in the day that the shop was mostly empty, and the area where we sat was private. I started to dig in before Officer Wang joined us with his soup and salad.

I checked out his chili. "What, no donuts?"

He grunted with a half-smile. "That's dessert, not lunch."

José put down his fork. "Officer Wang—"

"Carlos."

José huffed in acceptance. "Carlos, why did you want to talk to us?"

He lowered his voice. "Do...do you know what I am?"

José sighed. "Yes."

Carlos nodded quickly. "Are you...because you don't smell...like me. You smell normal, human. Well you—" he looked at me, "—smell of the forest, but mostly normal.

244

It's distracting."

José leaned back in his chair. His eyes glowed as he released part of his alpha power, flooding our vicinity with alpha essence.

My breath hitched as his power rolled over me, blanketing me with the need to obey. Carlos's chin hit his chest as he slid from his chair, shaking. I jumped out of my seat to catch him. "José, enough."

The power suddenly stopped. Carlos steadied and I sat back down.

Carlos's breath was choppy. He took a deep breath. "Holy hell, what are you? What did you do to me?" He looked ready to bolt.

José's neutral face twitched. "I just gave you my credentials. You asked if we were like you, even if we smell different. Now you know."

Carlos smelled spooked. He rotated in his seat towards me. "Can you do that to me, too?"

I smiled as I took a bite of my sandwich, then shook my head as I swallowed. "Nope. I'm no…" I looked to José who nodded in permission, "alpha. So, your turn. What are you? A lone wolf? Have you ever been part of a pack? What did you want to speak to us about?"

Carlos downed a bottle of water and then a cup of hot tea. After a couple of calming breaths, he leaned back and nodded. "Lone wolf, I guess. I've been on my own since I was turned. I didn't know there were packs I could join."

José placed his hand on Carlos's arm and the man visibly relaxed. The power of touch was so important for wolves. Carlos looked at where José touched him as if José were performing some sort of magic.

José shrugged, but left his hand where it was as he said, "Yes. We'll talk about packs later."

Carlos watched José hand on his arm in confusion as he continued. "I put up the cameras in that alley. Once I realized there were…well, wolves, I wanted to know what was going on."

I let out my breath in a whoosh. "So, it isn't something that the police force has in general, just you as a private citizen?"

"Yeah. The feed is attached to my phone. I…well…I saw the wolf attack that girl. Did she survive the attack?"

I rubbed my face. "You mean the blonde attacked right after the new year?"

Sadness flowed from Carlos. He must have read my actions as a negative and not just tired exasperation at having my actions viewed on a hidden video feed.

José's voice came out warm and tender. "It's okay, Carlos, she's alive. Jade's just upset that she was caught on camera."

Carlos slumped in relief. He checked his watch, and I heard his heart rate shoot up. "Okay, good. That's really good. Look, I have to get back to work. Can I contact you again?"

José immediately agreed and the three of us swapped numbers. Before he left, José asked, "Can we meet so that I can teach you what pack is about? I'd love for you to know more."

Carlos's eyes widened. "Yes. I'd like that." He shook my hand, then José's. He seemed like he didn't want to let go but then forced himself to release his grip. He slowly made his way to the door. Once the door shut, he shook himself before he ran off.

Watching him go, I asked José, "Do you think he'll call?"

José shrugged. "I hope so, but if he doesn't reach out, we will."

I met Greta and Quinn when they returned for spring semester. We had dinner together in the cafeteria. When I got to the table, there was a third person with them. I sat down, sniffing, and realized the third was a werewolf. I tried not to react. The number of wolves popping up was making my head spin.

"Jade, this is Quinn's best friend, Boden. He wasn't sure if he was going to college, but he was just accepted here and starts this semester."

I shook Boden's hand and was thankful, once again, for the bears and their soap that covered my scent. "How long have you all known each other?"

Boden held my hand a few seconds too long, as if he were trying to flirt. "All our lives. I used to babysit the twins."

At my look of confusion, Greta said, "He took off a few

years, and a semester, and then decided to start college here."

"What will you study, or are you undecided?"

"For now, undecided. How about you?"

"Pre-med."

His brows hit his curly brown hair. "Impressive." His deep voice rumbled. I'd rarely heard a voice that low.

"Thanks."

Greta hadn't touched me since I sat down, so I sent her a quick questioning look.

She shrugged with an apologetic, sad shake of her head.

Apparently, our relationship had gone on the DL. Whereas I had never been flamboyant, I had also never been in the closet. This was something I had to think about.

Fear rolled off Greta during dinner. It added a sweetness the cafeteria food didn't need. I'm sure I smelled frustrated. This whole situation infuriated me. Quinn smelled bored, like plain rice, and Boden smelled amused, his vanilla tea scent overpowering it all. Apparently, he was enjoying himself.

After dinner, I returned to the dorms. I was halfway there when Greta caught up with me. "Jade, I'm sorry. Boden got accepted two days ago. No one knew he had even applied."

"That's fine."

"You're upset."

With a sigh, I stopped to speak with her. "Yes, but not because you have a friend at this school. I think that's great. I have friends here as well."

"What do you want me to do?"

"I want you to figure this out." I waved my hand between us. "I may be private, but I've never been in the closet. I've never hidden who I've liked before tonight. It felt like I was wearing clothing a size too small. It made me itch. I really like you. I've made that obvious, but I can't do that again." I pointed at the cafeteria.

"So, what does that mean?"

"We have options. We can stay together as long as I never have to see Boden again. Or…I don't know, the ball is in your court."

I spun on my heel and continued my walk to the dorms, running up the stairs to my room. In the stairwell, I paused and finally let loose with a howl of pure pain, releasing all my frustration and rage. When I got into the room I fell into bed, curling up with my back to the room. Thankfully, the room was empty.

My phone rang. Checking the display, I saw it was Sarah.

"What?" I said in a clipped tone.

"You tell me."

It took a few minutes to fill her in.

"Oh, honey, that isn't good."

"That isn't helpful."

"Go to Pack House."

"Goodnight, Sarah."

"Night."

Five minutes later, Bevin walked in.

I grumbled into my pillow. "I need to start locking my door! Did Sarah call you?"

"No, José sent me."

I stayed curled in a ball on my bed and told him what I'd told Sarah. He plopped onto my bed, curling himself around me.

"Don't. I'm going to cry."

"That's okay."

"I don't want to cry."

One arm slid under my head, the other around my waist in a gentle hug. "Just pretend I'm not here."

"I don't want to pretend I'm not me. There is so much in my life I have to hide. This is the one thing I'm open about. I know I didn't tell you about me until Piper, but I wasn't pretending, I was just shy."

He hugged me tighter.

"Gods, Bevin, I just *can't*." I rolled over and cried into his chest.

After a few minutes, I froze.

He rubbed my back. "What?"

"Don't kill me. I just remembered. Boden…he's a wolf."

Five minutes later, I was in the car driving to Pack House. Bevin had allowed me time to splash water on my face before we headed out.

We met in the dining room. Zee was pacing. "Do you think he knew about you?"

"No. I spent years with Coach Nelson, and I'm here

with all of you. I know we don't leave scent markers."

"Why do you think he was amused?"

Frustration leaked from my every pore. "My guess is, he knows damn well Greta is gay and I'm her girlfriend. He loves messing with her. He can smell it on both of us. I can't tell her that. He won't let on that he knows. He's just going to sit there watching us squirm while he flirts with me."

Zee slipped his hands in his pockets and leaned against the wall. "Ah. Makes sense. He's being a manipulative jerk."

José was holding the ring from the second wolf. "Did he have one of these?"

I shook my head. "No."

"I think this could be a big coincidence. The other two stayed hidden; they didn't sign up for classes. If they had, then their scent would've been all over campus."

Violet asked, "Should we have someone approach Boden?"

José's voice took on that alpha edge. "Only if we can get someone from another pack. We still aren't in a strong enough position yet. I don't want to give away our pack's presence until we have an established Pack House." He sighed, as if in resignation. "The Were House."

Violet growled low in her throat. I was so shocked at that amount of emotion coming from her, I gaped.

She ducked her head, blue strands covering her face. "When Were House is established, we're going to have a command center. Then I can do a deep dive into who this kid is. We just don't have all the needed equipment or bandwidth I require. I can't do it at work because everything we do there is monitored. There would be questions as to why I was researching this kid."

José paused and his fingers tapped as he thought. "What do you need?"

Violet grumbled. "It's more than just that, I need equipment *and* space. I know there's the basement, but Luke has been down there most nights. There really isn't room in Pack House. We're using all the available space we have."

Bevin gazed off towards Were House. "I spoke with the builders. Originally, they said we could start moving in this month. When I told them we wouldn't need that date, they shifted how they built to be more efficient. It cut a few weeks off their timeline and dropped the total cost." He closed his eyes, thinking. "The project should be completed by our spring break."

I froze. I hadn't realized we had such a solid timeline.

He faced Violet. "A lot of the final pieces can be done at our discretion. I can ask them to get the command room done first. I don't know when it will be finished, but my guess is, once it's done, you can set it up to your standards."

Her eyes glowed. "What's my budget?"

José just smiled at her.

CHAPTER 22

Winter break ended, Sarah, Owen, and Brooke were gone, and classes had begun. Alex or Bevin were in every one of my classes. I wasn't taking any more I.T. classes, so unless I went out of my way, I wasn't going to see Greta. I told her she had to make a decision about how she treated our relationship and as far as I knew, she hadn't.

The full moon came halfway through the first week back in session. Alex's first. After our classes for the day, we all piled into José's car and headed out to Pack House. I had a few extra outfits stored there, and Alex's suitcase was already in the trunk.

On the way over, Alex sat next to me in the back, sending off sweet waves of sugary scented fear. We were too close to the full moon. I took a deep breath and released my calm.

The car jerked and José took in a sharp gulp of air. "Chica, warning next time."

"Yeah, sorry. But it's better, they aren't as afraid."

He sighed. "You are correct about that. The fear, do you know…never mind. Can you go in and talk to their wolf?"

"Now?"

"Have you ever done it?"

"Well, actually, no." I'd put it off because things had been so busy with having the full pack around. Then, when everyone had left, school and Greta."

Alex sat next to me, watching us talk, calmer, but their eyes still took up half their face. "What do I have to do?"

"Nothing." I reached over and placed a hand on theirs.

Alex's owl-like eyes tracked the motion as if my hand were a mouse. Their terror was making everything turn into prey.

I closed my eyes and felt Panther leap up, always the first to want to explore. *Wolf*, I directed. The last thing I needed was to scare her wolf with a cat.

We entered. It didn't take long for me to find the wolf. It looked like a snowball, as white as mine was black, except for some gray around the paws and down their nose.

Hi, beautiful.

The wolf bounced on its front paws, and I felt Alex stiffen and whisper, "What the…"

There were light chuckles from the front of the car.

The wolf said, *"Do I know you? I think I saw you once before, a long time ago. You helped but didn't stay. You smell similar, but you look different."*

Oh, gods, the wolf talked as much as Alex.

Would you like to come out for a run with me today?

"Can I?"

I sent a wave of friendship and acceptance. *Of course, young one.*

The wolf trotted in a circle, wagging its tail excitedly.

I will see you soon. We slowly backed out.

After I moved my hand away, Alex, whose eyes hadn't shrunk, just stared at me. "What did you just do to me?"

"What did it feel like?"

"It felt like you were tickling the inside of my brain and talking to my soul."

I looked up and realized the car had stopped. We'd reached Pack House. The boys were watching us. "Is that what it feels like?"

They both shrugged and nodded. Finally, Bevin said, "More or less. You either feel like a warm shower on the inside, or tickling. It never feels bad, but it's always odd."

I scrunched up my face for a second. "Huh."

José's demeanor changed. He became *more*, somehow, as he slid into his alpha mantle. "Are they ready?"

A smile erupted on my face, imagining the white fluff ball joining our run. "Oh, yeah."

José's eyes narrowed. "What aren't you telling us?"

I shook my head. "Nope. This will be awesome."

He grumbled as he got out of the car. We all followed. He took Alex's hand and led them near the tree line. Bevin and I sat on the logs around the cold firepit. José spoke to Alex for several minutes, rubbing their arms to help them relax.

Alex turned their back on us and stripped down, lowering themself to hands and knees. José placed his hand on Alex's head and said a few more words. And then the shift began.

I leaned over and whispered to Bevin, "Wait until you see their wolf."

Bevin slipped his arm around me. "Not another black one like us, then?"

I leaned in, resting my head on his chest. "Oh, no."

As always with a first shift, it took time. I knew from experience it didn't feel good. Then, the snowball of a wolf stood there. Alex was a bit larger than average, with ice-shard blue eyes sparkling out of mostly pure white fur. Alex crouched down, snarling, and launched a full attack at José.

Bevin froze. "Good gods, Alex is gorgeous. I can see why you were so excited."

José grabbed Alex's muzzle and squeezed it shut. He rolled with them until their mind finally caught up with their actions. Fear and guilt rolled off them. José knelt down and whispered something to them, welcoming Alex into the pack and making a connection at the same time.

Then the two of them came over.

I gave Alex a rub. "Alex, you are amazing." I pulled out my phone and snapped a few pictures. "I'll show you tomorrow. Beautiful."

They started to bounce with excitement.

José sat on the other side of Bevin. "The official run begins after dinner. Alex told me they would like Jade to show them around the property, or both of you."

Bevin and I stared at each other and shrugged. Then I eyed José. "Not you?"

He shrugged. "They don't know me as well. I also think they figure one of the alphas needs to stay back. I agree. This is better. Let me know if they're squeamish and you need me to put out food for your dinner."

This last was said with a layer of disgust. We all understood Pebble's distaste at killing in wolf form; she was nine years old. But Brooke had been a wolf for a few years now and needed to get over it.

At the word squeamish, Alex's lip peeled back from their teeth, and they snarled up at José. Though I could smell his amusement, he looked back at them. In human form, we could all make eye contact, in animal form, our dominance wouldn't allow for it. Alex started to shake and dropped their gaze, falling to the ground.

My brows went up. "Did Alex hold your stare for a few seconds?"

José snorted. "They were offended. But yes, they

aren't submissive."

Bevin and I found our wolves and the three of us, two black as night, and one white as snow, took to the woods. Before we left, José said, "Do a full sweep while you're out there."

We started off with a circle of the property. We let Alex take in all the scents. Their interest rolled off them as they ran from tree to shrub, smelling each item. After circumnavigating the property, we found a scent trail for a rabbit. We followed it. Alex bounded ahead, naturally silent. When they found the rabbit, they crouched low and attacked. They snapped the neck in a clean kill. Alex immediately backed off, looking at Bevin as if asking permission.

I wasn't sure if it was their taking the training more seriously, having grown up on a farm, or the wolf instincts being stronger, but this run was easier than either my first run with Brooke or Pebble. Bevin stepped forward and took a bite, as did I. We let Alex take the rest.

As Alex ate, I closed my eyes and connected to José.

Alex's wolf instincts are good. They took down a rabbit without being shown and seem to be enjoying it. Don't worry about dinner.

"Good."

And he disengaged.

There was no lake or stream on our property, like in Wisconsin, so we'd set up a trough of water outside Pack House. We ran back to drink and rinse off our faces before heading out to explore more.

It was getting dark as we continued to track through the property, finishing the sweep. Eventually, we met up with the rest of the pack. José took over the lead and we ran. Each member of the pack made sure to meet the newest wolf.

The next morning, I woke early and dressed. I slipped into Pack House to start up coffee and breakfast. I may not have been the best cook, but this was a meal I usually didn't destroy. I had placed a few plates of bacon, sausage, and pancakes out on the table, and was about to serve myself when Alex came in.

"It's seven in the morning and you've cooked all of that? I figured we'd eat on campus."

"Half the pack has to go to work. It's easier this way."

Alex dropped into a chair next to me and started filling a plate with food. They took a single piece of bacon, one sausage link, and an apple.

I snorted. "No."

"What?"

"You heard so much during training, but not this? Look at my plate."

"Your plate is empty."

I looked down. "Oh. Well, it wasn't. You know how I eat. It has nothing to do with track and everything to do with having wereanimals. I admit I probably eat more than most because I have two animals."

"Well, I'm not that hungry."

More of the pack started filing in to grab food.

Eventually, José came in and sat down next to Alex. He checked out their plate. "What did you eat?"

They shrugged.

I ratted them out.

José filled their plate with more food. Alex glared. José raised an eyebrow.

After Alex huffed, José explained. "You *will* be hungry in about twenty minutes. Especially after your first run. A hungry wolf is dangerous. We'll also be sending food with you. Make sure you have bars and nuts with you at all times, especially for the next few days."

They gaped. "You sound like my parents."

I threw my arm around them. "I know, right. Now you see what I have to live with. Don't worry, we can complain about them together."

Bevin snorted. "I see what's happening here. You'll replace me with Alex?"

I waggled my eyebrows.

After a couple of minutes Alex said, "I can't believe I ate everything you put on my plate. I never eat that much." Their stomach growled and they blanched. "I can't still be hungry."

"Alex, you ate about half of what I ate. You'll have to adjust your idea of eating…fast."

Alex slowly took a few more items onto their empty plate and tucked in. Their acceptance to eat more, though hesitant, seemed less hostile than some young female wolves new to the pack.

Once we'd all eaten, Alex insisted on helping Bevin clean up. The others all left for work. I sat and enjoyed my coffee with José.

"I don't remember your schedule. Do you have classes with Bevin or Alex today?"

"I always have some classes with Bev; we plan it that way. I can't imagine not spending some of my time with him every day. I think I'd go crazy. I actually set my schedule up so I would have a class every day with Alex as well. Not originally, but we redid our schedules after the attack. I spend my mornings with Alex and afternoons with Bev."

"Good. You can keep an eye on them and drag them to lunch every day. I fear this is the one area Alex isn't comfortable with. I'm guessing eating was something their friends or family gave them grief about back home. It won't do. Figure it out."

"Wow, you can be demanding."

He stood, kissing me on the head. "Yes, yes I can. Now, let's pack up and get to campus."

On the ride in, we discussed with Alex their new senses. It was part of pre-shift training, but in reality, there was no preparing for this.

We parked in the school's lot. Before we opened the door, I searched out where all the people were. Surveying the parking lot, I noted a dozen or so students getting out and milling around to meet up with friends.

We all got out. I opened up all my senses to approximate what Alex would be taking in. It was a lot, but so far, manageable. I closed everything down and looked over at them.

Alex's eyes were a bit wild and their breathing choppy, but they nodded, ready to move on. I gave Bevin and José each a hug and kiss on the cheek. "I'll see you two at lunch?"

José was focused on Alex. "We'll be there. Noon. Hopefully there will be an open area available without too many people."

I grabbed Alex's hand and their shoulders dropped. "What did you just do? Was it your special thing?"

"No, that was just being with a pack member. Touch is important. That's why you see the three of us touching so much."

Their eyes somehow got bigger, and their mouth dropped into an O.

I kept my hand in theirs as we walked to class. Alex knew I liked sitting in the middle and started walking that way, but I dragged them to the back corner. Once we were seated, Alex started to shake as the room filled with people.

"Remember what we've discussed. Close your eyes. Imagine the firepit at Pack House surrounded by boxes. Take each of the scents you smell, put them in one of the boxes and throw it into the fire; you don't need any of them. Once you've cleared them from your perception, build a wall around yourself. You are your own person. You don't need them. You can make your wall a castle with a moat. Just put a buffer between you and them."

Alex tilted their head. "Can it be a farmhouse, with animals? Like, protective goats and cows?"

I bit my lips and considered. "Well, yeah. It's your protection. You just need a mental separation from all the incoming information...give your senses a break."

Alex's breathing finally evened out. "I can do this?"

"Say it again, but make that a statement, not a question."

They nodded. "I can do this."

As they began to relax, I grabbed my phone. "Look."

Alex's whole face lit up. "Is that me?"

"It is."

"Oh, my god. I'm...But...Wow! I look like snow with crystal eyes."

I laughed. "You're gorgeous."

For the briefest of seconds, they completely relaxed. Then a student with strong cologne walked by. They froze, and then sneezed.

"This next week will be hard, but it will get easier. You showered this morning with the soap from Pack House. I want you to start using my soap as well."

"Why? You never mentioned soap before."

I quickly explained the reason without mentioning the bears.

And then class started, and we were both too distracted to think about anything else.

CHAPTER 23

On Saturday, I got a text from Greta. `Can we talk?` Alex and I were at Pack House and were planning a trip to San Francisco. We decided a walk down the wharf would be a good way to learn how to filter out the noise from other people's emotions and scents. She'd improved at school but wanted to practice in larger crowds and with different scenarios before something big happened. I was also looking forward to overpriced clam chowder in a sourdough bread bowl.

Bevin sat next to me as I gazed at my phone. I had stared at it long enough that the display went dark. He pulled me close. "You should talk with her. You need to figure this out. We'll take Alex into the city. You can have the soup another time."

I whimpered. I wasn't sure which part was troubling me more.

"I know, hon. It's a lot." He just cuddled with me on the couch and let me figure it out on my own.

Eventually I texted back. Yeah, we can talk.

Her reply came fast. Can we meet at the café? Thirty minutes?

Sure.

José dropped me off at the café. When I opened the door, I could smell Boden there as well as Greta and Quinn. A growl developed low in my throat as I made my way to the counter. There was a line. I knew my spike in anger had been intense when José knocked on my mental door.

What? I snapped. And stepped forward with the line.

"Do you need us to turn around?"

She isn't here alone. And no. See if Alex smelled me on you.

When I first started mentally connecting to people, we realized those I spoke with began to carry my epsilon essence, chamomile and a forest river. Not even the bear soap product could cover that scent. It would be interesting to know if Alex's abilities were sensitive enough to pick up that scent yet. José's chuckle rippled down the connection as I disconnected.

I placed my order, trying to calm down before grabbing

my coffee and heading over to the table.

I plastered a smile on my face and sat. I hadn't assumed such false cheer since I'd been sitting across the table from Cody, a rogue wolf who'd targeted us back in my junior year of high school. Apparently, junior years weren't my best lots in life.

"Morning, all, good first week of classes?"

Quinn leaned back, assessing me. "Absolutely. Though I miss seeing your cheery face. You sure you don't need another intro class?"

I laughed, genuinely. "I'm sure. My schedule is full. I'll be running ragged for the next three months."

He nodded, "I bet."

Boden's eyelids lowered. "So, you like my friend's sister. You're one of *those*?"

I leaned back in my seat and sipped my coffee, evaluating him for a few seconds. "You know, I've never been ashamed of who I am. I'm not going to sit here being judged by the likes of you." I turned to Greta. "I'm not sure why you invited me here today, but if this was the reason, I gave up a much better day for this."

As I stood, her hand shot out, grabbing my arm. "Please stay." She turned to Boden. "Stop being a jerk. You are not my keeper."

"You sure about that?" His voice wrapped around us with utter confidence.

"Yes, I am. I swear I'll make a phone call if you mess

with me at all this semester. I wanted you here for one reason. I wanted Jade to hear me say this in front of you. Now, try to keep quiet."

The two of them faced off, some message burning between them. Finally, Boden leaned back in his chair, disgust seeping from him, though his face stayed neutral, pleasant even.

"Jade, I don't care that Boden doesn't approve." She grabbed my hand. "He can stuff it. I want to continue dating you."

"Is he going to be a problem? Make your life harder?"

She shot Boden a quick look, then gazed at her brother. Quinn gave her a slight shake of his head. Finally, she turned back to me. "No, he won't be an issue. I can handle him, or Quinn can if it comes to that."

I leaned back in my chair and faced Quinn. "I don't understand any of this."

He shrugged. "I like my sister better when she's happy. You make her happy. Boden was an unexpected…gift this semester. We're all just trying to adjust. It took some debating to figure out where we all stood. This will be fine."

Everything he said was truthful. This didn't surprise me; Quinn had been honest and supportive from the start. The idea that he could control his friend was a bit of a stretch; the werewolf seemed a bit off his rocker. But since this conversation was more open than the last, I decided to give the discussion more consideration.

I knew I was missing something, something big, but I just shrugged it off. I had secrets, too. The cayenne pepper scent emanating from Boden's hate burned my nose. He did *not* like me, but it was not showing in his face or body language. I asked him, "And you're okay with all of this?"

One brow twitched. "If you two want to play for a semester or two," he shrugged, "what's it to me?"

Greta's face reddened, but she tightened her grip on my hand. She leaned over and kissed me. It seemed more of a show for Boden than care for me, but at this point, I understood her need. Halfway through the kiss, it softened. In the end she pulled back but rested her forehead against mine. "Sorry. I'm so sorry for all of this. Please forgive me."

I squeezed the hand holding mine. It seemed she was in an impossible situation.

I heard a chair scratch across the floor and footsteps stomp across the café. When Greta and I sat back, Boden was gone.

Quinn's scent was much cheerier. "Well, that's one way to get rid of him."

I looked between them. "I thought you liked him; you said he was your friend."

"Oh, I do like him, but not when he's near my sister. Boden with Greta, never a good match up. When it's just the two of us, it's great. The exciting part, the three of us have several classes together. But, without you there, Boden will only be annoying, not mean."

"Why are you friends with him if he's that awful?"

Greta kissed my cheek. "I've been wondering that for years."

Quinn just shrugged. "My lot in life. Okay, I'm off. You two have fun. Greta, I'm sure I'll see you...well, at some point, tonight, tomorrow, whenever. Jade, I'm glad Boden failed in this." And with that he cleared off his and Boden's mugs and left the shop.

Greta just collapsed into me like I was a lifeline. "Please tell me you'll forgive me for this week."

"Is that what life is like for you back home?"

"It's what it would be like if they knew." She finished off her coffee. "Can we talk about something else? Anything else?"

"Sure."

"How was winter break with Alexandra? Was it horrible? Did you end up spending all your time out at Bevin and José's place?"

I winced at the use of Alex's full name. It had been a while since I had heard it used. "Actually, things went well. You saw how they got along with Sarah and Owen."

"I thought that your friend and brother were just being nice."

"Naw, Sarah and Owen can be accepting, but it's more than that. Alex's had a rough life, kind of like you. Family and friends that don't accept decisions..." I didn't finish the sentence.

I decided I needed permission to finish the sentence. I

hadn't done this, and it might freak them out, but they were with their alphas. I reached out and connected with Alex.

Hi, Alex, it's Jade, please don't freak out.

I sensed Alex freaking out. I knew they were not handling my voice in their head well. I felt the knocking.

Hi, Bevin.

"*A bit of warning next time.*"

I'm with Greta, I don't have time.

"*What do you want?*"

Can I just ask Alex, or are they still not taking this well?

I waited, sipping my coffee.

"*Go ahead and ask them.*"

Alex, can I tell Greta about your pronouns?

It got very quiet in my head. "*Just Greta, or her brother?*"

Just Greta, but she may tell her brother.

There was a moan. "*No, yeah, okay, tell her. Tell her I'd rather Quinn didn't know, but if he knows it'll be fine. It isn't like I'll see them.*"

I sent a blast of acceptance and friendship down the two connections before releasing them both.

Greta started to smell worried. "Where did you just go?"

"I was debating a few things, sorry." I sighed. "Can I tell you something and have you keep it from Quinn?"

Greta, for her credit, paused to think for a minute. "I think so. As long as it doesn't endanger anyone."

I told her about Alex and the Youth Outreach Center. She was interested in the center, too. I finally explained about Alex's new pronouns.

Greta's eyes got huge. "That's…that's really cool. I had a friend who went through that last year. It's good that she, they, had you here to help."

"It's new and Alex's nervous about people knowing. I figure since you are in a similar position, they'd be okay with it."

"They don't know I know."

"No, Alex knows. I asked them before telling you… last night."

"Okay, good. You wouldn't want to go to the center, see if there aren't any activities happening we could attend?" Greta's whole demeanor changed, she sat a bit taller and her eyes widened with the question.

I smiled back at her. "Sure."

We cleaned off the table and headed out.

When we walked into the center, we read the different fliers.

Milo approached us. "Bringing in more people? We could hire you as our outreach coordinator."

"Not this time; we're just checking out what's happening around town this month."

They nodded and went back to their desk.

Greta watched them walk away, then whispered to me, "I hope you don't get offended, but I think they're hot."

CHAPTER 24

Sunday morning, I slept in. Alex woke me up. They shook me until I snapped awake.

"What?"

"José couldn't get ahold of you. We're needed at Pack House. Bevin will be here in a few minutes to pick us up."

I groaned, but ran to the bathroom to splash water on my face. When I got back to the room, I smelled coffee. "Alex, have I told you that I love you?"

They giggled as I quickly pulled on clothes.

We made our way down the stairs and out the door before Bevin arrived, which was a first. "Did he give any indication as to why we were being summoned?"

"No, just said to get your lazy bones out of bed."

The car pulled up and we got in.

Bevin searched my face. "Did the day get better?"

I quirked a half-smile. "Mostly. Boden is a real piece, but I guess Greta decided hiding wasn't worth it. He was just there long enough for her to tell him she wasn't playing any games."

Bevin squeezed my knee. "Good. You look like hell. How late were you two out?"

I groaned. "I got in...and slept."

Alex piped up from the back. "I heard the door close at about two."

I let my head flop back on the headrest. "Really? Was it that late?"

"Yep."

"No wonder I'm so tired." I yawned. "So, what's the emergency?"

"You'll see."

When we got to the house, Bevin led the way to the basement. My stomach growled as we passed the kitchen.

He heard and patted my head. "Afterwards, I promise."

We found the rest of the pack sitting around the computer displays. They were watching one of the feeds playing on a loop. On the screen, a gray wolf dragged the body of a dead man to our firepit and then loped away.

I leapt up, ran up the stairs, out the door, and to the pit.

The body was gone and police tape surrounded the area. I shut my eyes and envisioned the video we'd watched. I slowly circled the firepit. I kept taking in deep breaths through my nose. Pack, Pack, Pack. All I could pick up were the scents of the wolves in our pack. I had to dig deeper.

I stripped down and shifted to wolf. The world of scents went from black and white to technicolor. Everything became sharper. I continued to spiral out from the firepit, from the police tape. I could pick out the scents of the police officers, of the pack, of the cars that had come to our home. None of them were the scent I wanted to find.

Focus, Jade, focus deeper. Find the scent. I paused and thought again about the video. I oriented myself to where the body must have come from. I found the odor of the body and followed it away from the police tape. Five feet. Ten feet. The extra scents started to fall away. Muscles I hadn't realized I'd been holding tense relaxed as some of the background smells dissipated. I paused and cataloged every scent I could find.

There! I found it, the trail of the intruder. I breathed in deep and long, letting the smell of this wolf sink in to my scent memory. It was a familial match to the other two. We were dealing with a family of wolves. At this point, they had to know we were werewolves. We could hide our scent in human form, but not as wolves. I howled, announcing my success and releasing my frustration.

The other members of the pack approached me slowly.

I could sense them like a thickening of the air around me. Their scents let me identify who was who.

José knelt by me. "Did you find the scent?" He sniffed and shook his head.

I pawed the ground.

He lowered his nose and sniffed again, then froze, inhaling deeply. "Good. Family member of the first wolf."

He backed up as each person came to sniff, even Alex, though I wasn't sure they knew what they were sniffing for. "Is that the smell of the wolf from the video?'

Bevin came over and placed his arm over their shoulder. "It is. Jade's nose is amazing. We each came out and searched. No one found this. I didn't think it was possible. He obviously covered his tracks, just not good enough to hide from Jade."

Alex looked back at the police tape. "You called the police?"

Bevin nodded. "After dropping you off, we came home to find the body. We called the police right away. We aren't going to play games."

I growled low in my throat.

José, who still knelt next to me, wrapped an arm around me. "I know. None of this is a game. The body was another tourist. The police are thinking he snuck onto our land to build a fire and was attacked by a wild coyote. There are more coyotes than wolves around here."

Legs angled out, I stood there, shaking. Our land wasn't secure enough. This group kept slipping in. We needed to build a fence to keep the riff raff out.

José's touch became a hug. "Do you want to run it out? Do you want a partner?"

I looked up at him and rubbed my head against his chin. "Me?"

I rubbed again. I needed my alpha.

He headed back to drop his clothes. The others went back inside. The two of us ran for a couple of hours, letting me stretch my legs and release the aggravation that had been building over the last week. Frustrations about being asked to put myself in a closet. Frustrations about rogue wolves in our territory. Frustrations about Brooke. Even pent-up frustrations about Greta. Everything I had been holding in, I tried to let go.

After we returned to Pack House and found our humanity, I got dressed and sat on one of the firepit logs. José sat next to me. "Better?"

"Mostly."

"You were trying to run from a lot of things out there, chica."

I curled into him. "Who knew growing up would have so many things to deal with?"

"But you got the Greta issue figured out?"

"I think so."

"Good. She makes you happy."

"I was afraid the wolf that left the dead guy was Boden."

"I know."

"I just don't trust him. He seems so…I don't know. Controlling? Manipulative? Something."

"Just remember, he isn't someone you have to deal with." His arm slipped around my waist.

"Thank the gods for that."

I curled into him, taking comfort from the pack connection. "Thank you for running with me. I know you have a lot on your plate right now."

"Chica, I always have time for you. You just have to ask."

On Monday, all the scents and emotions from the other students still made Alex tremble. Their breathing was rough, and their eyes wild. "This is horrible. How did you get used to it? And you did this in high school with all the extra high school drama?"

I chuckled. "I had Bevin and José to help. Though, I did wear a shirt proclaiming I was gay one day early on. That was a singularly horrible idea…except for meeting my girlfriend at the time."

"You didn't. Did people react?"

I snorted. "Yes. Just a bit."

My distraction worked, she focused on me and my story of a school losing their collective mind over the quiet girl proclaiming that she liked girls. Once class started, there was too much going on for them to pay attention to all the people in the room.

Between classes, Alex asked quietly, "Jade, I can smell what people are feeling about me. It's…I don't think I like it."

I swung my arm around them. "You'll learn to block it out. It does come in handy when you finally find someone you're interested in."

They stiffened, then relaxed. "I kind of think everyone is attractive. That's my problem. I've never preferred… well, anyone."

"Why am I not surprised? Have you spoken to anyone at the Center about that?"

"Yeah, we've discussed different groups and such. I was just kind of embarrassed."

"Why?"

"I dunno. It's all still so new."

"Well, you do you."

They relaxed as we entered our next class and found seats away from everyone else.

At lunch we met Bevin and José. The four of us were sitting and enjoying lunch alone in a corner when I smelled Boden. Everyone at the table stiffened.

I shook my head. "Just ignore him. He's a jerk and he wants to provoke me. Do *not* try to protect me; he'll know what's going on."

Both Bevin and José bristled at the command in my voice, but before they could say anything Boden reached our table.

"Hello, pretty lady."

I glared up at him, but he wasn't looking at me; he gazed straight at Alex.

He placed a hand on their shoulder. "What are you doing sitting with these losers? You should come join me, I'm sure I can show you a *much* better time."

I gave him a flat stare. "Boden, why don't you go find Quinn and leave us alone."

"Quinn and Greta are in class, and they are not my keepers. It's more the other way around. I mean, they're kids, and I'm twenty-six. You all are babies."

I smiled gently. "That's good. Then you should leave us alone."

His hand tightened on Alex, and they winced. "Do *not* think to tell me what to do, Jade. You have no idea what you've gotten involved in."

José's chair scraped against the tile floor as he slowly stood up. He kept his eyes lowered to the table until he got to his full height. It wasn't as impressive as Bevin's height, or Boden's, but then he met Boden's eyes.

Boden froze.

José said quietly. "Take your hands off my friend." Apparently manhandling one of his wolves was beyond José's ability to ignore. The alpha took over.

Boden struggled, but finally said, "It's a free country. At least, it's *my* free country. Don't know where you come from...bro."

José didn't so much as twitch. Standing statue still, Boden's eyes widened. He snatched his hands back and he dropped to the floor, knees slamming down hard.

I turned to him and pitched my voice high. "Are you okay? Did you trip?"

His entire body shook, and shock oozed off him, like a ginger infused dream. "What? Um, yeah, I tripped over my own feet. My mistake. Sorry. I'll be off." He stood and vacated our area of the cafeteria fast.

José dropped to his seat, head in his hands, shaking. "That was a bad idea. I should *not* have done that."

Alex surveyed all our faces. None of us were smiling. "What just happened?"

Bevin patted Alex's hand and gave them a half smile. "José just pulled rank on the newbie."

A few days later, Greta invited me out to dinner for Valentine's Day. At first, I hesitated, but then Alex pushed, saying I needed a good night out with my lady.

I showered and searched my closet for something nice. I didn't have Sarah and Pebble's magic ability to climb into my closet and come out with the right clothes. I found a dark green silk dress that came to just below my knees with spaghetti straps and a small, high-waisted belt. It was stylized with a darker green pattern that looked almost black. I accessorized with a pair of black sandals.

I managed to not mess up my make-up too badly and contained my hair in tight twists in the front for about two inches, then let my hair fall free down my back. Alex looked me over, then found a black shawl in their closet for me to add to the ensemble, and a small black purse. The purse was pretty useless, but it was big enough for my phone, a credit card, and some cash.

Alex snapped a shot on my phone to send Sarah for final approval. As I focused on texting, someone knocked on the door. I texted the picture while Alex answered the door.

Not bad on your own. Glad you found the dress I left you.

I shook my head in disbelief. I can't believe you're dressing me all the way from Wisconsin.

She sent a laughing emoji.

I shut off my phone and slipped it into my purse. Gazing up, I gazed at lovely image of my date. She had on a light blue iridescent top and a navy mini skirt. I could see her belly button was pierced between the two items of clothing. She wore a matching necklace and bracelet set and knee-high velvet boots. *Wow!*

Stunned, I stood still for a few seconds, taking it all in. Then my face cracked into a smile and I gave her a hug. "Wow! You clean up well."

She chuckled low, and I felt it down to my toes.

"Right back atcha!"

Alex stopped us before we were out the door. They quickly snapped a photo and then let us go.

We walked the mile to the restaurant, the Mexican mole buffet I loved so much. The inside of the restaurant looked like the inside of a friend's house. The front area was the living room with maybe fifteen small tables that fit four people maximum. I had called ahead and reserved a table, which was good, because all the small kitchen sized tables were occupied. Then, through the double-door opening, was what looked like a formal dining room. Instead of a long table and chairs, there was a table along one wall, and a second table parallel to it. On these tables were large bowls of mole. Each had a board proclaiming the name of who made the mole and some of the ingredients in the cauldron of love.

The hostess led Greta and me to our small, round table. It was the only one free in the entire restaurant. We ordered drinks, placed our outer layers and purses down, and went for food. Next to the mole options was a bowl of rice. On the perpendicular wall was a table with a fruit bar, and a salad bar. I was going to be petite for about three seconds, and then went about my normal route and filled two plates.

I got to the table after Greta, carefully setting my two plates down.

Her eyes widened at my gluttonous amounts of food. "Two plates?" I blushed. "That's genius!" She leapt up, only returning after she'd filled a second plate with salad and fruit options.

I knew there was a reason I liked this girl.

We dug in, spending several minutes enjoying the food, not worrying about talking. As we ate, I focused on building up my blocks for the number of people, sounds and scents in the room. It was beginning to overwhelm me. With school, I practiced regularly, but the emotions in the restaurant were high.

Greta reached over and snared my left hand in hers, still eating. I felt her foot rubbing my leg. I stared at my plate for a few seconds, breath caught in my throat. I glanced at her, but she ignored me in favor of the mole. Slowly, I lifted my fork for another bite. Right before I put it in my mouth, she massaged my hand with her thumb in a light circular motion. I almost dropped my fork.

I grasped my fork a bit tighter. A bit of the chicken fell to my plate, but I managed to eat the remainder of the bite on the utensil.

Greta laughed lightly. "You are not used to flirting in public, are you?"

I swallowed quickly and took a sip of soda. "No, that's not it."

She raised an eyebrow. "Is it me?"

I laughed. "No, it isn't you." My eyes widened, and I tried to look sincere. "It's me." I couldn't hold the fake look and snickered. "It's the public bit I question. I can't flirt in public *or* in private…I just can't flirt. I can't believe you haven't figured this out by now." I shifted my eyes to where she kept making patterns on my hand. It distracted me and I kept losing my train of thought. My breath hitched, my face warmed, and my stomach was fluttering enough I wasn't really hungry anymore. "Yeah, not good at this."

Her smile got wider and a bit wicked. "You're fun to play with, you know."

I was about to answer when a sound and a familiar smell distracted me. A voice from the host stand caught my attention. "There has to be somewhere we could sit. I've heard this is the best place in town."

I froze and tried to breathe evenly.

Greta's brows dropped. "What is it? You looked like you left me for a second there."

"Sorry, nothing." I flipped my hand around and tried to imitate what she had been doing.

"You sure?"

The voice slithered over the crowd like a snake, low and invasive. "I think I see some friends, maybe they'll let us join them."

I suddenly squeezed Greta's hand. She yelped in pain.

I gulped. "I'm so sorry."

"What the hell?" She hissed. "That isn't flirting. You said you didn't know what you were doing, but that's taking it too far."

Boden approached the table. "Hiya, Greta. Mind if me

and my date join you?"

Greta stiffened then slowly tipped her head up until she was looking into the face of her brother's friend. "I'm on a date. Not a double date. You can wait for your own table."

"But you have two extra seats at this table. Why not be generous?"

"Because, Boden, it's Valentine's Day. We are having a romantic dinner for two. Please go away."

Boden's date looked like she wanted to run, but Boden was having none of this. "Greta, love, why are you being so rude? Just let us join you. The wait is over an hour."

"Then leave us alone and go somewhere else."

His eyes started to glow. His spicy anger rolled out of him in a cloud. He seemed like a guy who was used to controlling a situation. Or maybe it was Greta he was used to controlling.

Boden's upper lip curled in a sneer. "I'm letting you have your time with…her. I don't know why you're making this so difficult."

"Boden, leave."

"No."

I shifted my gaze between the two of them. I gently placed my hand on Greta's. "Hey, wanna go get some ice cream down the street?"

Greta was quivering and her eyes glittered. "Why do *we* have to leave?"

"Because if we leave he doesn't get this table."

Greta smirked and grabbed her things. We made our way to the front to pay. When we got to the sidewalk, Boden was right behind us. He grabbed my shoulder and tried to flip me around. I debated letting him know I was stronger than him, then rejected the idea, and spun to face him.

Boden's face was set in an ugly glower, and he reeked of anger. "I don't know what your problem is, girly, but you do *not* want to make an enemy of me."

"I don't know what you're talking about. I just want ice cream." I spun and, grabbing Greta's hand, flounced down the sidewalk.

CHAPTER 25

February settled down into a pattern of classes, studying, and seeing Greta. We found ways to spend time together while studying. Things had calmed down with Boden...mainly because we hadn't run into him, which made me happy.

Two weeks after the incident at the mole restaurant, we lounged outside the dorms with Alex, studying. I lay on a blanket beside Greta. Alex sat on another blanket cross-legged with their books scattered all around them. Alex and I studied vet sciences while Greta studied English.

"Wait, your answer for this section is wrong." They

threw my notebook back to me. "You forgot the notes the professor gave last Tuesday."

I groaned and lowered my head, leaning into Greta. She laughed. "This is fun. You two are both so damned smart."

I grunted.

She rubbed my back. "You know, I never did learn caveman talk when I was in high school; you'll have to use actual words."

I shifted to my side and gazed up at her, amazed again at how beautiful she was. "Alex's the brilliant one, I'm merely following their lead in this class."

Alex threw a pencil at me, and it jabbed me in the head. "Ouch!"

"You deserve it. I think this is the first mistake I've found in your work since starting college. You are a pain to have as a roommate. I've complained to Bevin about this, and he just said try growing up with you…sharing classes with you, especially when you were in a grade lower than him. Absolutely no sympathy."

I tried keeping a pitiful face, but neither of them believed it. I rolled back up to my elbows. "You complained to Bevin?"

"Yep. I would have complained to José, but he's not in any of your classes. Bevin is."

"Ever since ninth grade. I can't imagine not being in classes with him."

They both just gave me weird looks. I picked up my

notebook and found the page in my notes, comparing my answer with the notes I had taken from the previous lecture. "How can you remember which lecture these lessons come from? I can remember big picture ideas, but you always can remember specific days."

Alex blushed. "It's how my brain works."

"Do you have eidetic memory?"

"Sort of, but it's closer to hyperthymesia."

I slowly sat up. "You have perfect memory?"

"Maybe. A little."

"That's amazing. No wonder you're always telling me which day to look for specific notes."

"Yeah, but you can combine notes to create patterns. Your ability to understand intuitively is what I've had to develop."

Greta watched us, head going back and forth, like in a tennis match. "How did you know all those words and conditions?"

I shrugged. "I read a lot."

Alex shook her head. "Jade knows everything."

The wind shifted and I caught a scent I didn't want to smell. One I hadn't smelled since that night at the restaurant. "Hey, you know what? I think I'm going to head back inside. I've had enough sun for one day."

Confusion poured from Greta, minty and strong. Then her scent shifted to cinnamon with her disappointment. "Are you sure? I'm loving it out here."

Alex started to protest, then I saw them pause and

sniff. Their body froze and I smelled the nuttiness of their nerves. "Yeah. Um, I'd like to head in as well." She started stuffing her notebooks and papers in her bag willy-nilly. It all became a haphazard mess.

Greta's confusion turned from cinnamon to a slight sandalwood of concern. "Are you okay, Alex? You suddenly seem really flustered."

"Oh, I just remembered a meeting I was supposed to attend. I don't want to be late."

The lie came quickly but stunk of a sour bitterness. So many scents made me sneeze.

Before Alex finished zipping up their bag, Boden stepped from behind a tree and his deep voice wrapped around us. "Well, Greta, it's nice to see you studying with your friends. I wouldn't want you to fail."

She stiffened. "What are you doing here?"

He tapped his nose. "I was just coming to see if you were doing okay. I haven't seen you for a few days."

Alex quickly zipped her bag and started to stand. Boden's hand snapped out and landed on her shoulder. "Aren't you the pretty one? And you don't have that friend here to protect you."

"Protect me? What are you talking about? Do you mean the day you tripped in the cafeteria?"

Alex was doing her best to cover for our knowing what he was.

Boden sniffed, but I knew there was nothing to smell,

nothing but my epsilon scent, but I'd never been able to cover that. If he wanted to think something of that, there was nothing I could do about it. Alex just smelled sweet, like a scared mouse.

Alex tried to pull away. "I really have to go." "So soon?"

I stood and moved to get between them. "Yes, so soon." I placed my hand atop his. His grip was tight, but using a karate move, I twisted and released his hold. "Talk to you later, Alex."

As soon as his hand was off them, they ran.

Boden glared at me. "Know a bit of the martial arts, do you?"

"You just need to understand that when someone says no, that's what they mean. What's up with you, anyway?"

"I'm sure I don't know what you're talking about. I just wanted to check in with Greta. Her brother is worried."

She snorted. "That's not true. I see Quinn every day in class."

"Fine, *I* was worried."

I squatted down to collect my school supplies. Unlike Alex, I put everything away neatly. Boden was big and mean, but I doubted he would attack me here. Despite my assumption, I kept a wary eye on him. Once my stuff was in my bag, I stood slowly, and headed for the dorms.

Before I got to the door, his hand wrapped around my arm. "Just so you understand, your friend doesn't scare me."

"I don't know what you're talking about."

"He will. Tell him that it was a fluke. He's nothing."

"I'm sure he doesn't even remember you. It was a five-minute encounter, and you tripped. Why would that have left an impression?"

"You just tell him. He'll know what you're talking about. He'll remember me."

With that, he turned and walked away.

Greta came up behind me. "What is he talking about?"

I told her about his meeting us at lunch and tripping over his own feet. I didn't mention José standing up and staring him down. I had a feeling Greta would know what that meant. I had a feeling she was keeping as many secrets as I was. If Boden was a werewolf, there was a good chance she knew about them, but I wasn't yet ready for all our secrets to come out. I wanted this year to be easy…things just weren't going according to plan.

The next day, I went to Pack House to study math with Bevin. Alex came along with me. José and Violet were instructing them on pack and werewolf lore. After an hour immersed in differential equations, I was ready to pull my hair out.

Bevin punched me on the shoulder. "You usually pick up on this faster than me. What's up?"

"I dunno. Frustrated. I almost feel like Boden is stalking me. I know he can't know we're wereanimals, because of our smell, but he knows something. After what José did, maybe he has some sort of instinct?"

"It's possible, but without the scent, maybe not. Your dad and Pebble are studying the precognition of werewolves, so who knows."

"You were supposed to say I was crazy and there was no way he could know."

"Oh, you're definitely crazy."

I punched him on the arm, and he laughed.

There was a knock on the door. Bevin took out his phone and pulled up an app for the front video feed. Brow furrowed, he mumbled, "Who the heck is that?"

I grabbed his phone. "Hey, it's the werewolf cop, Carlos."

"Really? That's him? I thought he'd be shorter."

I jumped up and ran to the door. I opened it up and said, "Hi! Selling girl scout cookies?"

He quirked a half-smile as he said, "Made with real girl scouts."

My eyes widened. "I *love* that movie!"

We both laughed. "So, what brings you to our neck of the woods?" Particularly hilarious since we were sitting on the edge of a wooded area.

"I've been sitting at home each night since meeting you and José, thinking about the idea of a group of...a group of..."

"A pack of werewolves. Go on."

His head snapped around like he was staking out a crime scene. "I can't believe you just said that...out loud."

"You *are* standing in Pack House, but okay, we'll

continue to pretend…"

He gulped. "Pack House?"

Bevin came up behind me and placed his hands on my shoulders. I could feel his alpha mantle. There was something about him and José when they were being official. They stood taller and were somehow *more*. "Welcome, I'm Bevin." His hand reached over my shoulder towards Carlos.

"Wow, make a gal feel short. I'm not *that* short, by the way."

Bevin, standing over six feet tall, and Carlos, just under six feet, both towered over my five-foot seven. Bevin patted my head. "You just keep telling yourself that, champ."

Carlos said, "I'm Carlos Wang. I'm a police detective at the Arcoíris police department."

"I know, I've heard of you. Would you care to come in and talk?"

"Um, yes, if that's okay." He kept his eyes down, and sounded a bit awed at Bevin, similar to when he met José and experienced his alpha mantle.

He joined us in the dining room. Bevin and I cleared away our books. José and Alex came from the kitchen with a plate of pastries. Carlos stared at Alex for a few seconds like he was amazed they were really standing there, alive.

José came over by Carlos. "Welcome to our home. It's small, but only temporary. We are building something bigger. Hopefully, we'll be able to move next month."

Carlos nodded as José spoke. "I thought this place looked small. You seem young to be building for a…pack?"

José gave Carlos half a smile. "Bevin and I are the alphas of the pack. We *are* young, but that doesn't matter. We know what we want for our pack, and we're going to do it."

Carlos looked at each of us in turn. "Can I ask you all a question?"

Bevin's face broke into a huge smile and he dropped his alpha mantle. "I'm guessing you'll ask us lots of questions, but go ahead. Where do you want to start?"

When his mantle fell, his being transformed from an ageless powerhouse into a young twenty-year-old college student. Carlos just gaped at him for a few seconds before shaking his head and narrowing his eyes as if he was trying to get his mind around what he'd just witnessed.

Finally, he shook his head. "Barring whatever you just did, if you didn't tell me you were werewolves, I wouldn't know. Why do you smell…normal? I mean, I asked in the restaurant, but you never answered me."

José smiled. "We have a soap that neutralizes our scent. For now, we use it for safety."

"Interesting. So, you all are really werewolves?"

Bevin's head tilted. "Would you like to run with us at the next full moon? Have you ever run with a pack?"

Carlos was reaching for a petite fours but froze. "Could I do that? Join you for a run? Would I have to join your pack first? I'm not sure I'm ready for that kind of commitment."

José mumbled something unintelligible under his breath. He smelled annoyed and frustrated. Finally, he looked directly at Carlos. "I don't know what you've been told, but you can run with us. You don't have to join. You can join. If you do join and decide you don't like the rules, you can go back to being a lone wolf. Joining a pack isn't like joining the mob. I'd really like to know where the bad press is coming from."

Carlos's face scrunched up and his eyes danced back and forth. Then he smiled brightly, and a citrus scent filled the room. "Okay, maybe I will come out and run with all of you. Yeah. That could be good. I've only ever run alone. Is it scary with all the wolves?"

Alex gave him an earnest look. "Only if one of the panthers joins us."

CHAPTER 26

February in Wisconsin is a hard month. Bitterly cold. And although the month is short, it feels like there's no end in sight. The month was less miserable in California, but I was scarred from years in the Midwest and would always have a dark place in my heart for the shortest month of the year. It also was the month when I had to get into the swing of new classes, which was always rough. A new routine, the expectations from the professors, and homework...lots and lots of homework. The first week of March meant I had survived another February.

Alex did well during their second run. Their

transformation was smooth, and they were just as excited about their second run as their first. They were meshing well with the rest of the pack.

Carlos decided to run with us. Despite his fears, he learned that running with a pack was more enjoyable than trying to run alone. He still wasn't sure about joining the pack, but he did like the idea of running with a pack of wolves.

The following week, the head of the construction project informed us the main section of Were House was complete. The living room, dining room, kitchen, three of the bedrooms, and the main basement area, including the command center. There was even a secret escape tunnel behind a fake panel in the command center.

The three bedrooms included the one assigned to the alphas, and one assigned to me. Bevin and José were insistent that the three of us move in right away. I wasn't sure I was ready.

"But track has started up. How will I get to practice?"

They both groaned. José's face hardened. "You'll take my car, then drive back. Shower and we'll return together after Bevin or I make breakfast."

"What about Alex?"

José looked at everyone in the pack. "There is the third room available. If everyone here agrees, I say we offer it to them. Then everyone in the pack living in town is on the pack's land. I would be much happier with that."

Luke shrugged. "I'm fine with that."

Violet bobbed her head. "As long as I can set up the command center, I don't care where my bed is. Ultimately, I want a basement bedroom, not that third room anyway."

Like Luke, Zee shrugged. "You're the alpha. I follow you, bro. You and Team Kid."

We walked to the new house. The building was shaped like a big U. The arms of the U had two stories. The main center wasn't quite as tall, and only had one story. There was a door in the center of the U atop three steps. The double doors led into a grand living room. The back of the living room housed a wood dining room table. On the far side of the table were sliding doors leading out to the back porch. When I looked out the door, I saw a hot tub on the porch and a pool.

The backyard was partially fenced on two sides, the side that faced the road and the park with walking trails. The third side opened into the woods.

To the right of the dining room was an industrial sized kitchen, with an eight-burner stove, an eat-in table that seated at least ten people, and two double ovens. There was a walk-in pantry and a huge refrigerator. On the other side of the kitchen was a mud room. Walking back into the living room, there were hallways to the left and right; they each led to rooms. Eventually there would be single bedrooms and small family suites.

On the opposite side of the living room to the kitchen and mudroom was a staircase that led to the basement. The basement held the hangout for future family kids, a rec room, small library, and bedrooms. There was also a hangout room with a small kitchen, a movie room, and the command center.

Were House was huge. My mind could barely take in everything I saw, it looked like a fancy resort. The finished rooms had furniture, and I just walked around touching and sensing, barely taking in the details. There were areas for people to hang out in large and small groups. As I roamed around the public space, I felt overwhelmed. Eventually, I ended up in the main living room sitting on a couch. The others were still prowling around, but I just sat there getting a feel for my new home…our pack's den.

I closed my eyes and let my head fall back. The couch was comfortable. After a few minutes, someone sat next to me. It took a second for me to identify Bevin. He took my hand in his. "What do you think?"

I leaned over and rested on him. "What do *you* think? It's *your* Pack House. I could always switch packs or live close by. You're the alpha."

"Nope. You are not allowed to do either of those things. New alpha rule."

I snorted. "When did this rule come about?"

He hummed. "Oh, I don't know; about ten seconds ago, but I'm sure José will agree to put it on the books."

"Ah. Got it."

"Have you checked out your room?"

"No. I was just getting the feel of the house in general."

He shifted as if to get up. "Do you want to be left alone?"

I gripped his hand tight. "Yes, but not from you. Give me another few moments, then we can see this room of mine. If it's covered with geese I'm staying in the dorms."

His chest rumbled with silent laughter.

We got up and started in his room. It was large and modern. It overlooked the backyard. There was a walk-in closet and a private bathroom.

I poked around. "I'm never going to see you two again."

He grabbed my hand and dragged me next door to my room. It was painted a terracotta and had a queen size bed in the center. There was a mango wood dresser and a beautiful bed set. I also had a walk-in closet. When I poked my head in, it was partially filled with some of the clothes I had left back in Wisconsin.

I whipped around and stared at Bevin in confusion. Smiling, he said, "Sarah and Owen brought an extra box with them. We've kept it in storage. We thought it would help you feel more at home."

There was a second door that led to a private bathroom. It had a small vanity, a toilet, and a tub. When I looked closer, the tub had jets. I nearly swooned. My eyes heated with tears. I couldn't believe they had put together all of this for me. Most of the rooms wouldn't have this much privacy, only the alphas. Some of the rooms would share a private bathroom, but most would use communal bathrooms.

I just stood there in the doorway of the bathroom, dumbfounded. Bevin wrapped me in a hug from behind. I turned and buried myself in his hug, waiting to get control over my emotions.

Before I did, I felt José approach, and join Bevin in the hug. "Do you like it?"

"I don't even know what to say." My voice was a whisper, sandwiched between them. "I didn't expect even half this much. Why?"

José had laughter in his voice. "Chica, you are as much the heart and soul of this pack as me and Bevin. This pack is made up of three leaders, not two. There are two alphas and three leaders. You may not know this, but everyone else does. You deserve this, and we all love you."

It was too much; the tears started flowing. I hated the tears but accepted them.

The following weekend, Alex and I moved into Were House. It shifted the way we lived and related to classes, but it also strengthened our bonds with the pack. I quickly learned that Bevin was correct—this was something my wolf needed. A level of anxiety and tension seemed to leave me as soon as I was living with my pack.

Breakfast and dinner was often eaten with everyone. Even with track, I would be home in time to have breakfast with some combination of pack mates.

Alex and I didn't tell the school we had moved out, so we could use the dorms if we wanted. I didn't tell Greta; I felt that she was keeping secrets from me, and I didn't want it getting back to Boden. I could easily run home at night or call for a ride. We had never hung out in my room, so it now being empty wasn't something she'd discover.

The first weekend living in Were House, Carlos came over. Alex and I were sitting in the living room, relaxing, watching a movie. We decided to take him out to do a sweep of the land.

Carlos eyed Alex warily. "I've been meaning to ask, but didn't want to sound silly in front of the alphas...you know what I mean.... What did you mean, panthers?"

She smiled. "It's been weeks. Have you been sitting, worrying about panthers for all this time?"

He shuffled his feet and cased the room. "Maybe."

I shook my head and rolled my eyes. "Well, she hasn't come out to play in a while, so I was planning on running her today, anyway. You'll get to meet her."

"Wait, what? Alex wasn't kidding?"

"No. I have two animals: a wolf and a panther. I've only been running in wolf form lately because our pack is so small, and Alex is new. Since today is just a sweep of the territory, I thought I could switch up my form. Bonus, you can meet a new member of our pack."

He nodded quickly, as if this were not a big thing, but his hands shook, and his scent turned nutty.

José and Bevin came up from the basement and joined us in the living room. They sat in the small loveseat. José considered Carlos, sitting back warily. "You okay? What has you so jittery?"

Taking a deep breath, Carlos nodded. "Yeah. I'm just learning that werepanthers are a real thing and that I will be meeting one today."

Bevin quirked a half smile, but José just sat calmly. "Do you think you'll be okay with that?"

"I…um…I think so."

José leaned forward onto his knees. "Why don't we all head outside and let Jade shift. You can meet her panther, a beautiful beast I might add, and then you can decide. If it's too much, we can reevaluate the day."

Carlos appeared shocked. "Is that okay?"

The alpha mantle finally fell away and José smiled. "Of course." He hopped up. "Let's go."

When we got to the backyard, I piled my clothing to the side, got to my hands and knees, and let Panther flow out over me. This transition was easier and faster than my shift to wolf. Probably because she was my first animal, but after all these years, she flowed out almost painlessly. I shook out my muscles and stretched my back. It felt good to be feline again.

Carlos's fear smelled like candy. I slunk over to him, purring. I rubbed against his side. His scent slowly shifted away from sweet fear as he petted me.

José's disappointment washed over me. "I can't believe you just did that." Then I felt him knock on my mental door. I opened up and he continued. *"You do not cuddle up to lunch, it just isn't done."*

I chuffed out a laugh.

Once Carlos relaxed and smelled at peace, I moved away. If he only knew.

He and Alex shifted, and we were off. I showed them the boundaries, and we each took a section to run. As I was doing my sweep, I felt another knock on my mental door. Taking the distraction as an excuse for a break, I stretched and relaxed on my side. I was glad I'd had a big lunch. Opening the door, I answered.

Hiya Sarah, what's up?

"Apparently there was a fight at Pebble's school yesterday. Tensions are running high. I was hoping to drop a calm bomb on the room. You good with that?"

I think so.

"Okay, it'll probably be in the next couple of minutes. It takes me a few to figure out how to get it going, not to mention find any calm with all the tension in this house. Expect it soon."

I braced myself for the draw of energy. Unlike healing, when she pulled on the Soul Sharing for calming it took a lot of my energy, but didn't leave me completely incapacitated, as long as I knew it was coming and wasn't run down.

Pain stabbed in my brain. I shut my eyes to visit my mindscape, where my animals lived. Only Wolf was there right then, and the cave where I kept ghost-Piper. Suddenly, the cave exploded, and ghost-Piper emerged, howling in terror. Her fear infused me. I backed up a few paces, not knowing what was wrong, just knowing it was bad. I had to escape.

My eyes snapped open, my heart racing and my muscles tense. The trees, they meant safety. I leapt onto a branch, and then ran from limb to limb, from tree to tree. I had to escape, find a haven. I used all the energy I had at my disposal. My path took me at high speed through the tops of the trees, branches scraping my snout as I practically flew through the forest. Where could I find a refuge?

I ran. I had to escape. My mind fractured as I tried to focus on a destination, a plan, on anything.

A second explosion blossomed in my mind, my body, my soul, and more energy drained away. Sarah. Oh gods no! She tapped into my calm, taking whatever I had, regardless if I had anything to give. No! I couldn't. Not now, with ghost-Piper loose. It was too much.

Everything went black.

I woke up lying under a bush. My body was curled around

a tree. Naked and scratched-up, I felt abused.

I tried to reach out to someone, anyone. I had nothing left with which to call for help.

Thorns dug in deep as I wiggled out from under the bush. The red juices from the berries stained my skin. Dizzy from my lack of energy, I sat on the ground with my arms wrapped around my legs and my head on my knees. Looking up, I saw that the lowest branch was about fifteen feet up.

I gazed around to see if I recognized anything in the area. I didn't. If I started walking in a direction, I didn't even know if I'd make it back to Were House or end up somewhere else.

Deciding help was worth more than consciousness, I reached out to José. I put everything I had into the connection.

"Chica?"

Help!

Just as my vision went black again, I sent a solid connection with my location.

I woke up curled in a ball on my side. The forest felt the same; I was alone. Groaning with the effort, I pushed myself up. My head pounded and I shivered. Sitting in the shade, the cool air tickled my skin and tingles ran down my back. I pulled my knees up and rested my cheek on my legs.

After a few minutes, I heard a rustling. "Hello?" I asked. My voice barely above a whisper. If the rustling came from a pack member, they'd hear me. If it wasn't, I didn't want to be heard.

There was a crashing noise. A white wolf came up and rubbed against me. Tears burned my eyes. "Hiya, Alex. Are the others close?"

They leaned in so that they could answer me without using much energy. *José and Bevin will be here soon.*

They ran off only to return with Bevin and José ten minutes later. The boys had the green bag with food and a pile of clothes. I slipped into my clothes, then started in on the food. I ate some nuts and swallowed some liquid energy, a chocolate flavored shake that had nothing on what Tanner could make. Fast calories.

Once I felt solid, I stood. "Can we head back?"

Bevin slipped an arm around my waist. "You sure you're up to it? I can carry you."

I glared at him, but I did lean on him. "Don't make me hurt you. Yeah, I can make it."

We didn't talk on the way back. I was focusing hard on consuming calories and walking. Once we made it to Were House, a trek that felt like it took hours, I fell into a dining room chair.

Luke was in the kitchen, cooking. "My world famous goulash will be up in just a few minutes."

Once we were all served, I dug in. I moaned at the taste. "This is really good."

Luke smiled, "Why, thank you, m'lady"

Everyone sat at the table, eating, except for Carlos.

"Where did Carlos go?"

Alex wiped their mouth on a napkin. "Once we got back, he headed back into town. He wanted me to say 'thanks' for the experience."

José put down his drink. "Sarah called to apologize. She was already pulling on the Soul Share for the calming and didn't know how to stop it. Once everyone was calmed down, she texted Piper and Julez. Found out they are in Florida for spring break. I guess they decided to jump off cliffs into the ocean today, and Piper is afraid of heights."

I shut my eyes, letting his news fill me. Piper was safe. She had just been extreme in her activities.

Heat spread through my body. I didn't understand what I was feeling – low in my core and pulsating out in waves. My breathing grew rough. I dropped my fork. I felt my face blanch as I realized what was happening to me. I couldn't move.

José reached for me, but I snatched my hand away from him. "Chica, what's wrong?"

I whimpered. Bevin reached for me, but I jerked away from him as well. A tear slipped down my cheek. I was frozen in place. Taking a shaking breath, I started to tremble.

Searching the faces around me, I choked out, "Violet, help me. Room."

She looked bewildered but jumped up to help me to my room. José and Bevin followed at a distance.

Once I was separated from the group, I curled in a ball in

my bed, tears wetting my pillow. My voice was shaky. "José, contact Sarah. Find out what she did to the ghost in my head."

I heard him pull out his phone and Bevin swore. They must have realized what was happening. Of course, Violet didn't follow. "What's happening to her?"

Bevin's voice was low, concerned. "My guess? Piper and Julez are celebrating right now, and Jade is experiencing it along with them. Can you imagine experiencing your ex-girlfriend's celebration, emotion by emotion?"

Violet let out a sound of pity. "What can I do to help?"

"I don't know."

The bed dipped and José took my hand. "Jade, I have to lie down next to you. You need to bring me to the ghost."

I did. When he arrived at the mental landscape where my animals lived, his red wolf and my black one rubbed noses. José looked a bit freaked out. I sat, much like I had done in the woods, rocking and trying to ignore the emotions and sensations pouring through my body.

He gazed over my shoulder to where ghost-Piper stood, taking up a larger piece of my space. As the ghost grew, my control shrunk.

José squatted next to me. "Jade, start with putting the ghost in the cave you told me about before."

I nodded. It was hard. So, so hard. When she had broken out, she had torn through all my defenses. I squeezed his hand in the real world. I grabbed his hand in the dreamscape for extra "oomph." Closing my eyes, I finally released a pulse of energy, pushing out her emotions. With that push, I finally managed a full breath of fresh air. The cave appeared around the ghost.

Piper's emotions were still coursing through me, but I had stopped crying. I couldn't feel what she felt. It was an improvement.

José, still holding my hand, evaluated the area. "Better. Okay, let me see what I can do." He closed his eyes and did a push of his own power through me. It felt like I was being cleansed of any emotions or feelings that were not my own. I shivered and moved so that my head was on his shoulder, unwinding a bit with the severing of Piper from my being.

Investigating the world my animals lived in, I saw that José had built a cone of silence around Piper's cave. In the real world, I felt the tension drain away. I relaxed into my alpha, his arms wrapping around me. I heard the door open and close and then I felt my bed shift. This time when Bevin moved in behind me, he brought Pack, he brought protection, he brought friendship.

Still, he asked, "Is this okay?"

I nodded.

He placed an arm around my waist and cuddled in from behind. My alphas were both protecting me.

The week after my move, Greta and I sat in the dorm

commons theoretically studying. It was a week until spring break, and though there were several tests coming up, we both needed a mental break.

I stood to grab a soda and she yanked me down onto her lap. I yelped in shock. She covered my mouth so as not to distract the people who *were* focusing on classes. "Do you want to get out of here on Saturday?"

I leaned into her. "Where would you want to go?"

"We could go to the beach, like, Half Moon Bay."

"You do know that the water is freezing right now, right?"

She laughed. "I know, but we could sit on the beach and just enjoy being away from here."

The thought of getting away sounded amazing. I relaxed into her, imagining the day on the beach with her. "If we go to Santa Cruz, we could possibly go into the water and not freeze."

"Hmmm, tell me you own a bikini."

"I don't even know if I have a swimsuit, but I'll figure something out before then."

"So, we can do it—we can get away together on Saturday? No Quinn, none of your friends? Just the two of us."

"Yes, that sounds wonderful."

"I'll get the car from Quinn, I'm sure he'll be okay with it."

On Saturday, we met in front of the dorms. I arrived early

with a bag. I had searched all the clothes Sarah had packed and was unsurprised to find a swimsuit in one of the drawers. Because the suit had once belonged to Candice, my adopted older sister, it was a bikini. Thankfully it covered everything it was supposed to cover.

At breakfast, we had discussed the issue of me swimming.

José had placed a plate of scrambled eggs and toast in front of me. "If you go into the water, the soap will wash off you. If there are any other wereanimals in the area, they'll be able to scent you."

"I know, but it will just be the two of us, I don't think there's much risk."

"What if Boden is there?"

"She hates him; I don't think that that's going to be an issue."

Bevin placed his hand on my arm. "I don't either, but I still worry. You'll be pretty far from us, and we still haven't found the third rogue."

"True, but after that one guy, he seems to have quieted down."

I looked up at José. "I'm surprised that Boden hasn't confronted you on campus."

"Me, too, chica. Me, too."

As I adjusted the bikini under my clothes, I debated again if I'd actually swim or not. I was weighing the pros and cons when Greta shot out of the doors. "I can't believe how early you get up. I was going to get out here before you. I didn't even see you inside at all."

She grabbed my arm and dragged me to her car. Overall, the ride was quiet and uneventful. The drive from campus to the beach was just over an hour and we listened to music and talked. When we got to the beach, the day was unseasonably warm. The weather report said temperatures could approach ninety degrees before the end of the day. We spread out our blanket and settled in to relax.

As the day grew warmer, Greta leaned over. "Let's swim!" Her eyes were alight with excitement.

Despite the heat of the day, we had found a chunk of beach without many people and had walked to find a private area. It felt like Greta was trying to hide, but I just wanted to unwind.

I decided the risk was low. I quickly checked in with José, letting him know I was about to swim. Then I let Greta pull me up and drag me to the water. Despite the air temperature, the water was freezing. My toes hit the water and I yelped. Greta laughed.

We played in the surf, splashing and squealing. Eventually we were soaked, though we never jumped into the water. I tried to wring out my hair, but the cold water hitting my body made me squirm.

Greta came up behind me and gave me a hug, an ice-cold hug. I leapt up and she fell on her butt laughing. I turned and, shivering, tried to help her up. A cool wind off the water clashed with the warm air of the day, and my body didn't know which temperature to trust. Not even being a wereanimal helped with the coldness of the water.

Once Greta was standing, she said, "I'm going to grab some water. Coming?"

"Give me a sec, I want to rinse off some of this sand." I turned towards the ocean, and the wind shifted, coming from the other side of the beach. The wind carried the scent of wolf to me. I froze, then continued to splash water, straightened, and walked towards the towels. I knew I had deodorant there. If I could get to that, I could cover up part of my scent; it would help.

After getting the last of the sand off my body I looked up and saw Boden beside Greta. "Stop right there, Jade."

Greta jumped up, but Boden grabbed her around the waist. "You didn't listen to me girl, but you'll listen now."

Greta struggled and I started to move forward.

"Stop or I'll hurt her."

I stopped.

Greta's eyes widened. "Jade, no…"

But I didn't hear what she said next. A sharp pain exploded in my head, and everything went black.

CHAPTER 27

My head pounded. I woke up lying on my back. A chill seeped into me from the cold stone under my bare skin. Nothing about the situation was correct. Keeping still, I took a deep breath and smelled a strange wolf. *Not again.*

I tried to piece together what happened and where I was. *I need more information.*

"Greta, listen to me. She's a werewolf, I think. At least one of her friends is a werewolf. She lied to you."

"If she's a werewolf, then why didn't you find out until today?" The whine in her voice made her sound younger… and my suspicions of her having secrets was confirmed in that one statement.

"I don't know." The annoyance in Boden's voice amused me more than it should've. Such a piece of work—a bully, sexist, obnoxious—he deserved any amount of frustrations sent his way.

"And what the hell Quinn—a shovel? You hit her in the head with *a shovel*? You could've killed her."

"Sis, you know I was just worried about you. I wanted to protect you."

"No, you weren't. You two followed me down here. What for?"

Boden's voice became softer. "I need to protect what's mine. You were promised to me. I know you want to play at having a girlfriend, but when I was six, I was told that when you came of age, you were mine. That's twenty, Greta. You're nineteen now, so one more year."

"You can't even have kids anymore; what does it matter? You've already broken the rules. The marriage is off, and even if it wasn't…if *you* can break the rules, then why can't I?"

"The idea that a werewolf can give birth to a werewolf is a folktale. There is only one way to create a werewolf, and you know it."

"No, I don't know it. I'm not a guy, remember?" She finally sounded like herself as she snapped at him.

I decided I'd had about enough of their idiocy. Why were all lone wolves so dumb? I connected with José.

His voice was a bit frantic. *"Jade, you're alive?"*

Yes, now be quiet and listen.

I filled him in on what I had heard, and then I opened up the connection so he could listen along with me. I also made our connection visible so that he could follow it back to me.

Boden's grumbly voice blanketed the room along with his frustration. "Quinn, how hard did you hit her?"

It was hard to not twitch my nose as Quinn's sweet scared smell filled the room. "I don't know. You said she was a werewolf. Aren't they tough? I always heard they needed to be hit harder."

"I don't know. I'm not really an expert. This is pretty new to me, too. Remember, I found that guy who bit me and then I killed him. No one back home even knows."

Did he just casually say he killed a werewolf?

José snorted. *"Sounded like that to me...stand-up kind of guy."*

Greta sounded exasperated. "They'll know when you return. Won't they? You could smell it on Jade after she was in the water, so, that means the elders will smell it on you."

A loud crack nearly made me jump, and then Greta squealed. Did Boden slap her? "Hush, she may be awake and listening to us. Assume you are being listened to. That trick I played on the beach will only work once."

"Don't slap her, God, have you gone insane?" Quinn's fear evaporated, replaced by his frustration.

"I still can't believe you threatened to hurt me."

"You know I would never *really* hurt you, Greta, not

like her. She's probably the one who killed your cousin. And no one has heard back from your uncle. It was either her or her friend, that one who just stared at me and made me drop. I don't know how he did it. I need to get my hands on him, teach him a lesson."

José snorted in my mind.

You don't sound scared.

"*Chica, you could take him with one hand tied behind your back. He's a bully and an idiot. We're on our way. They didn't stay in Santa Cruz. Which was our worry.*" He sounded distracted, as if our conversation were only one of the things he was doing.

Are you close?

His growl vibrated down the line. "*Not close enough.*"

I heard sniffing. "I don't think she's out. I think she's awake. Hey, wolf-girl, I'll kill your girl if you don't sit up."

I didn't move. He was an idiot. He just said he wouldn't hurt her.

There was a thump that sounded like a punch.

"Why'd you punch me?" Boden sounded like a petulant child.

Greta sighed. "You are such an idiot. You literally *just* said that that wouldn't work again."

"Well, do you have a better idea?"

She harrumphed. I heard steps and a chair being dragged. "Jade, can we talk?"

Thoughts, alpha-man?

"May as well; we need time to get to you. See how long you can drag it out. We're going as fast as we can, chica."

"Don't see a reason."

"Are you really a werewolf?"

I let my head fall to the side and opened one eye. I was in a large and mostly empty room. Squinting to filter the brightness, I saw I was caged in an alcove. The bars were mere inches apart, so squeezing through in any form was out of the question. I slowly worked towards getting both my eyes opened. When I got her in focus, I noticed she wore a t-shirt and jeans. I, on the other hand, still wore my bikini.

"I'm in a cage?"

"It's not what you think." Her eyes pleaded with me.

"That my girlfriend's brother hit me over the head with a shovel, hard, and they, along with her fiancé, threw me in a cage?...Am I missing anything? Oh, wait, they think I'm a werewolf, and did the hitting before they knew for sure, and with a blow that hard didn't seem to worry about the potential of killing me…"

She winced. "Okay, that part is true, but that isn't the full story."

"It never is. Greta, my head really hurts. I'm not moving because I feel like my head will split open. Can you please explain this to me in simple terms, let me out, and let me go home?"

Boden laughed a belly laugh. I covered my head with my hands.

José, who was still listening in, said, *"Nice try, chica."*

Greta turned on Boden, "What's your problem?"

"She plays a great game, doesn't she?"

I took a calming breath. "You don't think everything I just said was true?"

He sniffed and cocked his head. "Say a lie."

"I like you."

His brow dropped as if thinking were hard. "Oh. Got it. So, yeah, until that last bit, you haven't lied."

José tsked in my head. *"No training your captors."*

I rubbed my forehead to hide my desire to laugh at José's comment. *No making me laugh!*

I slowly swung my legs down and sat up. I was a bit dizzy, but I wanted to be vertical when help arrived.

Greta watched me. She ran into the kitchen and came back with a bottle of water and an energy bar. She threw them into my cage before Boden could stop her.

"Girl, what do you think you're doing? She's in a cage for a reason."

She whipped around then slammed her fists on her hips. "Do you plan on killing her?"

"She's a werewolf, what do you think they do back home?"

"I don't know! Do *you*?"

"No, but I've never heard of other werewolves, so I can only assume."

Greta turned to me, eyes wild. "Jade, are you a werewolf?"

I sat on the bed eating the energy bar and drinking the

water. "Are you?"

Boden laughed. "Of course not, she's a girl."

I cocked my head. "If girls can't be werewolves, then how could *I* be one?"

Quinn approached the bars. "Well, that's what we're trying to figure out."

I focused on Quinn. "Is your family part of a," I waved my hands as if trying to find a word, "a pack, like a wolf pack?"

My head continued to pound as I gazed at my captors. "Are you asking if *my* family is like *yours*?" I couldn't keep the derision from my voice.

He paused in thought. "Well, no, we're part of a…" He gazed up to the ceiling and then over at Boden. "How would you describe it?"

Boden shrugged. "We're a group of families, a clan, who reward the elder men in charge with the gift of the animal."

"Elder men?" Disgusted, I spit out the word as the mere idea of it shocked me.

Boden could smell my disgust. "Of course. Only men can handle the beast soul inside."

I nodded. "Ah, of course." I stayed hunched over on the cement ledge, but the food and water had done the trick, and I felt much better. If only I could get the cage open.

Boden gripped the bars. "Did you kill the wolves who came into town to convince the twins to come home?"

"I thought girls were too weak. Isn't your question counter to the premise of your group?"

He growled low in his throat. "Answer me, did you kill the two wolves?"

I sighed. "I did not kill the two wolves."

He paused and sniffed the air. "That isn't a lie."

"Did that friend of yours kill them?"

"Who? José?"

"Yeah, him?"

"No, he didn't kill either of them."

I heard another snort come from José. He was enjoying the back and forth.

"Were they killed by a werewolf, someone from, what was your word, someone from your pack?"

"Why are you assuming I know how these wolves were killed? I can tell you that I didn't kill them both. I can tell you that José wasn't involved. These answers don't tell you that I know who did the killing. You are making interesting assumptions. Better question: why were they killing tourists? Why were they being so splashy?"

His forehead wrinkled as if he tried to concentrate on what I was saying and find fault in my words.

"What about you?" I asked. "You said you killed the, what did you call him, the guy who bit you. So, if you could kill that one, you could've killed the others. Did *you* kill all these wolves you are asking me about?"

"What? No. Why would I kill members of my clan? That would be a death sentence!"

"Well, you obviously went behind their back and

became a…" I waved my hand up and down at him, "a wolf…a werewolf?" I tried to skip over the word as if it were foreign to me. I added a hint of mocking as if I didn't really believe the word.

"Just because I want to start a new group with different rules, better rules, doesn't mean I want to kill people from my old group."

José spoke then. *"We're outside. It may get noisy. It's me, Bevin, and Luke."*

I'm locked in a cage; I won't be of much use.

"We'll get you out, chica."

Boden sniffed. "Why do you sometimes smell more like trees and the river? It's like your outdoor scent takes over for a few seconds. Why is that?"

I shrugged, trying to look as confused as he was projecting. "I smell like trees and rivers? What does that even mean? I thought you said I smelled like a wolf. What's next? A bird?" I snorted. "Can I ask a question?"

Quinn stepped forward. "What?"

"What's the point of all of this? Why hit me over the head? Why bring me here?"

Quinn rested his head on the bars. "I don't know about Boden, but I wanted to know if one day Greta could be a werewolf. We've been told only certain men can…but I think my sister should get a chance. I think Boden had darker desires."

Quinn smelled sincere in his concern for his sister. It

was too bad this was how this all went down.

"My suggestion to you is: if you do find a female werewolf in the future, try asking her—instead of locking her up in a cage. You'll probably get a much better response." My facial expression and voice were flat.

At that point, the door slammed open and the calvary rushed in. Boden confronted José, who knocked him out with a single punch. The rest of the fight was uneventful. Quinn and Greta simply put up their hands, their fear filling the room with a sweet sugary scent.

José sighed. "Let her out. Now."

Greta pulled the keys out of her pocket and unlocked the cage. Greta had the keys. Greta. She could've let me out at any time, but had let me sit locked up instead. *Maybe she thought she'd kept me safe?*

I stepped out and walked into Bevin's hug. José was too scary right now.

José directed Luke to carry Boden out with us.

Quinn tried to stop us. "Where are you taking him?"

José stared at him. "Next time, don't play in grown-up games."

With that, we all walked out.

CHAPTER 28

The first area the builders had finished, but that I hadn't yet explored, was a garage—a huge garage that housed up to eight cars across and two deep. In the back of the garage, there was a soundproof locked room where we'd built a few cages. Into one of these cages went Boden. The cage had a cot bed so he could rest, and we checked on him regularly and took him to the bathroom if he needed it. We'd also made sure he had food and water. That said, he probably wouldn't survive the cage.

When we left the building, Bevin saw my bag and grabbed it, so I had my phone and clothes back. Once home, I was about to take a shower, when José led me to the hot tub. I crawled in and was quickly joined by the rest of the pack.

Eyes closed, I addressed no one and everyone. "You know, every time we spoke, he said I smelled more of trees and rivers. He knew when José and I were talking. It was one of the only things his nose was good for."

Bevin, who lounged next to me, mumbled, "Tell River, he needs to set up a training program."

Everyone laughed except Alex. "River? Who's that?"

"River is my dad. He's the one who started Owen down his path of torture and destruction."

"Ah," Alex said. "So, we should tell Owen so *he* can set up your training program." Their chin dropped. "I kinda like my training program, I've been feeling better…stronger, and it makes me feel more like I'm part of the pack."

I groaned. "Who invited *them* to the party?"

There were chuckles all around the hot tub.

CHAPTER 29

Sunday, José and Luke tried to get information from Boden, but he wouldn't talk as much as he did on Saturday. We decided to give him another day to stew.

Monday morning, I woke up early for track practice. I pushed through the weights harder than normal, but I was off in the corner, and I didn't think anyone saw.

After alleviating a bit of my frustrations, I trudged to the head of the running path, turned on my watch, and started to run. There weren't any other people on the path, and I stretched my legs, thinking through what I'd heard while in the cage. The run was an hour stint, so I went out thirty minutes, then turned and came back in. Before Coach could see my watch, I saw that I had run just under fifteen miles. I snapped a photo on my phone and cleared out my watch's memory of the run. Coach was disappointed, but my sweat and panting told a story he liked to read.

I jogged back to the car and found Greta leaning against the driver's side door. "I've been trying to figure out why I don't see you around the dorms as much. You've moved out, haven't you?"

"Can we talk about this later?"

"Why later?"

I looked down at myself. "I need to shower, and I slept at José and Bevin's last night."

"Just last night?"

"Well, you see, my girlfriend and her crazy family threw me in a cage. It kinda freaked me out. I want to stick near my friends…if you don't mind."

"I do mind. I don't think you were freaked out in the cage, or now. Part of me thinks you had more control of the situation than any of us thought, even though you were locked up."

I closed my eyes. "Not now. I need to go shower and get back for class."

"You'll talk to me later?"

"Sure, whatever. Yes."

"Four, when we're both out of class, at the café."

"I'll text. I may be busy then."

"Are you blowing me off?"

"No, but considering what happened yesterday, would you blame me? Right now, I'm just tired, and will text you after I've eaten and had coffee."

When she didn't move, I gently pushed her out of the way, slipped into the car, and drove away. When I got to Were House, I ran inside and straight to the shower. I didn't want to discuss what had happened with anyone. Once I cleaned off and got my emotions in line, I dressed, and joined the others for breakfast. It was a fend-for-yourself morning, so I prepared a bagel, cream cheese, and coffee.

While I ate, the others shuffled in. We munched in silence, then Alex, Bevin, José, and I piled into the car. In the parking lot, I got a whiff of the rogue werewolf from Pack House on the wind. It was faint and directionless. I froze. "Did any of you catch that?"

Bevin and José searched the lot, noses up before returning their gazes to me faces drawn. Alex just shrugged. "I'm not sure what you all are sniffing."

"Sorry chica, I didn't smell anything, should we be worried?"

"No, I'm probably just jumping at proverbial shadows." Shrugging, I gave him a small smile.

Bevin stared at me like he could see into my soul, but eventually sighed. "If you say so."

On the way to our first class, Alex asked if I was okay.

"I'm fine. It was just a rough weekend."

They nodded and we finished our walk to class in silence.

On the way to lunch, I caught the scent again. It was stronger this time, and I grasped Alex's arm. They sniffed the air, but their memory of the scent wasn't as strong as mine.

"Maybe. There is something strange in the air today, a weird tension, but I don't know if I actually smell something or just feel something."

At lunch, I told them all about track practice.

José massaged his temples. "You cleared your watch's memory?"

"Yeah, but I took a picture for Owen."

He gave me a half-smile. "He'll be happy. Just under fifteen miles, he may even say you weren't slacking... maybe. But what got into you this morning?"

"I don't know, I was, I am feeling weird. I keep scenting that smell too...you know the one from the house." There were too many people at tables nearby to be more direct in my explanation.

José paused, lids narrowing to slits. "Anything else happen this morning?"

I took a moment to breathe, just staring back. Bevin reached across the table, placing his hand on top of mine. I swallowed. "Greta was leaning on your car when I got there. She wants to talk to me this afternoon at four at the café. She doesn't think I was freaked out in the cage and wants to know why."

"You're not going."

"Why not?"

I saw José fight to keep his alpha mantle from showing in public. His eyes glowed a bit and his jaw tightened. After a sharp breath, he tilted his head at me. "It isn't safe. The last time you saw her you ended up *in that* cage." He repeated with a snarl, "It isn't safe."

"What if I don't go alone? What if you or Bevin come with me?"

His expression softened. "Why?"

"I don't know. Maybe I just want closure. Maybe I want to get that exact answer. Why would she lock me in a cage?"

José thought for a second. "It hadn't occurred to me. She had the key to let you out. Not Boden, not Quinn."

I nodded. "That's pretty much all I've thought about."

Bevin spoke quietly. "I'll go with her. We have class before then together anyway."

José sighed. "Fine, but I'll be close, and then we'll all drive home together."

Alex sighed. "I'll be at the library studying. Just let me know when you're ready to leave."

I sent a quick text to Greta saying I could meet her at four.

After our classes for the day, Bevin and I walked to the café. We got our drinks and snacks and found a table near the back. We made sure our backs were to a wall so no one could sneak up on us. We had discussed his sitting at a different table, but decided it wasn't worth it.

At just before four, Greta walked in, grabbed a coffee, and joined us. "I guess I shouldn't be surprised you aren't alone."

"The last time I was alone with you didn't end well. Not to mention, you had two others with you."

"I don't know who ended up with the worst lot in that deal. No one's heard from Boden since your friends took him." She looked pointedly at Bevin.

"You do know he was planning on killing me, don't you? It was one of the things he said."

She flinched back as if slapped, then pursed her lips. "He was kidding."

"No, he wasn't. He also explained to us that the wolves around town who've been killing tourists—who killed Elroy—were part of your family. So, before you start calling my friends killers, look at your own family." My voice grew softer with an edge of a growl as I finished my statement.

"I know. This's why Boden wants to start a new group. One with different rules. He thinks even women can be werewolves, though we aren't sure. It's never been done. We're afraid it might kill me."

Bevin leaned his head on his hand and started to rub. "I'm not sure what you are telling us, or why. You kind of sound crazy."

Greta's eyes narrowed. "Jade didn't freak out. She was hit over the head with a shovel and thrown in a cage. She pretended to be passed out longer than she actually was and then she was sane and lucid—no freaking out. Then when there was talk about werewolves, she took it in stride. I want to know why."

I took a long pull of my coffee, sighing with the pleasure of the taste. "I'm just a naturally calm person. It's also part of my training. My uncle is a former ranger and a bounty hunter. He likes all of us to be prepared for anything."

She tilted her head. "Is that true? I know you said Boden could smell a lie, but I can't. And how did you know that?"

"I said nothing of the sort; I just asked him if he thought I was lying. He then asked me to lie, and I did. Big difference. If it was a cool skill I knew about, do you think I would teach it to my jailor?"

"Huh. I guess not. But I also think you're clever and dangerous when you ask and answer questions."

I raised an eyebrow. "Oh?"

"And Boden is an idiot."

That made me smile. "In that, we agree." I raised my mug in a salute, and took another gulp of ambrosia.

"Will you answer one question for me?"

"No guarantees. I won't say anything that will incriminate me."

"You said you didn't kill both of the wolves. Did you kill one of them?"

I just stared at her, face blank.

She continued. "You see, I was really good at puzzle books when I was younger. Then, when I was older, I liked books about people who couldn't lie, but could lie with the absolute truth. The more I thought about your words, the more they felt like that. You were telling the absolute truth, but not the whole truth. You weren't answering the question being asked of you. You were lying by omission."

"The answer is either 'yes' or 'no.' If it is 'yes,' I incriminate myself, which I said I wouldn't do. If it is 'no,' you know the answer, and the question, the one question you have, is redundant. So, knowing this, you know it isn't a worthy question. Why don't you try again?"

"If I ask a question that won't incriminate you, will you answer it truthfully?"

"Probably…that is, if I'm willing to answer it, yes."

"Can women become werewolves?"

"Easily."

Her eyes widened.

Frustration and anger poured off Bevin. I took it in, knowing it was my due. I'd just given away more information then I had to.

"Are you a werewolf?"

"Now that is a second question. And one I can answer 'no' to, depending on how I want to interpret it. What you need to focus on is, why your family is coming to town and killing people. From my count, they've killed at least seven people so far. They've attempted to kill more."

Her breath caught and she shook her head. "That can't be right."

"Oh, it is. Check out the news. There have been at least seven people killed by wild animals. Remember the family Brooke told you about on the trail? They're part of your families' count. Anyway, I didn't freak out in the cage because it wouldn't have helped the situation. Moreover, if my guess is correct, Boden would've enjoyed it, and I wasn't about to give him pleasure of any kind. If you think harder, you'll realize that, too, wasn't your best choice of questions."

Her face scrunched up in concentration. "I'm confused."

I stood. "Bev, let's go."

Bevin collected our mugs. "Finally."

Greta reached out and grabbed my arm. "Wait, Jade. Is there any chance…"

I slowly turned. "There were three people in that room. One wanted me dead, one hit me with a shovel, and one locked me in a cage."

She blanched, looking stricken.

I shifted my gaze to her hand. After a beat, she let me go. I gave her my back, following Bevin out to the car.

We drove in silence for barely five minutes before Bevin's anger erupted. "What the hell, Jade?"

I drooped. "Bevin, I didn't tell her anything she didn't already know about me."

"You told her you know about werewolves. Information she didn't have."

José tensed at the wheel of the car. Bevin seeing the tension quickly filled him in on our conversation. José relaxed instantly.

Bevin's ire increased. I could almost see his hackles rising. "Why aren't you mad at her, too?"

Alex's small voice came from next to me. "Because Jade didn't freak out."

Bevin froze and looked at her. "What?"

"That's what Greta kept saying. Jade didn't freak out. It wasn't just about being hit over the head and being thrown in a cage, was it? It was about learning about werewolves. They were talking about werewolves in front of you and you had no reaction at all, did you?"

I shook my head. "I questioned them, but I stayed mostly neutral. When I did act confused it was too little too late. When Cody and his dad caught me, I played up being scared. This time my head just hurt, and I was tired. Tired of everything. I also figured since Boden knew about José, there wasn't much point."

At the mention of Cody and his dad, Alex's scent turned confused. I grumbled at the thought of one more thing to explain to them, both so they understood the history and for a lesson in safety.

Bevin fell back into his seat. "So, you gave Greta the one piece of a puzzle she's been seeking."

"She was either going to ask about that, or how you found me so quickly. I would rather her focus on that. I wouldn't answer the other."

José laughed. "I don't know; listening to you give

misleading answers is my new favorite pastime."

We spent the rest of the ride to Were House in silence. When we arrived, José parked outside the garage. The three quickly scrambled out and headed to the house. I took off my seatbelt but wanted to take a minute to myself. I put my heels on the seat and placed my forehead on my knees. I hugged my legs and began to shake from everything that had happened over the last few days.

I heard my door open. "I'm com…"

I was cut off by a hand over my mouth and a second one around my waist. "Hey, girly. All alone in a car in the woods." After pulling me out, he gently closed the door behind me.

I connected with José and Bevin. It drained my energy faster connecting to both at once, but I didn't think this would take that long.

José asked, *"Is it the third werewolf?"*

Yes.

I felt the breeze on my face and realized we stood downwind from the house. The wolf was dragging me towards the garage. "Not much struggle in you. I don't see what my nephew sees in you." He sniffed. "But it smells like you've spent time today with Greta."

Great, smarter than the other wolves we've dealt with. Just our luck. Both boys snorted back.

When we reached the back of the garage, he let me go. "Now, if you scream, I'll kill you. It's really as simple as that.

338

It would be easy with that twig-like neck of yours. It would be a shame, though. Not enough meat on your bones to even make you tasty."

I tried to play this better than my last game. I took a choppy breath and widened my eyes. I imagined this man getting his hands on Pebble. It was the only way I could fake being scared, as tired as I was. It was how Tanner trained me in emotions. "What do you want?"

He licked his lips. "Mmm, that tastes good. I want my nephew. There is this coded door between him and me."

"I...I...I can't get through it."

"Why not?"

I forced my body to shake. "Because. I'm just a girl. They don't tell me everything."

José laughed.

I really hoped he was as sexist as I'd heard. The idea that only men could do anything rankled, but right now his blind spot was my best advantage.

"I worried about that. But how do you clean in there?"

That almost threw me. "Um, huh? Oh, clean. I'm not allowed in there."

"The men can't be expected to clean themselves."

Trying to think fast, I opened my eyes wider and hunched my shoulders. "The only time I've seen the inside of that room, someone else has opened the door for me."

"And you didn't see the code they used? I heard you were smart; getting a medical degree of some sort. You aren't acting smart. What degree are you getting, girl?"

"Don't you know?"

"A nurse, isn't it?" he spat.

Gods, I wanted to slap him. Nursing was a tough degree. Nurses knew more about some areas of the hospital than doctors. Doctors specialized, but that didn't mean nurses knew any less. I couldn't imagine growing up with this attitude.

"Nurses are amazing." I said it with such reverence, that he could taste my honesty.

His face fell. "Smart…right. Whatever. Well, we told Quinn he could find his own girl, didn't say it had to be a smart one."

I didn't have to fake the shivers this time.

José and Bevin were nearby. This wolf could use his senses if he wanted, but didn't. He was so focused on me; it didn't occur to him to pay attention to his surroundings.

"So, how do we get into that room?"

I straightened, dropping all pretenses. "You don't."

"What?" He jerked back a step, staring me up and down as if trying to figure out what was different.

"How about you tell me why you and your family have been leaving dead bodies around our property?"

"At first, to punish you for killing Billy. Well, not you, one of the men of the house. But then, your group took down my brother, Lonny."

Intrigued, I narrowed my eyes. "How do you know?"

340

"We found the ring in that other house."

"The ring with the V? Which stands for Verater."

Through the pack bond, I felt both boys tense. They were close enough now, I could smell them. We hadn't discussed what the V could stand for.

"Who told you this, girl? Was it Quinn, or was Boden bragging?"

"How many wolves in your clan?" I needed answers, not to answer his questions.

"I've had about enough of that. How about I kill you now, then go to the house and find a real match-up."

José snorted. "You really think you can take her down. Just you? Alone?"

His eyes widened a moment before his mask of control slammed in place. "Well, if it isn't the boys. I smelled your bed; you two like to share one room."

José checked out Bevin, head to toe, then shrugged. "Was that an insult? Because look at him." He grinned.

I bit my lip, but my amusement filled the room. I can hide my expressions, but not the emotions behind them.

"You think that's funny, girl?"

I shrugged. "I think a lot of what you say and think is pretty amusing…either I laugh or shake my head at your ignorance."

He turned back to José. "So, which one of you took out Bill and Lonny? I want to face you mano-a-mano."

It was Bevin's turn to have to work to control his expression.

I sighed, loudly. "You know the problem with you and your clan? You are so sexist."

He continued to watch José, who was oozing his alpha power. "Quiet girl, this is between the men."

"But you said you wanted to know who took out the trash."

He froze. "What?"

"You see, Billy attacked me, and in a fight to the death, I wasn't about to die just because I'm a girl. Then, Lonny attacked my roommate, and one of our friends—female again—took him out. Your pack, your clan, for all your macho posturing, aren't that great at fighting, are you? So, you have me here, or my friend, but she's in Wisconsin. You could fly out there, but that would take more time than you may want."

He slowly turned, straightening to his full height, which came perilously close to Bevin's six-four. "You killed a werewolf? Then we are going to fight, just us."

José snorted. "Don't you know anything about wolves and how packs work? Do you think you can come onto our property, into our garage, onto *our pack territory* and set the conditions of *your* death?"

His eyes widened as he focused first on José, then on Bevin, and finally on me. Narrowing his eyes a small growl escaped him as if it didn't bother him to be surrounded. "But I'm a werewolf, what are you? You're three kids. I can easily..."

José huffed, "You are an idiot who knows nothing."

Before the stranger could say anything else, I ran in and punched his Adam's apple. I had the shot, and I took it. I knew it was a sucker punch, but I didn't care. This wolf had killed innocent people to test us, and I was done with him.

He dropped to his knees, clutching his throat, unable to breathe. Bevin walked up, grabbed his head, and twisted until we all heard a crack.

When I looked up, José had turned away. He talked a good game, but his biggest fear in becoming a werewolf was the fighting. He didn't want to do it. None of us did, but Bevin and I had decided, if we could fight for him, we would.

Luke ran in with Zee behind him. "We have clean-up duty. Will it be one body or two?"

We all faced José, whose face was hard as stone. "One, I hope. Let's go talk to Boden."

CHAPTER 30

José entered the code into the door. When the door swung open, Boden started yelling to be let out.

We closed the door and stood around the cage that had become his home. Once he realized his yelling wasn't getting him anywhere, he quieted down.

José stood in full alpha command. His mantle made him feel eight feet tall. The power he emitted infused the room. He may not have smelled like a wolf, but he made his presence known.

Boden's eyes went crazy. "Me and mine will not be separated so easily! My family will come for me! They will destroy you!"

Bevin rolled his eyes and muttered, "Melodramatic piece of..."

José's voice cracked out. "Bevin!" He stepped up to the cage. "We aren't going to kill you, Boden. We're sending you back to your group with a message."

"I'm not your messenger. And if I go back, they'll brand me a traitor...say I betrayed them by even talking to you and surviving. I'm not going to betray my own for you."

I rubbed my temples and mumbled, "Didn't you already do that when you became a werewolf against your family's rules?"

Another wave of alpha essence flowed through the room. Boden shook, then dropped to his knees. His breath became choppy. "Not your messenger."

"Then we'll leave you here until you agree." José started to turn, and we followed suit.

"Wait, no, wait, let's talk. What's the message?"

"Arcoíris and its surrounding land is our pack territory. No wolves are allowed here without a check-in with one of the three of us. We are the leaders."

"All three of you? Even her?"

A low growl came from José's belly, but on his face, he only smiled. "Yes. Even her."

"What about the twins? Are you sending them off or only forcing me to quit school?"

"Are the twins werewolves?"

"Of course not. Quinn hasn't had kids, and Greta's a girl."

"And do you have kids?"

"Well, no, but I'm not supposed to be a wolf either; it's why I don't want to go back."

"You're not the smartest in your clan, I hope. So, two options, stay in the cage or take our message."

"Fine, I'll take the message."

We all sighed. He was lying. We turned and left him.

When my dad realized he needed to be able to communicate with the other packs securely, his security firm developed an ink that was visible in a spectrum outside human sight but within werewolf sight. The ink was used in pens and printers. It was developed so that if anyone tampered with it, the ink would self-destruct, destroying the document as well.

When I was young, I would draw pictures with one of the pens. I could see an echo of the line right as I drew, the moisture of the pen leaving an image behind on the white paper, but it quickly dissipated, leaving me no idea what I'd drawn. After I'd created my masterpieces, I would hand the blank sheets of paper to my dad. He hung the clean sheets around his office like rectangular snowflakes, ooohing and aahing in appreciation. When I'd been tiny, I'd giggle.

After being bitten, I went to speak to my dad and was amazed when I walked into his office and gazed at the images of my childhood. There was the tree in a field with mountains in the background, a horse running across a field, a sun shining on a flower. Image after image, all gray lines on white popped out at me. I was stunned that the paper in his office suddenly came to life. The amusement erupting from me mixed with the pleasure from dad as he realized what I was seeing for the first time since I had created the artwork decorating his office all those years ago.

We used the same ink when we wrote our letter to the San Mateo Clan.

The next day I found Greta and handed her an envelope. "Take this to your leaders, or elders, or whatever."

She had been sitting in the library, studying. I'd followed her scent from the dorms to find her. Her head snapped up when I spoke. "What is it?" She looked down at what to her was a blank envelope, but what to me were the clear words: *To the leader of the San Mateo Clan.*

"A warning."

She bit her lip. "I don't want to get you hurt, Jade."

"Trust me on this one. I won't get hurt."

She looked down at the envelope and then back at me and nodded. "Okay, sure. This is a good faith move to prove to you I can be trusted. I want to fix what Boden broke."

I sat next to Zee as he drove a few cars back, following the twins. "How did you learn surveillance?"

"I've had a few odd jobs in my life, this is just one of them. We're just making sure she delivers the letter."

We parked on the same street they did and saw them approach a large white house. I rolled down my window a pinch to listen.

A woman answered the door.

"Quinn, Greta, what are you doing here? Shouldn't you be in school?"

"Hi, Willa, we need to talk to Jerry. We have a letter for him."

Willa stared at them for a few seconds before turning and heading back into the house. A mean-looking man came out. He was in his late fifties or early sixties. It looked like he'd gotten into some fights in his life with a scar running down the side of his face and a permanently broken nose.

I mumbled softly, barely loud enough for Zee to hear. "Those had to have happened pre-shift. Never thought to ask the wolf to help."

"Nah" Zee drawled. "Probably marks of pride."

Jerry eyed the twins with a look of distaste. "What do you two want?"

Greta, hand shaking, held out our letter. I saw her mouth open and close a few times, but she didn't say anything.

Jerry snatched it from her. "Is this it?"

She nodded.

"Then get out of here!"

They ran.

We didn't know the clan's name so we wrote to them by location.

The letter read:

To the San Mateo Werewolf Clan,

You are a group of lone wolves unaffiliated with a werewolf pack. There are several in North America, and we know them all. As long as you stay in your area and do not harm anyone, we will not have a problem with your existence. Werewolves that kill and feed on (eat) people, are a danger to us all. If you don't know, they are called rogue wolves and are hunted down by pack wolves.

The wolves that invaded our territory fed on their kills and were summarily dispatched. Our territory is the city of Arcoíris and the lands surrounding it. If you or your wolves enter this area, we expect a formal introduction, and request for visitation, as is deemed proper in all werewolf society. If you refuse such an action, we will assume you come with hostile intent, and will act accordingly.

Any non-werewolf members of your clan will not be held to such high standards, but the conduct we have presented above is considered polite for any affiliated with your clan.

José Cortez, alpha

Bevin Green, alpha

Jade Stone, epsilon

Whitewater had the same spring break as ours, and Sarah and Owen decided to come home for a visit. We'd finally let Boden go with a warning; if we saw him again, he'd go the way of his uncles.

Owen started his visit with a walk-through of the gym, a building on the other side of Were House from the garage. It was half again the size of our parents' gym, as per his instructions; I hadn't realized he'd given the specs to José and Bevin. Like their gym, the rooms and equipment were surrounded by a track.

Owen started to quiver in glee. "Think you can get your hour run over fifteen miles?"

I groaned. "Can we put Owen's room out here?"

After everyone found their rooms, we all met at the pool. After a few laps, I climbed into the chairs near everyone else.

José stood and started pacing, then he stopped. He pulled his alpha mantle around himself again. "I think we need to be more present in the community."

I sat up. "What do you mean?"

"I've registered Were House with the city. We are officially Mondaris Estates. Any werewolf who knows anything will know that we've claimed territory. It is time me and Bevin stop hiding." He raised his chin, his eyes gleaming. "We're going to stop using the werebear soap."

I cleared my throat. "And me."

José nodded. "You sure?"

"Yes. We're in this together."

Please review to help other readers to choose Jade Stone Chronicles!

Continue Jade's adventure:
Book 5: Pack: mybook.to/pack
Book 6: Battlefield: mybook.to/battlefield

Find back stories and updates on my website: https://huckleberryauthor.wordpress.com

Find me on:
Facebook: https://www.facebook.com/Huckleberry-Rahr-Author-129482262301549
TikTok: https://www.tiktok.com/@huckleberryrahr
Instagram: https://www.instagram.com/huckleberryrahr/
Twitter: https://twitter.com/huckleberryrahr

If you missed the first three books, find them here!
Book 1: Wolf Healer: mybook.to/WolfHealer
Book 2: Epsilon: mybook.to/Epsilon
Book 3: Alphas: mybook.to/Alphas

ACKNOWLEDGEMENTS

The list of people I want to thank is ever increasing. As always, the top of my list includes my family, especially my son Gavin Rahr. He saw something in my writing when I'm not sure there was anything to see. Then came along Angela Grimes, who took my slapped-together words and found beauty, or at least something that could be cleaned up to form something fun to read. You add a bit of Wes Imrisek, and then my writing comes to life. The Jade Stone Chronicles takes a village. To this book I add the YA readers group, Monica Boothe and Sarah Welch, who added their thoughts and comments to the story, and finally Corona Rivera, who's taken on a bigger and bigger role as family supporter, reading the stories and giving her support before the book is finished.

ABOUT THE AUTHOR

Huckleberry Rahr is a mathematics instructor at the University of Wisconsin-Whitewater. She spent many years teaching math around the Midwest and in Papua New Guinea with the Peace Corps. Her parents instilled a love of reading from a young age.

She grew up with lesbian moms who had a huge collection of women authors with heroines as the protagonist. Her favorite genre was fantasy and science fiction, that is, until she discovered urban fantasy. What her mom's library lacked were books with characters that looked like her family: diversity in background, gender identity, and sexuality. She decided if she couldn't find that series, then she would write it.